Praise for *Final Impact*
Book Three of the Axis of Time trilogy

"The multilayered plot flows smoothly along.... If you're a fan of Harry Turtledove, [the Axis of Time trilogy] will make you happy."
—*Contra Costa Times*

"Take the time to read this explosive conclusion to the 'Axis of Time' trilogy.... I enjoyed this story and highly recommend it and the other two books in the series."
—*SF Revu*

"This third and final installment in John Birmingham's insanely clever alt. history mashup of WWII and the twenty-first-century war on terror isn't your typical time-traveling techno-thriller."
—*Wired* magazine

"Birmingham is exemplary.... The descriptions of combat—both from an executive remove and up close—are terrifyingly gruesome and detailed.... Birmingham succeeds in restaging WWII in a manner as gripping as, say, Herman Wouk's *The Winds of War* and *War and Remembrance*."
—*Sci Fi Weekly* (grade A)

Praise for *Designated Targets*
Book Two of the Axis of Time trilogy

"Good culturally speculative stuff is woven deftly into a sprawling war saga with hyperkinetic and brutally entrancing battle scenes. . . . [Birmingham's] detailing of both 1942 and 2021 military technology, strategy and tactics makes for captivating, even fetishistic reading."
　　　　—*Sci Fi Weekly* (grade A)

"*Designated Targets* fulfills the promise of *Weapons of Choice*. A mutant 1942 develops with layer upon layer of surprise and dementedly ingenious and plausible culture-clash, as 2021 meets the Good War. The action scenes are formidable, and the characters show hidden depths that shock and yet ring true. This is a series, and an author, to watch. And incidentally, buy it."
　　　　—S.M. Stirling,
　　　　　author of *Island in the Sea of Time*
　　　　　and *Dies the Fire*

Also by John Birmingham

FINAL IMPACT

A NOVEL OF THE AXIS OF TIME

JOHN BIRMINGHAM

BALLANTINE BOOKS • NEW YORK

Final Impact is a work of historical fiction. Apart from the well-known actual people, events, and locales that figure in the narrative, all names, characters, places, and incidents are the products of the author's imagination or are used fictitiously. Any resemblance to current events or locales, or to living persons, is entirely coincidental.

2008 Del Rey Books Mass Market Edition

Published in the United States by Del Rey Books, an imprint of The Random House Publishing Group, a division of Random House, Inc., New York.

DEL REY is a registered trademark and the Del Rey colophon is a trademark of Random House, Inc.

This book contains an excerpt from the forthcoming edition of *One Day*. This excerpt has been set for this edition only and may not reflect the final content of the forthcoming novel.

Originally published in trade paperback in the United States by Del Rey Books, an imprint of The Random House Publishing Group, a division of Random House, Inc., in 2007.

ISBN 978-0-345-45717-2

Printed in the United States of America

www.delreybooks.com

OPM 9 8 7 6 5 4 3

FOR ROSE AND ANGUS MACKAY,
neighbors, friends, and deadline firefighters

DRAMATIS PERSONAE

ALLIED COMMANDERS

Arnold, General Henry H. (Hap). US Army Commander of the Army Air Force.

Churchill, Winston. Prime Minister, Great Britain.

Curtin, John. Prime Minister, Commonwealth of Australia.

Eisenhower, Brigadier General Dwight D., US Army. Head of War Plans Division. Appointed Commander of US Forces, European Theatre of Operations, June 1942.

King, Admiral Ernest J., USN. Commander-in-Chief of the US Fleet and Chief of Naval Operations.

Kolhammer, Admiral Phillip, USN. Task Force Commander, Commandant Special Administrative Zone (California).

MacArthur, General Douglas, US Army. Commander, Allied Forces, South-West Pacific Area. Headquartered in Brisbane, Australia.

Marshall, General George C., US Army. Chairman, Joint Chiefs of Staff.

Nimitz, Admiral Chester, USN. Commander-in-Chief, US Pacific Fleet.

Roosevelt, President Franklin D. Thirty-second president of the United States of America.

Spruance, Rear Admiral Raymond A., USN. Commander, Combined Pacific Task Force.

Stimson, Henry. US Secretary of War.

ALLIED PERSONNEL

Black, Commander Daniel, USN. On Secondment as Chiefs of Staff Liaison to Special Administrative Zone.

Danton, Sub-Lieutenant Philippe. Ranking officer on *Robert Dessaix*.

Denny, Sergeant Adam, USMC Force Recon.

Flemming, Chief Petty Officer Roy, RAN. CPO HMAS *Havoc*.

Francois, Major Margie, USMC. Combat surgeon and Chief Medical Officer, Multinational Force.

Grey, Lieutenant Commander Conrad, RAN. Executive Officer, HMAS *Havoc*.

Groves, General Leslie. Director of the Manhattan Project.

Halabi, Captain Karen, RN. Commander, British contingent; Deputy Commander, Multinational Force; Commander, HMS *Trident*.

Harrison, Sergeant Major Aubrey. 82nd MEU.

Howard, Lieutenant Commander Marc. Intelligence Officer, HMS *Trident*.

Ivanov, Major Pavel, Russian Federation Spetsnaz. On secondment to US Navy SEALs.

Jones, Colonel JL, USMC. Commander, 82nd Marine Expeditionary Unit.

Judge, Captain Mike, USN. Commander, USS *Hillary Clinton*.

Kennedy, Lieutenant John F., USN. Commander PT 101.

Kicji. Guide to Pavel Ivanov.

Liao, Lieutenant Willy, USN. PA to Admiral Kolhammer.

Lohrey, Lieutenant Amanda, RAN. Intelligence Officer, HMAS *Havoc*.

McTeale, Lieutenant Commander James. Executive Officer, HMS *Trident*.

Mohr, Chief Petty Officer Eddie. Transferred to Auxiliary Forces, Special Administrative Zone.

Müller, Captain Jurgen, Deutsche Marine. On Secondment to Special Operations Executive.

Nguyen, Lieutenant Commander Rachel, RAN. Multinational Force Intelligence Liaison to South-West Pacific Area HQ.

Rogas, Chief Petty Officer Vincente, US Navy SEALs.

Snider, Sergeant Arthur, USMC. 1st Marine Division. (Contemporary.)

St. Clair, Sergeant Major Vivian Richards, British SAS force.

Steele, Captain Colin, USN. Commander JDS Siranui.

Viviani, Lieutenant Colonel Nancy. Production Chief for Admiral Kolhammer.

Willet, Captain Jane, RAN. Commander, HMAS *Havoc*.

Windsor, His Royal Highness Major Harry. Commander, British MNF SAS contingent. Commander Training Squadron.

GERMAN COMMANDERS

Göring, Reichsmarschall Hermann. Chief of the Luftwaffe.
Himmler, Reichsführer Heinrich. SS Chief.
Hitler, Reichschancellor Adolf.
Oberg, General Karl. SS Commander in Paris.
Speer, Albert. Minister of Armaments.
Zeitzler, General Kurt, Wehrmacht Chief of Staff.

GERMAN PERSONNEL

Brasch, Colonel Paul. Engineer. Reich Special Projects.
Skorzeny, Colonel Otto. Personal bodyguard to Adolf Hitler.

JAPANESE COMMANDERS

Hidaka, Commander Jisaku, IJN. Interim Military Governor of Hawaii.
Homma, General Masaharu. Commander of Imperial Japanese land forces in Australia.
Oshima, General Hiroshi. Japanese ambassador to Germany.
Uemura, Lieutenant Masahisa, Squadron leader, "Thunder Gods," Special Attack Squadron, Sapporo.
Yamamoto, Grand Admiral Isoroku, IJN. Commander-in-Chief, Combined Fleet.

USSR

Yukio, Lieutenant Seki, Commander Special Attack Squadron, Caroline Islands.

COMMANDERS

Beria, Lavrenty Pavlovich. Head of NKVD.
Khrushchev, Nikita Sergeyevich. Prisoner.
Molotov, Vyacheslav Mikhaylovich. Foreign Minister.
Stalin, Josef Vissarionovich. General Secretary of the Soviet Communist Party.

CIVILIANS

Davidson, James "Slim Jim." Formerly Able Seaman, USS *Astoria*. Chief Executive Officer and principal shareholder Slim Jim Enterprises.

Donovan, William. Chief of the Office of Strategic Services.

Duffy, Julia, *New York Times* feature writer. Embedded 82nd MEU.

Halifax, Lord. British Ambassador to USA.

Hoover, J. Edgar. Director, FBI.

Natoli, Rosanna, CNN researcher/producer. Embedded 82nd MEU.

O'Brien, Ms. Maria. Lawyer, former USMC captain, 82nd MEU. (Retd.)

Stephenson, William. Churchill's personal representative in the USA.

PROLOGUE

Captain Jane Willet came awake in an instant—even before the chime rang at her cabin door. At least that's how it seemed.

It's probably just my mind getting bent of out shape.

Willet was groggy from a fortnight of broken sleep. Gone were the days of dialing up a stim surge from her implants. Indeed, most of the things she had taken for granted were long gone. Close friends and family outside this boat. Six hundred channels of bad TV. Thai food. No-fuss contraception.

The chime rang again.

"Enter," she said, her voice cracking badly. She had to repeat herself, after a cough. "Come in, please."

The door slid to the side, and a female sailor stuck her head into the cabin. "Begging your pardon, Captain, but the XO says we've picked 'em up again. He said you'd want to be on the bridge."

"Thank you, Bec."

Willet sat up and ran her fingers through her hair, gathering the thick, shoulder-length mass of tangles and split ends into a workable ponytail that she tied off with an elastic band. The sailor stepped into the room and over to the counter, then poured a mug of coffee—the last of the boat's stock of premium-blend Illy. She handed it to the captain.

"Ah. Thanks again. Champion effort." Willet took a sip, and it felt as though the caffeine went straight to her cortex. Young Sparrow brewed a very mean cup of coffee.

Jeez, I'm gonna miss this when it runs out, thought the submarine commander. *Wonder how long it'll be after the war before anyone imports a decent Italian blend.*

Aloud she said, "Tell the XO to keep his finger off the trigger until I've got some pants on. I'll join him in two minutes."

"Aye, Captain."

Her orderly disappeared, closing the door as she left. Willet took a long slug of the coffee, brewed warm rather than hot so she wouldn't scald herself. She set the mug down in a recess on the small table beside her bunk. She grabbed a 'temp-made energy bar and peeled back the waxed paper, then started chewing joylessly on her so-called breakfast at the same time as she climbed into a pair of gray combat coveralls. She checked her watch.

Zero four thirty-one hours, local.

She'd been asleep for less than two hours.

Washing down a mouthful of the bar with the last of her coffee, Willet gathered up her flexipad and left behind the small personal space of her cabin. Some novels, a few black-and-white photographs of the Sydney Harbor Bridge, a picture of her sister, and a small watercolor of their parents' beach house painted by her dad back up in twenty-one marked out the room as her private territory. She was never far from work, however.

The cabin was located all of fifteen meters from the sub's Combat Center, allowing her to arrive in a shade under the promised two minutes.

"Captain on deck!"

"As you were. Mr. Grey, I hear we've got them by the short and curlies again."

Lieutenant Commander Conrad Grey stepped aside from a bank of flat-panel screens, a quick nod inviting her to take his place. She could see that he was tense, like everyone present.

"The sea's calmed down a fair bit up there, skipper. We're getting clean capture on the sensors now, the best we've had in three days. Their cocks are on the chopping block, ma'am. Just waiting for the magic word."

Willet took in the sensor feed with a glance. Once upon a time, they would have made this kill from a much safer distance, but in such foul weather, without satellite cover, they'd been forced to come within six thousand meters just to use the boat's own sensor suite. Tracking something as dangerous as a *Sartre*-class stealth destroyer was like snuggling up to a nest of vipers.

At least it would have been under normal circumstances.

The *Dessaix,* however, wasn't under the command of its normal crew. Mostly their fates were unknown, but it didn't take much to imagine what had become of them. The Nazis had captured the ship while they were all still comatose from the Transition, so there wouldn't have been a chance to resist. If any still lived, they were probably hanging by their thumbs in a Gestapo cell somewhere in Germany.

Willet leaned back into the gelform seat padding and peered intently into the multipanel display. There was no video feed to examine, only animations of the boat's electronic intelligence haul. The *Havoc* had five small drones left, but they weren't robust enough to cope with the extreme conditions above. Three days earlier two giant storm cells had merged to create a supercell within which the *Dessaix* was trapped. Sitting two hundred meters down, the submariners had enjoyed an easy time of it. Conditions topside, on the other hand, would be evil.

They were bad enough that tracking the ship had been near impossible. They'd lost contact again and again. At last, when the weather showed signs of abating, they had her—and the chance of taking her down.

"You know, Mr. Grey," Willet mused, "we may not have to bother with this after all. Mother Nature might just do our job for us. It looks to me like the *Dessaix* is struggling."

"Better safe than sorry, ma'am," her XO cautioned.

"Of course. It was just a girlish whim." She smiled, then her features took on an altogether somber cast. "Weapons?" she said crisply. "Confirm target lock and torpedo status."

"Aye, ma'am. Both confirmed. And we've reached firing depth."

"Well, then, let's not drag it out. Open tubes."

Though she couldn't actually hear or feel it, she knew instinctively when the giant submarine had bared its fangs.

"Tubes three and four open, ma'am."

Willet did not hesitate. "Fire."

"Firing three. Firing four, skipper. Clean shots. Tracking now."

The Combat Center was normally a hushed environment, but when a warshot was loosed, a preternatural stillness came over the dozen men and women working there. In the bad old days a sub captain would have followed the torpedoes to their victim by watching through a periscope. Just two years ago Willet herself would have observed the killing stroke on the ship's holobloc, where the action would play itself out as a ghostly, three-dimensional image. But now all she had was a crude computer-generated simulation as her last pair of Type 92 torpedoes accelerated toward the hijacked French vessel that was struggling through the waves.

"Countermeasures?" she asked quietly, although there was no need. The *Havoc* was fully stealthed.

"None deployed yet, ma'am. They haven't made us."

She nodded, but couldn't help chewing her lip. She had just fired off the last of their offensive weapons. There were no more shots in the locker—the cruise missile bays and the torpedo room were empty. If they missed with this strike, and the pickup crew of the *Dessaix* were any good, she would have to dive deep and hide out down there for a *very* long time.

Two indicator bars, showing the distance to the target, crawled across the nearest screen. Five millimeters before they reached their goal, the chief defensive sysop cried out.

"They're onto us! Threat board's red."

Willet's heart rate surged, but then her weapons officer spoke up.

"We got a double tap, skipper! Clean hits." He added, "She's gone."

Willet's crew were disciplined, and nobody cheered, but the commander of the HMAS *Havoc* spoke for them all. "Outstanding piece of work everyone," she said quietly. "Congratulations."

Lieutenant Commander Grey stayed bent over the schematic displays until he was entirely satisfied. Standing upright, he asked, "Shall we search for survivors, ma'am?"

It didn't take long for her to consider the question. "No, I'm afraid not, Mr. Grey. The seas are still running at twelve meters up there. We can't take the chance. Bring us around, and let's get back to the lake. Prepare an encrypted burst for Pearl, San Diego, and Sydney, then send it when we get within range.

"And have Ms. Sparrow brew me a hot chocolate. I'm going back to bed."

1

The lead helicopter hammered across the English Channel at the edge of its performance envelope, close enough to the waves that Lieutenant Gil Amundson thought he could feel a fine mist of sea spray stirred up by their passage through the darkness.

The seven men in his chalk were quiet, each alone in his own cocoon of anticipation and fear. Amundson could hear Sergeant Nunez beside him, reciting rapid-fire Hail Marys, working through a set of rosary beads in what looked to the young cavalry officer like record time. Across the cabin Private Clarke was nervously tapping his heel on the steel plating of the floor, the tempo increasing until it sounded like one of those rock-and-roll drummers. Then he'd curse, punch himself on the leg, and go still for a moment before starting all over again.

On either side of him a couple of the boys were dozing fitfully. Or at least pretending to.

That's how it went the whole way across. Each man playing out what might be his last hour as he saw fit. Some checked their equipment, before checking their buddy's. Some leaned over to get a view of the invasion fleet as it headed for the coast. Corporal Gadsden craned his head skyward, the bulky lens of his Gen2 Starlite goggles tracking his gaze as he picked out Dakotas, gliders, Mustang night fighters, and, at one point, a squadron of Sabers miles overhead, all screaming toward France.

Amundson forced himself to go through the plan again. The rapid insertion, the assembly point for his platoon, the mental map of their objective.

He used what little space he had in the chopper to perform a set of isometric exercises, lest his butt fall asleep before they jumped into Hitler's front garden. He stretched his arms and legs and craned his neck from side to side, a full extension in each direction, which gave him a clear view of the rest of the cav squadron as it thundered toward the enemy in 132 Hueys, with another forty Cobra gunships riding shotgun.

It seemed that the demonic roar of so many engines, the great thudding of all those rotors, could surely be heard in Berlin itself. But as quickly as the thought came to him, it was gone.

A quick glance forward through the armored glass canopy revealed the firestorm that was engulfing the Pas de Calais. So much high explosive had been dropped on that small region of France, it would be a wonder if anything bigger than a flea still lived down there. There'd even been talk back in England that Ike might bust a nuke over the krauts, although Amundson doubted that. They hadn't been outfitted to fight in radioactive terrain.

That wouldn't stop the Nazis, though, he supposed. Axis Sally had been taunting the Allies for weeks now, claiming that the Reich was just waiting for them to set foot on the Continent, giving them an excuse to use the first of their many, many A-bombs. Amundson glanced down, then back at the lead elements of the great fleet headed for the beaches of Calais. At least *his* squadron was probably too small a target to justify the use of such a weapon.

No, they were probably just gonna get chewed to bits by German jet fighters.

Ah, screw it.

He figured the same doubts were gnawing through every man in the operation. Eisenhower himself was probably being tortured by the same sort of fears. Ever since the Transition, so much was known, but so much more was unknowable.

There was one person who didn't seem to give a shit, though, and she was sitting directly across from him. She was a civilian, but she'd seen more combat than any of them. Maybe even anyone in the whole squadron. Amundson knew a few guys who'd fought in the Pacific, but almost everyone else in the Seventh had never fired a shot—not in combat. Nor had they come under fire themselves.

But they'd trained as hard as any outfit in the world. And in one of those weird, head-spinning paradoxes, they'd learned the lessons of another D-Day, one that had taken place on another world. Amundson knew, for instance, that a field full of French cows most likely wasn't mined, but if those cows kept staring at a bush or a hedgerow, there was probably a German hiding there. Their equipment was without a doubt the best. The poor old infantry, down in those Higgins boats, they didn't get any Starlite goggles, or even body armor. And they were still armed with the M1 Garand, not the brand-new assault rifles with integrated grenade launchers.

But even though he'd been honed to a razor's edge and was riding at the head of the most powerful cavalry unit ever assembled, Gil Amundson couldn't help but wonder. Would he crumble when the first bullet zipped past? Would he freeze up over the Landing Zone? Would he fail his men? And would he look like a coward in front of this woman who seemed not to give a damn that they were less than an hour away from certain death?

The chopper banked sharply as the dark sky to the north suddenly filled with dozens of beautiful, sinuous lines of light. Tracer fire. Where the hell had that come from? They'd been told that the air force was going to bomb the coast back to the Stone Age.

He struggled to get a view back to the rest of the squadron, which followed the lead chopper. He heard the copilot calling in a position estimate for the antiaircraft batteries and half expected to see a couple of gunships peeling away to deal with them. But everyone stayed in formation, pressing on toward the objective.

They left the lead elements of the fleet behind them. The only movement on the sea was a rippling crescent of reflected moonlight as they sped on. The pilot's voice crackled out of a speaker above Amundson's head. "We'll be over the coastline in five minutes."

Amundson looked south as four gunships pulled ahead, their job to rake the ground clear of defenders. When he looked back at the woman, she was talking to Gadsden. Or rather he was yelling something in her ear. She smiled and nodded.

Amundson felt a brief, irrational surge of jealousy. He slowly and deliberately stamped it down. She wasn't his girl, after all. They'd shared a bed in London for a couple of nights, made love in ways he hadn't thought possible—and which wouldn't have been, if he wasn't in such amazing physical shape. But she'd made it clear that she wanted nothing more than sex. She didn't even like to cuddle. The couple of times he'd tried, she had rolled on top of him, fucked him insensible, then rolled off and gone back to sleep.

When he'd told his best buddies, lieutenants Savo and Lobes, they'd stared at him like he'd just won the Kentucky Derby. And actually, it kinda bugged him, them just looking at him like he was out of his mind.

Julia Duffy was famous. And beautiful. And rumor had it that she was as rich as a Rockefeller. So if he didn't feel like sharing her bed, then Savo and Lobes reckoned they'd be more than happy to volunteer. After all, if she was good enough for the president of the United States of America—well, he'd be president someday, at least, if he survived the war—then who were *they* to turn her away?

Amundson caught himself staring at her just before she locked eyes with him. He glanced away guiltily.

Julia kicked him. It would have hurt if he hadn't been wearing a thick rubber knee pad.

"You and your boys, you'll be fine, Lieutenant," she called out over the noise. "Don't sweat it. You're gonna eat those fuckers alive. *Garry-fuckin'-owen.*"

The men in his chalk roared back.

"Garryowen!"

Amundson smiled. But he felt sick in the pit of his stomach.

About three months after the Allies had retaken Hawaii, a package had arrived for Julia at *The New York Times*. She'd been back home for a month by then. After the slaughter on Oahu, the paper had insisted that she take a proper vacation, and to everyone's surprise she had agreed.

She'd still been with Dan at that point, but she hadn't gone out to the Zone. Hadn't even bothered to phone and tell him she was back. Mostly, she just stayed drunk.

She did manage to visit Rosanna's family, and for about three hours in their company she felt half human. But she fell apart when Poppi Ugo brought out the family album and insisted on taking her through every shot they had of Rosanna. She'd guzzled down nearly three-quarters of a bottle of grappa, crying hysterically all the time, and had passed out on the couch. She woke up at three in the morning, shivering under the Natoli family quilt, then vomited and snuck out the front door, leaving twenty dollars to cover the dry-cleaning bill. Hours later she remembered that dry cleaning as she knew it didn't exist yet.

She'd gone back to apologize, but the Natoli clan refused to hear it. They tried to talk her into staying for another 188-course dinner, but—fearing a meltdown—she had begged off and fled back to the city. The next she heard from them was when this package turned up at the *Times*.

The mailroom cleared about a thousand items a week for Julia. Letters from servicemen she'd written about. Cookies baked by their moms. Crayola drawings by little girls who said they wanted to grow up and be just like her. And at the other extreme, hate mail and death threats from fans of the former FBI director who blamed her for his ruin, or from nutjobs who just didn't like her. There were plenty of those. Many of them working for the same paper as her.

The package from Rosanna's family lay on her desk for about two weeks before she could bring herself to do anything about it. Worried that she might fall apart in front of her colleagues, Julia had carried the parcel back to her apartment and left it in a closet for nearly a month.

It took a fifteen-hour liquid lunch at the Bayswater before she could get it back out of the closet, and two pots of black coffee before she could take a knife to the packing tape without cutting a finger off.

She had no idea what was waiting in there. Part of her thought the Natolis might have sent the quilt over for her to clean up. But the package wasn't big enough, and when she spilled the contents of the thick, padded envelope onto her Castiglioni coffee table, a small "Oh!" escaped her, and she had to run to the bathroom to be sick again.

The snoring man in her bed stirred but didn't wake as she lost a whole day's worth of Manhattans and finger food in the bathroom. She sucked a few mouthfuls of cold water straight from the faucet, thought about taking a shower, and decided to go without, lest she wake up the asshole in her bedroom.

Walking very unsteadily back into the lounge area of her huge open living space, Julia studied the sad collection of personal effects that lay on the tabletop. Rosanna's flexipad and a dozen data sticks, a traditional leather-bound diary, some jewelry, an

Hermès scarf, her imitation Bordigoni handbag, a wristwatch, a small piece of notepaper, and some cosmetics.

Julia stared at the pile of detritus for a long time while her stomach threatened to rebel again. She tried to think, but it was as though her mind could gain no traction. It kept slipping over the sight in front of her, refusing to latch on to anything in particular. After a few minutes, with a shaking hand, she picked up the piece of paper.

Rosanna's great auntie Tula had written on it in her large, looping style.

> Dearest Julia.
>
> A very kind Captain Schapelli from the army came by today with a large carton of little Rosie's belongings recovered from Hawaii. She had made out a will and hidden it in her apartment. The Japanese killed everyone there, I hear, but they never found Rosie's last testament or the things she had hidden away. Captain Schapelli, a lovely boy, but Jewish, insisted that we send them to you. He's quite a fan. There is a larger box, which we could not afford to send because of the postage being what it is these days, and Captain Schapelli says there are some things in there for you, too. We would love to have you around for dinner again, and you could collect the things little Rosie wanted you to have. Please do call or write.
>
> Love and best wishes,
> Tula

Eight months later Julia sat braced against the forward bulkhead of the lead chopper. It was the Seventh Cav's first charge since they'd gone tearing around after Pancho Villa.

She adjusted a shoulder pad as Corporal Gadsden yelled something into her ear about a couple of London barmaids he'd screwed a couple of weeks earlier. *What a dick,* she thought, but she just smiled and nodded.

Her titanium weave armor was way past its expiration date. It'd been repaired time and again with reactive matrix panels and patches bought, borrowed, and occasionally stolen from other twenty-first-century reporters who didn't share her enthusiasm for front-line action. So it had taken on the appearance of a camouflage quilt. The ballistic plating was brand new, though, thanks to Rosanna, who had left all her own mostly unused equipment to her friend.

A brief, sad smile died at the edge of Julia's mouth.

Still lookin' out for me, babe.

The copilot's voice crackled inside her powered helmet. "Ten minutes to insertion."

Amundson repeated the call and held up both hands. Everyone nodded.

Julia could see that the young officer was trying to control his nerves. She guessed it had less to do with fear of being killed than with fear of fucking up and letting everyone down. He was a sweet kid, really. They'd had some good times in London, even if he was a little clingy. In fact, thinking about it, she'd spent more time with Gil than any man she'd been with after Dan had died.

And now the poor kid was shitting himself.

"You and your boys, you'll be fine, Lieutenant," she yelled over the uproar. "Don't sweat it. You're gonna eat those fuckers alive. *Garry fuckin' Owen.*"

She punched the air between them.

The men grinned fiercely and called out the Seventh Cav's war cry.

As the troopers began yet another round of equipment checks, Julia performed her own precombat routine. A software aid scanned all her built-in combat systems, most of which were useless now anyway for want of tac-net coverage. She unsheathed her knife. The monobonded carbon blade was a dull gray, but more than razor sharp. Her Sonycam was powered up and loaded with four blank data sticks—again thanks to Rosanna—enough for two days' continuous filming. Her medikit was an eccentric mix of original 21C supplies, some AT stuff, and some plain old-fashioned 'temp gear—assorted twentieth-century items she'd scavenged here and there.

Apart from a gene shear contraceptive, which of course she couldn't switch off now—and hadn't that been a fucked-up decision—her bio-inserts were tapped out. If she took a round in the guts, there'd be no warm flush of anesthetic from her thoracic pips. She'd be screaming for a medic and a shot of morphine, just like the best of them.

"Five minutes."

Amundson repeated the gesture he'd made before, except this

time he held only one hand up. A harsh burning smell reached them, and one of the cavalry troopers, Private Steve Murphy, asked her what the hell was going on.

"Be cool," she called back. "And learn to love the smell of napalm in the morning."

When nobody got the reference, she rolled her eyes.

"It's the air force. They would have come through here and bombed the shit out of the place. That's what you smell. Toasted Nazis. *Mmmmmh. Crispy.*"

Gadsden sniggered. Murphy seemed to ponder the point before nodding his approval.

The chopper banked to the right and began to lose altitude as it put on speed.

"Just passed over the release point," reported the copilot.

In the cabin, the pilots were now free to ditch their maps and fly by dead reckoning. They were close. The door gunner primed his .30 cal. Amundson glanced around quickly to catch a look at the whole squadron as it formed up for the assault. Like the others, Julia tugged at her chinstrap and cinched her pack just a little tighter.

Cobra gunships roared past them on both sides as she waited for the familiar snarl of miniguns and the *whoosh* of rockets leaving their pods.

"Lock and load," Amundson cried at two minutes out as a dense black canopy of trees sped beneath the skids.

The cav troopers tapped their mags against their steel pots before slapping them into place. Julia did the same, pulling the charging handle back along with everyone else. The bolt carrier slapped the first round into place. After Hawaii she'd switched over to using the same 'temp weapons as the units she covered.

Other than a small stock of ammunition kept for research purposes, none of the original loads that had come through the Transition remained. All the marines coming out of the Zone, and a few of the 'temp forces like the cav here, now loaded out with AT gear like the M4 assault rifle, a workmanlike copy of Colt's venerable old martyr-maker.

Indeed, fitting her goggles and sweeping her eyes over Amundson's chalk, it was hard to separate them from some of the units she'd covered as a young pool reporter in Yemen. Swap their olive drab battle dress for Desert MARPAT, and you were almost there. The knee and elbow pads, camel backs, combat goggles, webbing, and weaponry were all uptime variants, manufactured decades ahead of their time.

The Seventh Cavalry Regiment, along with all the other regiments in the First Air Cavalry Division, were still 'temp units, however, which meant that some things were very different. There were no African American cavalry troopers riding in this or any other helicopter. And no women. Other than Julia.

"Thirty seconds!" Amundson yelled.

"Clear left," the crew chief called.

"Clear right," the door gunner added.

The world turned opal green inside Julia's Oakleys when she powered up the low-light-amplification system. They were descending rapidly onto a large field, where dozens of black-and-white—or rather, dark-jade-and-lime-green—dairy cows scattered in fear. A wire-guided rocket, a stubby little SS-11, swished overhead and detonated behind a copse of oak trees. Secondary explosions followed, and the night erupted. The chopper flared over their LZ, and Julia stood up.

"Let's go!" Amundson yelled.

2

D-DAY + 2. 5 MAY 1944.
SPECIAL ADMINISTRATIVE ZONE (CALIFORNIA).

It was a hell of a thing, the way the smog had come back to Los Angeles.

Well, not *back,* he supposed. Most Californians were getting to know it for the first time. When Kolhammer had arrived in mid-'42, the air over the LA basin and the San Fernando had been so painfully clear, you could hurt yourself breathing it in too quickly. That had changed.

It still wasn't anything like the carcinogenic soup of his era, but when he flew in these days there was a definite brown haze hanging over the mountains to the east, and a blurring on the horizon out in the Pacific. Nevertheless, the admiral shrugged and took a long, deep breath, just because he still could. To his leathery old lungs the air tasted sweet.

Perhaps after the war there'd be a chance to slow down and do things differently. Some people were already headed in that direction. He'd met some of the pointy-heads up in Berkeley who were looking at fusion, and he knew there was a small but well-connected group in the National Security Office studying options that would help the United States avoid ever falling hostage to the whims of the Saudi royal family "again."

On his infrequent trips to downtown LA, he never failed to notice some manifestation of the future folding back in on itself. Last time it had been a billboard advertising the arrival of disposable diapers. Before that it was a restaurant that proclaimed its "all-microwaved" menu to the world—very unwisely, in Kolhammer's opinion. Some days it seemed as if the postwar economy was already with them. Despite the demands of war production, some resources were now being allocated to manufacturing consumer goods like automatic washing machines and pop-up toasters. They weren't available in great numbers, but that scarcity only added to the hysteria of desire for each new arrival. He'd read somewhere that each of five hundred "experimental" color television sets made by General Electric had been bought before they rolled off a special assembly line last month. Even though there were no network broadcasts for them to tune in to yet.

Every one of the top five hundred companies in the United States now had a wholly owned subsidiary resident in the Zone. Some, like GE or Boeing, were there to exploit their own future intellectual property. Others were simply hydra-headed monsters like Slim Jim Enterprises or McClintock Investments, which had moved quickly and aggressively to cash in during the confusion of the months following the Transition. They had accumulated enough wealth, and with it power, to protect their often dubious claims to ownership over myriad products and patents.

So much money had been pouring into the Zone via its own stock exchange—an offshoot of New York's—that regulators in Washington had been forced to step in and stem the capital tide, lest it unbalance the outside economy.

It was amazing what happened when hindsight became foresight.

"Refill, Admiral?"

It was all he could do not to jump. The female seaman had appeared at his elbow without making a sound.

Kolhammer swirled the dregs of his cold coffee around in the bottom of a mug he'd taken off the *Clinton* nearly two years ago. The gold-plated motto IT TAKES A CARRIER was patchy in places, and there was a chip right where he put his mouth, but he couldn't bring himself to part with it. It was a rare link to the "old" world.

"No thank you, Paterson. I'd best be getting back inside, anyhow."

It was really too hot to be standing around in the midday sun, sipping coffee, but Phillip Kolhammer was a creature of habit. When he was buried in work, he tended to eschew a sit-down lunch in favor of a ham sandwich and a quick cup of joe, taken out on the balcony of his office. It was a fine view from up here on the eighth floor, all the way back to the Santa Monicas. In between there lay a patchwork of undeveloped farmland, industrial estates, and miles of cheap tract housing for the hundreds of thousands of workers who'd migrated here.

Kolhammer poured the last of his drink into a much-abused potted plant, then turned to go back inside, momentarily closing his eyes to help them adjust to the darker interior.

He stepped through into his air-conditioned office, pulling the glass door closed behind him. Paterson took his mug and disappeared through the main office door, telling his personal assistant, Lieutenant Liao, that the boss was back on deck. Kolhammer strode over to his desk and dropped into the gelform swivel chair—another piece of *Clinton* salvage, as was the enormous touch screen that dominated his work space.

On that screen, multiple windows ran the first images from D-Day, mostly in color and V3D. That meant the source had to be twenty-first-century equipment, since it still took them a few days to convert contemporary black-and-white film coverage. So for now he was restricted to whatever came down the wire from Washington—and even that had to be encoded on a data stick, then physically flown across the Atlantic before it was sent via cable to San Diego.

There, at last, it could be laser-linked to the Zone.

Any assets that might have been used to grab the take from Halabi's Nemesis arrays were fully engaged in-theater, meaning that even the *Trident*'s data bursts had to travel by stick. Coaxial cable just wasn't up to carrying encrypted quantum signals, not without significant degradation. Still, despite the time delays, he had an excellent overview of the titanic struggle Eisenhower insisted on calling the "Great Crusade."

That phrase brought a quirk to his lips whenever he heard it. Back in 2021, after twenty years of the jihad, you still weren't allowed to use the C-word.

Kolhammer traced his fingertips across the screen, bringing three windows to the fore, filling most of the display. One carried raw vision from the air assault over the villages of Coquelles, Peuplingues, and Frethun, towns that sat astride the main road leading into and out of the port of Calais.

The window next to it ran footage of the mass parachute drop by 101st into the same area, just two hours later. And in the third and smallest window, a continual loop showed the first wave of Higgins boats coming ashore on the wide sandy beaches of the Pas de Calais, where a half-built section of the Atlantic Wall had been reduced to smoking rubble by a six-hour-long storm of precision-guided five-hundred-kilo bunker busters and fuel-air explosives, the "poor man's nukes."

A chime sounded, and Lieutenant Liao appeared in a pop-up.

"I have your conference call, Admiral. General Jones and Captain Judge on screen. Links verified secure."

"Thank you, Lieutenant." Kolhammer collapsed the D-Day coverage into thumbnails as his two closest friends and colleagues took over 90 percent of the screen in two separate windows. Judge was down in San Diego on board the *Clinton,* while Jones was in his office at Camp Hannon, the Eighty-second's induction and training facility just a few klicks over in Andersonville.

"Morning, Lonesome. Mike. You've been following the progress in Calais, I suppose."

"As best I can, Admiral," Jones replied. "Things are a little hectic over here, but I've been getting the highlights from your guys. It looks like it's gonna work. I can't believe Hitler bought the Normandy fake-out, but then you never could tell what that fuckin' loon would do, could you?"

Mike Judge, sitting in Kolhammer's old cabin on the supercarrier, shook his head. "Nope, it's true. Bookies are still six-to-five that he'll go nuclear, though."

"You taking those odds?" Kolhammer asked.

"Nah. My bet's that if he had 'em, he'd a used 'em already," Judge said. "I doubt he'd even wait for the invasion. That guy's got poor impulse control. He woulda lit up London as soon as he got the wrapping off his first bomb."

Kolhammer had to agree. Herculean efforts had gone into determining the status of the Axis powers' atomic weapons program. Nearly as much energy had gone into disrupting that program as had been devoted to the invasion, and to the search for any more "missing" task force ships like the *Dessaix*.

Of course, the great unknown was still the Soviets. Stalin undoubtedly had his own atomic plans, and while it was extremely unlikely that he'd really cooperate with the Nazis beyond the elaborate charade of the Demidenko facility, just about *everything* they'd been dealing with had been unlikely, ever since the moment Manning Pope's wormhole had dropped them eight decades into the past.

"I think you're right, Mike," Kolhammer said. "But I still get that sick feeling in my gut every morning when I get out of the rack. You have to figure Groves is going to deliver any day now, and then what? When we first got here, I used to dream about Marie every night. Now all I see in my dreams are mushroom clouds springing up over Europe."

"Yeah, me too," Jones agreed, with a somber cast to his features.

None of the three was privy to the progress of the Manhattan Project, the Allies' own race for the bomb. Despite the resources Kolhammer had transferred over to General Leslie Groves, the man in charge of the project, a wall of impenetrable secrecy still surrounded it. Nobody outside the inner circle had any idea when the first bomb would be dropped, or where.

But thanks to the records they had brought with them, the whole world knew it was coming. This had induced a state of generalized panic that reminded Kolhammer of the days following the destruction of Marseilles, back in his own universe. The genie was out of the bottle, and everybody was well aware that he wasn't a friendly spirit.

"Okay, gentlemen," he said, putting an end to the maudlin exchange, "we deal with what we must, and what we can. Mike,

I'll be handing things over to Nancy Viviani tomorrow and heading down your way, so you'll need to get out of my room and change the sheets. I know you Texans love sleeping rough, but we admirals, we prefer our little comforts."

Judge grinned. "It'll be good to have you back, sir."

"Lonesome," Kolhammer continued. "You got everything squared away there? I've been talking to Spruance, and he's looking forward to seeing your people at work. But some days it feels like he's a minority of one."

"Admiral, I've had the First and Second battalions locked down for three days now. Everyone is back from R and R, and we didn't have a single straggler. I think that's a record. My boys and girls, they've got some shit to prove. Not to me. But like you say, there's a lot of folks don't think they're up for it. We'll prove 'em wrong, *if* we get the chance." The marine growled out the last line with real anger.

"You'll get the chance," Kolhammer promised.

"That's not what I hear. What I hear is that you've been taking heat to send us to fucking Persia. For garrison duty with the Brits."

Kolhammer shook his head emphatically. "Look, you've heard right. There's been some pressure, but it doesn't mean a damn thing to me. You've got to stop chasing your tail, Lonesome. It's been two years, and it never stops."

Frustration flashed in the marine's eyes. "That's *why* I can't stop chasing my goddamn tail, Admiral. Every time I look back, there's someone trying to fuck me in the ass!"

"Nobody here is going to allow that to happen. True, I got leaned on. And when it happened, I did what I always do. I told 'em to take a leap. You're coming to the Marianas with the rest of us, so get used to it.

"Now, Mike," he continued, shutting down the subject, "how's my old girl? She ready to rumble?"

Judge nodded. He looked uncomfortable, though, at having been caught up in the crossfire. "Even my wife was impressed when she stopped by, sir. And those Royal Navy types, they don't impress easy."

Jones's deep bass rumbled out. "So what, you gonna have to keep your pants on forever now?"

Judge's expression didn't change a bit. "I think the phrase *yo mama* covers it, jarhead," he replied calmly.

It was a rare day when Kolhammer could think of anything positive that had come of the Transition, but Mike Judge's wooing and winning of Captain Karen Halabi qualified as A Good Thing. Their giddy, teenlike infatuation reminded him of his own marriage, back in its first hot flush, and he felt sure that, like his, theirs would endure. He had kept to his vows, forsaking all others even though he was lost to Marie, and for all she knew he had died off East Timor.

Though Judge had already been married for six months, Kolhammer still saw the intensity there, despite the fact that they'd been able to spend very little time together. Halabi's last two weeks of leave had been spent on board the *Clinton* while her husband bedded down the last of the retrofit and prepped the great warship to go back out to sea. She'd worked just as hard as he had, lending her invaluable experience in re-equipping the *Trident* with what the locals called "Advanced Technology" but the uptimers all thought of as museum pieces. Like the six-barreled 20mm Vulcan cannon that replaced the *Clinton*'s laser packs and Metal Storm mounts.

It hadn't been much of a honeymoon, as Judge admitted, but at least they had managed to get one day and one night to themselves, staying at the log cabin Kolhammer had bought for himself up at Clear Lake.

Jones broke in on Kolhammer's train of thought. "I saw the new fighter squadrons out at Muroc the other day, Admiral. It was a beautiful thing, watching those Skyhawks get busy. Of course, my guys were all over yours, Mike."

Before Judge could respond, Kolhammer cut him off. "You can lay your bets later, gentlemen. I just wanted to make sure nothing's getting jammed up here at the last moment. So, Mike, you happy with your aircrew? They're about ninety percent 'temp, aren't they?"

"Yes, sir. And I've got hundreds of requests from the ship's original complement, asking to return to combat duty, but we still can't justify putting our own people in harm's way. Not when they're of more use in research and development. It *does* make for some sore feelings, though, Admiral."

"Bruised egos," Kolhammer grunted.

"Nothing to be done about it," Jones said. "It's been the case since we got here that anyone with an engineering degree—or *any* technical qualifications, for that matter—is going to be of more use in the lab than out on the battlefield. I've lost some of my best combat engineers to Caltech because of it. And one of my best company commanders, too, who just *happened* to major in fucking fluid mechanics, all because he was hot for some bimbo surfboard designer back in college."

"You know, it's been noted—rather uncharitably, I might add—that the three of *us* are all going back into combat," Judge observed.

Kolhammer shrugged it off. "We've been through it a hundred times. Somebody has to command this battle group, and it's a very different gig from running Spruance's task force, even with the AT stuff they've been bringing online. The whole world is watching Calais right now, but soon enough they'll be watching us, too. Tojo isn't the only one who wants to see us fall on our asses.

"So if there's nothing else I can do for you gentlemen, I suggest we all get back to work. And I'll see you in San Diego."

Both men nodded in agreement, then signed off. Kolhammer returned to the business of handing over the Special Administrative Zone to his deputy, Colonel Viviani. She would be empowered to act in his stead for the duration of the deployment. That meant he was almost free. There were about two hundred documents requiring hard-copy signatures, a final sit-down with the colonel, a quick tour of the campus to say good-bye to his department heads, and then he was *outta* there.

The only way he could be more excited was if they'd let him fly one of the new Skyhawks out onto the Big Hill. But that was an indulgence reserved for younger men. No, he'd be catching a C-130 down to the base.

Kolhammer pulled the stack of documents toward him and reached for his fountain pen. He brought the D-Day coverage back up and noticed that the byline on the air assault video was Julia Duffy's.

Dan's ex.

That had been a hell of a piss-poor show, their breakup. It had gutted Dan, killed him if truth be known. The big doofus had insisted on going back into combat afterward, whether to prove himself or to escape, Kolhammer wasn't sure. Didn't matter, though. Poor bastard never even made it to Pearl. His transport had crashed on takeoff from Muroc. Still, it wasn't his place to judge. What chance had they really had, coming from such different worlds? It had been noted, more than once, that almost all relationships between uptime women and contemporary men failed in the end—although, intriguingly, the reverse was not true. Perhaps the angrier feminists of his time had been right and all twenty-first man had really wanted was an old-fashioned wife. God knew there were any number of movies being made about it now. They screened as straight romances throughout the rest of the country, but were marketed as comedies inside the Zone. In the same way that *Reefer Madness* had once played so well with stoned college students.

Kolhammer watched the feed as he methodically worked his way through the stack of paper, signing wherever Liao had indicated. It wasn't something that took much of his attention, so he could follow Duffy's raw vision quite closely. The 'temps had adopted the embed system pretty much intact, so she got total access to the Seventh Cav. But all her unedited data became government property.

The fight outside Calais looked intense. There was no way most of this footage would be released outside the Zone, to the general public. It was way too graphic for the 'temps, who still hadn't seen a picture of a dead GI. While he scratched away with his Mont Blanc, a savage hand-to-hand battle played itself out on the screen in front of him. He couldn't tell which village she was reporting from, or even whether the cav and the 101st had made it into the port itself at this point. He kept the sound turned down while he worked. A part of him, detached from the repetitive task of signing off documents, wondered whether Julia Duffy was working through the same sort of impacted emotional damage that had driven her husband back to combat, and on to his death. She would doubtless carry a heavy load of guilt for the breakup. Dan had told him that she was already messed up over her friend Rosanna getting waxed on Hawaii. Blamed herself and couldn't get over the fact that she was still alive when Natoli was gone.

That was only normal. But did she blame herself for Dan getting killed, too? There was not a shred of doubt he'd demanded a combat assignment because of the breakup. And they had broken up mostly because of her refusal to accept that with marriage came family commitments. At least according to Dan. Kolhammer had never discussed it with Duffy. He had always found her to be a really tough bitch when they dealt professionally, and they'd had occasion to do so a lot when she was on Hoover's case last year. But he had to admit she was always a pro. The grunts loved her. And a lot of readers did, too, because of that. He shrugged the thought off. It wasn't relevant.

Having grown up with global media coverage, Kolhammer was more than capable of sitting in his comfortable office, watching men die thousands of miles away while he calmly attended to paperwork and personal thoughts. Some called it callous, and even the contemporary military personnel thought of it as a defining characteristic of the people who had come through the Transition. For him, however, it was just the way the world turned. The way it always had.

Other than Halabi and the *Trident,* none of "his" units were involved in the invasion. The only personal connection he had with the D-Day landings was there on his flat-panel display. The ex-wife of his late chief liaison officer.

Julia Duffy.

She was firing a weapon, silently. A helmet-mounted camera rendered the scene into something reminiscent of the video games he'd played as a teenager. The barrel in the center of the screen spat long tongues of fire, tracers leaping away, the impacts clearly visible around the window of a stone cottage a hundred meters in the distance.

He wondered when Dan had last spoken to her, and what they had said to each other.

All the heavy equipment had already been loaded onto the Eighty-second's newly commissioned heavy littoral assault ships down at San Diego. The *Falluja* and the *Damascus* were based on a long-hulled *Essex*-class keel, with substantial modifications to fit them out for the requirements of Jones's marine expeditionary brigade. The president had approved the change from unit to brigade when the First and Second battalions came online. And Jones's promotion had gone through in the same sheaf of orders.

There had been times, plenty of them, when Jones had wondered if they'd ever be allowed to leave. Or whether, when they did, they'd be pushed off into some sideshow like Persia or Burma. He'd have to apologize to Kolhammer for snapping at him like that before, but even his considerable reserves of Zen calm were being drained dry.

Still, at long last, they looked good to go. The Super Shermans and AT-LAVs were all stowed away and chained down on the *Kandahar*. The last supplies were being loaded. Only a few heavy-lift choppers and Jones's own command Huey remained to be flown out from Muroc Field, along with the twelve Skyhawks that would join with his remaining Super Harriers to provide organic air support. Another thirty-six of the "modern" Skyhawk fighter-bombers were embarking with Kolhammer on the Big Hill, making them the first carrier-borne jets in the Pacific. They were also the most powerful military planes in the world, a generation more advanced than the Sabers that were increasingly coming to dominate the skies over Europe.

Regardless of the matériel they had amassed, Jones was most concerned with the beating heart of his command—the three battalions of the Ninth Regiment, Fifth Division, United States Marine Corps.

He pulled the brim of his cap down lower as he stepped out of the Quonset hut onto the gravel path, turning away from the regiment's administrative buildings toward Camp Hannon's parade ground. Conditions at Hannon were primitive, especially when compared with the increasingly settled and luxurious campus informally known as "Area 51" or just "51," the control center of the Special Administrative Zone, which had attracted dozens of aeronautical and "high-technology" firms—a term he found more than a little ironic.

More often than not these companies had established West Coast offices in downtown LA or elsewhere in the Valley. However, with the Zone operating as an autonomous region where twenty-first-century U.S. law and custom prevailed, a lot of outfits like Douglas, IBM, Boeing, and McDonnell had spun off stand-alone companies with their offices here.

Despite wartime restrictions on building materials, they had still managed to run up some very impressive-looking buildings dotting the grounds of 51. Even so, they were dwarfed—both physically and conceptually—by a publicly owned entity, the Intellectual Property Trust, or IPT. By an act of Congress, IPT now held "deemed" patents over all those remaining processes and creations where ownership was contested or even nonexistent. Prime examples were Microsoft's operating systems and applications, which had yet to be invented, yet had come with them through the Transition. From what he had heard, the plan was for the trust to be broken up and floated on the open market sometime after the war.

Frankly, it was all beyond Jones—he had no idea how these guys worked out who owned what. One of his former captains, Maria O'Brien, had been a legal affairs officer attached to the War Crimes Unit on the *Clinton,* and she had tried to explain it to him once, without much luck. She'd been just a few weeks from finishing her hitch in the corps when the Transition had ripped her out of whatever life she'd been *supposed* to lead. Now she made more money than God as a civilian lawyer, smoothing out the intersection between the economy of 1940s America and twenty-first-century intellectual property law. Her personal "Death Star"—as she jokingly called it—was a weird, contorted mass of polished concrete and black glass out on the fashionable western edge of 51, amid a streetscape of expensive restaurants and lush parkland. Jones always thought her building, which had been designed by some very important architect whose name completely escaped him, resembled a bagel turned inside out, if that made any sense. It looked to be about six floors high, although he doubted it ran to anything as mundane as actual "floors" on the inside.

As far as he was concerned, she could have it all to herself. The less Jones had to do with the 'temps, the better.

A born conservative, even as a kid in the projects he'd never had time for politically correct bullshit. In *his* America men and women, black or white, got the chance to make a success out of life. And if they didn't succeed, it was probably their own fucking fault. He'd gotten no special treatment from the corps, but he'd suffered no discrimination, either. Every decoration he had pinned to his dress uniform had been honestly earned, mostly by killing people who badly needed it. The Bible at his bedside table had lain beside his daddy's pillow, and like his daddy he allowed himself one reading every night that it was possible, starting at Genesis and slowly working his way through to Revelation, before going back and starting all over again.

He had supported the same baseball team—the Cubs—for thirty-five years. The same basketball team—the Bulls—for thirty-six. He loved his country, his corps, his friends, and his family, most especially his wife who was, as he never tired of telling people, as white as the Grand Cyclops of the Ku Klux

Klan. By way of contrast General J. Lonesome Jones disliked whining left-wingers, network news broadcasts, and steamed brussels sprouts all about equally.

He wasn't the sort who saw himself as the victim of anything.

Yet nearly every time he had to deal with the 'temps, it seemed like he was instantly cast in bronze as the object of their fear and loathing. At the very best they treated him with a stiff reserve. That was the standard response whenever task force business took him down to Camp Pendleton to meet with the "old" Marine Corps brass. He was treated with courtesy, and every formality due his rank. But never once were the informalities observed. Even after Hawaii, he'd never been invited to take a drink or share a meal with anyone at Pendleton.

Jones pressed his lips together as his boots crunched along the gravel path. The insults to his own dignity he could suffer in silence. He didn't give a shit about the opinions of ignorant assholes. But the endless shitcanning of his marines was intolerable.

The sun burned the back of his neck, and he could feel sweat beginning to stream between his shoulder blades, under his uniform. His eyes remained hidden behind a pair of powered-down sunglasses, but anyone who ran across his path would have had no trouble telling that he was mightily pissed about something. Around him the camp was relatively quiet, a counterpoint to the seething anger that threatened to get the better of the Eighty-second's commander.

A platoon jogged by, singing cadence, a tune he recognized from his earliest days in the military. The lyrics had changed, though, in this post-Transition world.

We care a lot
About the Nazis and the fucking Japanese.

He really hated the fucking song, truth be known, but an old roomie had played it incessantly many years ago, and in a strange way hearing it calmed him down a little as he returned the salutes of a couple of lieutenants he passed on his way to the final staff meeting. Mary Hiers and Nikki Christa from the landing support team. Good young officers. 'Temps, but most of the brigade were, nowadays. They'd taken 20 percent casualties on Oahu. Added to the losses in Australia, it meant he'd

come home with an effective fighting strength of one reinforced company.

He was still humming the old "Faith No More" standard sev-
eral minutes after the platoon had passed by.

They'd had no choice but to rebuild from the ground up.
There'd been no shortage of volunteers from among the
'temps, allowing his recruiters to skim off the cream.

And given that so many of his newest marines were never
going to be welcome in the old corps, you might have thought
they'd have been left in peace. But no. He and Kolhammer had
been forced to wage a series of small bureaucratic wars just to
keep the Eighty-second alive. Everything was contested. For instance, there was no Fifth Marine Division when they had arrived.
It would not have been established until November 1943 for the
Battle of Iwo Jima, but the contemporary corps insisted on placing a caveat over the designation anyway, demanding that Jones
give up the "Fifth." Indeed, he and Kolhammer had been forced
to fight battles over lineage for virtually every one of the "new"
units they'd spun up. In every case they'd refused to give ground.

The Eighty-second MEU had fought as part of the Ninth
Regiment, Fifth Division of the United States Marine Corps,
since it was raised for the Second Afghan War in 2012. They
had earned the right to be who they were.

He noticed that his speed had increased when he'd become
angry again, stirring up a small storm of gravel as he double-
timed it over to the First Battalion ops room. Jones screwed a
lid on his temper. He reminded himself that for every dumbass
he'd encountered, there were old-fashioned Americans like
Mary Hiers and Nikki Christa, or Master Chief Eddie Mohr, or
even Dan Black, God rest his soul, who were good people. As
good as people ever got, really. He slowed his breathing and
dropped back to a normal pace. It wouldn't do to go charging
into battalion in such a foul mood. Somebody was liable to get
an ass chewed off for nothing.

D-DAY + 2. 5 MAY 1944.
LOS ANGELES.

The view from the top floor of the Davidson Building—which
had, until recently, been the Oviatt Building—was nothing
compared with his New York base. Back east the company had

leased about twenty floors of the Empire State, and on a clear day Slim Jim could stand at the window of his personal office suite and almost see his own power as it pulsed outward across Manhattan, racing away toward the horizon like a blast wave. That was what real wealth and power were like. A force of fucking nature that swept everything in front of them. He'd always known that, of course. But only because for most of his life he'd been the one getting blown away. By cops. By judges. By bigger, tougher, meaner crooks. By wardens. By parole officers. By the whole fucking system.

"Now I am the fucking system," he said with a grin.

"What was that, Mr. Davidson?"

"Sorry," he said, turning away from the window in his LA headquarters. The place was on Olive, near Sixth, and afforded him a good view of Bunker Hill, which looked like a natural rampart laid across the western edge of the old pueblo. Downtown Los Angeles lay at his feet, but it was obvious that his building was going to be dwarfed before too long by the skyscrapers rising around her. Not that he cared much. He owned a couple of construction companies now, and he loved looking out at all the cranes soaring over the city's rooftops. It was sorta like they were there to scoop money up off the streets and dump it into his pockets.

"Sorry," he said again. "What were we talking about?"

His lawyer, Ms. O'Brien, looked exasperated, as usual. He often thought that uptight was her natural state of being. Their relationship had changed some since the early days, though, when she'd acted more like his drill sergeant than his employee. O'Brien was a player in her own right now. Probably one of the richest women in America, if you didn't count heiresses. And he didn't. They tended to be stuck-up bitches who wouldn't give him the time of day. But as his business got bigger and he grew more and more powerful, she came to . . . what? Admire him, he guessed. She was only a little more deferential than she had been, but if he didn't know any better he'd say she almost respected him for the way he'd handled the last few years.

"We were discussing your testimony in the Rockefeller suit, Mr. Davidson," she said. "It's important. You can't slide through this one on a boyish grin and southern charm. These guys are out to snap you like a twig."

He shrugged. "Assholes like this been beating on me since—"

"Oh please. Let's not do your E! channel bio today. Let's work through the brief I zapped over. You did read it, didn't you? They're not going to let you wear your Oakleys in court, so I can't send you notes up on the stand."

"Yeah, yeah, I read it," he grumbled. Most of what he did nowadays seemed to be reading and signing big piles of paper. Most of it he didn't understand. He preferred sitting down with a couple of guys over a beer and talking shit through like men. He was a good listener. You had to be when you'd made your living as a grifter.

Ms. O'Brien started in on him like a prosecutor going after an ax murderer. It'd been a little scary the first time she'd done it, but she explained it was just like in the navy when he'd trained for war. The courtroom was no different. He had an enemy that was coming after him, trying to destroy him. He had to be ready. She kept firing questions at him. Real curly ones, too, and he practiced saying as little as possible that'd get him in trouble. The only real joy of it was contemplating what a bloody pulp Ms. O'Brien was going to reduce those Rockefeller assholes to when they got onto the stand. She had a well-earned reputation for brutality in the courtroom. It was partly why he expected this bullshit case to settle, and why only part of his mind was really on it. Another part, the old Slim Jim, was thinking about the party he was gonna throw in his penthouse over the weekend. He had half of Hollywood coming over to rip it up in his rooftop pool and artificial beach. They were the only original features he'd kept when he bought the Oviatt Building. Everything else—the Lalique chandeliers, the art deco bar, the exotic woods in the floors and walls—he'd had torn out and replaced with the closest facsimiles of twenty-first materials his personal designers could find. Ms. O'Brien had been aghast and argued vehemently against the "vandalism," as she called it, but Slim Jim wasn't having a bar of it. The next century had been very kind to him, whereas this one had done nothin' but kick his ass from the moment he'd crawled out of the cradle.

And anyway, 21C was the hottest style in modern architecture. Nobody built old anymore.

"Are you concentrating, Mr. Davidson?"

"Nope," he admitted.

"Are you thinking about your party this weekend?" she asked, putting down the flexipad she'd been holding.

"Uh-huh."

"You thinking about copping a blow job from Hedy Lamarr again?"

He grinned. "No, but now that you mention it—"

"Well, knock it off!" she barked. "Because if you can't, the only blow jobs you're gonna be getting will be from the jail-house cat in a federal pen."

Chastened, he apologized and tried to focus on the questions. But before long he was daydreaming about Hedy Lamarr again. And splitting beers with Ernest Hemingway. And sailing with Errol Flynn. And playing poker with Artie Snider, the war hero he'd met at a Kennedy fund-raiser. They were all great fucking guys. And unlike those society snobs, they didn't look down on him for what he'd once been.

3

D-DAY + 4. 7 MAY 1944. 2045 HOURS.
BUNKER COMPLEX, BERLIN.

It was no longer safe at the Wolfschanze.

Indeed, there *was* no Wolfschanze to speak of—not now. Allied bombers had struck there in a massive raid just three months ago. Had the führer not been delayed in Berlin, he might even have been killed. More than a thousand men of the SS had died on that day.

Himmler rubbed the hot, grainy feeling from his eyes. This bunker offered none of the comforts of Rastenburg, but it had one major advantage. The British and Americans did not know of its existence. Or at least he thought they didn't. One could never be sure these days . . .

The *Reichsführer-SS* grunted. It was pointless trying to second-guess one's opponent, especially in wartime. The enemy rarely did what you wanted. You could study them, and plan for contingencies based on their capabilities, but once you began fantasizing that you actually knew their intentions . . . well, that was a folly for decadent novelists, not for statesmen.

The rough concrete walls of the underground bunker oozed with condensation. Here in the map room, it wasn't so bad. Fans turned constantly to suck the stale atmosphere away and drag fresh air down from the surface. But there were places in this complex—as in all the subterranean hideouts in which they had been forced to take sanctuary—where he found himself close to passing out, so vile were the stench and the heat. Every breath tasted as though it had already been inhaled a hundred times over. Fastidious in his personal habits, Heinrich Himmler found the press of unwashed humanity one of the hardest burdens he had been forced to bear in this conflict.

Thirty or more people were crammed into the map room, an area not much bigger than a sizable parlor. The overcrowding was made worse by the huge map table, which dominated at least half the floor. A large, flat televiewing screen hung from the wall, displaying much the same information as the little wooden blocks that were being pushed around the table, but it wasn't updated nearly as frequently. Even with the bounty they had taken off the *Dessaix* and the "Indonesian" ships, the Reich simply did not have the Allies' ability to monitor the "battle-space," as they called it.

Göbbels had come up with a suitably Teutonic alternative to the Anglo-Saxon phrase—*Kriegsgebiet,* the realm of battle. And standing by Hitler's side as the führer marshaled his response to this violation of the Reich, Himmler could appreciate the cor-rectness of the phrase. Battle was not joined across a simple field, as it had been in the days of Bismarck. No, it was being fought on land, in the air, on and under the sea, where millions contested the future of the world, in blood and iron.

The mood in the room was tense. They had known this was coming, since their own lunge across the channel was foiled. The memory still gave him shudders. The führer's screaming. Göring getting drunk and becoming more dangerous as his vaunted jet fighters were scythed out of the sky. Göbbels saying nothing, his eyes sinking back into those darkened pools. The military high command making one excuse after another. One fool of an admiral had even dared to question the wisdom of launching the operation in the first place. He, of course, was no longer numbered among the living. Indeed, a great many of the men who had been in the war room at Rastenburg had received their final rewards: a firing squad and an unmarked grave.

This would be different, however. He breathed slowly through his mouth, lest a sudden gulp give away how nervous he was. The führer ordered the Second SS Panzer Corps moved up out of Le Mans. A moment later he countermanded the order. No one said anything.

Himmler let his eyes traverse the room, settling on anybody who seemed even half inclined to question their leader's judgment. One Wehrmacht colonel blanched under his gaze.

"It is a ruse," Hitler muttered, biting his lower lip. "I am sure of it." He was staring at the table with such febrile intensity that it was a wonder the surface did not begin to smolder.

General Zeitzler, the army chief of staff—who looked about two decades older than his forty-nine years—seemed about to say something, jumping into the space left clear by the führer's uncertainty. But then Hitler folded his arms and jutted his chin.

"Yes. A ruse. This business in Calais is a feint, don't you agree, Herr General? Just as it was with their Operation Fortitude in the Other Time. I saw through that one, too, you know. The historical documents make it quite clear. I knew they would come ashore at Normandy, and tried to get that traitor Rommel to reorder the defenses. But no! He would not listen. So it is here, at Normandy, that the real blow will fall."

The führer brought his pointer down with a sharp crack.

Himmler, along with everyone else in earshot, jumped slightly.

The tip of the pointer was resting on the stretch of shoreline the Allies referred to as Omaha Beach. It was the logical point of access, and much work had gone into luring them there. The defenses in the dune system had been allowed to degrade, to make Eisenhower think that the Wehrmacht's center of gravity had shifted north of the Seine, just as it had in the Other Time, *die Andere Zeit.* Close study of the archives captured from the French ship and corroborated by the Japanese had taught them that fixed defenses were a death trap. No matter how much concrete was poured, no matter how many thousands of miles of razor wire were laid, in the end such defenses could be negated by high explosives.

No, it was mobility that had won the Reich all the prizes in the opening phase of this war, and it was mobility—the doctrine of blitzkrieg—that would win this next battle.

Himmler mopped at his greasy brow with a gray handkerchief. It had once been white. The accursed "drones" sent out by the mud woman Halabi made everything much more difficult, but the Soviets had been unusually helpful in providing creative camouflage, what they called *maskirovka*. They were acknowledged masters of the field. Himmler shook his head. He was tired, suffering from nervous exhaustion, and his mind had a tendency to wander. He forced his attention back onto the map table.

Four divisions of Allied infantry had come ashore at Calais. Two American, one British, and one Canadian. It appeared as if another two airborne divisions had leapfrogged the diversionary assault, one by helicopter attack, to infest a number of villages outside the port city. A division of *Fallschirmjäger* had been tasked with defending the area and had given a good account of themselves—much better than their pathetic showing during Operation Sea Dragon. Six enemy divisions, equipped with some quite amazing new weaponry, had been held up for two days. But six divisions were less than 4 percent of Eisenhower's order of battle.

No, the führer was right. The main blow would fall on Normandy.

Wouldn't it?

D-DAY + 4. 7 MAY 1944. 2156 HOURS.
CALAIS.

The small living room looked liked something out of a crackhouse nightmare. Every stick of furniture was broken. Fires had been set everywhere but in the fireplace, which was full of human excrement. And everything was covered in a thick dusting of plaster brought down from the ceiling and walls by the seismic shock of the Allied assault.

"Fire in the hole!"

Julia turned away and covered her ears. The shaped charge went off with a head-splitting roar, temporarily smothering the sounds of gunfire from the street. The hammering of three or four Colt carbines on burst kicked in while her ears were still ringing from the detonation, followed by the flat *whump* of an M320 grenade launcher. Another crash and someone cried out.

"Satchel charge! Fire in the hole!"

Another explosion shook the house, perhaps the whole row of terraced houses, reminding her of the time a mud brick house in Damascus had come down on top of her just like this.

"Go, go, go!"

The fire team rushed forward and leapt through the hole they'd blown in the wall dividing this house from the next. A brief burst of gunfire, and then the familiar call.

"Clear!"

She swung around the door frame where she'd been sheltering, automatically checking to make sure the battery indicator for her Sonycam was still showing blue. A time hack in the corner of her heads-up display told her there was just over an hour's worth of storage left on this stick. Her last.

Moving toward the smoking fissure, Julia forced herself not to look at the spot where Gil Amundson had bled out on the floor, waiting for evac. They'd covered him with a rug.

She bent and stepped quickly through into the next house, the muzzle of her own Colt sweeping the room as she did.

A three-round burst sounded upstairs, immediately followed by the *thud* of something heavy hitting the floor. Plaster chips and fine white dust floated down, coating her goggles.

"Clear!"

A windowpane shattered and sprayed her face with shards of glass. She felt the sting of lacerated flesh, and the warmth of blood that was beginning to flow freely. Julia whipped off her glove and ran her fingers over the skin of her neck. Nothing cut there. Just more facial scars to add to her collection. She cleaned herself up with a couple of medicated wipes and a small tube of spray-on skin.

"You okay, Ms. Duffy?"

It was Steve Murphy, the trooper who was now an acting corporal, in charge of twelve men from two other remnant platoons. With Amundson dead, nobody from their original chalk was left.

"I'm fine, Murph," she said, wiping the last of the blood away. "Just making myself beautiful."

A pair of boots came thundering down the stairwell in the narrow, darkened hallway outside what looked like a dining room.

"Alcones coming through!"

Another cav trooper, one of Murphy's strays, came back into the room, being careful to stay out of the line of sight provided by the broken window.

"There was a kraut upstairs, Corporal. He was saving this for company."

Alcones flipped a potato masher grenade in the air and caught it with the same hand.

Murphy nodded. "Good work. Let's take five and wait for the others to catch up. This is the last house in the row, if I'm not mistaken. Anyone think different? Alcones, could you see anything from up there?"

The trooper nodded. "We're at the end of this block of houses, or what's left of it. We got ruins on all three sides. The next stretch of buildings is a block to the west, maybe fifty yards or so to reach them."

Murphy risked a quick glance across the cobbled street. It was coming up on midnight, but there were hundreds of fires burning all over this part of Calais, and they lit the night. Besides Duffy and himself, there were four others in the room. The rest of the platoon had taken up defensive positions throughout the ruined house.

"Okay. Ammo check?"

Prufrock checked his pouches. "Two mags, two frags, Corporal."

"Three mags and the LAW," Chalese reported from his covering position by a door.

Juarez, by the window, had "one mag and fuck-all else."

Murphy pulled one of his own magazines and tossed it to Juarez. "That leaves me with three. What about you, Al? Ms. Duffy?"

Alcones had two and some spare change.

Duffy didn't need to check. "I got three full reloads and four grenades. Plus an hour's worth of video left, if anyone's planning on doing something dramatic."

Murphy sighed and took off his helmet. "Ms. Duffy, can you tell where we are or where Reynolds's squad is? They should be across the street by now. But I can't see shit with these goggles."

He tapped his Starlites with a bloodied fist.

She shrugged. "Dunno. Let's find out."

If they'd had a workable tac net, she could have just brought up the drone coverage and located her own biosensors in the battlespace display. Duffy was a popular embed for a lot of reasons, partly because she had access to the Fleetnet interface at a 21C level. Unfortunately, that only worked when she was near enough to a relay node to make the link. They were out on their own here, and she hadn't had a tickle from Fleetnet for—she checked the counter—nearly thirteen hours.

Julia bent low and crept over to the window, pushing aside the torn lace curtain with the muzzle of her carbine. She was the only one with a powered helmet and integrated tac set. It wasn't her original rig—that had been based on a standard-issue Advanced Combat Helmet, which looked too much like the Nazi "bucket" for comfort. Wearing something like that, she was just asking to get shot in the ass, so she'd paid an engineer from the Eighty-second big dollars to build her a new mount that fit on a contemporary M1 helmet.

She removed the Sonycam from its base and, holding it so that only her hand was exposed, focused it on the cottage across the way. The smart sensors adjusted to the light, and she concentrated on a small pop-up window in her goggles. The nearest house looked deserted.

Then a flash of light drew her attention, and she shifted the camera.

"All-righty then. Two doors down to the northwest, your two o'clock, Murph. Looks like a coupla *Fallschirmjäger*. And second floor, center window, an MG-Forty-two. Got good intersecting fields of fire. They'll chop us to dog meat if we go out there."

She shook her head.

"Man, I wish Fleetnet was up. I could tell you where your other squad is. But as it is, I got nada."

"Reynolds is going to run into those guys," said Alcones. "They've got to know we're here, Murph. With all the racket we made getting in here."

"The kraut by the door is slumped. I'd say he is either sleeping, wounded, or both," Julia said.

Murphy pondered his options for the moment. Julia had enough confidence in him to shut up and wait. She'd seen way more combat than him, but he'd proved himself a natural the last few days. The corporal put his helmet back on.

"Okay. Alcones, Chalese, get yourselves upstairs. Prufrock, get back out into the hall, give the rest of the guys a heads-up. Tell them to get a bead on that house Ms. Duffy just tagged. On my mark we're going to put a world of hurt on that joint. Half-'n'-halfs. High explosive and flechette. Got it?"

They nodded and dispersed.

"Ms. Duffy, could you keep an eye on things, make sure no friendlies get into that place before we hit 'er up?"

"Sure thing," Julia said, checking her batteries and memory blocks again.

Murphy and the lost paratrooper from the 101st, Private Juarez, took up positions by the window, with Murphy loading a fat gray HEMP slug into his grenade launcher. Prufrock poked his head through the hole in the wall to indicate that the rest of the platoon was ready. Murphy nodded and poked his carbine through the shattered window.

The M320 made a thumping sound. Julia followed the round as it crossed the forty or so meters until it sailed through the center of the open window. A flash followed by a *crump* signaled the start of the fight.

"Open fire!" he yelled.

A crash upstairs preceded long knives of glass falling past her into the street by half a second. Five dull *thuds* sent the 40mm grenades on their way. The underslung M320-type launchers some of them carried on their carbines weren't a patch on the programmable 440s she was used to, but they still shot a variety of bomblets up to four hundred meters, with a muzzle velocity of seventy-six meters a second. The target building—no more than forty meters away—shuddered under the impact of the handheld artillery barrage.

Five flashes and peals of thunder rolled into one as a dozen automatic rifles opened up.

"Again!" Murphy called out.

The volley was a little more ragged this time, each man firing independently. Five staggered *whumps,* five more detonations.

Julia raised the camera to the window again, just before Corporal Murphy hoisted his rifle and squeezed off a three-round burst. A German soldier who had come running out of the house covered in blood and beating at flames on his arms was thrown back inside. Only the soles of his boots showed in the darkened doorway. They twitched for a few seconds before going still. His burning uniform threw a guttering light on the shambles inside.

"Okay. All right. Stand down," the corporal yelled.

"Well, that's that, I figure," Murphy went on a little more quietly, sliding down the wall to sit with his legs splayed out in front of him. "If Reynolds is alive, he should be able to get here now."

Juarez, the paratrooper, kept watch.

Julia took a sip of chilled sports drink from the tube at her left shoulder. She was exhausted, too. They'd been fighting their way into Calais for two days, literally blasting a passage through the long rows of terraced houses. It was a murderous business, but marginally less dangerous than moving out in the open.

Amundson had explained that they'd trained for this scenario back in England, using a village that had been specially constructed by the army. She wondered idly whether some genius had picked up the details in an old soldier's memoir, or whether the marines back in the Zone had passed on the lessons learned from twenty years of urban warfare in the Middle East and South Asia.

Didn't matter, really. As long as the job got done.

She paused the Sonycam, saving lattice space, and pulled an energy bar out of one of the many pockets on her matrix armor. Before they'd embarked, she'd stuffed about a dozen of the things wherever she could find space. It was wrapped in waxed paper rather than foil, but other than that it was exactly like the energy bars she'd chewed through when running half marathons back up in the twenty-first. She chuckled at the thought.

"Something funny, Ms. Duffy?" Murphy asked.

She broke off a piece of the chewy snack and waved it at Murphy and Juarez. "I've got shares in this company, that's all," she said. "Eat up, boys. Make me rich."

Her eyelids were twitching, the way they did when she went without sleep or stimulants for too long. There were uppers you could get, ripped off the formula for stims, but she didn't like them much. The effects were crude, and the crash was brutal. With her inserts tapped dry she was better off going back to basics: sugar, caffeine, nicotine, and Hooah! bars.

The uproar increased again outside. Two huge bangs shook a broken mirror off the wall above Murphy's head, and it shattered against the floor. She could hear animalistic screams under the sound of a brief but savage firefight.

"Heads up!" Murphy called out, hauling himself up from the litter on the floor.

Julia powered up her Sonycam again and flicked off the safety of her carbine.

They waited for some word from Reynolds's guys on the far side of the street, to let them know who had won and who had lost that small, discrete encounter in a very long, strange war.

D-DAY + 4. 7 MAY 1944. 2354 HOURS.
BUNKER COMPLEX, BERLIN.

There were more than a hundred individual unit markers on the *Kriegsgebiet* display, and every one them jumped when the führer pounded his fists down on the map table, hammering at Norway like a vengeful God.

"I say it is a diversion, and so it must be!"

"Yes, yes, of course, *Mein Führer,* but they are still a worthy target," Zeitzler babbled. "Just imagine the blow to their morale if they were to be wiped out. They are weak, the democracies. They cannot absorb the damage as we can. If we were to release the *Panzer Lehr,* they would annihilate—"

Hitler turned on him.

"*Enough!* You will execute my orders, or you yourself will be executed. Do you understand?"

Himmler thought the army chief might save them the cost of a bullet by falling dead with fright then, right in front of the assembled high command.

The lights in the room faded out for a second, causing them to glance around nervously. But a quick check confirmed that no Allied bombs were falling. Most likely it was just some problem with the wiring, a common enough occurrence in these hastily constructed bunkers.

As the exposed bulbs hanging over the map table flared again, Himmler regarded the situation in Calais with a dismal eye. He did not like to question the führer, and would never do so publicly, of course. But uniquely among the Nazi elite, he prided himself on being able to broach unpleasant subjects, even with Adolf Hitler.

Indeed, it was he who had suggested the temporary cease-fire with the Bolsheviks, allowing them to secure themselves in the West. And it was he who had first admitted that the Allied air strikes on the rail lines leading to the Jewish processing facilities in Poland were appreciably slowing the Final Solution. He had led the counteroffensive against their enemies within, revealed by the electrical archives on the *Dessaix*. And he had been the first to recognize that, to preserve the forces they had moved into northern France, they would need to withdraw beyond the range of the *Trident*'s sensors and Churchill's Bomber Command.

Hitler had not enjoyed hearing any of it, but he had to be told. Was it the same now?

The *Reichsführer-SS* examined the map table, comparing it with the televiewing screen. He wasn't a military genius—he knew that only too well. But he would not shy from doing whatever was necessary. Around him the business of the war continued. The führer curtailed his diatribe against Zeitzler and started in on Göring, demanding to know why the Luftwaffe was making so little headway in cracking open the Allied air defense network.

"They are in our *Kriegsgebiet* now, *Herr Reichsmarschall*. But where are your jet fighters? Where are the dive-bombers?"

Himmler didn't even bother attending to the fat fool's reply. It would be a waste of time. Göring had no operational control of the air force anymore. He was only here because he had survived the purges. Himmler shut him out now, along with the dozens of war room staffers who scurried about. Instead, he concentrated on the situation unfolding in front of them.

The Abwehr reported that Allied preparations for a massive assault on Normandy continued unabated. A *real* army was gathering in the hinterland of Falmouth and Dartmouth, ready for the channel crossing. There would be no repeat of the *Fortitude* deception—not in this war. The Reich would not be caught unawares or misled into thinking the invasion would fall in one place, when all along it had been meant for another. The crushing weight of the greatest military machine the world had ever known was poised to fall on Eisenhower as soon as he commenced his main thrust.

Still, Zeitzler had a point. To destroy the landing at Calais might prove a crippling blow to Allied morale.

But then, the führer was right, as well. Thousands of Allied warplanes infested the sky above Calais and Dover, just waiting to pounce. To commit the best of their armored and heavy divisions into Calais meant feeding them to the sharks of the RAF and the USAAF.

If only they could match the Allies' surveillance cover. Unfortunately, while providence had delivered the *Dessaix* into their hands, only a handful of the crew had proved cooperative, and some of *those* had turned out to be saboteurs. As a result, they had not been able to fully exploit the ship's capabilities, and now she was lost to them forever. Sunk by that criminal whore on the submarine *Havoc*.

One could go mad thinking about the squandered opportunities. With just a few "surveillance drones," and the men trained to use them, they could have logged every ship and aircraft movement out of southern England.

Himmler sighed.

The führer had calmed down and was standing at the table again, arms folded, chin on his chest as he bobbed up and down on the balls of his feet and pondered the diabolical strategic problems of the hour. The Allies must be kept from the Fatherland a little while longer. Soon the Reich would have its first atomic weapon, and there would be no more talk of unconditional surrender. Churchill and Roosevelt would be the ones groveling, begging for an accommodation.

Then, with the democracies checkmated in the West, they could turn their attention back to Stalin.

The map table did not extend beyond Poland, yet the vast steppes and the brooding Communist giant were never far from anyone's mind. The cease-fire with Moscow was still holding, but it was beyond argument that the Red Army was using this time to prepare its defenses against another Wehrmacht attack, at the same time that the two states "cooperated" on a number of technical projects—all in the name of facing the "common enemy." It was all horseshit, but the pause in hostilities suited them both.

Or rather, Stalin *thought* it suited him.

When the atomic warheads were finally delivered, the Slavic buffoon would be made to realize just how wrong he had been.

4

D-DAY + 5. 8 MAY 1944. 1833 HOURS.
PARIS.

Brasch had read somewhere that those who can eat well, and those who cannot, exist at all times on opposite sides of a gulf that can never be crossed.

It had been more than three and a half years since pastries had been legally sold in Paris, and about the same interval since fish, meat, chocolates, tobacco, and wine had been rationed almost out of existence. Nonetheless, sitting by one of the large windows in Maxim's Le Bar Imperial, Major General Paul Brasch found himself adrift on the odors of fine French cuisine. The Parisians in the street below might have been getting by on starvation rations, but when *Reichsmarschall* Göring was in town looting the art treasures of the Republic, he loved to dine at Maxim's, and so the wartime restrictions did not bite as heavily here.

Brasch nursed his Kir Royale and wondered whether or not he would ever have set foot in this place—or any like it—had it not been for the war.

Not likely, he mused. And truthfully, it wasn't the war that had delivered him to this stool at the end of a dark wooden bar. No, it was the Emergence. Without the miracle of the time travelers' arrival, he would probably be a frozen corpse somewhere in Russia by now. Instead he sipped at a cocktail, enjoyed the sour look on the face of his latest bodyguard, *Hauptsturm-führer* Neumann, and wondered whether his data package would arrive before his dinner guest.

He would never know, really. The encryption software protecting his communications stripped off any identifying tags such as datelines. He alone would be able to read the file, and then for only ten minutes, before it disappeared from history altogether. And of course, he wouldn't be cracking open his latest instructions from the British over a late supper with General Oberg, the SS commander in Paris.

Dining with human filth like Oberg was a necessary sacrifice. Brasch was a very privileged Nazi nowadays, one of the trusted few. He had even been invited to share a table at the Palais Luxembourg with the morphine-addled Göring, resplendent in his white *Reichsmarschall* uniform, encrusted with jewels and medals over which the fat criminal had vomited during the dessert course. The engineer had long ago learned to control the sensation of his balls crawling up into his belly, his flesh seeming to swarm with lice, whenever he mixed with the likes of Göring and Oberg. Since he had received word that his wife and son had safely reached Canada, he had even begun to *revel* in the double life forced on him as the price of their deliverance. It was a wonderful thing, mixing with these pigs, conniving in their downfall, and all the time knowing that the only people in the world he cared about were beyond their reach.

Indeed, as far as anyone in the Third Reich was concerned, Willie Brasch and little Manfred had been killed in a British bombing raid in November 1942. A tragic loss for a hero who had already given so much to the cause, and an explanation—as if any were needed—for his fanatical devotion to duty.

"Ah! So good to see a smiling face at last. We can always depend on you, Herr General."

Brasch's smile only grew wider as he turned on his bar stool and stood to salute *Oberstgruppenführer* Karl Oberg, the man who would probably set Paris aflame in a couple of weeks to deny its liberation by the Americans. The room was crowded, and so thick with cigarette and cigar smoke that the patrons in the farthest corners were almost obscured. Oberg stood out, though. Even the *Wehrmacht* officers gave him a wide berth.

"Inventing some new V-weapon while you wait for dinner, I imagine," Oberg said. He resembled nothing so much as a squashed, fattened caricature of Heinrich Himmler. He had been a fruit seller before joining the party and the SS, and he was the embodiment of all the poisonous irony inherent to the term *master race*. Nevertheless, the smile never left Brasch's face as he opened his mouth to reply.

"No! No, don't tell me," Oberg interrupted, waving a hand. "I understand well that you cannot discuss such things."

In fact, Brasch was imagining what it would feel like to take Oberg's close-cropped porcine head in his hands and twist it so violently that the spinal cord shattered instantly. How many of the people in this bar would applaud?

Some, but not all. Neumann there would probably put a bullet into his head before Oberg hit the floor. And of the handful of Frenchmen and -women who were taking an aperitif in the baroque splendor of the Imperial, how many would be pleased, and how many horrified?

It was impossible to say. Only the most significant collaborators were given entrée to these rarefied circles, and with the invasion under way, only they would care to be seen with the Germans.

Even so, you couldn't trust the waiters, or the prostitutes, or even the fascist leaders of the French Popular Party. Any of them might be secretly working for the Resistance. Dozens of collaborators and their German overlords had been killed in the last few weeks. Brasch himself was a target of great value, because of his role in the Ministry of Advanced Armaments Research, so the SS had assigned Neumann to protect him out of a genuine fear that he might be lost to such an attack.

Yet none of this meant anything to Brasch—he had numbered himself among the dead back when he served on the Eastern Front. In truth, his secret life, and the knowledge of his family's escape, made each day a gift from above.

"Actually, Herr General," he said, pumping Oberg's arm in a firm two-handed grip, "you are entirely correct. You should consider a career in counterintelligence. Clearly you can see right through me."

"Of course, of course!" the SS commander replied. "So we must talk our way around such things, over dinner.

"I understand you are leaving for Berlin tomorrow," he continued. "I just wanted to thank you for all of the help you have given my staff while you were here and, if I might impose upon you, to pass along a personal note to the *Reichsführer*."

Brasch clicked his heels. "Of course, Herr General. I shall be seeing *Reichsführer* Himmler almost as soon as I return. I shall make certain he gets your letter."

He pocketed the slim envelope in his jacket, next to the flexi-ipad that still waited for the signal from Müller.

He had less than an hour to live. The blood leaking into his shoes made a squelching noise as he dragged himself up the street.

There was no pain, thanks to an analgesic flush from his spinal syrettes, but Müller knew that the knives had struck deeply. As much blood as had flowed out of him to soak his clothes, he was losing even more to the internal bleeding that would surely end his life.

A lamppost loomed, the glow of its light a soft sphere in the summer night, tempting him to stop for just a little while. But he pressed on. If he gave up now, even for a short rest, there was no guarantee he'd be able to get moving again.

The three Frenchmen who had set upon him earlier had meant business. Whether they were Resistance fighters or simply street toughs did not matter. It had been a short, brutal encounter. He hadn't hesitated to defend himself when they came at him out of the dark alleyway. Many people would have paused, and died on the spot, but when the oldest, most primitive parts of his brain began screaming at him that he was in danger, Müller *acted*. His fighting knife had appeared in his hand instantaneously, and without conscious thought he had decided which of the three was to die first, even before they had closed the short distance between them.

If they were Resistance, there was no point trying to explain that they were all working toward the same end. He'd dispatched two of them with his knife and killed the third with an open-handed strike to the throat that had crushed the man's larynx. However, he wasn't fast enough. At least two of the stab wounds he'd suffered felt as if they had cut something deep and vital. As he fled the scene, gray space bloomed at the edge of his vision, and cold chills racked his upper body with increasing violence despite the warmth of the evening.

Müller could not be certain that he would get far enough to establish a point-to-point link with Brasch's flexipad. He stopped in the doorway of a boarded-up tailor shop, a Jewish business, and automated the contact routines, just in case. He might not make it all the way to the dispatch point, but as long as the engineer passed within seven hundred meters the link would set itself up.

Drawing breath felt like hauling a great weight up into himself at the end of a long rope. His feet dragged, and more than once they threatened to become tangled up with each other.

People were beginning to stare.

He tried to calculate the distance he had left to travel. Maybe another four hundred meters. Supercoagulants gathered at the site of his wounds, to slow the loss of blood. Another flush of stim coursed into his veins, pushing him on and clearing some of the gray from his vision.

But blood was beginning to show through the coat he had taken from the body of the man he'd killed with the blow to the throat. As the stain spread, and his discomfort became obvious, the reactions of those passing by became more pronounced. In short, they avoided him. There were many Parisians about, but none approached him to help, for which he was grateful. The last thing he needed right now was some Gallic busybody complicating matters further.

Actually, the *last* thing he needed was for another German to do so, but as he staggered down the way, that was exactly what occurred.

Someone hurried across the street toward him. "Hey! Wait there. I'll help you."

The figure swam in and out of focus, but the black uniform of an SS officer was unmistakable.

Fuck it.

Müller cursed his bad luck. He was wearing a civilian jacket over his gore-stained Luftwaffe captain's uniform. In his breast pocket was a British flexipad, and he was heading toward the most valuable spy the Allies had in Nazi Germany. This was not going to end well.

"Resistance," he coughed as the SS man ran up and grabbed his arms to steady him. He had been very close to toppling over.

"What happened?" the man demanded. Müller recognized him as a *Hauptsturmführer*. A captain. A definite buffer existed around them now, a circle about twenty meters in diameter into which none of the locals would dare step. They all found some reason to cross to the other side of the street.

"Resistance," Müller repeated. "Three of them. Back at the Rue la Bruyere. I killed them."

"I don't doubt it," his would-be savior said, supporting most of his weight. "We must get you to an aid station. Quickly, come this way."

The man began to force Müller back the way he had just come. There was an aid station two blocks down. He attempted to resist, but his helper was too strong.

"No, this way, *Herr Kapitän,*" he insisted. "You are in shock. You need to come with me—let me carry you."

Finally Müller allowed himself to fall over the other's shoulder, his arm around the man's neck. He let his body go limp, allowing his full weight to burden the SS officer, who grunted a little with the effort. Müller let himself be carried away from his objective, acting in character, cursing the Resistance, vowing revenge, demanding that the SS hunt down those who were responsible.

"But you said you killed them," his rescuer grunted.

A wet, wounded chuckle bubbled up out of Müller's throat. "So I did."

Then he drove his fighting knife deep into the man's sternum, twisting and ripping up and out. The screech of pain became confused with the cries of onlookers, who could not believe what they were seeing as Müller suddenly locked up his victim's head, using the arm he had draped over the shoulders, before slitting his throat from ear to ear. The man's screams were cut off as Müller severed the windpipe. The body dropped with a sick *thud* as the head hit the pavement.

Müller's world tilted then, and threatened to fall out from under him. He let his momentum carry him into the road, where he stopped a velo-taxi, one of the faintly ridiculous three-wheeled, pedal-powered cabs that had taken over the city during the Occupation. The driver attempted to swerve around him, but a shot from Müller's pistol pulled him up.

A shrill whistle sounded in the distance, and he thought he could hear hobnailed boots hammering toward him. He half lunged, half fell into the passenger's seat.

"Just get me up the road," he croaked in his passable French.

"B-but . . ." The driver tried to stammer out some excuse, but a wave of the pistol set him to his job. They lurched away just as rifle fire cracked past them.

"They will kill me," the driver protested.

"No, *I* will kill you if you don't hurry up. Just to the next corner, and then you can get out. I'll shoot you in the ass if you like, to prove that you were hijacked."

"To prove I was *what*?"

"Just fucking pedal."

More bullets whistled past, some of them sparking off the cobblestones and shattering shop windows, sending the native Parisians scurrying for cover. More bullets chewed great chunks out of the little wooden passenger's cabin. Müller painfully forced himself to twist around in the seat.

About two hundred meters back a detachment of German soldiers had outrun a couple of gendarmes and were taking aim.

They weren't going to make it.

Crack!

The top of the velo-taxi driver's head flew off in a fantail of blood and gray matter. Immediately they decelerated, and Müller allowed himself to roll out of the cab onto the hard stone roadway. A bullet struck him a glancing blow on the shoulder, knocking him forward. He managed to scramble a few more meters as he hauled out the flexipad.

No signal lock.

Crack!

An enormous iron fist slammed into him, bringing darkness.

He came to, expecting to find himself in a Gestapo cell.

But he was still in Paris, on the street. The pedicab driver's body was just a few feet away, gushing blood like a ruptured pipeline. A squad of German infantry had surrounded him, their guns leveled at his head.

He blinked slowly and his head swam.

"What have we here. A spy? A Resistance pig playing dress-up. A traitor?"

An officer was speaking, advancing on him. Müller realized he was still holding the precious flexipad in his outstretched hand. He tried to get to his knees, but the Wehrmacht officer, a lieutenant, sailed in and launched a vicious snap kick at his ribs. His inserts protected him from the worst of the pain, but he felt at least three ribs break as he flew over onto his back and rolled another half a meter away, ending facedown in a puddle of mud.

The pad began to beep.

It had locked on to Brasch's device and initiated a linkup. The file transfer began.

It was complete within half a second.

"What the hell is *that*?" the lieutenant demanded.

Müller coughed up a thick blood clot.

"*That* is the end of the world," he said, rolling on top of the flexipad with the last of his energy and triggering the explosive weave vest he routinely wore under whatever disguise his mission required.

Everyone within thirty meters was atomized by the blast.

"What the hell was *that*?" Oberg asked as the rumble shook the crystalware on their table at Maxim's.

Brasch had no idea, but he instantly assumed something had gone wrong with Müller. There was no reason to think so, really. Bombs were constantly going off in Paris. The Resistance had been tutored by instructors familiar with insurgencies from the far future that had paralyzed much more formidable opponents than the Nazis. It might be a truck bomb twenty-five kilometers away, or a suitcase bomb in a café or bistro favored by the Germans. It might even be one of the Existentialists, seeking vengeance for the murder of Sartre and de Beauvoir by blowing himself up in a brothel favored by the occupying forces. Everybody feared being caught up in one of their mad attacks. It was said that the last thing you ever heard was the crazed existentialist screaming "To do is to be!" before he triggered his suicide device.

Brasch stood up and pushed aside the drapes that covered the window nearest their table. He had to press his face right up to the glass, but in doing so he could make out the telltale signs of a detonation a few blocks away.

His stomach turned over.

"An existentialist," he sighed, not believing it for a second.

Something *had* gone wrong. He could sense it down in his core.

"Madmen," Oberg hissed. "Cowards, all of them. If only there were some way to stop them. To detect them before they set themselves off," he complained.

"As I understand it, no foolproof solution was ever found in the future," Brasch commented. "When a man is willing to die to harm his enemies, there is always a good chance of taking some of them with him."

"Pah!" spat the SS commandant. "When will these bastards accept that they are *beaten*? You know the most frustrating thing about this, Brasch. It's that we cannot identify the bombers postmortem. Believe me, if that were possible we'd thin out the ranks of their recruits. Execute every last one of their friends and relatives. Then they mightn't be so enthusiastic about blowing themselves up."

Brasch returned to his seat, itching with the desire to take out his flexipad and see whether his data burst had come through. He pushed at an unfinished plate of *boeuf bourguignon* with his heavy gilded fork. "A lot of money is going into DNA research." He shrugged. "Eventually it will help, and then we will have the ability to trace back to the culprits and take the appropriate measures."

"Yes, yes, so I have heard!" Oberg said approvingly. He had returned to his own meal without missing a beat. "It is a very exciting field, this genetic science. I understand you have been instrumental in pushing it forward."

Brasch smiled abashedly. "It's not really my field. I am a combat engineer. But any good German could see the importance of investing in such a thing. For starters, it will mean there is no hiding for the Jews. And the weaklings—the infirm, the cripples, and the mentally defective—will be detected before they have a chance to be born. Although I do not understand the science, I understand the opportunities for the Reich—"

"As do we all!" Oberg interrupted. "For me, personally, it is one of the most exciting developments to come from the Emergence."

"*Reichsführer* Himmler shares your enthusiasm," Brasch remarked, suppressing the death head grin that wanted to crawl over his face.

He had championed the cause of genetic research because it was an exact fit with the worst of the Nazis' paranoid fantasies, and because it was the perfect sinkhole into which he could pour billions of Reichsmarks. Every pfennig spent on a wild goose chase—like the search for a homosexual gene—was money lost to the development of lighter body armor or improved jet turbines. Brasch had never received any explicit instructions from Müller's controllers to sabotage the Nazi war effort in this way but, quietly, it was the work of which he was most proud.

"There are, of course, those chattering fools who do not see the historic importance of such research," he continued. "Admittedly, atomics are a more pressing concern at the moment, but even that research cannot be allowed to detract from our advances in the genetic realm."

Oberg nodded sagely, like the fat, bigoted fruit seller he was, trying to prove himself the intellectual equal of his esteemed dinner guest. "Yes, yes, I understand," he replied. "I've even heard that the atomic bomb itself will cause terrible damage to the breeding line of anyone who is exposed to it."

"Exactly!" Brasch agreed. "So while we must push on with the atomic program, the purity of the race can only be guaranteed by a genetics program that proceeds apace with our nuclear research. There is no point to winning an atomic war if we all turn into mutants afterward."

"My point precisely." Oberg nodded, sloshing some of his wine onto the white damask tablecloth.

They continued like this for another two hours, with Brasch encouraging the wildest flights of lunacy to which he found most high-ranking Nazis more than a little prone. The entire time, however, he could feel the flexipad digging into his hip. The urge to haul it out and see whether he had received a secure transmission from Müller was nigh on intolerable.

What had happened out there?

Was Müller involved?

Was he dead? Or perhaps captured and already being tortured?

What would Brasch find waiting when he finally broke free of this odious little man?

5

**D-DAY + 7. 10 MAY 1944. 2355 HOURS.
DORSET.**

The airfield lay ten miles outside of Bournemouth, on the coast of southern England, almost directly across the channel from Cherbourg. Thousands of aircraft flew overhead, all of them heading out and on to targets in France.

Hundreds of thousands of men and incredible tonnages of

heavy tanks and trucks and other vehicles were on the move through the countryside down to the ports at Southampton, Portsmouth, and Bournemouth itself. But nothing moved out of the airfield for three days after the invasion commenced.

Then, on D-Day plus seven, the dull, bass thudding of a massed helicopter flight drifted across the green-and-brown patchwork of tilled fields and green pasture that surrounded the base. Two extended V-formations of heavy-lift choppers swept in from the northeast and set down on the makeshift helipad, which had been a village cricket pitch before the war.

"All right," Prince Harry said to himself. "Game on." He hadn't thought it possible to find a more uncomfortable form of transport than a Chinook heavy-lift chopper, yet here it was: a reinvented 1940s analog of a Chinook.

Pounding up the rear ramp into the dimly lit interior at five minutes to midnight, Colonel Harry Windsor envied his 'temp troopers their lack of familiarity with the uptime version of the helicopter. To him, these facsimile CH 47As felt smaller, slower, and altogether more likely to fall apart in midair.

He'd studied the aircraft specs before the first operational squadron arrived at the regimental HQ in Kinlochmoidart, and it had made for unpleasant bedtime reading. The engines, although a significant advance on anything available locally just twelve months ago, were still underpowered. The craft could carry only twelve men, as opposed to sixteen. But there was an upside to that, he mused wryly—it meant there would be fewer casualties when the things fell out of the sky like fat, broken-backed dragons.

He cast around looking for the crew chief. Yes, there he was checking a galvanized-steel drip pan. The big helos were notorious for hydraulic leaks, and it was standard procedure for the chief to check the level of fluid in the drip pan before takeoff. If you didn't see any leakage, the lines were probably bone dry and you were all going to die.

Harry adjusted his Bergen pack and automatically checked the safety of his personal weapon, just to get his mind off the hydraulic problems. The AK-47 copy was designated the AW/GLS—for "Automatic Weapon/Grenade Launching System"—by the Royal Ordnance Factory where it was manufactured, but the popular tag *Ivan gun* had caught on, in recognition of its Russian heritage. The stamped-metal version of the infamous

Kalashnikov was now standard issue throughout most of the British and commonwealth forces. They were much easier to build than the Americans' more glamorous Colt carbine. His sported an underslung M320-style launcher.

Every other SAS trooper was likewise equipped. The launchers were harder to find outside the Special Forces. For the time being they tended to be restricted to squad and section leaders in the Main Force infantry units.

The chopper's interior was bathed in a soft red light. His half troop of eight men were seated with their backs against the fuselage, packs between their legs, guns pointed down so that a misfire couldn't damage the rotors or engines above. Of these men, only the Jamaican giant Sergeant Major Vivian Richards St. Clair, his senior NCO, had come through the wormhole with him. The others were all 'temps, but they were every bit as good as the troopers he'd left behind in the twenty-first. They'd have to be—he'd trained them himself.

"Evenin', lads," he called out over the whine of the Rolls-Royce Osprey engines. "So, anyone fancy a trip to France? I thought we might pick up a bit of duty-free, maybe catch a show at the Follies, and then pop down to Donzenac to kick the living shitter out of a couple of fuckin' Nazis. What do you say?"

St. Clair roared from the front of the cabin, *"We say cry God for Harry, England, and Saint George!"*

For just a second the cheers of his men overwhelmed the sound of the engines cycling up. Harry grinned hugely and hauled himself the rest of the way up the ramp, giving each man a pat on the shoulder, or a nod, or a wink. Like the Special Air Service of his day, nobody walked into a squadron straight out of the recruiting office. In this here and now, in the Second Regiment at least, they had to have at least five years in service already, and a proven combat record had been a big plus on any application.

There was still an original, contemporary SAS, still being run by David Stirling, and it operated under slightly different rules—their own. There was a good deal of interplay between the two outfits, and constant traffic in training cadre, but in the end they did what they did, and Harry got on with his own business.

He shrugged off his pack and settled himself down next to

the two French nationals who'd be going in with them, Captain Marcel Ronsard of the Free French First Army and Mademoiselle Anjela Claudel of the Bureau d'Opérations Aériennes, a Resistance group responsible for coordinating special ops in northern and, more recently, central France. His own French—workmanlike before the Transition—had improved to near fluency in the years since. He shook hands with both Ronsard and Claudel. The huge drooping four-bladed rotors began to turn faster, and Harry indicated that they should power up their tac sets if they wanted to speak in anything less than a bellow.

He was still wearing the powered helmet he'd brought through the wormhole. Unlike the Yanks, his British headgear didn't make him look like a German paratrooper. Ronsard helped Claudel plug in and power up. She was unfamiliar with the comm rig, but the Frenchman had been training with the SAS for nearly twelve months and was as much a part of the regiment as Harry, or Viv, or any of the half a dozen Free French officers the prince had sought out to join him for the "Great Crusade."

As they fiddled with the earphones Harry looked past them, out through the rear hatchway to the nameless airfield where another thirty Chinooks were spooling up, adding the thunder of their takeoff to that of his own. Two full squadrons of the Second—close to 240 men— were on their way to seize control of one of Hitler's strategic jewels, the Missile Facility at Donzenac in south-central France on the western fringe of the Massif Central.

D-DAY + 8. 11 MAY 1944. 0110 HOURS.
LONDON. CABINET WAR ROOMS.

"I think you are to be congratulated, General," said Winston Churchill. "This will be a victory for the ages."

Eisenhower looked uncomfortable with the praise. His shoulders rolled around nervously under his jacket. "Our men . . . and women," he replied after a pause, "are the ones who deserve congratulations, Prime Minister. They're out there fighting for us."

Churchill grinned wickedly. "I don't know how you expect to become president if you refuse to take credit for others' good work, General. You still have a lot to learn."

Eisenhower didn't so much as twitch a facial muscle in reply. Instead he focused on the drama of Europe's liberation.

The map table in the war room was crowded with hundreds of wooden unit markers. Female RAF officers still pushed them around with long pointers, but most of the high-ranking staffers watched the video wall, where eight large flatscreens had been linked together to make one giant battlespace monitor, displaying the take from HMS *Trident*. The screens weren't locally manufactured—that capability was still a few years away. Maybe even a decade. No, they had been borrowed from the Zone especially for this event. Churchill wondered how he might hold on to them afterward. British industry would benefit tremendously from being able to study them.

He caught himself, however, thinking as though the future were settled. They still had this grim business to be done with, of crushing the Nazis. It was entirely possible, he knew, that at any moment one of those screens would light up with the news of an atomic blast somewhere in France, probably directly over the Calais pocket occupied by growing numbers of Allied Forces.

Churchill rarely slept more than a few hours a night, as a habit, and the specter of a Nazi A-bomb prevented him from enjoying what little sleep he *did* get. He'd read thousands of pages of secret reports indicating that they simply did not have the resource base or industrial capacity to produce even one such device, and thousands more warning of an inevitable atomic attack some time in the next few weeks. Or even days.

An aide appeared, and the British prime minister nodded for another cup of coffee, with a shot of Bushmills. For the moment the operation was running as well as could be expected—better, in some ways. The Germans were still maintaining the bulk of their forces in the Normandy area, waiting for a blow that would never fall there. The Allies had established air superiority—if not total dominance—of the Calais battlespace. The Germans had put many more jet fighters into the fray than had been expected, and they had cut to ribbons whole wings of old prop-driven fighters, but they simply could not prevail against the huge numbers of Allied, mostly American, F-86 Sabers that confronted them. And the Germans didn't have anything like the numbers of heavy and medium bombers that the

RAF and USAAF could bring to bear. Nor had they invested in any kind of airborne warning and control systems like the Allies.

The great strategic surprise of the campaign, however, had been the airlift. The heavy, coordinated investment in just three types of helicopter by all of the Allies had paid handsome dividends. In just four days an extra six divisions had been lifted directly into the combat zone, including three artillery regiments with all of their howitzers and ammunition. It was a miracle.

"Prime Minister, Prince Harry and his regiment are en route."

"Thank you," he replied to the young army captain who had brought the news. Then he turned to Eisenhower. "And now we reach one of our trip wires, General. We shall see whether Donzenac is the bogey we all feared."

Eisenhower nodded, pressing his lips together. "I sincerely hope not, Prime Minister."

D-DAY + 8. 11 MAY 1944. 0232 HOURS.
SOUTH-CENTRAL FRANCE.

Fifteen silver darts shrieked over the evergreen forests of Correze, blue cones of superhot exhaust pushing them toward their target at a thousand kilometers an hour.

Squadron Leader Fiona Hobbins nudged the stick over slightly, shifting her heading two degrees to the south. The moonlit landscape blurred beneath her, the shimmering surface of a small lake rushing toward the nose of her fighter-bomber and vanishing beneath in just a couple of heartbeats. She paid it no heed, instead concentrating on the world she could see in the heads-up display of her powered goggles, a precious set of Oakleys on loan from the *Clinton*.

Behind her the other pilots wore identical sets, linked via the flexipads in their cockpits to one of the *Trident*'s high-altitude drones. It was a slipshod half-arsed arrangement, in Hobbins's opinion, but there was no avoiding it. Until somebody built a plant capable of fabricating quantum chips, or even old Pentiums, they were stuck with these sorts of kludges.

Bottom line, though, they worked.

Mostly.

Her visuals resembled an old flight-sim game from the days

before V3D, but that was enough to allow them to thread through the tangled mess of the air battle over France and into the target box, a short, shallow valley in the quiet south. As the squadron flashed over a small French hamlet, designated in light blue outline by the *Trident*'s Combat Intelligence, she craned her head to the left, where twenty-eight small green triangles were converging on her heading at about a quarter of her airspeed.

The Chinooks carrying Prince Harry and the SAS. Five minutes late and two choppers short. She quickly checked a status display and found that one of the big birds had been forced to turn back with hydraulic failures. Another had crashed in the channel.

Hobbins performed a few constrained isometric stretches to work out the kinks and some residual nervousness. If she fucked up, the men in those helicopters were all going to die. If not in battle, then soon thereafter. The Germans were still summarily executing any "Kommados" they captured.

A chime in her helmet sounded, and the voice of the *Trident*'s Combat Intelligence spoke up. "Five minutes to release point. Arm warheads."

A small flashing red box appeared just above the virtual horizon in her HUD. She nudged the stick again, lining up the yellow arrowhead with the target designator. Back up in the twenty-first, a CI would have handled all of this, with the pilot riding along just in case something went wrong. Of course, back up in the twenty-first she wouldn't have been on a mission like this. She wasn't a jet jockey—or hadn't been, anyway. But thousands of hours flying light transport planes in and out of Third World death traps like Damascus and Addis Ababa had marked her out when the talent scouts had come calling. So now she flew jets.

Specifically she flew the contemporary version of the F-86F Saber jet.

"Three minutes to release. Slaving mission package to CI."

The *Trident*'s CI, still speaking in the voice of an as-yet-unborn Lady Beckham, informed the squadron that she had taken over the bomb release. Hobbins wanted to grip the stick harder, but she forced herself to breathe out, to relax her hold on the plane, and let herself flow through the moment.

A quick check of the heads-up confirmed that all fifteen

Sabers were in formation and lined up for the final run in. High above them, the *Trident*'s Big Eye tracked the jets feeding the data back to the stealth destroyer's CI, which measured their progress against position fix emitters set in place by the Resistance, and calculated the time left to release while keeping the squadron on the correct heading.

The Chinooks had fallen well behind now. Hobbins would need a top-down view of the battlespace if she wanted to track their progress. Instead, she concentrated on the darkened world that was rushing past her bubble canopy, and the objective that lay just ahead. It was a cloudless night; the stars were pinpoint emeralds in her LLAMPS vision, the Central Massif a wall of lime-green negative space, blotting out the heavens to the southeast. Tactical readouts and rendered terrain display overlaid the soft luminous French countryside, where every human-made structure was drawn on her goggles in hard schematic outline. A dry stone wall. A tumbledown barn. A burned-out church.

And then, rushing toward them at a seemingly insane velocity, the target box and nearly two dozen smaller icons: flashing red triangles where the Big Eye had detected and designated antiaircraft guns and concentrations of armored vehicles.

"Begin climb. Begin climb. Begin climb."

She pulled back on the stick, and the nose of the F-86 turned skyward. She could feel the g-force pressing her back into her seat, trying to squeeze the blood out of her brain and down into her butt, despite the pressure suit she was wearing.

"Begin dive. Begin dive. Begin dive."

She pushed forward, and the virtual horizon floated up in her display as all the blood rushed back toward her head. Soon she was lancing down toward her objective, a hardened concrete silo system housing two dozen V3 missiles.

Hobbins centered herself as the final chime sounded.

"Bomb release in five, four, three . . ."

Lazy streams of wandering, badly directed tracer fire searched for her in the darkness.

". . . two, one. Release. Release. Release."

Hobbins felt the tug as her seven-hundred-kilo Penetrator dropped away. Concentrating furiously on the nav display, she pulled up and rolled to the west while the first explosions ripped apart the giant hidden complex beneath her. The shock waves buffeted her as she sped away, shaking the airframe so violently that she wondered if she might lose a wing.

There was a sharp stab of pain in her mouth, followed by the rush of something warm and salty. She'd bitten her tongue. Pouring on the acceleration, weaving around to follow the yellow arrowhead designator that kept her away from the rapidly diminishing flak streams, she dialed up a feed from the Big Eye, an infrared view from ten thousand meters up.

All fifteen jets were still flying, but one was trailing flames. It exploded as she watched, the detonation lost in a storm of much larger blasts as more Penetrators drilled deep into shattered concrete and went off, focusing their destructive energies down into the missile farm.

Secondary explosions of rocket fuel and warheads tore up the valley, negating the attacks on smaller individual targets.

"Shit," muttered Hobbins. "That was a bit excessive."

"Sweet Jesus," Ronsard breathed.

"Nope," Harry corrected him. "Professor Barnes Wallis, and about twenty years of uptime experience digging reinforced bunkers out of the Hindu Kush."

Anjela Claudel's voice, shocked and a little shaky, came in over his helmet systems. "But everyone will be dead. The scientists, too."

"Not everyone," said Harry. "We'll lose everybody in the silos, but three-quarters of von Braun's team live off-site in Complex B. That's still standing."

"How many of the Boche will be waiting for you, though?" asked Claudel.

Harry smiled. "Enough for everyone. Now, if you'll just excuse me a moment."

He pulled his combat goggles down over his eyes, the gelform seal molding itself to the contours of his face. He linked to the Big Eye and back to the *Trident* via flexipad. A dense, multicolored V3D representation appeared, showing the threat bubble out to eight kilometers. In smaller windows, live video ran of the blazing bunkers and the residential complex that was their objective. He was presented with immediate damage surveys, estimates of the number of enemy killed and incapacitated, the disposition of his own forces, and live intel from the *Trident*'s CIC. To the uninitiated it would seem an almost impenetrable mass of data, but it was as familiar to Harry as an old and much-loved children's picture book.

The second squadron, under Lieutenant Colonel Hamilton, was already setting down in their Landing Zone away to the west. The first choppers had disgorged their troops, who'd formed up just below a ridgeline overlooking Complex B.

Harry switched his view to a live feed of his squadron's own LZ, overlaid with tactical and threat assessment data. They would be setting down another six hundred meters away, in a large field to the south.

The copilot's voice cut in. "Strobe sighted. Verifying."

An infrared strobe had just lit up, identifying the LZ, and Harry knew that the Big Eye had just focused at least half of its lenses and sensors on that area. All being well, one of Claudel's Resistance cells would be down there, ready to lead them in. If that didn't check out, and the Intel Division back on the *Trident* decided that the contact had been compromised, the area would be hosed down with autocannon and rocket fire, and they would move on to an alternative LZ.

He could sense Claudel's tension next to him. "It is okay?" she asked.

Harry waited for the signal from the *Trident*.

The strobe kept flashing.

"It is okay?" she repeated. *"Oui?"*

A green ALL CLEAR finally appeared in his HUD.

"Oui," he answered. "Lock and load, gentlemen. And mademoiselle, of course."

Claudel smiled brilliantly as she prepped her old Sten gun with a metallic *kerrchunk*. Her white teeth and bright green eyes were quite arresting, even in the red light of the cabin. Harry checked himself, grinding down on a spark of attraction. He normally didn't feel like getting a leg over until well after an op. But this had been happening a lot since his inserts had run out of neurochem inhibitor.

Oh well, perhaps if he lived . . .

"One minute."

Suddenly they dipped and swooped to the right, leaving his stomach where it had been somewhere above them. The combat chief hit a switch, and the rear door of the Chinook opened with a slow, heavy whirring noise.

Dozens of people back in England were watching the

ground below, alert for the slightest hint of a trap, but even so Harry was glad to see the chief giving it a severe eyeballing himself. That sort of attention to detail was how you got to be an old veteran rather than one of the poor fucking glorious dead.

A sick shudder ran through his body, a momentary aberration he recognized from the three or four times he'd experienced it before. It felt like a premonition of his death, but he suspected it was just a deep-body realization of his mortality.

After all, he was still alive, despite the previous visitations.

He noticed Claudel making the sign of the cross and whispering what looked like a Hail Mary. Of his own men, he could see four who were making their own peace with God, but like the remainder of his troop—and Captain Ronsard—Harry drove away his demons with a last equipment check.

"Thirty seconds," the crew chief called out.

The pilot wiped out almost all of their forward momentum, dropping them into a hover over the thick grass of the field. Harry could see cows gallumphing away in fear. A good sign. The chopper assumed its landing attitude, with the nose elevated so that the rear wheels would touch down first.

The chief and his two offsiders stood at the rear door, scanning the ground closely.

"Clear left!"

"Clear right!"

"Clear in the arse, guv!"

They began the last few meters of their descent. Nobody was praying now. Everyone had their warrior's mask firmly in place beneath the greasepaint and night vision goggles. Harry hooked an arm through his pack, getting ready to go. In his headphones, the copilot counted them in to touchdown.

". . . four, three, two, one, *down.*"

The front wheels struck ground. The chopper jumped forward a meter or two, then came to rest.

As soon as he felt the soft bump, Harry was up. They all rose as one, some more gracefully than others, who were caught off-balance and wobbled slightly as they hauled up their packs. Everyone dropped into an old-fashioned runner's stance: legs bent, knees flexing, ready for the starter's pistol. The chief pulled on a lever, dropping the tailgate onto the ground.

"Go, go, go."

The members of the heavy-weapon team ran out first, dropping to the ground, ready to start laying fire on the enemy if he had somehow gone undetected. Two by two, the remainder of the troop charged out behind them.

"Good luck, Your Highness," Anjela Claudel said.

"Vive la France," Harry replied.

They moved out into the night.

6

D-DAY + 8. 11 MAY 1944. 0341 HOURS.
DONZENAC MISSILE FACILITY,
SOUTH-CENTRAL FRANCE.

No plan survives contact with the enemy. Harry was going to have that tattooed on his arse if he survived this right fucking teddy bear's picnic.

He had twelve men to protect thirty-four German rocket scientists from an estimated eighty or ninety SS troopers, all of whom seemed to have gone to Plan B: kill everyone in sight. Harry himself was holed up in some sort of canteen on the second floor of the residential complex, with Nazis above and below him, and the rest of the squadron cut off on the other side of the H-shaped building.

The crash of small arms and Mills bombs did not let up. The scientists huddled together behind a makeshift barricade at the very rear of the mess hall, where Anjela Claudel and three of Harry's men, who would have been better used up here on the firing line, guarded them. Harry crouched behind an upturned table, a solid oaken slab of cover that protected them from the German Mausers. For now. There was only so much damage it could take, however, before it was reduced to splinters.

"Bit of a cock-up then, guv," Sergeant Major St. Clair commented.

"Just a fucking bit," Harry agreed.

Captain Ronsard shrugged theatrically. "Such is life, *non*?"

There'd been no warning that two companies of *SS Panzer-grenadiers* were posted at the residence, and before the two sides got themselves sorted out there were probably forty or fifty casualties in the mêlée. Now Harry's squadron was split over three floors, in a dozen different rooms. What looked like two full-strength platoons of Waffen-SS were blocking them from linking up with the other squadron, and tac net was blaring warnings of a battalion-sized enemy force racing toward Donzenac from Tulle. Gunships had peeled away to attack them, but there would be more to follow.

Harry had already ordered six of the Chinooks to depart with his wounded troopers and those captured rocket scientists they had managed to get out. But he needed to see the remaining prisoners away, too, because numbered among them were two of the Reich's foremost missile researchers, perhaps even their best: Wernher von Braun and Major General Walter Dornberger. Both had worked for the United States after the war, in his time. Since this was common knowledge now, the fact that they were still alive spoke volumes for their importance to the Third Reich. Harry was determined to get them out of here and back to England, no matter the cost.

If that proved impossible, as a last resort he'd put a bullet into each of their brains.

The sounds of close-quarter battle were so loud they penetrated his helmet's gel seal, making it difficult for him to communicate with his men, even using the throat mikes. The upturned table shuddered under the impact of concentrated rifle fire. At first he'd wondered why the *Panzergrenadiers* hadn't just tossed a couple of potato mashers over and finished off all the white coats he'd put in the bag. They'd done just that on the floor below, killing half a troop of his men and the six technicians they'd been shepherding.

But then, von Braun and Dornberger hadn't been part of that group. The Germans must have had orders to keep them alive no matter the cost. A mirror image of Harry's own mission brief.

For the moment, then, they had arrived at a stalemate.

The frenzy of small-arms fire and hand-to-hand fighting that had marked the opening minutes of the encounter had settled down into a more measured exchange, with each side trying to pick off the other, man by man. Harry couldn't even rely on his lads' night vision to give them an advantage. The SS were kitted out with their own Gen2-type goggles. He and St. Clair could have blinded them with flash-bangs, which their 21C optics were smart enough to blot out. But the rest of his men were equipped with NVGs no more advanced than the Germans'—perhaps a little less so.

An SAS trooper next to Ronsard who'd raised himself up to take a shot suddenly flew backward, a gout of dark fluid jetting from his splattered skull.

"Merde," grunted the Frenchman.

"Who was that?" Harry asked St. Clair.

The giant noncom glanced over. "Looks like Asher, guv."

"Bugger. I've had enough of this, Viv. They just have to keep us here long enough, and they win. That's why they're not pressing the issue."

St. Clair nodded. "Fair enough."

Captain Ronsard lifted his Ivan gun above the table and squeezed off a three-round burst. "You have a plan?"

"It's a bear hunt. We can't go through them. Can't get around them. We'll have to go over them."

"Sorry, guv," said St. Clair. "Left me jet-powered backpack at 'ome."

"Not to worry. I have a cunning plan. Is Private Haigh still in the land of the living?"

It was a bugger of a thing not being able to call up his men's biosigns. It meant he was never quite sure at any given moment who was drawing breath and who wasn't.

"Gideon!" St. Clair cried in a harsh whisper. "What are you up to, you nasty little man? Not 'aving another wank, I 'ope."

"No, Sergeant Major," came the reply over the tac net. "I'm down by the big fridge at the back of the room."

Excellent, thought Harry. "Private Haigh, it's Colonel Windsor," he said as softly as he could while still being heard. "Stay right there, and try very hard not to get killed. You're coming with me."

"With you? Where, sir?"

"On an adventure, my boy. Just keep your fucking head down."

Harry wormed his away over to St. Clair. Guns still barked all around them, and a shower of hot splinters pattered down on his helmet.

"I'm going up into the ceiling with Haigh," he said. "He used to be a coal miner, so the confined space shouldn't bother him. We'll try to work our way over behind the krauts and drop down on them. You'll have a second or two before they recover, more if they don't kill us right off the bat. You need to clean them out, Sergeant Major, and quickly. The old-fashioned way. Like we did in Surabaya."

Harry couldn't see St. Clair's eyes behind his combat goggles, but the grim set of his jaw was enough to confirm that he understood. Ronsard glanced up dubiously.

"Be ready in . . . twelve minutes," the prince said.

"Yes, sir. Good luck, Colonel."

"Cheers," Harry replied with more verve than he felt. He pressed himself down as low as he could and began to crawl across the debris-strewn floor. St. Clair tapped the shoulder of the man next to him and, with a series of hand gestures, told him to be ready to fix bayonets in ten. The trooper nodded and repeated the order back. When St. Clair gave him the thumbs-up, he turned to the next in line and passed it on.

Bullets snapped through the air just above Harry's head, some hitting stainless steel or chrome with a metallic ring, but most just thudding into plaster and woodwork. The German scientists all lay prone on the tiled floor, twitching and flinching when a round cracked close by, attempting to burrow under one another as they forgot themselves in the extremity of their terror. Two of them were dead, their throats cut as a punishment for trying to help the SS. Anjela Claudel was bathed in their blood. Harry had to pass through them all to get to Haigh, who was one of the few Englishmen actually standing, protected as he was by the mass of an industrial-sized refrigerator in the farthest corner of the hall.

The SAS troopers keeping watch over the scientists trained the muzzles of their Ivan guns on the men immediately around their commanding officer as he forced his way through. If any of them tried to interfere, they'd be shot without warning.

Harry checked his watch.

He'd used up two minutes twenty seconds covering the short distance. Haigh loosed off one more round before backing into the cramped V-shaped nook he'd made for himself by pushing the fridge away from the wall. Harry crawled in as far as he could, then hauled himself up like a rock climber, so as not to expose his back to the direct fire of the *Panzergrenadiers*. The uproar of the gunfight never once abated.

"Sorry to be so forward, Private, but I can't leave my arse hanging out. Some cheeky fucker would shoot it off."

"Very good, sir," Haigh responded. He was a tall, thin young man from the north of England who'd ended up in a Welsh coal mine before he was old enough to get into the army.

"No time to piss about then, Private. We're going up into the crawl space—" He pointed at the roof. "—at least there should be a crawl space. There's an access hole over by the servery. They probably use it for storage. We're going to get ourselves over behind those bastards and drop in on them for a bit of sport."

"Right you are, sir," Haigh replied, surprising Harry, who'd expected him to protest it as a damn fool idea—which it was. Instead he clicked the safety on his weapon and began to crawl up the exposed piping at the back of the refrigerator.

There was a fifteen-centimeter gap between the top of the unit and the roof, which exposed them to stray rounds, but Harry was pretty sure that in the chaos they wouldn't be noticed through the small break. Haigh took out his bayonet and carved through the roof tiles without much trouble.

They were probably made of asbestos, Harry thought as the dust drifted down on him. Well, that was the least of their worries. When he had an opening large enough to crawl through, Haigh disappeared inside the black hole like a snake into a rat's nest. Harry followed him, amazed at how easy the young miner had made it seem. It was really quite difficult just getting up there. He had no sure footholds. No room to maneuver. The din of pitched battle was painfully loud. He could feel every bullet that smacked into the fridge, and just before his head popped into the gap between the unit top and the ceiling, at least two rounds caromed through and punched into the plaster wall a few inches from his face.

He scrambled up through the hole, expecting to be hit.

He hadn't known what they'd find in the crawl space. In fact he hadn't been entirely sure there would *be* a crawl space up here, despite what he'd told Haigh. But there was, about half a meter of it.

His goggles rendered everything bottle green. Hundreds of bullet holes appeared as faint jade circles. The roof, which was now supporting him, felt very insecure, as if it might collapse under his weight as soon as he shifted position. He felt a light tap on his arm.

Private Haigh was lying along a thin wooden beam, beckoning him over. Very carefully, but with as much haste as he dared, Harry inched across while the trooper moved forward to give him room.

Haigh gestured *Forward* and Harry nodded, checking his watch. They had six minutes. The private wriggled along the narrow beam without any apparent effort, snaking around the joists that blocked their advance every ten meters or so. Bigger, older, and less flexible, the heir to the throne had slightly more trouble, almost rolling off the beam more times than he'd care to remember. He could imagine himself crashing down through the ceiling and dropping with a bone-cracking *thud* into no-man's-land. Just before the Germans blew him apart.

The crawl space was a deadly, surreal environment, jammed with plumbing, duct work, and electrical wiring, the last of which sparked and fizzed as ricochets and misdirected bullets sliced through live circuits. Harry felt as though he were sneaking between tectonic plates that might shift at any moment and crush the life out of him. He switched from low-light to infrared, to better keep track of exposed electrical wires, which could kill him just as quickly as the gunfire. Creeping around the joists slowed him even further, and, checking the time hack in the corner of his goggles, he cursed softly.

They had a minute and a half left.

Three rounds punched through the ceiling next to his head and he tensed, assuming he'd been spotted and was about to get stitched up. The heat of the gun battle below produced eerie cones of infrared illumination, including the spot where the burst had punctured the roof. But nothing further happened.

He scurried forward to catch up with Haigh, who was waiting for him a few meters ahead. The youngster had even managed to spin himself around so that he was facing his commander.

"I reckon this is it, Colonel."

Harry risked leaning out from the beam and pressing the lens of his NVGs up to a couple of closely spaced bullet holes. He discovered that if he shifted uncomfortably—and precariously—to his left, he could just make out what might be the camouflaged back of a German below them.

The time hack counted down.

04

03

02

01

00

"Go! Go! Go!" Harry cried. They both rolled off the beam and let their full weight collapse the flimsy roof tiles.

Sergeant Major St. Clair gathered what men he could at the up-turned table: eight in all, including Ronsard, leaving the French bird and three troopers to watch over the prisoners. They had orders to make sure von Braun and Dornberger did not survive if the colonel's plan didn't come off.

As the tac-net time hack flashed a two-minute warning, he pressed his throat mike and whispered, "Fix bayonets."

The men all quietly drew out their new standard-issue saw-back blades. Captain Ronsard fitted his with commendable alacrity—for a Frog. *Must be all that time in England.* Nobody loved a bayonet charge like the British army.

St. Clair unsheathed his own custom-made 21C Dark Ops fighting knife. It felt like an old mate's handshake. The double-thickness blade was forged from a hybrid alloy of five high-tensile metals and a surgical-grade monobonded carbon, nanonically hardened to give it a superfine edge without any brittleness. Back up in twenty-one it had been his habit to polish the blade in pig fat, a practice he'd given away shortly after the Transition. Only ragheaded nutjobs cared about getting stuck by "Ol' Porky," as he'd christened the evil-looking weapon. The boxheads, on the other hand, just didn't like it up 'em at all. For a supposedly warlike super-race, they turned into a bunch of fuckin' girly-men when things got up close and sticky.

The time hack counted down.

03

02

01

00

They held fire, lest they hit their own men. St. Clair heard a loud crash as Private Haigh and the colonel suddenly dropped out of the roof about three meters behind the German barricade. The rough staccato trip-hammer of two Ivan guns, pounding out six hundred rounds a minute each, started up as the Germans' own rate of fire trailed off in confusion and panic.

A war scream, a bellow, and St. Clair was up, leaping the barrier. Ronsard and the other men were right there with him. It was a potentially suicidal attack. The Germans were now caught in a rough crossfire, but that meant that his men were firing in the direction of Windsor and Haigh. He couldn't locate them in LLAMPS view, and hoped they'd dropped into cover of some sort, but for now his job was simple.

Close with the enemy, and destroy them.

Harry stayed low, shooting up, angling his fire across the *Panzergrenadiers* and hopefully not into St. Clair and the lads. Haigh had dropped to the floor beside him and cried out as he snapped a bone. He seemed a game type, though, and he'd started firing almost immediately.

The prince had been a bit luckier, landing on a couple of dead krauts who broke his fall quite nicely. He could hear the approaching bayonet charge as he slashed at the legs of the SS goons with a stream of automatic fire. The mêlée played itself out in a series of jump-cuts and jerky, disjointed images. A glimpse of a German half turning toward them. His head flying apart as Haigh took him under fire. A leg cut in two by tracers. Blood splatters. Chunks of flesh blown free and flying up to stick on the ceiling. Guttural screams. Panic. Outrage.

The next shock came as his men arrived, crashing into the SS line. He took his own fighting knife in his hands, the ground-quartz grip inserts cutting into his palms, a flash of light on the laser-tooled blood grooves. He smelled the foul exhalation of somebody's dying breath as he slashed through their throat. His gun, swung like a club, caved in a skull. Then there were fingers clawing at his goggles, hands at his throat. A clearing sweep of his arm and two short elbow jabs into his attacker's nose.

He kept firing his sidearm, firing and firing until the hammer clicked on a dry chamber. Then he was struck by the sudden realization that quiet had descended and that, for a few seconds at least, nobody was trying to kill him, and he didn't need to take anyone else's life.

St. Clair appeared. Breathing heavily, grinning like a cannibal. "Nice one, guv."

"Thanks, Viv," he gulped, taking in the full extent of the carnage for the first time. "Best we get a move on before they regroup outside. How many did we lose?"

"Three, sir. Robbins, Jezza, and Haigh, I'm afraid, guv'nor. He copped one in the throat."

"Bugger!" Harry grunted. "Okay. Make a note, Sergeant Major. We're putting Private Haigh up for a DCM."

"Very good, sir."

Harry picked his way across the killing floor, his boots beginning to stick on the blood and gore that were already congealing. Two of his troopers were guarding the doorway, making sure the krauts didn't get another look in. Ronsard and Claudel were smoking and chattering away quietly. They were both covered in blood.

He still had to get his charges up to the roof, and he had a squadron scattered all over the shop, but for the first time since they'd blundered into this five-star cock-up, he felt as if they might have a reasonable chance of pulling it off. He wished he could bring up a schematic of the building, not to mention the bio-indicators of everyone in his command, but he'd left that sort of convenience behind on the other side of the wormhole. He'd have to gather his forces piece by piece.

"Round them up," he ordered, pointing to the German scientists.

"I'm afraid we had to neck a couple more of 'em, guv," said St. Clair. "They got a bit uppity."

"Fair enough. What about the principles?"

"Dornberger's unconscious. Trooper Watson had to give him a smack. Von Braun is fine."

"Okay," Harry said. "Let's go."

7

As the California coastline slipped below the horizon, a freshening breeze built out of the southwest, tugging at the overalls and colored vests of the crew while they wrestled with the never-ending traffic down on the flight deck.

A Seahawk chopper, one of the few remaining aircraft from the *Clinton*'s original complement, was disappearing down the number one elevator, while a pair of Skyhawks waited in front of the jet blast deflectors of catapults three and four on the angled runway. Another twelve of the fighter-bombers were chained down along the starboard rows. Kolhammer had a full-time job just keeping track of the technology mix on board these days. The FAX catapult systems damaged at Midway had been completely replaced by steam catapults, and he was only too glad to admit that they were more reliable than the skittish, high-maintenance beasts with which the *Clinton* had first been outfitted. And they weren't exactly *contemporary* technology, having been redesigned by a specialist R&D shop back in the Zone to handle much greater stresses than the "old" launchers on a ship like the *Enterprise,* which was plowing into the swell three and a half thousand meters to port.

The "Big E" was still throwing old-fashioned Corsairs into the sky, too, not heavier, more powerful jets like the Skyhawks. And like most of the U.S. Navy's principal combatants, even the venerable *Enterprise* had been refitted with a suite of AT upgrades, such as simple rolling airframe missiles and radar-controlled Close-In Weapons Systems to protect her against the *kamikaze* attacks that had become a problem in the Pacific.

Kolhammer crossed his legs and eased back into his old

command chair as he took in the scene. The Combined Task Force consisted of three carrier battle groups, two that were contemporary and his own "retrofitted" group, now rebadged as Task Group Twenty-one. The USS *Hillary Clinton* was the beating heart of Twenty-one, with the Nemesis cruiser JDS *Siranui* and the three original ships of the Eighty-second MEU—the *Kandahar, Kennebunkport,* and *Providence*—making up her twenty-first component.

Four brand-new *Halsey*-class multimission guided missile destroyers rode shotgun on the group, their classic lines a close match with Kolhammer's boyhood memories of the old *Charles F. Adams*–class destroyers on which they were based. All four threw back fans of white water from their bows as they charged about, shepherding their flock and generally showing off.

For the moment the USS *Curtis* and her sisters the *Garrett,* the *Chandler,* and the *Reilly* were listed as Auxiliary Force vessels, which meant their crews were mixed and they operated under 21C laws and customs. Kolhammer used a pair of powered binoculars to follow the *Curtis* as she took up station a few hundred meters forward of the *Damascus,* one of Lonesome's new littoral assault ships. He could have dialed up battle-cam vision from the ship herself, but he preferred the glasses. They felt more intimate, even though they couldn't pull in as tightly as a camera. The great bulk of the *Clinton* meant that the relatively gentle swell had little effect on her, but the *Curtis* was already beginning to climb and plunge through the long, rolling waves. He watched as some of her crew ran through a simulated bomb strike on the ship's stern. He could just make out that a few of the sailors were black, and perhaps a couple were women. It was hard to tell at that distance. They all seemed to be working well together, but he worried that without inserts to dampen the sex drive, and given that they were crewed almost entirely by 'temps, there would inevitably be some trouble.

Hell, he'd had trouble with his own people when their spinal syrettes all ran dry, and everyone had to go back to being on their best behavior without neurochemical support.

"Admiral," said a young freckle-faced sailor, whose nervousness at approaching him for the first time seemed to be causing some violent gulping on her part. "A m-message from the *Enterprise,* sir. Admiral Mitchell sends his regards, and reminds you that you owe him a . . . a . . ."

"A six-pack, yes, thank you, Petty Officer Maguire." He smiled, trying to appear as harmless as possible. There seemed a very real chance that the young woman would pass out if he startled her. "Tell Admiral Mitchell that I'll . . ." He paused as her eyes bulged with a low-grade horror at the prospect of having to tell Mark Mitchell anything other than what he wanted. "Tell you what, I'll call him myself. You're dismissed."

"Thank you, sir." She gulped again before making her exit as quickly as she could.

"And Ms. Maguire?"

"Yes, Admiral?" she squeaked, turning so quickly that she almost fell into a bank of flatscreens.

"Relax, at least for now." Kolhammer smiled. "Nobody's shooting at you just yet."

"Yes, sir!"

She scurried off the flag bridge.

Mike Judge grinned after her, tugging the brim of his baseball cap down over his shades as he turned back to the blast windows. "And she was never seen or heard of again," he said.

Kolhammer suppressed a smirk, but a few of the bridge crew grinned. Judge was becoming well known as a captain who appreciated his own wit. It was a trait Kolhammer had noticed almost as soon as he'd met the *Clinton*'s former executive officer back in the twenty-first. That sort of thing could be very annoying, but Judge somehow managed to pull it off with a dash of Texan charm.

"I remember the first time I had to speak to an admiral," Kolhammer said. "I was twenty years old, fresh out of Boat School. I'd been an ensign for all of three minutes, and I do believe I may have wet my pants just a little bit."

Mike Judge's shoulders moved as he chuckled to himself while watching the great armada form up for their trip west. "Met me a lord admiral in London when I was wooing my good lady wife," he said. "Had a castle and everything."

"And did you wet your pants just a little bit, Captain Judge?" Kolhammer asked with a commendably straight face.

"No, sir, I did not."

"Good for you, son."

A screaming roar of jet engines announced the launch of the two Skyhawks on combat air patrol. They peeled up and away from the flight deck, two AT Sidewinder missiles hanging from hard points under their delta wings.

Kolhammer watched them enviously. They were the undisputed kings of the air, at least for the next little while. He doubted the Germans would ever build anything more advanced than the 262s they were desperately throwing into the skies over France, but it was a righteous certainty that old Joe Stalin would have armies of engineers playing catch-up with the West. The intelligence reports he'd read implied that the Commies had done a great job so far.

Before long-range bombers flying out of Tabriz in northern Persia had destroyed it, the Demidenko facility had apparently delivered a huge boost to the USSR's research base. It was another of the enduring mysteries they faced. What the hell had the Germans been doing there when everyone—even the Russians—knew the Reich was going to turn on them at first opportunity? Kolhammer had lost count of the number of theories he'd heard. He might have been better placed to answer such questions if he'd been able to keep his own covert teams in place in Russia, but he'd ordered Ivanov's people out eighteen months ago on the direct orders of President Roosevelt.

What a dark fucking day that'd been. The admiral shook his head as he recalled the meeting.

FDR was furious.

The president had dismissed all of his aides from the Oval Office as soon as Kolhammer arrived. It was the first week of the new year, and Washington was very quiet, with snow lying heavy on the lawns of the White House, deadening the sounds of the city. The heavy blanket of white powder was a given at this time of year, but the exact snowfall and temperature weren't predictable in the way they had been immediately after the Transition. Meteorologists had been left to twiddle their thumbs for at least six months back then, because archival weather data proved to be more accurate than their forecasts.

And then, in December 1942, a typhoon had blown through the New Hebrides during a week that had originally been recorded as having been "sunny and warm." Global warming had nothing to do with it, but the Transition must have. After that, the archives were of less use than the various weather sensors on the ships of the onetime Multinational Force, and the division of those assets became something of a political cage-wrestling match.

Roosevelt didn't smile when Kolhammer entered. He didn't return his salute or bid him to sit down. There was nowhere to sit. The president remained in the chair behind his heavy wooden desk, his legs kept warm by an old three-bar heater pointed through the well in the center.

Kolhammer waited.

Roosevelt said nothing for a long time after the door closed behind his secretary. His lips were pressed so tightly together that all the color was forced from them. Muscles knotted along his jawline, and he repeatedly clenched his fingers with such slow deliberation that Kolhammer wondered if he was in pain.

"You did not tell me, Admiral Kolhammer, that you were running a black operation within the Soviet Union."

"Ah," Kolhammer said, understanding at last. "No, I did not, sir."

"And why not?"

"Because then you would have known."

If possible, the president looked even angrier. "Is that your idea of a joke, Admiral?"

Kolhammer shook his head. "No, sir. But it has been my experience in dealing with the executive level of government that they prefer to remain ignorant of operational details when such knowledge might prove unworkable."

"Unworkable, or uncomfortable?"

"Both. Sir."

President Roosevelt looked no less irate, but at least he didn't appear to be getting any angrier. He was still clutching at an imaginary stress ball with his left hand. He seemed to notice the unconscious gesture, and deliberately placed both of his palms on the top of his desk, which was clear of any papers.

He sighed.

"Tell me what you were doing in Siberia, Admiral. I can't imagine you'll have a good explanation."

Kolhammer resisted the urge to look around for a chair. It would have been an expression of weakness. He stood foursquare in front of the president and delivered his bad news straight, as he had twice in his own time, in this very room.

"When we discovered that the *Dessaix* had arrived here, out of sync with the rest of the task force, it became necessary to ascertain whether any other twenty-first assets might have come through in a similar fashion, and fallen into enemy hands. So I authorized a small covert team to enter the Soviet Union and begin searching."

A noticeable tremor ran through Roosevelt's upper body.

"You authorized a hostile act, against a friendly power, which could easily have led them into declaring war on us? When we already had our backs to the wall because of your arrival?"

"I did, sir. Although I respectfully submit that you should probably stop thinking of the Soviet Union as a friendly power, and accept that there is a war coming. Sooner, rather than later."

Roosevelt's nostrils flared as he sucked in air to control the flash of anger that showed in his eyes.

"If I wanted to bring a crazy man in here to start yet another war I'd have called up General Patton," he barked. "I expect *better* of you, Admiral. And I'm not getting it. I know all about your little mission, more than you're letting on. Because Major Ivanov wasn't just looking for lost ships out on the tundra, was he? He was actively building a resistance network, opposed to Soviet rule."

"He was," Kolhammer admitted.

Roosevelt's hand slammed down on the desktop with a loud crack.

"*Damn* it all, Kolhammer, when were you going to tell me about *that*?"

The admiral controlled his own rising temper and forced himself to concentrate on the matter at hand, rather than speculating as to where Roosevelt had picked up his information. That line of thought threatened to spiral rapidly down into panic. If he knew about Russia, then he could know about the Quiet Room. But if that was the case, Kolhammer wouldn't be standing here; he'd be in handcuffs. Unless of course Roosevelt had decided to let the Room be, or he'd somehow found out about Ivanov but nothing else. The next few minutes would tell. Outwardly, Kolhammer forced himself to remain phlegmatic.

"My special action team was supported for six months, Mr. President. After that, we could no longer sustain them in the field and they were withdrawn—most of them, anyway. Major Ivanov and Lieutenant Zamyatin, of the Russian Federation Defense Force, chose to stay of their own accord."

"You ordered them home?"

"I recalled them. They didn't come. They maintained, correctly, that their attachments—to the SEALs in Ivanov's case, and the Royal Navy in Zamyatin's—had expired. And that they were more than just free to stay in Russia, but obliged to do so."

"Obliged to stay?" Roosevelt said, his tone incredulous.

Kolhammer nodded, carrying on regardless, determined not to give away any advantage. He privately wondered if Roosevelt had been briefed in on this by the Brits. They'd had an SAS guy called Hamilton in-country with Ivanov. A Russian specialist, detached by the then Major Windsor to help in the search for any Multinational Force assets that might have gone astray.

He'd know nothing of the Quiet Room's domestic operations in the United States.

"Ivanov and Zamyatin regarded the Communist government as a hostile, occupying power," he continued. "And they consider it their duty to protect the Russian people from all enemies, foreign and domestic. So they stayed."

"Good Lord," Roosevelt muttered. "It never ends with you people, does it?"

Kolhammer took that as a rhetorical question best not answered. He remained at attention while Roosevelt seemed to turn inward for a minute, examining the problem like a puzzle with a piece that just didn't fit.

"And your missing ship? That would be the British vessel, the *Vanguard*?"

"Yes, sir, and possibly the two nuclear subs from our group. The *Vanguard* was our primary concern, though, since she was located within the area of the Transition's effect back in twenty-one, as best we could tell. The nukes were a hundred miles away."

"And you didn't find her? Or any trace of her?"

Kolhammer shook his head, but all the old worries he had learned to suppress came bobbing back up to the surface. "We got nothing during the six months the team was in-country. A few wild rumors, but those are like Elvis sightings back in my day, if you'll excuse the uptime reference, sir. People are forever reporting new ships, or planes from the future, winking through another wormhole. The *Dessaix* turning up like she did really bent everyone out of shape.

"Then again, the Soviet Union is a very big country, and they have an *excellent* security apparatus. They could be hiding any number of secrets in there, and Beria and Stalin would think nothing of killing ten million people to protect them.

"I'd be a lot happier if we had some U-Two coverage over them," he continued. "And I—"

Roosevelt held up his hand to cut Kolhammer off. "No! I go through this every few days with the Joint Chiefs, Admiral. We have only a handful of those planes, and every last one of them is needed for hunting down the German A-bomb assets—even the two aircraft we assigned to monitoring the Nazis' extermination camps. *After* your repeated demands, I might add—both here and in the press. Or have you forgotten that?"

"No, sir," Kolhammer said, keeping his voice neutral, though only with the greatest effort.

The 'temps, he had found, were more than happy to play on the Holocaust for propaganda purposes, but getting them to commit assets to disrupt the program was another matter entirely. The whole thing was a waking nightmare, and his own intervention—which he considered a matter of unavoidable moral duty—had occasioned a personal tragedy.

His uncle Hans, who would have survived this war had it not been for the Transition, had been removed from the death camp at Treblinka and publicly executed as an American spy, some six months earlier. The German propaganda minister, Josef Göbbels, had personally seen to the release of the film footage into the free world, via Spain. Even now Phillip Kolhammer could feel an ungovernable rage gathering inside him as he remembered the first time he'd heard the news. He doubted that fate would play him an even break, but if it did, and he ended up in a room with *Herr Doktor* Göbbels at the end of this conflict, there was a very good chance he would beat the little rodent to death with his bare hands.

When he regained control over the poisoned wellspring of his feelings, he found that Roosevelt was looking mildly abashed.

"I forget myself, Admiral," the president muttered. "I apologize."

Not knowing what to say, Kolhammer merely nodded, but he remained stiffly at attention.

After another few seconds of uncomfortable stillness, Roosevelt eventually broke. "Can you at least assure me that the Russians don't have your ship?"

"No, sir. I cannot. As you know, we're still doing all we can to find out whether it came through and fell into the wrong hands. If it did, it might not necessarily be in the USSR, of course. It could be in Colombia, or China, or buried under a mile of ice at the South Pole. I suppose it's possible it could turn up tomorrow or a hundred years from now, given the temporal anomalies of the *Dessaix*'s arrival. We just don't know."

Roosevelt shook his head and held up his hand again. "Please, spare me. I just need to know that you're not still running some undercover operation in Joe Stalin's backyard."

"I am not."

"And what about *my* backyard?" the president asked, his voice suddenly cold again. "Am I going to wake up tomorrow and find that your Ms. O'Brien has done away with yet another inconvenient foe, like Mr. Hoover or Congressman Dies?"

Kolhammer could sense a trapdoor creaking beneath his feet. He carefully avoided answering the first question by concentrating on the second.

"Ms. O'Brien is her own woman, sir. She's a private citizen now. Not mine to command."

"Really?" FDR tilted his head. A reflection of the fire burning in the Oval Office hearth filled one lens. Kolhammer resisted the urge to shrug. He knew Roosevelt was using the expanding silence as a weapon, hoping to make him blurt something out as the discomfort grew more intense. Did the old man know about the Room, or was he just fishing?

He chose his next words carefully. "I'm sure Director Foxworth could tell you all about Ms. O'Brien," he said in a monotone. "I understand he has a considerable number of the bureau's agents assigned to watching her full-time."

Roosevelt didn't bite. "And how would you know that, Admiral?" he countered. "Surely Ms. O'Brien's affairs aren't a matter of concern to your Zone security officers."

"No, sir. They are not. But Ms. O'Brien is no wallflower. I doubt a week goes by that she doesn't complain in the press—about harassment by the FBI or the IRS."

Roosevelt didn't so much smile as stretch his lips back to bare his teeth. "You seem to sympathize with her, Admiral Kolhammer. You don't think Internal Revenue should have investigated her companies."

Still standing rigidly, Kolhammer had little trouble avoiding *that* trap. In a way, being forced to remain at attention focused his mind. "I don't see that it would be appropriate for me to comment, Mr. President, for any number of reasons."

"Oh, come now, Admiral. You *must* have an opinion. I know you think very highly of Ms. O'Brien. You were quoted at length in that *New Yorker* profile of her, as I recall. You can't be happy to see her name dragged through the mud."

"If I had a personal opinion, it would be just that, sir. Personal . . . and private."

"I see," Roosevelt said, fitting a new cigarette into his holder. "That's odd, because you were quite free with your opinions when Director Hoover resigned."

Kolhammer ground out his reply like an ogre chewing rocks. "Director Hoover misapplied public resources in the surveillance and harassment of Zone personnel. He compromised the security of a significant number of research programs. And he did untold damage to the operations of other intelligence agencies through his incompetence, malfeasance, and utterly inappropriate use of bureau resources. You are correct, Mr. President. I expressed these opinions publicly, under oath, during hearings in both the Senate and the House. It was my duty to do so."

"Was it your duty to repeat them and expand on them for Miss Duffy in *The New York Times*?" Roosevelt demanded.

"I believe so, sir. Where I came from, considerable harm was done by military officials who did *not* speak their minds when they should have."

"Well, you're not there anymore, admiral!" the president barked. "You are *here,* and we do things differently, as you are forever reminding me. You may not have liked Hoover, but he was a patriot, and he didn't deserve what your people did to him. Julia Duffy drove that man to his grave. In the end, I believe she as good as put that gun in his mouth and pulled the trigger."

A single twitch at the corner of one eye was all that gave away the roiling surge of anger behind Kolhammer's mask, but he held his tongue.

Roosevelt was breathing hard, one fist clenched on his desk blotter. What Kolhammer wanted to do was pound the president's desk so hard it cracked in two. He wanted to demand that Roosevelt sign an order directing as many resources as it took to dismantle the transport system that fed the Nazi death camps in Poland. He wanted to tell the president to stop fucking around, to face the inevitable and sign Truman's Executive Order 9981. He wanted to do about a thousand things that he knew were vitally important, but that nobody born here seemed to care two figs about.

Most of all, Kolhammer wanted to know why Roosevelt was allowing the killer of Daytona Anderson and Maseo Miyazaki to continue walking around as free as a fucking bird, fêted as a *hero* while he did so.

Roosevelt had known the murderer's identity for well over a year, and Kolhammer had suppressed it for the entire time, much to the disgust of the only other two uptimers who also knew: Doc Francois and Lonesome Jones. The commandant of the Special Administrative Zone felt sick whenever he thought about it. He had given his word that he wouldn't go public with the information, and he had extracted the same promise from both Francois and Jones, on the understanding that justice *would* be done.

But it hadn't been, and now he had to stand here being dressed down about Hoover when the vicious old fag had brought ruin on himself. It was enough to make him throw up his hands and walk away.

And he might have, too, if not for Roosevelt's next move.

"I want you to sign this, Admiral."

"Excuse me, sir?"

Kolhammer came back to earth with a thud. The president had taken a piece of paper out of a desk drawer, and he was holding it out for the admiral.

"It is an undated letter of resignation," Roosevelt explained without preamble. "I'm afraid I'm going to have to shorten your leash, at least until I feel I can trust you to—"

"No, sir," Kolhammer interrupted.

The president looked genuinely stunned. "What? What do you mean?"

"I mean, no, sir. I will not sign this letter. If you wish to dismiss me, I would ask you to do so now. Terminate my commission as of this minute. But I will not be a party to *this*." He dropped the paper back onto the desktop.

"Well, I . . . I . . ."

Clearly Roosevelt was at a complete loss.

Kolhammer expected to be dismissed, cashiered on the spot, but the president simply gawked at him.

The two of them faced off over the letter for what seemed like an awfully long time. Kolhammer knew he was supposed to pick it back up. You don't just throw documents back in the face of the president of the United States.

Finally a long sigh leaked out of Roosevelt. He leaned back in his chair, nodding slowly.

"All right then."

He took up the letter and tore it in little pieces, dropping them into a wastebasket by his side.

"All right," he repeated. "But understand this, Admiral, your days of running off like Lord Jim are well and truly over. You have no idea of the political capital I have spent protecting you and your little kingdom out there on the West Coast."

Kolhammer opened his mouth to speak, but this time Roosevelt wouldn't allow him to get a word in.

"No. Just be quiet and listen for once. This war is drawing to a close, if the whole planet doesn't burn inside a nuclear fireball. I won't be here much longer—"

He held up his hand to forestall any objections.

"—another year or two, most likely. Maybe three depending on the treatments your physicians have been supervising. But I can feel myself winding down like an old clock. My time is passing."

Roosevelt paused, and seemed to notice for the first time that Kolhammer was still standing at attention.

"Please relax a little, would you, Admiral. You're giving me a stiff neck just watching you stand like that."

Kolhammer allowed some of the tension to run out of his body, but he still didn't look around for a chair.

"The sunset clause on your enabling legislation for the Zone will come into effect one year after the unconditional surrender of whichever of the Axis powers lasts the longest—probably Japan, as in your time," the president said. "So on the stroke of midnight of that day, a little more than one year hence, the Special Administrative Zone will cease to exist."

He seemed to be waiting for something from Kolhammer, watching him like an old dog eyeing a fox at the henhouse door. When he didn't get it, he continued.

"You're not going to be able to trick the American people into doing what you want. You certainly won't be able to *force* them, no matter how hard Ms. O'Brien and her friends may try."

For the first time in the evening, he smiled. A dry, desiccated wasteland of a smile.

"You're going to have to do things the old way, Admiral Kolhammer. When you disagree, you are going to have to convince them that you are right, and they are wrong. And while setting out to destroy men like J. Edgar Hoover might *seem* to clear a path to that goal, I can assure you that it is a road to perdition. I would caution you against walking any farther down it."

Kolhammer's eyes narrowed imperceptibly. Roosevelt had not come out and accused him of running the Quiet Room. He had certainly danced around the issue, but he'd done nothing directly. He wondered where this was heading. Was Roosevelt trying to sound him out about some sort of political future? Or was he simply warning him against misadventure?

The president produced another letter, this one sealed in an envelope.

"Since you'll be staying on, you have new orders, Admiral. You'll be going back to sea when the *Clinton* is ready. *If* that's all right with you, of course," he added, loading the phrase with a heavy dose of patrician sarcasm.

"Thank you, Mr. President," Kolhammer said, not entirely sure whether he'd just been tested, disciplined, or comprehensively outmaneuvered.

D-DAY + 9. 12 MAY 1944. 1915 HOURS. SPECIAL ADMINISTRATIVE ZONE.

The food in Wakuda's was some of the best in the Zone, which meant it was some of the best in the country, and certainly on the West Coast. Maria O'Brien had tried out the new restaurant at the Ambassador with Slim Jim and Ronald Reagan, and it was probably as good as Pacific cuisine got outside the Zone, but it still wasn't a patch on Mr. Wakuda's place, an eighty-seater run by a former petty officer from the *Siranui* and a couple of local partners, some gay guys who'd been among the first wave of 'temp refugees beating down Kolhammer's doors when he set up shop out here. Styled after an Asian longhouse, Wakuda's was open on three sides, with covered decks spilling down into a manicured garden through which a lily pond wound a sinuous course. She could spy the blue glass atrium of the newly opened Burroughs Corporation building through the foliage, just around the corner from her own firm's landmark site.

O'Brien popped a small piece of freshly baked bread liberally slathered with truffle butter into her mouth. The truffle shavings and a dusting of Parmigiano-Reggiano gave the butter a thick, obscenely rich dark taste, vaguely reminding her of an old mustard without the heat.

"You're not having the beef, dear?" her companion asked. "It's quite wonderful, you know. And you need your strength. You can't possibly get by on green beans and radishes, with all the work you do."

O'Brien smiled and shook her head, reaching for a small white disk of rice topped with a confit of wild mushroom, resting over grated apple and olive.

"I still don't eat meat, Eleanor. I'd like to, but I just can't."

The first lady nodded sadly. "I suppose I understand, dear. You must have seen some awful things."

O'Brien shrugged. "It's no biggie. Are you enjoying the ocean trout? It's his signature dish, you know."

Eleanor Roosevelt forked a small mouthful away with obvious pleasure. The dining room buzzed with conversation, but most of the noise was coming from a cocktail bar, separated from them by a huge wooden slab carved from Oregon pine and covered in plates of complimentary bar snacks. The foldaway glass doors were all opened to let in a pleasantly balmy evening.

"I wish we had food like this back at the White House. It's all so very stodgy and old there. Not like out here. You young people are doing a marvelous job, I must say. I always feel so vibrant when I visit the San Fernando. There is so much energy here. And you can feel it over the range in Los Angeles, too."

O'Brien took a sip of her wine, a nicely chilled chardonnay, and nodded. "That's partly what I wanted to talk to you about, Eleanor."

"Oh, how so, dear?"

The old girl seemed completely ingenuous, but O'Brien could tell that her radar had just gone to full power. Almost every table in the restaurant was full. Only a couple with reservation cards perched on the starched linen tablecloths were empty. The crowd was mixed, with quite a few uptimers to break down LA's white power homogeneity. There were more than one or two WASP holdouts on the far side of the Hollywood Hills—clubs, resorts, hotels, and restaurants that maintained a bar against "undesirable" elements, including the movie industry's Jewish moguls. But they were dying. The Zone was the new center of the universe in California, and like Roman rule, its power was prescriptive and imperial. Twenty-first-century law stopped dead at the boundaries of the Special Administrative Zone, but twenty-first-century custom was spreading up and down the West Coast like a wildfire. It was money. It was always about money, thought O'Brien. If you wanted to tap into the insane wealth that was being generated in the Valley, then you had to play by the Valley's rules.

"You see a lot of things that you like out here, don't you, Eleanor? The way that men and women of all colors and creeds are judged on the basis of their character?"

The first lady nodded, not warily, but with just a hint of reserve. "I've often said to Franklin that the first principles of America have found their truest expression out here," she said. "But why do you ask, dear?"

O'Brien didn't bother sugarcoating it. "Because we will need your help in preserving all this," she said, waving a hand around the restaurant but implying much beyond its confines. "This war is going to end soon, and the sunset clause in our enabling legislation will suddenly begin to tick. A year later, everything we've built here, all those *principles* you find so appealing, will be exposed to attack by those who do not agree with them. You know what these people are like, what lengths they will go to. Hoover was one of them. He had you followed. He read your mail. He would have destroyed you, given half a chance. He did the same out here—or he tried, anyway—a thousand times over."

The first lady acknowledged the point with a dip of her head as a server appeared with a small square plate, in the center of which sat a tangle of roasted pepper shavings and arugula leaves, framing a small roll of daikon, celery, and carrot. O'Brien took the plate and thanked the young woman. Jazz played over the sound system, and the tables were far enough apart that they could speak in low voices without being overheard. O'Brien knew quite a few of the other diners as bigname players from the emerging aerospace and electronics industries. They were doubtlessly hatching their own plots and schemes over the fourteen-course banquet. Some may have even been discussing this very issue. The first lady was not the only person whom she had lobbied on this matter.

"I can understand your anxiety," said Mrs. Roosevelt. "But what can I do?"

It was O'Brien's turn to smile shyly, a gesture framed entirely for effect. "Come now, Eleanor. You have the president's ear, and you speak with many people around him. Plus, you're a significant figure in your own right. You've campaigned very hard to establish many of the things that already exist here in the Valley. All I am asking is that you consider helping us, where you can, when you can, back on the East Coast."

President Franklin Delano Roosevelt's wife nodded. "Of course I will, dear. I would have done so anyway. But I must say it's a pleasure to find a young woman unafraid to put herself and her case forward in such a forthright manner. It gives me hope for the future."

"Thank you," said O'Brien. "That's very flattering."

She maintained eye contact with Eleanor Roosevelt while she spoke, but she noted that a waiter was showing guests to an empty table just behind the first lady. "Stiffy" McClintock, the CEO of McClintock Investments, was dining with a couple of guys from Combat Optics and IBM. She would definitely have to arrange a drink with them afterward. They were all on her list of people "to do" over the sunset clause. She topped up her glass of wine, satisfied with her efforts for the evening so far, as she mentally checked Eleanor Roosevelt off the same list.

8

The planning room of the *Yamato* did not run to flat-panel plasma screens or digital projectors. In fact, it looked very much as it had in the first days of June 1942, before the Emergence.

Well, that wasn't entirely true. The plotting table looked infinitely worse for Imperial Japan. Yet Grand Admiral Yamamoto betrayed none of the fears eating at his insides as he surveyed the situation. Elements of the army continued their assault against Australian forces in northwestern New Guinea, on Bougainville, and in Timor. But they had been reduced to a sideshow by MacArthur, and were operating almost as guerrilla forces—a task made all the more difficult by their complete lack of support among the native populations on those islands.

He bit down on a disgusted grunt as he pondered the situation in the Dutch East Indies, or Indonesia as it was now calling itself, where that scabrous dog Moertopo had come back to haunt him. Yamamoto could feel his heart begin to beat faster as he contemplated the depth of Moertopo's villainy. They should have just executed him in 1942, as Hidaka had suggested.

Instead he'd been installed as the puppet governor of some obscure Javanese province. From there he had secretly built up his own peasant militia, which had arisen and stabbed the Imperial Japanese Army in the back when MacArthur invaded in November 1943.

At first nobody paid them any heed. Loyalists under the local general Sukarno were dispatched to deal with them—and were slaughtered to the last man. Only *then* did the scope of Moertopo's betrayal become clear. He had clandestinely hosted a large deployment of Australian SAS troops, who had been training and equipping his rebels for almost as long as the little wretch had been taking the emperor's coin. Now he sat in Jakarta, the puppet president of the so-called Republic of Indonesia, having declared independence from Holland and Japan—with the full backing of his new protectors.

Yamamoto's humiliation at having been played for a fool by such a creature was compounded by his total inability to do anything about it. The emperor's forces were in retreat on so many fronts, they didn't have the resources to do anything about Moertopo.

For the moment all his energies were devoted to the looming Battle of the Marianas. If and when they fell, two things would follow. The U.S. Army Air Force would begin its systematic destruction of Japan's industrialized cities, and the Philippines would likely be taken by Allied forces, robbing Japan of her most important colonial prize and cutting off a vital source of raw materials. Staring at the diabolical state of affairs represented on the giant tabletop display, Yamamoto wanted nothing more than to collapse into a chair, let his head fall into his hands, and scream out his frustrations.

But he stood impassively as his underlings pushed markers around this miniature world, while others argued minor points of strategy and tactics. Directly across the table from him generals Takeshima and Obata continued their never-ending feud over the relative importance of reinforcing Guam, Saipan, or the Tinian Islands. No matter how much he tried to get them to think in terms of "joint warfare," as the Allies now called their combined arms operations, the two men were emblematic of the Japanese army's failure to comprehend how much had changed in just two years. He regretted ever inviting them to his planning meetings.

Soon, however, they would understand that no matter how formidable they made their defenses, they would be overcome. Only the most ignorant xenophobe still believed in the myth of the decadent democracies. They had proven themselves more than capable of inflicting and absorbing the most grievous harm. Yamamoto didn't know whether the arrival of the Emergence barbarians—to use the popular phrase—had added anything to the hardening of the democracies' warrior spirit, but he doubted it. Everything he'd read from the documents of the future, about how this war would have gone, told him that Japan and Germany had been doomed, simply because they couldn't beat the Allies in the atomic race.

As the iron behemoth of the *Yamato* pitched gently beneath his feet on the Pacific swell, he wondered if he had done enough. Realistically, no. Despite everything that had changed, in many ways things had proceeded just as they'd been "meant" to. He was about to fight the Battle of the Marianas at roughly the same time it had been fought in Kolhammer's world, and the Allies were actually ashore in France a month earlier than would otherwise have been the case. He, of course, had had nothing to do with the defense of the Marianas in the original time frame, having been killed in 1943. But he spent very little time worrying about his personal fate. The world was now full of those who should be dead, but weren't, and those who were dead when they should have lived.

His old enemies Nimitz and Halsey were numbered among the latter, and he could not help but feel some residual shame about that. Unlike many others, he did not blame Hidaka for the loss of the Hawaiian Islands. The young officer had been appointed as the civil governor of the colony, not its military ruler.

That responsibility had fallen to General Ono, and the phantom soldiers of the Negro marines' unit, the Eighty-second, had murdered him just before the first rocket impact. A terrible thing it had been, too, the way they had ritually humiliated him in his death, and then openly proclaimed their savagery as a valid punishment for his "crimes." Yamamoto often wondered if that was to be his fate one day. At any rate, Hidaka could not be held responsible for losing the islands. He *could,* however, be blamed for the abuses of the Americans held under his control, which had done so much to enrage their countrymen and allies, spurring them on to greater efforts in retaking the territory.

Similarly, all the blood and treasure spent in the failed conquest of Australia had come to naught. His forces had been driven from that island continent, and Prime Minister Curtin had then turned around and released the Australians who came through the Emergence, allowing them to assist in the retaking of Hawaii and the hunt for the *Dessaix*—it was exactly what Yamamoto had hoped to avoid. All of it attributable, in his opinion, to the ham-fisted brutality of Hidaka. Yamamoto's vision glazed over. His mind wandered away from the hot, rank planning room and back to the images of Japan's short-lived occupation of Hawaii. He could not help feeling some approval at the form of Halsey's death. The man had lived up to his nickname, charging like a bull at a company of Japanese marines, pistols blazing in both hands as they shot him down. Nimitz, however, had been summarily executed, as had hundreds of other high-ranking officers. It was an act of criminal stupidity, given the intelligence that might have been extracted from them, and—Yamamoto fervently believed—it was barbarous. Unworthy of a true warrior.

Hidaka had no excuses for that. Like Yamamoto, he had been educated in America, and he understood the nature of his enemy with much greater fidelity than many of their countrymen. Perhaps, more to the point, he did not understand *himself* and his own culture well enough. There was nothing in the code of *bushido* that should lead a true samurai to commit such grotesque atrocities as Hidaka had visited upon his vanquished foes.

A sigh at last escaped Yamamoto. A small exhalation of stale air, and a slumping of the shoulders under the weight of his own responsibility for all that had transpired. Around him, preparations continued without pause. Messengers arrived. Junior officers attended to the demands of their superiors. Staff officers worked through scenarios they had examined from every possible angle uncountable times before. Intelligence about the enemy's movements arrived as the tiniest drops of ice water on the swollen tongue of a man dying from thirst. It wasn't just that the Allies had access to unbreakable cryptography, thanks to Kolhammer. Not every unit in their order of battle could be so equipped. But there was also a tsunami of disinformation to be picked through, hundreds of thousands of false radio messages sent quite openly, to distract and disarm.

And regardless of the restrained but growing excitement around him, Yamamoto was transfixed by something that frightened him more than all else, something nobody here seemed to see: the specter of the world he was working to create. A world in which men like Jisaku Hidaka and Heinrich Himmler were armed with atomic weapons.

"A grim business, yes, Admiral, but I place my faith in the Cherry Blossoms and the spirit of Shikishima."

The voice of the First Air Fleet commandant, Vice Admiral Takijiro Onishi, cut through Yamamoto's maudlin self-indulgence. The grand admiral lifted his chin off his tunic, where it had been resting while darker thoughts got the better of him.

Yamamoto had not been looking forward to this conversation. Vice Admiral Onishi was that most dangerous of creatures, a romantic. To Yamamoto's way of thinking, he was nigh on obsessed with the martial virtue of self-sacrifice—a reasonable thing, one might have thought, except that Onishi took it to unreasonable lengths. He was known both here and in the twilight world of the Emergence barbarians as the father of the *kamikaze*—although nobody in the Imperial Japanese Navy used that insulting form of words. To them he was the creator of the *tokkotai*—the special attack units.

Suicide bombers.

He stood in front of Yamamoto, seemingly entranced with the evolving cataclysm on the map table. His eyes positively sparkled as he contemplated the presumed westward passage of Spruance's main strike force, the *Clinton* battle group. It was thought to be somewhere between San Diego and Hawaii by now, as the Allies gathered their might for a sledgehammer blow on the empire. A long time ago Yamamoto might have shared Onishi's enthusiasm for the coming fight. It was shaping up as the *Kassen Kantai,* the decisive battle, which he had advocated in the first days of the war. But unlike Onishi, who had yet to taste the ashes of defeat, Yamamoto was sanguine about their chances for success.

"You have heard from Manila, then, Admiral?" he said, tipping his head in reply to Onishi's bow. "How go your plans?"

"Very well, Admiral. They go very well. The last of the *Ohkas* are ready. We have nearly a hundred of the Type Twenty-twos and forty of the turbojet Forty-threes. I have seen a test flight myself, and they are magnificent. Fearsome. The Americans will not be able to withstand them."

Yamamoto's eyebrows crawled toward the ceiling. "So you have only a hundred and forty all together. Admiral Onishi, almost none of them will survive the air screen. Kolhammer's people have been dealing with rocket swarms of much greater sophistication than anything we can invent."

Onishi looked insulted. "That is not *all* I have been doing," he protested. "There are two and a half thousand *tokkotai* ready to fall on the enemy in the conventional way. And many of *them* will get through. But their role is really to overwhelm the Allied defenses and create a gap for the *Ohkas* to exploit. That they will do—I assure you. I have studied the archival material and concluded that it would not be sensible to send our men in piecemeal. They must come upon the American fleet as a typhoon comes upon a fishing boat, with overwhelming power."

His eyes glistened as he spoke, and Yamamoto feared that he was about to cry again. He had famously soaked the ground with his tears when told of his own act of *seppuku* in the alternate world at the end of the war. Something had fused in the vice admiral's mind since then, and he had become unbalanced on the subject of "his" *tokkotai*.

"And where have you disposed your forces, Onishi?" he asked, hoping to forestall any possible blubbering.

His subordinate rapped out instructions, and three junior officers began to place unit markers on the map table throughout the islands of the Marianas.

"The Germans," he said as they worked at their task, "were most helpful in speeding up the development of the Type Forty-three, as you would expect given their expertise in the field. However, they were also of great assistance in helping us disguise the airfields from which the *tokkotai* will embark. I suppose they have learned something from the Soviets in that regard. At any rate, if you examine the map, you will see that the approach to the islands will naturally funnel the Allied ships to this point"—he tapped at the map table with a long wooden pointer—"where we shall suddenly appear as a great swarm of hornets buzzing about their heads."

Yamamoto examined the display, and was not entirely unhappy with what he saw. Onishi had dispersed his forces well, so that they could not be destroyed at a stroke with some Emergence superweapon. They would have a reasonably short flight to intersect the American advance, and although the pilots were not the best in the empire—far from it, in fact—they could probably be trusted to follow their pathfinders. Since the full weight of Spruance's airpower would most likely be given over to demolishing the bunkers and sandbagged gun pits that generals Takeshima and Obata were so lovingly building, there might even be a chance that some real damage could be done.

"Have you assigned your men to their targets yet, Admiral Onishi?" he asked.

"Not only have they been assigned, but they have also been training to press home their attacks as best they can, given our resources. My study of the archives led me to understand that I had previously underestimated the importance of piloting skills, to ensure that a higher percentage of them penetrate the air defense screen. I imagine that Spruance will use his jet fighters for long-range strike missions, and his lesser aircraft to fly combat air patrol around the fleet."

Yamamoto could not stifle a snort at that.

Lesser aircraft! Onishi was talking about F-4 Corsairs and Skyraider fighter-bombers, both of which were vastly superior to the Zero that was still the mainstay of the Japanese fleet. He was glad that Onishi had planned on having so many *tokkotai* in the attack wave, because most of them were never going to make it through the American defenders.

It was encouraging, however, this small lift in spirits he received from contemplating what might be done, outclassed though they might be. They would lose the battle for these islands—of that he was in no doubt. But perhaps, with some luck, he could make it a Pyrrhic victory for the Allies.

"So you will concentrate on the *Clinton*?" he pressed.

"On the *Clinton* and the other carriers in the first instance. And on the troop transports in the second. I studied the history of the Falklands War from the nineteen eighties," Onishi said, "and I believe that if the Argentineans had concentrated on sinking the British transports, rather than her destroyers and frigates, they would have kept those islands. We see that point made again with the Chinese attack on Taiwan in the following century, except that there the rebels *did* concentrate on the Communist transports, and prevailed because of it."

Yamamoto said nothing. He, too, had studied the conflicts of the coming decades, examining them for whatever insight they might give him regarding new opponents. And Onishi seemed to be forgetting that it was Americans like Kolhammer—possibly it even *was* Kolhammer—who had turned the Taiwan Straits into a mass grave for the Communist Chinese.

"Send me the full report on your preparations, Admiral," Yamamoto said. "I should like to study it this afternoon, before I contemplate the final disposition of the fleet."

"Hai!" Onishi barked in reply, firing off a series of commands to his juniors to see that a full briefing was made ready for the grand admiral.

Yamamoto returned to studying the map table again, stifling another sigh as he watched the noose tightening around his neck. To the south, MacArthur was straining at the leash with an Allied army of one and a half million men. To the west, China had collapsed into a civil war between the Nationalists and Mao's Red Army, after the effective withdrawal of Japan from Manchuria. And to the east, *somewhere* to the east, Spruance was in the final days of building a titanic force, a fleet such as the world had never seen. An armada that could have swept aside the great Combined Fleet that Yamamoto had led to Midway, in the days before the Emergence.

He could not match that force.

But could he cripple it? Could he hurt it badly enough that his enemies might be delayed long enough to secure the empire?

Grand Admiral Yamamoto did not know.

D-DAY + 16. 19 MAY 1944. 1410 HOURS.
CAROLINE ISLANDS.

The camouflage was impressive, but that was no guarantee of success. The Americans enjoyed unbelievable advantages in surveillance technology.

Lieutenant Seki Yukio knew that his men could not afford to harbor any doubts about the success of their mission. Even so, he often found himself awake late at night, wondering whether they would even get off the ground. His inevitable death did not rob him of sleep. He had accepted that the moment he had agreed to Commander Tamai's request that he lead the most important of the special attack forces, the *toku-betsu kogeki tai.* No, what concerned him was the prospect that they would be detected and destroyed before they were even airborne.

He walked around the Type 43 *Ohka,* running his hand over the smooth metallic surface. It felt cool in the tropical heat. Painted in a disruptive green jungle pattern on top and light blue underneath, it sat in a partially buried hangar under a canopy woven from palm fronds and jungle creepers. Arriving on the atoll by flying boat, he'd been unable to make out any sign of human habitation, let alone a military buildup. And once on the ground he understood why.

Years of work had gone into preparing this site. Walking around above ground level was strictly prohibited. Tunnels and caverns dug into the ancient, rock-hard coral protected the island's defenders from prying eyes. There wasn't even an airstrip in regular use. One had been constructed a year earlier, when the front line was a thousand miles away, but it was now covered by an ingenious system of wheeled garden beds—giant planter boxes on old vehicle chassis in which lay thousands of tons of soil, plants, and even wildlife. Come the day when they were ordered into the skies, the gardens would be pushed down a slightly cambered slope at the edge of the hidden runway. It was a brilliant ruse, and Yukio could only wonder who had come up with it.

Leaving the deadly aircraft behind him, he walked the length of the hangar to a sunken observation bunker near the water. He mopped at the greasy sheen of sweat on his brow and peered out to sea. The admiral's seaplane was a faint speck to the north, growing larger as he watched. All of the garrison's supplies arrived by seaplane or submarine, negating the requirement for an airstrip or any obvious docking facilities. In fact, there was a dock in a large, flooded cave on the far side of island, but it was rarely used.

Yukio stood in the bunker, shaded by netting thickly threaded with camouflage scrim and vegetation. The two sailors standing beside him trained oversized binoculars on the horizon to either side of the growing dot that was the grand admiral's plane. There was no control tower to bring them in. No radio contact with the outside world. A fully equipped communications room lay in the jungle about two hundred meters away, but the antennae had never been erected and not a single message had ever been sent or received from the secret base. You had to assume these days that if you spoke on a radio, the enemy would hear you, locate you, and, if they felt like it, destroy you.

As frustrating as their isolation could be at times, it was a deadly necessity.

He fancied that he could hear the drone of the seaplane as it dipped through the hot, moist air, its pontoons feeling for the first kiss of the waves. It was still a couple of hundred meters up, but closing rapidly. The angle of approach would take it into a cove on the far side of the soaring headland under which this part of the base had been built. Yukio watched the plane grow larger, its engines sounding louder and louder as it came in. Just before it disappeared from view, cut off by the near-vertical slopes of the heavily forested headland, the pontoons touched down, raising great sails of spray from the green-blue waters of the Pacific.

The two sailors never once broke the rhythm of their ceaseless metronomic scanning of the horizon. He supposed it made sense, although if American jet planes suddenly appeared it would have to be assumed they'd been discovered, and there would be nothing to be done. Stealth was everything. How many times had that been drummed into him, into everyone on the island?

Yukio hurried down the flight line. Dozens of *Ohkas* waited for their first and last flight. Ground crew tinkered and fussed about them like new mothers with a firstborn. In the end, the only way to be sure the planes would work was to use them. They couldn't really be tested, could they? But day and night, the technicians were here, including a handful of German officers who very much kept to themselves. When he'd arrived and seen them for the first time, he knew that he was involved in something very special. There was a lot of talk of how closely the Reich and the empire were working nowadays, but you still rarely saw a German in this part of the world. Yukio had never been introduced to them, never spoken to them. He didn't even know what role they played here, other than that they were somehow involved in maintaining the *Ohkas*.

They ignored him as he marched past.

The hangar dipped slightly as he headed inland. At the rear, four wide tunnels led underground, reminding him of the mine shafts in his old hometown of Kitamatsu. He hurried into the opening on the far left. It was about three meters wide, two and a half high. Low-wattage bulbs strung out every six meters provided a minimum of illumination.

The temperature dropped as he penetrated farther into the island's foundation. He was probably under fifteen meters of limestone by now. The walls were damp with condensation. He passed other men moving through the network of tunnels. You could always tell the newcomers. They had to stop and check the maps fixed to the walls at every intersection. Yukio had been here three weeks now, and was intimately familiar with all of those areas he was authorized to be in. There weren't that many places where he might get lost.

A few turns, a long, almost blacked-out section—three bulbs had blown and not yet been replaced—another turn, and a climb up a spiral staircase carved right into the rock, and he emerged into the reception area. A grand name for a small, buried room in the jungle at the edge of the cove. He saluted the base commander, General Kishi, and his direct superior, Commander Tamai, who were already there. A small launch puttered in toward the shore as the seaplane quickly made ready to leave again, lest its presence be detected.

Yukio's heart was nearly bursting with pride as he waited for the grand admiral to arrive. And when he saw that Admiral Onishi, the father of all the *tokkotai,* was with him, it was nearly too much. He was positively levitating.

"Careful," Tamai whispered. "If you stand any straighter, you'll snap."

The two older men chuckled coarsely while the admirals were still out of earshot, but they smartened up when the launch motored in under the overhanging canopy and ran up on the small sandy beach. Yukio was thrilled to see that neither of the visitors stood on ceremony. They alighted from the craft as quickly as possible and hurried deep into the cover of the jungle, their pants and shoes thoroughly soaked by the stagnant water that lay just inside the tree line. They were true fighting men, not just bureaucrats.

The profuse and elaborate greetings took up some time when Yamamoto and Onishi made it inside the reception area. The pounding in Yukio's chest was almost painful as Yamamoto stood in front of him, sizing him up.

"So, Lieutenant," he said, smiling. "You are to be my divine wind."

9

He kept the cave as clean as possible, which meant having to go farther and farther into the jungle to perform his ablutions. It was a dreadful indignity, being forced to shit in a hole and live like a monkey, but he probably deserved nothing more.

He had failed the grand admiral. Failed the emperor. Failed his ancestors and the code of *bushido*.

Jisaku Hidaka—he could not bring himself to use his military rank anymore—huddled in the shadows of the damp, fetid cave, hugging his knees, shivering with fever, and wondering if it were even possible for him to atone for his miserable faults. *Seppuku* would not do it. His failure was of so great a magnitude that even the ritual suicide would not attenuate his shame. That was the only reason he had not taken his life.

At least twice before he had written his death poem, laid out his *tanto* for the killing stroke, and kneeled on a makeshift *tatami*—in reality, an old cardboard box. But the temptation to live, the thought that he might strike one more blow against the barbarian hordes, had proved too great. Plus, of course, he had no second, no *kaishakunin* to observe his sacrifice or perform the *daki-kubi*, the final cut that would all but decapitate him, with his head left hanging by just a thin strip of flesh.

No, Hidaka was alone in this cave, alone with his grief.

He'd fled up here into the Choshiu Range—known as the Ko'olau to the *gaijin*—during the chaos of the Americans' counterattack. He had intended to lead an insurgency that would have rendered the islands useless as a base for the Allies, but he had been cut off, and as far as he could tell all his forces had been destroyed—a good many of them in the first thirty minutes of battle. His personal protection detail, six *Tokubetsu Rikusentai* marines of the Sasebo Regiment especially trained in bodyguard work, were all gone. Four had died just getting him up here into hiding, when a Wildcat had strafed their jeep. The other two, Corporal Okumi and Sergeant Tsunetomo, had sacrificed themselves in two separate incidents over the last few months, leading search parties away from his hideout.

So now he was alone in the world.

Hidden deep within the folds of the central Choshiu, his cave was large, twisting back nearly a hundred meters into the volcanic rock face of the mountains, the entrance protected by a thick canopy of jungle growth. The army had chosen it early in the occupation to serve as a redoubt in the event of a successful American invasion. A large number of fresh mountain streams ran nearby. His daily trek through the soft, boggy undergrowth to fetch water took him through an alien landscape of fat glossy leaves, creeper vines as thick as a man's torso, and ancient trees that seemed to hunch over as if ready to come alive and crush him with the swing of a great bough. It was all so different from the world he knew, the smell of oil, metal, gunpowder, and the honest stink of fighting men on board His Majesty's Imperial Japanese Navy ships.

Hidaka sat near the cave's entrance, morosely searching the airwaves with his flexipad for a sign that his comrades were still fighting somewhere on the Hawaiian Islands. Every few days he would be "rewarded" with news of a small gun battle or the capture of another "nip holdout." At least it meant that somebody somewhere was putting up a fight. When his time came he was determined to take at least fifteen or twenty of the white pigs with him. Okumi and Tsunetomo had set up some very clever traps to guard the approaches to the cave, and Hidaka kept a small arsenal behind the solid barricade of black volcanic rocks that they had built up when they first arrived here. Between the razor wire, the spike pits, and the new claymore mines, which were known as "cherry blossoms" to the Japanese, Hidaka was confident that he would give a good account of himself, even though he was a sailor, not a soldier. In the end they were all the emperor's men, and they bore a sacred duty to carry on the war, no matter how hopeless it might seem. Something, somewhere would turn the tide. The Germans might finish their atomic bomb. The Russians might come out of their coma and attack the West. Yamamoto might yet achieve his strategic masterstroke, the *Kassen Kantai*.

As he played with the touch screen of the flexipad, however, running through the civilian radio stations he could pick up, all he heard was music and inane chatter. There was no mention of the great fleet he had observed arriving offshore a few days ago, but that was to be expected. The Americans weren't *entirely* incompetent, and they would not want to give away such information, even if the passage of the *Clinton* and her "battle group" had probably been observed by a dozen Japanese submarines.

Two days before, Hidaka had crawled and climbed through four valleys to reach a ridgeline high enough to observe the enemy ships. He had made meticulous notes of the enemy's order of battle, including the presence of the traitor ship, the *Siranui,* and had returned to his cave ready to send the vital information into the ether with the radio he'd brought up here.

But as he sat in the cave, surrounded by enough provisions to sustain an entire company for two months, he'd decided that the time was not yet right to make contact. He was only too aware of how easily the *gaijin* found it to trace rogue electronic signals, and it would be a waste, wouldn't it, for him to give himself away when there might come some other opportunity to strike at the enemy, or confound his plans.

On balance, if he had selfishly committed *seppuku* when the island fell, he wouldn't have been here to observe the arrival of the enemy fleet. What might he miss now, if he gave himself away at this juncture?

His observations, and the photographs he'd taken of the task force at anchor around the *Clinton,* revealed that the Americans had made great strides in the design of their warships and aircraft. He counted at least fifteen destroyers that had obviously been laid down to plans based on ships from the future. They shared the same swept lines and featured strange-looking weapons mounts, possibly rocket launchers. Some of them even had tiny flight decks on which he'd observed helicopters landing and taking off.

No doubt the imperial navy had advanced many decades in its technology, too. How he wished he could see the first Japanese jet fighters carving into the enemy's flanks. After all, Japan had built the Zero, the greatest fighter aircraft in the world, and she would certainly have something to match the delta-winged jets he'd photographed on the deck of the *Clinton*.

Wouldn't she?

D-DAY + 21. 24 MAY 1944. 1024 HOURS. USS *HILLARY CLINTON*.

"She's a beautiful fighting machine," Admiral Ray Spruance said. "The Japs have got nothing to match her."

The commander in chief of the U.S. Pacific Fleet stood with a large group of officers on the flight deck of the supercarrier, inspecting one of the *Clinton*'s A-4 Skyhawks. It was only mid-morning, but the sun was already high, baking the men and women pink. Kolhammer could feel sweat leaking out under his arms, and he was glad he'd thrown on a pair of sunglasses before stepping out into the glare. Most of his people—nearly three-quarters of them 'temp these days—were hiding behind wraparound shades, but he noted that Spruance and everyone who'd come aboard with him made do with simply squinting into the fierce light.

He supposed there was some cultural point to be made there, but he was long past worrying about such things. You could spend your whole life cataloging the micro social changes that had occurred since the Transition. Indeed, just as they were leaving San Diego, one pinhead at UCLA had scored a research grant to study the "transplant effect" of unwritten French New Theory by unborn French postmodernists on unwritten texts.

Lord forgive me for the things I have wrought on this world.

"Did you have a hard time putting them together?" Spruance asked, jogging him back to reality. "I can't imagine that you had the blueprints just sitting around somewhere."

"No," Kolhammer answered. "Not exactly. That'd be like you keeping the plans for a Sopwith Camel on board the *Enterprise*. But we had a lot of relevant technical material, and some corporate memory spread across the Multinational Force, too, including some pretty grizzled old salts who'd actually worked with the Skyhawk early in their careers. Aussies and New Zealanders mostly, but a couple of Lonesome's aeronautical engineers on the *Kandahar*. There was one master chief called Madoc, he was like some sort of obsessed fan of the things.

And we had a Malaysian crew chief who was on detachment to us. He was a big help. It wasn't as hard as you'd think."

Spruance patted the fuselage just below the muzzle of a 20mm cannon. "Like riding a bicycle?"

"Same principle, I suppose." Kolhammer shrugged. "But it helps when you've got all the processing muscle we brought. And a blank check with the president's moniker."

Spruance nodded.

The Skyhawks were the navy's new glamour weapon, but for the moment they could only fly off the *Clinton*. It would be another three months before the first *Hawaii*-class flattops capable of handling them would come into service. In the meantime propeller-driven Corsairs and Skyraiders would do most of the navy's dogfighting and tactical bombing. Kolhammer wondered when the leapfrogging would end, and technological development would settle down into a steady curve again. When they all caught up with the next century, he supposed.

For once, the flight deck wasn't frenetically busy with landings and takeoffs. A squadron of the *Clinton*'s Skyhawks was flying CAP out of Hickam Field for the next few days, working in with Super Harriers from the *Kandahar*'s VMA-311 group, as the 21C Marine Corps fliers trained up their contemporary colleagues. The *Clinton*'s battle group hadn't berthed in Pearl, which was fully occupied by Spruance's other task force elements. Instead they'd pulled up about six klicks offshore, and Spruance had flown out by chopper to inspect them.

The loose knot of naval officers walked forward for a hundred meters or so, past another six Skyhawks chained down along the starboard rows. Heat shimmered up from the nonslip deck.

"It's an incredible-looking force, Admiral," Spruance said. "You can be proud of the work your people have done."

"I am, sir," Kolhammer replied. "It's a hell of an achievement, really. But it's a job half done. There's the fighting to come yet."

He let his gaze traverse the task force, of which the *Clinton* was but a part. When they sailed, Spruance would lead the entire fleet from the *Enterprise,* which had been refitted with both AT and some twenty-first technology taken off the *Leyte Gulf,* 3CI stuff mostly—equipment to improve his communications, control, command, and intelligence capabilities. Almost thirty ships lay around them, including three carriers and the heavy littoral assault ships, the *Kandahar* and her new sister ships, the *Falluja* and the *Damascus*—which looked much like carriers to the casual observer.

Four contemporary heavy cruisers and two *Iowa*-class battleships with extensive AT retrofits provided the big-bore artillery, although Kolhammer was certain they'd be restricted to shore bombardment once they reached the Marianas. If it got to the point of trading shells with the *Yamato,* something would be seriously wrong. The *Siranui* lay about a thousand meters to port, her flags limp in the hot, humid air. Like the *Clinton,* she'd been retrofitted, after firing off all her missiles during the assault on Hawaii in late '42. She now carried a very basic harpoon-style antiship missile, designated ASM-1 and called the Barracuda. Kolhammer's Skyhawks, the remaining Harriers, and the *Siranui*'s missile bays were the reason he never expected to get within range of the *Yamato*'s long guns. She'd be sunk long before she ever saw the force that was coming after her and the last of the Imperial Japanese Fleet.

A few hundred meters behind the *Siranui,* a *Halsey*-class guided missile destroyer swept past a couple of vintage destroyers, almost appearing to taunt them. She was "Old Navy," not Auxiliary Forces, but that didn't stop her lording it over the *Fletcher*-class rust-buckets as she passed them by. Spruance halted in his walk toward the bow just to take in the sight.

"Amazing," he said to himself. "Bill would have been proud, although he would have liked to have a carrier named after him. Or at least a cruiser."

He tore his gaze away from the sleek, dangerous-looking warship and turned back to Kolhammer. "Have you been out to the cemetery yet, Admiral?"

"Not yet, no. I was planning on taking a private trip out there later. I haven't even made it ashore yet."

Spruance nodded and began walking back toward the ship's island superstructure. On the *Clinton* it had the appearance of a raked-back shark fin. Kolhammer had seen the next generation of American carriers being built back in the States, and they imitated this radar-baffling design, as well, although contemporary materials science wasn't yet up to synthesizing the advanced RAMskin that coated the Big Hill's island.

As they walked back past the jet fighters the dull thudding of a helicopter reached him. He saw Jones's command Huey, an uptime original, coming in from the *Kandahar* for the O Group conference.

D-DAY + 23. 26 MAY 1944. 0302 HOURS.
KO'OLAU RANGE.

Fire demons chased him through his dreams, massive slump-shouldered ape creatures, covered all over in flames, except for two small black pools for their eyes.

The former Japanese governor of the Hawaiian Islands awoke with a shudder on the fold-up cot. It was nighttime and pitch black. He fumbled beside his bed for one of the last of the light sticks. Finding the little plastic tube, he bent it until something inside it snapped and flooded the sleeping chamber with soft green light. An old army blanket hanging across the cave at a natural choke point prevented the light from leaking out and giving him away, although any observer would have to be right inside the valley to see it anyway.

Hidaka shook his head to clear the memory of the nightmare. He'd suffered from vivid dreams ever since the Americans had returned. Their initial assault was so powerful, so paralyzing in its violence, that he sometimes feared it had unhinged him. He was never meant to fight on land. He would surely have done better on the bridge of a cruiser or a battleship.

He swung his legs over the side of the cot and felt around with his toes for the sandals he had been wearing. It was chilly and damp in the cave and he started to cough, as he always did on waking up. He wheezed almost constantly, but for some reason it was worse when he slept on his left side. Perhaps that lung was infected.

He slipped his feet into the wooden sandals and pulled a blanket around himself as he stood up. He checked his watch: three in the morning.

The nightmares often woke him at this time. It was when the first rockets had struck, destroying the encampment at Pearl Harbor and killing thousands of his men in the opening moments of the battle. Try as he might, it was impossible to rid himself of the memories. The fire demons of his fevered sleep were incarnations of the men he'd seen burned alive by some kind of incendiary bombs. If he lived to be a hundred, which was unlikely, he would never forget the horror of seeing one man, completely wreathed in liquid flames, melting away like candle wax.

The area he'd blocked off as living quarters was quite roomy, if Spartan. He had intended to run an insurgency campaign from here, so it had been fitted out accordingly. Ten empty bunks, for other officers who never made it, lay beyond his. He had maps of the islands, radio equipment, and food and weapons stores to spare. If only a few more had reached this hidden fortress. If only his protection detail had survived. They were all good men and even with just a handful of them, he could have caused havoc for the Americans. Instead he was reduced to hiding out, waiting for the moment when he might contribute something other than infamy to the emperor's cause.

Hidaka fired up a small gas oven and put a pot of water on to boil. He would have some green tea and noodles and ponder his dilemma some more. Perhaps he might even be able to get back to sleep before the dawn.

While the water was heating he played around with his flexipad, flipping through the radio stations in a desultory manner. Those few still on the air at this hour were mostly broadcasting slow dance tunes. At least there was no music from the future. He always found that harsh and unsettling.

He consoled himself with memories of the short time he'd been the absolute ruler of Hawaii, the way he had smashed all resistance, the luxury of playing God with vanquished foes who had thought themselves so very superior to the "little yellow men." He stirred the water and poured off a cup to make his tea, then added a packet of dried noodles and powdered pork flavoring to the pot. He treasured the memory of Nimitz being led to his execution, and lingered over the details of the many comfort women he had taken in the officers' facility at Diamond Head. It had been a wonderful thing, to crush the spirit of the enemy as thoroughly as that, to have his way with some *gaijin* slut while her man was forced to look on. He grew hard just remembering.

He was about to pleasure himself with the memory when he jumped at a whispered sound.

Phhhht!

Two silver prongs projected from his chest, and thin wires led from them back to . . .

He tried to leap to his feet, but a terrible shock surged through his body, robbing him of the ability to stand. As he fell into blackness he caught sight of his assassins, three black-clad men.

Ninjas, perhaps?

They advanced on him, weapons raised, faces obscured behind glasses that made them look like giant insects. Hidaka was vaguely aware that his penis was erect and pointing at them as he slid into darkness.

D-DAY + 23. 26 MAY 1944. 1101 HOURS.
USS *HILLARY CLINTON*.

The meeting took place in the main conference room of the *Clinton*. Although it was Spruance's briefing and should have been held on the *Enterprise,* he had agreed that it made more sense to bring everyone together on the much larger and better-equipped vessel.

Kolhammer stopped counting the number of officers sitting around the huge table after twenty-five. He hadn't been to an O Group of a comparable size in this room since the first emergency sessions after the Transition. It was a very different crew who'd gathered today, though, to work through the Marianas campaign. Jones, now a general, was still sitting next to him, and Mike Judge was acting as chairman. But the Brits, the Aussies, the French, the Japanese, and many of the U.S. commanders of his original task force were gone. Some dead. Some captured. Most just scattered to the four corners of the globe. In a perfect world Captain Willet of the Australian submarine *Havoc* should have been here, as she would be joining the task force later, but without satellite conferencing that was impossible. HMAS *Havoc* was stalking the Japanese fleet in the western Pacific.

The dark ages really did get him down sometimes.

A Marine Corps full-bird colonel—a 'temp, not one of Jones's men—was describing a Force Recon mission to plant position fixers around the Marianas, so that the fleet's gunnery officers would have solid coordinates to lay down their computer-controlled barrages.

Kolhammer could feel the tension radiating from the man sitting beside him. Jones had his own special-ops-capable marines who were not only trained for that sort of work, but had years of experience in it to boot. But the 'temps had gone with their own people again, as they did so often when the Eighty-second was involved.

Looking around the room, he could identify two distinct groups: Spruance's people and the AF personnel. The latter weren't all 21C. Most of the men and women he and Jones now commanded were 'temps, but they had volunteered for service in the Auxiliary Forces, putting paid to the caricature of the 'temps being nothing more than a bunch of boneheaded rednecks.

On the other hand, there *were* a lot of boneheaded rednecks around, some of them in this very room.

Another briefing officer, an Old Navy commander by the name of Chalmers, replaced the marine colonel at the lecturn to detail the Japanese order of battle as it was currently understood. It was another frustrating experience. Kolhammer knew Stuart Chalmers quite well. He'd acted in Dan Black's liaison role for a while, and he was a good man. But it was exasperating having to sit and listen to him guesstimate the size and strength of Yamamoto's forces. That was the sort of information he could have dialed up on the web in a public library back home.

"We have good intelligence on enemy land forces," Chalmers said. "Apart from some minor technological enhancements such as claymore-type mines, better radios, and an M-Seventy-nine-style grenade launcher, the Japanese army remains largely unaffected by post-Transition technical developments."

Jones snorted quietly beside him. "Commander Chalmers never walked into a fucking claymore," he whispered.

Chalmers carried on without seeming to notice. "However, the Japanese navy has made some significant advances in the use of radar-controlled gunnery, Close-In Weapons Systems, night-fighter operations—both submarine and antisubmarine warfare—and ship-launched missiles, probably through close cooperation with Germany, which has poured a lot of effort into rocket research."

Kolhammer had to admire Yamamoto for the focus he'd brought to Japan's defenses, if nothing else. The Pacific War was a naval battle. As savage as the fighting had been through the island chains, the side that controlled the seas would prevail. Japan could not hope to keep up with America's accelerating technological superiority. It simply didn't have the industrial or research bases to compete. But Yamamoto, for all of his talk of staging a *Kassen Kantai,* had instead fought a tremendous holding effort since the Japanese had been kicked out of Australia and Hawaii. Whatever internal battle he'd had with the Japanese army, he'd won, because hundreds of thousands of troops had been pulled out of China and redeployed into the Pacific, not to take new territory but to keep the Allies away from the Home Islands long enough for the Axis powers to develop their own atomic arsenal.

As MacArthur and Spruance fought their way toward Japan, it became obvious that most of the bounty from the Emergence, as the Japanese called the Transition, had gone to Yamamoto's surviving fleet rather than to the army. Yamamoto knew that slowing the Allies' inevitable advance on Japan meant slowing the U.S. Navy.

It always came back to the bomb, though, didn't it?

Who would get there first? He didn't believe for a minute that Germany could hope to compete with the combined industrial and scientific muscle of the English-speaking world. Not with the advantage the Allies enjoyed in raw computing power. Yet . . .

The admiral pushed aside these thoughts. They weren't his immediate concern, whereas the next five minutes of this briefing were. He gave Jones a light pat on the shoulder as he stood to make his way to the lectern. Slotting home a data stick, he nodded to Spruance, his only superior in the gathering, and waited for the PowerPoint files to arrange themselves on the screen behind him.

"I'm going to quickly run you through some of the capabilities of the *Clinton*'s battle group," he said, "and outline how these will be used in strategic support of Admiral Spruance's plan, as well as tactical support from General Jones and the Eighty-second Expeditionary Brigade's attack on Guam.

"First, a strategic strike on enemy capital ships . . ."

He ended up speaking for twenty-five minutes, mostly in answer to questions from the floor. Jones seemed distracted during the presentation, even taking a couple of silent messages on his flexipad. Kolhammer would have been pissed off, except that the hulking marine flashed him a private message that immediately explained his agitation. The text came up on Kolhammer's flexipad as it was resting in front of him.

Hidaka captured. Rogas queries Sanction 5?

Oh shit, Kolhammer thought.

10

D-DAY + 23. 26 MAY 1944. 1554 HOURS.
WAIPAHU MEMORIAL CEMETERY, HAWAII.

Neither Chester Nimitz nor Bill Halsey was buried on Hawaii. Their remains had been found, after much distressing effort, and flown home to be interred at Arlington National Cemetery.

The short rule of the Japanese had been as horrific here as it had been in northern Australia, New Guinea, the Philippines, and Indonesia—or the Dutch East Indies. As a matter of fact, thought Kolhammer, it had probably been worse. The civilian death rate had run to 90 percent, and almost no military personnel had survived to greet the liberators. Some of the higher-ranking officers had been transported to Japan for interrogation. With them had gone anybody from the Multinational Force, civilian or military. Almost everyone else had perished in a long orgy of abuse and mass murder to rival the Rape of Nanking.

A memorial to the dead and the missing had been erected. It stood near the ghost town of Waipahu on the site of one of the many mass graves that covered Oahu. The Japanese had used the former sugar-milling town on the north shore of Pearl Harbor's Middle Loch as a gigantic slave camp. At least twenty-five thousand people had been interred there while they worked on clearing debris from the harbor. As they died, they'd been dumped in a series of open pits to the west of the town. Kolhammer could only imagine what a hellish sight it must have bcen. The death pits contained thousands of children, women, and old folks.

War crime investigators, trained by his own people from the *Clinton*'s WCI Unit, had determined that at least half of the dead from the Waipahu Site had been summarily executed in the days before the Liberation—killed simply to deny them the hope of freedom.

Kolhammer had thought himself inured to horror by thirty years of active service, most of them spent fighting medieval savages with a fetish for degrading their victims. But standing with Jones on a small rise outside Waipahu, where more than a hundred of their own people were buried, he knew that he had but a scant understanding of the evil of which humans were capable. And now he had within his power the man responsible for this atrocity.

Jisaku Hidaka.

It was a glorious day to have to contemplate such dark matters. A cool southerly breeze ruffled his shirt and dried the sweat on his exposed forearms. Thin strands of altocumulus clouds softened the hard blue sky. The mass graves, six of them combining to make one enormous burial ground between here and Pearl City, had been declared part of the national cemetery and were now tended by the Department of the Army with the same care it lavished on Arlington. Blinding white gravel paths meandered between lush green lawns, small stands of shade trees, and dozens of memorial sites devoted to honoring specific acts of sacrifice and resistance that were deemed especially notable. Other mourners moved slowly though the site, stopping here and there to pay their respects, to pray, and to grieve. Almost all of them were in uniform. Very few civilians remained on the island nowadays. A short distance from Kolhammer and Jones a contemporary marine kneeled in front of a small marble plinth commemorating five Boy Scouts who'd hidden out in the Ko'olaus, reporting on Japanese ship and troop movements via a salvaged army radio until they were captured and beheaded. His shoulders hitched and shuddered violently as he wept. He might have been a father or uncle to one of the boys. He might have been a complete stranger. Even Jones had rubbed his eyes after reading their story on the little brass plaque at the base of the plinth. It was nearly buried in flowers and wreaths, and at some time in the past few months somebody had draped a military medal over it. A Silver Star. Hundreds more had joined it.

"So what are we gonna do about this fucker?" Jones rumbled. "I don't think I can remember a man more in need of sanction than this evil little shit."

Kolhammer watched the weeping man cross himself, climb to his feet, and walk away from the Boy Scout Memorial. High above them two contrails traced the flight of a couple of jet fighters. Skyhawks probably. He thought he could just make out the delta-winged silhouette.

"I don't know, Lonesome. You're right that hanging's too good for this little bastard. He's a living, breathing argument in favor of Sanction Five . . ."

"But?"

Kolhammer chewed his lip. "But, as much as we have a claim on him, the 'temps have a stronger one. Look at this place, would you. I don't know that I've ever been anywhere sadder than this. Don't know that I ever will. I passed sanction on Hidaka, but I'm thinking that for once, their way might be better than ours."

The Eighty-second's commander examined the tips of his polished shoes. An original Humvee and its driver waited for them back at the entrance to the cemetery. Jones lifted his head and stared out across manicured lawns, their gentle slopes covering a heinous crime.

"Do you even know how we would have sanctioned him?" he asked. "He's not some raghead jihadi. If we stitched him up in a pig carcass before killing him, he'd just think we were weird."

Kolhammer nodded. "I had some people working on it. Chances are, we're going to be dealing with a few of Tojo's finest at level five when we get back out there. It's one of our little eccentricities the 'temps are happy to indulge for now. I think they believe it spreads an exemplary terror among the natives."

"They weren't always so happy about it," said Jones.

"Not all of them, and not always," Kolhammer conceded. "You're right. I reckon they used to think we were monsters. But it's amazing the difference a few years and a couple of standout atrocities can make, isn't it? I don't recall anyone bleating about Ono's human rights when your boys put the blade on him for all this." He swept one hand around to take in the cemetery and everything beyond it.

"But you think they'd want to deal with Hidaka themselves."

Kolhammer didn't answer for a while. Like Jones, he had been deeply affected by the cemetery. In a way, they were responsible for it. This had never happened in their world. From a distance, the two men probably looked like pallbearers contemplating the load they were about to lift.

"I promised Roosevelt we wouldn't go off the reservation," Kolhammer said.

"He knows about the Quiet Room?" The big marine's eyes widened in surprise.

"No. As far as I can tell, it's never leaked. He didn't mention it by name when we spoke about Ivanov. But there was no doubt that we were being put on some sort of notice."

Jones folded his arms and pursed his lips as he took this in. Kolhammer recognized it as his Deep Thought routine. A couple of Jones's best men and women had been drafted as Roomies, with his full knowledge and consent. If anything, he was more enthusiastic than Kolhammer about reshaping this world into something more amenable to their way of thinking. Given the shit he'd had to put up with, it was understandable. "Okay," he said. "So, Hidaka? Do we take him into the Room, or not?"

Kolhammer looked past his friend's shoulder to the mass of flowers and medals heaped up around the Boy Scout Memorial. *What would they have done?* he wondered.

"Give him to the 'temps," he said at last. "But not straightaway. If we can't go to Sanction Five, we can at least get a *little* medieval on his sorry ass."

"Okay," Jones agreed. "I'll countersign."

D-DAY + 23. 26 MAY 1944. 2212 HOURS.
KOʻOLAU RANGE.

Hidaka had heard all about the barbarity of these people. It made sense. Their parent society was degenerate and so, having hailed from its future, they would naturally be even more thoroughly debauched than the *gaijin* of his time.

He sat on the edge of the wooden cot, his hands cuffed with some sort of light plastic tie that dug painfully into his wrists. He tried hard not to shiver from the damp chill of the cave, lest they imagine he was shaking from fear. Two of the soldiers—he knew now they were just marines, not assassins—kept their weapons trained on him. They wore combat goggles and never moved, except to strike him once when he attempted to stand up and go to the toilet. They had made him foul himself instead of allowing him that dignity.

They were animals. Much worse than the *Sutanto*'s Indonesians or the Frenchmen on the *Dessaix*.

He knew from having read the reports out of Australia what fate awaited him. These Emergence barbarians would not bother with a sham trial and formal execution. They would soon take him outside and shoot him in the back of the head. If he was lucky. Perhaps they would torture and disfigure him until he begged for mercy, as they had with Ono, forcing the man to shame himself in front of his comrades and his ancestors, indeed in front of the whole world. After all, in their eyes he was a "war criminal." He almost laughed at the poisonous irony of it, except that would only have earned him another swipe across the face with the butt of a weapon. These animals thought nothing of burning entire cities, and yet they had the audacity to accuse him of "a crime against humanity."

He had to wonder, though, why it was taking so long. Surely they couldn't be planning to torture him? He had been cocooned up here in the mountains forever. What could he tell them about anything? All his plans to lead the resistance from this dank little fortress had come to nothing. He was worthless as a prisoner.

And, he thought, *as a man.*

The blanket he'd hung as a blackout curtain twitched aside, and three figures entered. He couldn't help himself. Before he could control his reaction his eyes widened in shock. It was the giant black barbarian—the marine called Jones. And the famous Kolhammer right behind him! What could this mean? Did they intend to carry out the—what did they call it?—the "sanction" themselves? He'd heard that about those, too. Their death squads in Australia had been made up of all ranks, even the highest. He assumed the same had been the case in Hawaii, but he'd had no way of confirming it, isolated from events as he was up here.

"Get up," Kolhammer said.

The man's voice was harsh and deep, reminding him of Grand Admiral Yamamoto. Hidaka climbed to his feet with difficulty, ashamed of his nakedness, his poor physical condition, and the running sores on his legs and feet. They would not allow him any clothes to cover himself.

"You are Jisaku Hidaka?"

He nodded, flinching from a cracking blow that never came. More shame heaped upon unutterable shame.

"You know who we are?"

He stood as straight as he could. "Admiral Kolhammer and Colonel Jones," he said.

"General," the black man corrected him.

"Congratulations," he said with as much scorn as he could muster. "But I shall wager that you promoted yourself, *Colonel*. I doubt that your countrymen would be so generous to a *nigger*."

He grinned, pleased with himself for the first time in many long months. They knew he spoke English, but they couldn't have been prepared for his mastery of their colloquialism, or the unpleasant realities of their adopted society. His satisfaction lasted all of half a second, until Kolhammer stepped forward and drove a fist into his face. The blow was powerful, knocking him off his feet and through the air. He flew over the wooden cot and fell in a tangle among the beds lying next to it. White, scalding-hot pain filled his head, and he could no longer breathe through his nose.

"You will keep a civil tongue in your head, or I will have it cut out. Do you understand?"

One of his guards was already holding a dagger. Hidaka nodded, sending spikes of pain through his head and neck again. He crawled back to his feet. The knife disappeared back into its scabbard like a marvelous conjuring trick. He waited for them to do whatever it was they did before murdering their prisoners. But nothing happened.

"You can consider yourself a lucky motherfucker," Jones said. "We caught you, but you're going back to Pearl and we're turning you over to Admiral Spruance's folks. They'll deal with you their own way."

Hidaka's head wobbled, and he thought he might lose consciousness. "Why?" he asked. "You do not take prisoners. Not prisoners like me, anyway. You just kill them."

"Oh, don't tempt me," Kolhammer said. "You're right, we would normally sanction you under protocol five of the standing rules of engagement. And believe me, by the time that was done with, you'd wish we had just put a gun to your head. But other people have a claim on your sorry carcass. And we're giving you to them."

"No," he said, his voice breaking. "This is not *fair*. I cannot become a prisoner. Not after the shame I have already brought upon myself."

Hot tears welled up in his eyes. He blinked them away impatiently. Kolhammer and Jones seemed surprised. But what would they know of *bushido*? After all the dishonor he had brought upon his name, to be cheated now of death's release— it was unbearable.

Even with his hands cuffed he launched himself at Kolhammer, but he had covered only half the distance across the cave to him when a freight train slammed into him and drove him backward. He struck the wall painfully and looked up, expecting to see the admiral advancing on him like a common brawler. Instead, to his horror, a woman stood in front of him, the third American who had come through the blackout curtain. He had ignored her, thinking her some minor functionary. She bent down over him and released the uncomfortable plastic restraints.

He moved to push her aside and she broke his arm, snapping it at the elbow.

Then she went to work on him.

D-DAY + 24. 27 MAY 1944. 0902 HOURS. CINCPAC, PEARL HARBOR.

"What do you mean you've got him? How?"

Admiral Ray Spruance stared at Kolhammer as though he'd grown an extra head.

"Lonesome's mountain troop was on a training run through the Ko'olaus. Just stretching their legs after the voyage. They picked up his trail. Figured they'd stumbled across another holdout. Tracked him. Bagged him."

"That's it?"

"That's it," said Kolhammer. "Luck of the Irish."

"Master Chief Vincente Rogas is Irish?"

"Could be Black Irish . . . I suppose."

Spruance frowned, not appreciating the joke, as he shuffled

the photographs of Hidaka on his desk at fleet HQ in Pearl. "And these injuries?"

"He fell down," Jones said, from the chair next to Kolhammer. Spruance leveled a cold eye at him.

"A lot," Jones added with a poker face.

"Has he complained of being beaten?" Kolhammer asked.

Spruance looked vaguely troubled. "No. No, he says he fell down a lot, too."

Kolhammer dared not look at Jones. Spruance eyed them like a principal with two of his most difficult students, who also happened to be his main hope for the pennant. It was midmorning, the day after Jones's mountain troop had stumbled across Hidaka—that much at least was true. They were meeting in a prefab hut that substituted for Spruance's office while permanent facilities were being built—or rather, rebuilt. His office, like theirs, was a mix of old and new. A flat-panel display took up a big piece of real estate on the old wooden desk while paper maps of the Pacific theater were pinned to corkboard on all of the walls. His phone was a heavy old-fashioned lump of black Bakelite with a rotary dial, which sat next to a Siemens C65 flexipad. In the window behind him Kolhammer could see a flattop being nuzzled into its berth by a small flotilla of tugboats. It looked like the *Intrepid*.

"Well, I suppose congratulations are in order, then," Spruance said finally. "This news will be very welcome back home. Hidaka is the first high-value war criminal we've managed to capture alive out here."

"They don't give up easily," Jones said. "Same thing where we came from. Our bad boys used to just blow themselves up."

"Is that why you take so few prisoners?" Spruance asked coldly.

"That's not the simple question you think it is, Admiral," said Kolhammer, who could tell that Spruance was quite steamed about something, presumably the injuries to Hidaka. "There's a lot of history behind our policies. I can understand that you'd find them off-putting at first, but they've served us well in a war that's run much longer than yours. And of course, we'll be reviewing them after the end of hostilities here, when our forces are folded into yours."

"I think you'll be doing more than reviewing them, Admiral. I think you'll be leaving them behind for good."

"Perhaps," Kolhammer conceded. "They were appropriate in context."

"And they have their uses here," Jones added in his rumbling growl. "Otherwise I doubt Congress would have approved the extension of our rules of engagement."

"The Australians certainly didn't complain," Kolhammer said, turning to Jones. "As I understand the situation, there was a lot of public pressure to turn all the Japanese captives over to you and the Second Cav for field sanction."

Jones nodded. "There was."

Spruance gathered up the photographs of a bruised and bleeding Hidaka. "Well, as you say, everything in context, gentlemen." He didn't sound as angry.

He placed the prints in a buff-colored envelope and dropped them into his top drawer. Then he turned his attention back to the two men.

"I wonder if I might prevail upon you to be a little more circumspect in the application of field punishment when we reach the Marianas, though?" He shook his head as Jones opened his mouth to speak. "I'm not asking you to alter your rules of engagement. I'm just concerned that we don't end up indicted for the sorts of things we criticize in our opponents."

Kolhammer saw genuine discomfort in Spruance's eyes. He didn't want to be a party to sanctioned field executions of any type.

Jones was not so diplomatic. "We could run any sanctions through your office, if you'd like, Admiral. Have your counsel sign off the warrants."

Spruance paled at the suggestion. "No. No, I don't think so, General. All I'm asking, all the *president* is asking, is that you don't . . ." He groped for the words needed in such an uncomfortable moment. ". . . that you don't . . ."

"Admiral Spruance," Kolhammer said. "We will fight the good fight. And where justice needs to be done, it *will* be done. But we won't embarrass the navy or the country."

Spruance nodded, clearly relieved. "Thank you. And thank you for this," he said, indicating the report Jones had brought on the capture of Hidaka.

Later on, out in the corridor, Jones muttered to Kolhammer, "Country would probably vote us all medals if we capped off every one of those murdering assholes."

"No doubt," Kolhammer agreed.

"So then, why not just tell Spruance we authorized a Sanction Three on Hidaka? It was legit."

"It was," Kolhammer said. "And if he asked directly, I'd tell him. But he didn't. And now the blood's on our hands. Not his. You and I can live with that. He shouldn't have to."

"We told him the little prick fell down."

"Well, he did fall down. De Marco kept hitting him. He kept falling down."

Jones took that in silence, grinning just a little as they walked through a secretarial pool. Tinny music followed them from an old radio. A disco tune, "Born to Be Alive," covered by Glenn Miller and his big band.

"Kinda weird, ain't it," Jones said.

"What?" Kolhammer asked. He sensed a change of subject.

"The way disco, of all the possible music we brought, should be the one to catch fire here. Did you notice Hidaka had a disco station playing when we walked in?"

"Well," Kolhammer mused, "they're all over the dial. And I suppose it sounds a bit like swing. Plus, it's an optimistic sort of music. People want that at the moment. Who needs death metal when you've got the Nazis?"

They passed through the main entrance of the building and into the fierce white light of the morning. "I don't see old Hidaka being much of a fan. Not after Gina De Marco tooled him up like that."

Kolhammer grunted quietly at the memory. The female marine had beaten Hidaka senseless while singing along to the radio. It had been an entirely punitive retribution with the primary purpose of humiliating the man and breaking his spirit. A level three sanction. They had assumed, correctly, that he would never speak of it, shamed into silence, but even if he had, it was within their accepted rules of engagement.

"Something funny?" Jones asked.

"Not really," Kolhammer said as he fitted his powered shades in place. "I was just thinking of serendipity. Do you remember the exact song that was playing?"

"Not really," Jones said, looking nonplussed.

"Well, I don't know whether you heard or not. I think you were talking to Chief Rogas at the time. But Hidaka, he was sort of whimpering after she broke his arm, begging De Marco to tell him what she was going to do."

"And?"

"And so she leaned into him and told him they were going to boogie-oogie-oogie until they simply could not boogie no more."

Jones's rich baritone laughter rolled out over the naval base.

Kolhammer allowed himself a chuckle, too, now that they were out of earshot of the typing pool and any other 'temps who might be listening. They just wouldn't understand.

11

D-DAY + 24. 27 MAY 1944. 1954 HOURS.
NORTHERN FRANCE.

Julia had missed the first day of the offensive—she was stuck on the road from Dieppe to Abbeville, which, in her humble opinion, blew chunks. She didn't like to stand still for very long these days. It gave her time to think about all the mistakes she'd made. It didn't matter what anyone told her, she knew that she was to blame for Rosanna's death. She could have gotten her off the island for sure if she'd really tried. God knew she'd wiggled out of tighter situations herself over the years. And as angry as she'd been with Dan over the whole pregnancy thing, in the end he'd been right. What had she married him for if not to start a family? She certainly hadn't needed to walk down the aisle to get him into bed. And now he was dead because he'd had the shit-awful luck to fall in love with her.

She shook her head in the back of the jeep and cursed softly.

"Y'all okay there, Miss Duffy?" her driver asked. He was a pimply black kid from Detroit, name of Private Franklin, and he was still in awe of his unexpected passenger.

She smiled kindly at him. They were stuck in a seemingly endless traffic jam. Thousands of vehicles stretched away in front of and behind them. GIs trudged alongside the road in an unceasing line. Some of them slowed down to talk every now and then, usually until some noncom bawled at them to haul ass again. It would have been an irresistible target for the Luftwaffe . . . had the Luftwaffe not ceased to exist in any real sense in this part of the world. High above them countless numbers of Allied fighter aircraft described long, lazy figure eights, "guarding the parking lot," as Julia explained to her companion.

"We'll be out of this soon, ma'am. I'm sure of it," Franklin promised.

"S'okay," she said, staring across the plowed fields that surrounded them on both sides. "Gives me a chance to tally up all my regrets."

"You, ma'am?" he gasped. "You couldn't have any regrets! Damn, excuse me, ma'am. But damn, you're famous and all. And rich. And pretty, too, if you don't think me too forward for saying so, ma'am."

Her smile touched the corners of her eyes for the first time in many days. "Thanks, Franklin. But I'm not Sinatra. I've had more than a few regrets."

The jeep lunged forward a few feet as a pulse of movement crept along the jam.

"Hey, you know, that's my favorite song, Miss Duffy. You want me to sing it for you? I can sing it real well. My mom says so, anyway."

Before she could shrug and say *Sure* he was into the first verse, beating out a kickin' version of the old tune, which had bounced around in the top ten for the last six months. She couldn't help but laugh and join in the chorus. A couple of grounded paratroopers picked it up as they marched past, and within moments it had spread up and down the almost stationary line of traffic. Thousands of tired, bloodied men ripping out an a cappella power-ballad version of "My Way."

Julia quickly unpacked her Sonycam, blocking out a precious few minutes of lattice memory to record something other than blood and horror.

There was more than enough of that waiting for her up ahead.

For six days the combined air forces of Britain, Canada, and the United States had carpet-bombed a corridor 120 kilometers long and 30 wide. Within that target box lay twelve armored and motorized divisions the Nazis had released from the "defense" of Normandy to attack the Allied Forces around Calais.

The first concerted air strikes had begun as the lead element of the German counterattack—the *Panzer Lehr* and the *Panzer Korps Hermann Göring*—approached the town of Abbeville. The lead three tanks, Tiger IIs, rumbled onto a ridge to the east of town, but never even made it to the downslope. High above them, fifteen Lancaster bombers, protected by a squadron of Saber jet fighters, all of them controlled by the Nemesis battle-space arrays of HMS *Trident* three hundred kilometers away, released the first of tens of thousands of dumb iron bombs that would fall on the Germans over the next week.

The Tigers, their crews, and the armored personnel carriers traveling behind them were obliterated. The quantum arrays of the *Trident* delivered the weapons package in such a focused manner that most of the initial target mass was atomized, so tightly compressed was the storm of high explosives.

The strategic bombers hammered the centerline of the advance, all 120 kilometers of it, while hundreds of Cobra gunships and ground attack aircraft buzzed viciously on the flanks, chewing over any smaller formations that escaped the crucible. Nearly twelve hundred Tiger and Leopard tanks were destroyed in the first hour. By the end of the engagement two thousand more had been reduced to scrap metal, and approximately forty thousand German soldiers were dead.

Allied losses ran to two dozen bombers and fifteen helicopter gunships. The first press reports in London actually understated the scope of the victory, because nobody could bring themselves to believe it. Once the devastated corridor was secured by a highland regiment, Julia had hopped a flight over to see for herself the realities of what the tabloids had dubbed "the Great Turkey Shoot."

When she'd finally escaped the corps-level traffic snarl, she'd recognized the first signs of destruction from twenty klicks out—a great burned-out scar on the face of the earth.

"Holy shit," she muttered as her chopper bled off altitude and dropped down toward the ruined countryside. "Those boys really did do it their way. Anyone know how many Frenchies bought it?" she asked in a louder voice.

The pilot's voice came back over the intercom. "Nobody's saying, Miss Duffy. But I don't see how anything could have survived inside the target box. I've flown twenty miles in, and all the way out to the horizon on both sides that's all you see. Scorched earth. It's fucking amazing."

She nodded. The highway into Damascus had looked a bit like this when the air force had trashed the Syrian First Armored Corps. But at least that wreckage had maintained a sort of integrity, like a long drawn-out junkyard. You could see, as you flew over it, each cohesive unit that had been set upon and destroyed.

The devastation stretching across northern France was something entirely different, something she was only just getting used to, along with the 'temps. They might be a little backward in many ways, but when they put their minds to it they could do violence on an apocalyptic scale. It was funny, in a really dark way, thinking back to how horrified they'd been when the uptimers came spilling out of the wormhole with their detached, postmodernist, unemotional approach to warfare. There'd been quite a run of little books and magazine articles by the sniffier sort of contemporary intellectual about the "refined barbarism" of future morality and culture. Some days reading *The New Yorker* was like being trapped in a stalled elevator with Harold Bloom—and that had happened to her once, so she would know. As a genuine uptime celebrity Julia had even been dragged into the debate, arguing on radio with some idiot professor who wanted to ban television for fifty years to allow society time to "prepare" for its arrival. For all their initial squeamishness, however, the 'temps had proven themselves fast learners in the arts of savagery.

And when all that savagery was directed—as it had been over northern France—by twenty-first-century Combat Intelligence, the effect was exactly what she'd come to observe and report on: a genuinely biblical catastrophe.

"Holy shit," she repeated.

"Yeah," the pilot agreed, "that's what everyone says."

After they landed, Julia bivouacked with a British intelligence unit tasked with picking over the scrap metal and body parts, not that there was much of either to analyze. Over the next two days she shot a few megs of imagery that was eerily reminiscent of footage she'd seen from the First World War, then tried and failed to gain access to the handful of prisoners who'd been taken. There weren't many, and she believed the

Intel Division colonel who told her they weren't speaking to anyone yet. Most were under sedation, he told her in confidence.

She filed a thousand words for the *Times* on her impressions of the Great Turkey Shoot, which were really no different from anything anybody else had to say. No matter how she tried to spin it, it all boiled down to "holy shit."

She did a hometown puff piece on the crew of the Huey she'd ridden in with and filed a great bit on Private Franklin's impromptu cover of Frank Sinatra on the road to Abbeville.

Then, while waiting for a lift back to Calais, she missed the opening shots of Patton's breakout and drive toward Belgium.

D-DAY + 24. 27 MAY 1944. 0411 HOURS.
BUNKER COMPLEX, BERLIN.

The führer was screaming. The object of his rage, a poor Luftwaffe colonel with more bad news from the Western Front, looked gray, perhaps even feverish. Certainly he didn't look healthy.

Rather than creating a pall over the crowded underground room, however, Hitler's outburst actually lifted a few spirits, because it meant that the focus of his rage had shifted safely away from everyone else, at least for a brief moment. It had no effect whatsoever on Himmler, though, since he had long since stopped paying any attention to the führer's rants. They were like a constant background refrain, similar to the rumble of the British bombs during the night.

Still, the SS leader felt nearly as sick as the Luftwaffe officer looked. It was he who'd convinced Hitler to release the forces from Normandy for a strike against the Allied foothold. He had even committed his own prized Waffen-SS divisions to act as the vanguard for the assault: *Das Reich, Totenkopf,* and the *Leibstandarte SS Adolf Hitler.* The finest units in the whole world.

And now they no longer existed. It wasn't that they had been broken or suffered crippling damage. They had simply ceased to exist. Men and machines, they were all gone. Erased by a rain of bombs that fell with inhuman accuracy.

Ah, but that was the point, wasn't it.

Inhuman accuracy.

The British press had gone on at great lengths concerning the role played in the wreck of his elite forces by that half-caste mud creature, Halabi. Their arrogance was unbelievable, the way they openly boasted that the so-called Combat Intelligence on board the *Trident* had controlled every air strike.

He scowled over at Göring, drunk and probably insensible with morphine again. He was slumped in the corner of the map room. If that fat fool had only done his job and sunk the damn ship two years ago, this disaster would not have come to pass.

His attention returned to the map table that stretched out in front of him. It was a sorry sight. They were still pushing around little wooden blocks denoting tens of thousands of men who were already dead. Whole armies of ghosts haunted central and northern France. The display was so disconnected from reality as to be worse than useless.

Now the führer was blaming him—*him!*—for the failure to contain Patton and Montgomery in Calais. It was intolerable. He couldn't exactly wave a magic wand and conjure up the Reich's equivalent to the Allied surveillance drones and computer technology. There simply wasn't time to develop such things. And hadn't he delivered a treasure trove of other advances to the German war industries anyway? Didn't that count for anything?

Apparently it did not.

He came out of his self-pitying fugue with a shock when he realized that everyone was staring at him now. The führer was still screeching, but the tone had changed somehow. It was more threatening, more . . .

Direct.

With some alarm, he understood. Hitler was yelling at him again.

"I am sorry, *Mein Führer,*" he mumbled. "I was distracted by the map."

A terrible stillness came over the supreme leader of Nazi Germany. "Distracted, you say?" he sneered.

"Yes," Himmler answered uncertainly. "I, ah—"

"Perhaps if you had been paying attention, we would not be losing this fucking war!" Hitler smashed his fist down on the table, upsetting a handful of unit markers. Then he gathered himself and resumed in a quiet, cracked voice. "I asked you what happened to my missiles. I ordered the strike on London

two hours ago. Everyone in that city should be dead by now. But they are not. I . . . want . . . to . . . know . . . *why.*"

"Yes, *Mein Führer,* of course. But I . . . but I did tell you that the Donzenac facility was destroyed by British commandos. Do you not remember?"

The führer's already strained eyes seemed to bulge inhumanly, as if they might pop out of their sockets and roll across the map table.

A shudder passed over him.

"Of course," he said in a small, cracked voice. "I lost my train of thought. The air in here, it is . . ."

The release of tension in the room was palpable. Himmler could feel others' muscles loosening just like his own.

"Just go, *Herr Reichsführer,*" said Hitler. "Find out what is happening to my atom bombs. I need them. German civilization needs them."

Himmler used the opportunity to meekly bow and back out of the room, his ears and face burning with embarrassment. He had exposed the führer to potential ridicule, correcting him like that. But what was he to do? He had stood at the exact same spot one day ago and explained why there would be no V3 strike on London. He remembered the ashen faces of the assembled staff as he explained how Prince Harry had escaped with so many of the Reich's top scientists after the RAF had destroyed the missile silos. How could the führer have forgotten that?

He scurried out of the bunker, with its foul air of stale sweat and rising fear, glad to get away from it all. If only for a little while.

D-DAY + 25. 28 MAY 1944. 0205 HOURS.
CALAIS.

Julia made it back to Calais at two in the morning. Dismounting from the jeep, she thanked the driver, a garrulous Pole, and looked around for her next ride toward the front. Her status as an official embed of the Seventh Cav wasn't of much use. They'd been pulled from the line and were already headed back to England to take on replacements. The regiment had suffered close to 40 percent casualties and wouldn't be rated to fight again for months.

She hadn't been able to find her old minder, Sergeant Murphy, who'd apparently come through without any major injuries and was due some serious leave time. It might have been nice, she thought, to have split a few brews with Murph and Gadsden, but then she remembered someone had told her that Gadsden had caught an RPG round in the chest at Guines. No more brews for him, and no more barmaid sandwiches back in London.

She stretched, shook her head to clear the cobwebs, and looked around. The driver had dropped her in a small square on the outskirts of Calais. She thought she recalled it from the street fighting early in May. The war ran 24/7, so even at this hour the place was alive with jeeps and trucks, with hundreds of soldiers in different uniforms: American, British, and Free French mostly. Or maybe Canadians. Quebecois. They had a couple of battalions nearby.

A good number of civilians were also about, shopkeepers for the most part, doing business from wooden carts and stalls even if their stores had been destroyed. Trading by candlelight in windowless, pockmarked shopfronts if they were comparatively lucky. The night sky was clear, but lit by the persistent flickering of artillery barrages, bombing raids, and a massive tank battle to the east. The rumble was constant, occasionally flaring into something even deeper and more profound, sounding like a quake down in the very core of the world.

She was eager to get back to work, but she also realized that she was starving. Her last energy bars were gone, shared with the Pole on the long, uncomfortable drive back. She hadn't eaten a hot meal in days, and her eyes were watery with lack of sleep. A sit-down meal, some wine, a cup of coffee? She'd sell her fucking soul for less.

Julia hauled out her flexipad and checked for a Fleetnet link. Two small green lights in the rubberized casing told her she had power, and even a local connection. Her eyes flicked up, but she was too tired to actually gaze skyward for a drone. She'd never spot it, anyway.

The square was surprisingly festive for a place that had so recently hosted open combat. The tinkling of pianos came at her from two different directions. Somebody else was doing something cruel to an accordion, and rather than the harsh, hoarse bark of orders, or the animal screams of mortal combat, she could actually hear laughter and conversation. It was almost

normal. A shifting breeze brought with it the smell of hot
mulled wine and some sort of meat roasted with garlic and
rosemary. Saliva filled her mouth, and her stomach growled as
she smelled bread baking, too.

All right! I can take a fuckin' hint.

It was such a mild night she decided to take advantage of the
lull, track down some food, eat well, and see if a bed might be
had somewhere in town. Or a couch. Or a pile of straw. A hundred meters or so from where she stood, a relatively well-lit
stone cottage was rocking and rolling, with all sorts of officers
coming and going. Some clearly were rear-echelon motherfuckers, and others were just as obviously back from the fight
of their lives. Two knots of men and a few local women were
gathered around a couple of steaming cauldrons sitting atop
open fires on the flagstones in front of the building. That would
be the mulled wine, if her sense of smell was right.

So Julia picked up her pack, shouldered her carbine, and
wandered over.

The women were French girls, probably not in their twenties
yet. She wondered idly whether they'd had German boyfriends
a few weeks ago, but dismissed the thought as uncharitable.
The collaborators would have all been shaved bald and run out
of town by now. A fucking travesty in her opinion. These ma-
demoiselles were staying close to the Americans they'd picked
up. A couple of Rangers by the look of them. A smart move.

They stopped giggling abruptly as she approached, huddling
in closer to their protectors.

"Vingt-et-un," one said in a stage whisper. Twenty-one.

"Oh, for fuck's sake," Julia muttered.

She pushed her way through. The conversation around her
didn't stop, but she was aware that it had trailed off noticeably.
Admittedly, she looked like shit. She'd managed a change of
clothes since the air assault on the fourth, but that had been two
weeks ago, and she was filthy again. Her body armor, helmet
rig, and electronic gear also gave her away.

There were no female combatants in the European theater.
That was strictly an AF gig out in the Pacific, with Kolhammer's battle group.

"Une coupe, s'il vous plaît," she said to the wine seller.

He picked up a copper jug on the end of a long wooden handle, dipped it into the steaming brew, and swirled it around. A

giant cinnamon stick bobbed to the surface as he withdrew the jug and poured her a generous serving. He handed over the drink, and as she was about to pay a Frenchman in a British uniform put his hand on Julia's arm and shook his head. He spoke in accented but still perfectly understandable English. "Please, allow me."

He gave the man a couple of coins.

"There you are, mademoiselle. However, you should be careful," he said. "Gaston, here, he makes a heady brew. I doubt an American woman would be able to stand up after drinking even half a cup of it."

The small crowd burst into laughter, not all of it good-natured.

Julia took the drink and said nothing, cocking an eyebrow at the French officer, a captain, before draining the cup in one long swallow. The young women gasped, and one of the Rangers hooted with laughter.

"Ha! Give 'em hell, lady!"

She handed the empty mug back to Gaston and smiled, waiting for the hubbub to die down before nodding and smiling politely to the Frenchman. *"La réalité et toi, vous ne vous entendez pas, n'est-ce pas?"* Reality and you don't get on, do they?

This time the laughter came as a roar, and she felt a meaty hand slap her on the shoulder as she made her way toward the front door of the makeshift bistro. She knew, however, that on an empty stomach the wine would go right to her head if she didn't get something solid inside her in the next few minutes.

As she stepped into the street she heard her name mentioned in an American accent, but ignored it. It wasn't like someone was calling after her.

But the French captain suddenly appeared beside her again. "Please," he said. "Let me buy you dinner. That was a stupid jest, and you showed me up for a fool. I should not have tried to embarrass you. It was—"

"Okay," Julia said in French that was as good as his English. "Look, whatever. I'm tired and hungry, and I'm only carrying greenbacks. I'd probably end up paying fifty bucks for some fucking prewar pickled escargot. So yes, Captain . . . ?"

"Ronsard," he answered.

"Okay, Captain Ronsard, you may buy me dinner. Or rather

you may order, and I will pay, and that way there shall be no misunderstanding about copping an easy fuck from the future."

"But of course!" Ronsard protested, in English again. "The very idea of it!"

"Yeah," Julia replied. *"Quoi que."*

"Whatever?"

"No. What*ever*. Get the inflection right, *mon capitaine*."

She woke up next to him in a narrow bed, in the loft of a two-story cottage a few minutes' walk from the square. Light was streaming in through the shattered windows, and for a moment she had the unsettling experience of not knowing where she was, or *when* she was.

She'd spent a year studying in France as a postgrad, and stayed on for two more freelancing for a couple of magazines in Paris. The first Intifada hadn't been enough to drive her away. Indeed, that simply meant more work, as she began to file copy for a couple of the metro dailies and the blog portals back stateside. But after the bomb went off in Marseilles, Julia decided enough was enough. She'd joined thousands of other expatriates streaming out of Continental Europe, which was looking increasingly medieval with each new atrocity in the war.

She'd missed it, though, for a long time thereafter. She'd dated a young editor at *Vogue* for a while, and his family owned a cottage in the Pas de Calais, near Oignies, at the other end of the province. Waking next to Ronsard, she'd experienced a state of free fall, dropping through the years and thinking she had fallen back into the life she'd lived in her midtwenties. It was a delicious sensation, in a way, like half waking from a dream of immense wealth, but it dissolved as she blinked away the sleep and saw the bullet holes and scorch marks in the ceiling.

Her boyfriend had been young and thin and blond. A non-threatening, floppy-haired romantic. Ronsard was shorter, more powerfully built, and coarsened—most likely by a much harder life. He'd been a better fuck, though. No question of that.

He'd screwed her insensible and she'd fallen into a deep, dreamless sleep from which she had not woken, not even once. He was only now stirring beside her. She regarded him dispassionately. However ardent their lovemaking had been—and it was pretty fucking ardent—she awoke as always these days, disconnected and keen to be elsewhere. It had been that way with every man since Dan. A small pang penetrated the scar tissue she'd built up around his memory and, to her own surprise, tears began to well.

She slipped out of bed, naked, and hurriedly pulled on her pants and filthy gray T-shirt. Ronsard yawned and rolled over.

"Julia? Would you like to make some coffee?" he mumbled. "I have a sachet somewhere."

"De quoi est mort votre dernière esclave?" she asked as lightly as she could manage. What did your last slave die of?

Mercifully he rolled over and went back to sleep. She hurried across to the ancient narrow spiral staircase that led to the floor below. More tears came as she descended, and she slapped a hand across her mouth to smother any sounds that might escape. She could hear other people moving around the house, and wondered whether Ronsard's colleagues were billeted here. They hadn't discussed it last night in the hot drunken rush to be free of their clothes. She almost ran into the tiny bathroom at the end of the second-floor hallway. It was small and disgracefully dirty in the French fashion, but there was a latch on the back of the door that she fumbled into place just before a torrent of silent moans broke over her like a wave.

She slumped to the floor, arms wrapped around herself, her whole body shuddering with spasms of violent grief to which she could give no voice. The effort of restraining herself, of staying silent while this emotional hurricane blew through her, felt like a crushing weight on her chest. But she refused to lose that last vestige of her control. She *had* to have something to hold on to, after losing everything else because of her own stupidity: her husband, their baby, a far, far better life than the one she was currently living.

And so she curled into a tight fetal ball on the cramped floor of the bathroom, raking furrows in her own flesh and refusing to utter even the smallest squeak in protest over the desolation she could feel spreading inside her.

D-DAY + 25. 28 MAY 1944. 1014 HOURS.
CALAIS.

"Are you certain you cannot stop in Calais for a while?"

Ronsard was preparing a toasted baguette as he spoke, spreading the rich yellow butter with such loving care that

Julia suspected he hadn't eaten real food in a long time, at least not until the previous evening's meal. With knobs of melting butter still floating on the warm bread roll, he scooped strawberry jam out of a small stoneware pot and plopped a generous dollop at one end before closing his eyes and slowly biting into it.

When she didn't answer he opened his eyes as if from a very happy dream. "Not even a *little* while?"

Julia smiled and shook her head. "I'll get my ass kicked if I don't get up to the front and file some copy soon. I got held up by the Turkey Shoot, and my editor's convinced Patton's gonna be in Berlin by the end of the week."

Ronsard curled his lips down in a very Gallic gesture. "That long, eh? And here it is only Wednesday."

They sat on the small balcony of Ronsard's room, overlooking a park that was pockmarked with craters from multiple mortar rounds. All the trees had been stripped of their leaves, but a few birds still sang on the bare branches. It was a fine morning, and promised to be a glorious day.

The Frenchman hadn't asked her anything that indicated that he was aware of her little meltdown, but she was certain he knew. Still, people often went to pieces around combat zones, and each dealt with it in his or her own way. Julia didn't give off a needy vibe—at least she *hoped* she didn't—and Ronsard seemed happy to respect her privacy. Instead of pawing her and fussing about when she'd returned to the bedroom, he had simply busied himself with rustling up a marvelous breakfast. Fresh oranges, boiled eggs, the baguettes, butter and jam. And a pot of freshly ground coffee from fuck-knew-where. It was exactly what she needed.

"Thank you, Marcel. You've been a dream. But we both have work to do. Or I *assume* you have work to do. The Brits don't normally hand out those sandy berets to slackers."

She nodded in the direction of the light tan beret with a winged dagger badge, hanging from a bedknob behind him. The Special Air Service was recognized as an elite force, but it hadn't yet become shrouded in myth and mystery, as was the case in her day.

Ronsard didn't bother looking back over his shoulder. He just spooned more jam onto his baguette.

"I have another few days before I have to get back to England,"

ie said. "So I thought it might be nice to spend it with a beautiful woman."

"You know, Marcel, I think you'd be just as happy spending
t with your baguette. Here, now, don't Bogart the fucking
am."

He passed the small pot over with a grin. "It is good to have
you making fun of me, again. You have your—what is the
word—*mojo* back."

"Maybe if I were an Austin Powers fembot, but thanks. I'm
feeling better."

"Would you stay if I could get you back to Scotland? To do a
story on the regiment?"

"On Harry's Own?" she said, suddenly interested. "I might
be. I'm supposed to link up with a Captain Prather this afternoon. He's going to give me a ride up to the front on a Super
Sherman. He helped design them, you know. I was going to
cover the Seven Sixty-first."

"Ah, the Negro tankers."

"African American."

Ronsard shrugged. "But of course."

Four Sabers roared overhead, and Julia looked up. They were
high, but she thought she could make out the bombs and rockets positioned under their wings. Ground attack craft.

"Do you think I could write up the story of what happened
down at Donzenac?" she asked.

All she got was a sly, furtive grin.

"Well?"

"I know nothing about this Donzenac," Ronsard answered.
Then he finished the last of his roll and washed it down with a
mouthful of coffee.

"Spare me, Marcel. Everyone knows about Donzenac. Or
they *think* they know about it. There was a piece in the *Times,*
but it was small, and they couldn't get any details."

As she spoke, she leaned over the cramped breakfast table,
and he leaned back as much as was possible on the tiny balcony.
He closed his eyes and seemed to enjoy taking his time, soaking
up the rays.

"I am sure there would be no trouble in getting you to Scotland," he said. "His Royal Highness has allowed one or two
other reporters through before, and you are an embed, yes? So
you have been cleared. What young Harry agrees to discuss

with you once you are there, however, that would really be his business, would it not?"

Julia nodded, satisfied with half an answer. "Okay," she said. "You get me into the regiment, and we can spend a bit of time together up there. But first I have this job with Prather. They've blocked out half a page for me back in New York. Can you work with that?"

Ronsard's sleepy eyes opened slowly.

"But you do not have to meet this Prather until this afternoon, right?"

"Right," Julia said, uncurling herself from her chair and walking back into the room.

12

D-DAY + 25. 28 MAY 1944. 1533 HOURS.
761ST TANK BATTALION, BRUGGE, BELGIUM.

Captain Prather was a believer.

Julia had met a lot of them, both here and uptime. There was a USAF major in Syria who wanted to air-drop billions of genetically engineered "attack" scorpions on Damascus, to paralyze the entire population before a coded gene sequence killed all the stingers two days later.

There was the CIA contractor who wanted to raise a private army of orphaned Arab children, to run as deep-penetration agents when they were old enough to send back into their parent societies. He thought that eleven or twelve years old would be just about right.

There was Manning Pope, of course, the scientist who'd marooned them all here. And there was an armored division colonel named MacMasters who came up with the idea of sewing jihadi insurgents into pigskins before burying them. Actually, he'd borrowed the idea from "Black Jack" Pershing, who'd done the same thing to Islamic guerrillas in the Philippines back in the 1900s.

She had no idea what happened to the scorpion guy, or the spook, or even to Pope. The colonel, however, had gone on to become the Republican senator for Kansas, where he'd made certain that his favorite tactic became a "sanctioned field punishment" available to U.S. commanders when dealing with Islamic extremists. Last Julia knew of him, he was still confounding the liberal press with his boyish enthusiasm for the never-ending war, back up in twenty-one.

Captain Chris Prather still had his boyish enthusiasms, too. She found him atop the reinforced turret of one of "his" Easy Eight Super Shermans, in a holding area about fifteen klicks back from the front—although the way Patton kept driving forward, "the front" wasn't a stable concept. When she located him, after slopping through a muddy parking lot full of tanks, jeeps, and deuce-and-a-halves, he was bent over with his head buried inside the turret, talking to the crew. This gave her a wide-screen view of his butt.

"Hey," she called out. "Does that big ass up yonder belong to a Captain Prather?"

Two African American tankers, members of the 761st 'Black Panther" Tank Battalion, were standing by the treads. They favored her with flashing white smiles.

"Well picked, madam," the taller one said with an incongruously polished Bostonian accent. "You clearly know your asses."

He stepped forward and extended his hand. She returned the firm grip as Prather extracted himself from the turret. Snatching up an old rag, he called down to somebody inside the tank. 'Take five, Robinson. We got company."

Prather was a good-looking white boy with a southern accent. Kentucky, perhaps. He stood about five-eight with black hair and hazel eyes. He had broad shoulders and looked like he punched in around 180 pounds. He was a 'temp but seemed perfectly at ease surrounded by his black comrades. Not for the first time Julia had to remind herself to stop thinking of the 'temps as a nation of rednecked buttheads. You'd have thought she might have learned that from Dan, if nothing else.

"Miss Duffy, I guess?" Prather used the rag to wipe grease from his powerful hands.

"*Ms.* Duffy," she replied, "but Julia or Jules will do."

Prather jumped down from the body of the tank, landing softly but still splashing up a little mud. He nodded to the two other men. "You've met Lieutenant Burnett and Sergeant Turley."

The noncom smiled shyly and dipped his head. "Ma'am," he said softly.

"Hey, Sergeant." Julia nodded toward the tank. "So what's up with my ride?"

Prather looked a little surprised. "Oh, nothing. We're just fixin' a few things. I love to fix things. And anyway, this ain't your ride—that's over by Dog Company. But this baby's a beauty anyway, don't you think?"

"Guess so," she answered.

Prather gestured theatrically. "Aw, come on. This is a work of art, *Miz* Duffy." He turned back to his colleagues. "You guys gonna help Jackie with that wet storage sealant? I gotta take Ms. Duffy over to battalion. We'll meet you there in an hour."

"Jackie? Jackie *Robinson*?" she wondered aloud as they headed away at a brisk pace. "The ballplayer?"

"Will be, one day soon," Prather confirmed. "They say he's gonna play the majors. One of the first black guys ever. For now, though, he's working for me. He's a good guy, too."

A cold front was coming in from the Atlantic, ruining the perfect weather. The first cool gusts had whistled through the streets of Calais as Julia had said good-bye to Ronsard. She'd hopped a Huey that took her up to the staging area just outside Brugge, in Belgium, and it had seemed like they were running just ahead of the weather all the way up. Now a towering wall of dark gray clouds filled the sky to the west, behind them, while in front the sun still shone brightly down on the Belgian countryside. Along the way she had noticed that some villages and farms had been destroyed, but not others, reminding her of flying over Oklahoma twister country.

Fifteen minutes before reaching the armored depot, they passed over a five-kilometer-wide tract of dead earth littered with the burned-out hulks of Shermans and Tigers. Almost every building in the area had been destroyed, except for one small farmhouse, which remained untouched.

The fortunes of war.

Julia was glad for her thermopliable combat jacket: there was a good chance the cold weather would intensify over the next few days. *Bring on global warming,* she thought. Prather talked excitedly as they walked along the lines of tanks.

"It was a hell of a fight after you guys turned up," he said. "There was a strong push in the army for scrapping the Sherman and going straight to the Pershing, which would have been a match for the krauts. But in the end, momentum won the argument."

"Momentum?"

"Thirty thousand Sherman chassis already built by 'forty-three. All those plants already tooled up, Allied armies depending on them. It made more sense to go with what we had."

Julia stepped around a large pool of oily mud. "That was your argument, then."

Prather smiled. "Yeah, well, mine and others'. Nobody really listens to me, though. I'm just an engineer. Anyway, the M-Four, your classic Sherman, she had a few problems. Even I have to admit that. A low-velocity seventy-five-millimeter pop-gun, wafer-thin armor, and a gasoline engine that just loved bursting into flames. In the long run I would have recommended discontinuing some of the Sherman production and switching over to the M-Twenty-nine Pershing heavies, with a ninety-millimeter high-velocity main gun. And that's just what's happening with some outfits. But there are quite a few mods that can be put in place on the Shermans, since we've been churning them out so fast."

Julia wondered where he'd picked up the term *mod.* That was uptime gaming slang, as best she knew. But Prather was just a kid really—in a way he was a gamer, yet he was playing for life and death. She'd already decided she liked him.

He pulled up in front of a tank with a crude painting on the turret of a big-busted woman. She took a few still shots with her Sonycam.

"Check it out," he enthused. "We got some slat armor. Simple, you know, but it really messes up the krauts' RPG shots. We redesigned the turret to accommodate a high-velocity hundred-and-five-millimeter gun, and a lotta frame reinforcement went into that, but it means they can go toe-to-toe with old Fritz, although a lot of the time, you know, the Germans just use their tanks as pillboxes. They're still a lot slower than the Easy Eights, even with all the changes we made, and we tend to get around in back of them, messing with the infantry, while the choppers hammer them with rocket fire."

"So you do a lot of combined ops now, with airborne?"

"Been training for it from the day the first Cobras rolled off the line. Earlier, in fact, but that was just sandbox and theory."

A chill wind blew wet leaves onto her legs as she studied the tank. She lined Prather up in the pop-out display window of the video recorder.

"What about armor? What happens if a shell gets through the cage? Those slats will stop shoulder-fired rockets—I saw that a lot in the Middle East—but I'm guessing they don't stand up real well to an eighty-eight-millimeter round or worse." She couldn't help wondering what it'd be like, trapped in a big iron coffin with a shell bouncing around at the speed of sound, chopping everyone up into loose meat.

Prather patted the glacis plate at the front. "Whole hull's been revamped with appliqué armor," he said proudly. "There's a more sharply angled forward slope, side skirts to defend against RPGs, and some composite shielding beneath that and at the rear—which was a real problem area. We switched over to a diesel engine, too. Much safer. Doesn't brew up the same way."

"I guess," Julia conceded as they started walking again.

They reached the end of a long street formed by the row of dormant tanks, and Prather took them around to the left. A small clutch of tents lay ahead. Battalion headquarters. Prather narrowed his eyes and smiled gently.

"You don't seem to be reassured, Ms. Duffy. What's the matter? You've seen a lot more combat than me, after all. Doesn't seem as if a ride in a tank would bother you at all."

"Yeah," she said, "but usually I go out with the infantry. I've never been in an armored battle before. Not a fair one, anyway. They just didn't happen where I came from."

Prather nodded. "Oh well, if you don't want to go . . ."

"No—no, it'll be cool. Can't be a wuss, after all. So when do we head out?"

"Tonight. Twenty-two hundred hours."

She'd been expecting a silver helmet and six-shooters, but Patton was dressed for the front. His fatigues were filthy, and he'd managed to acquire a prominent bloodstain on one trouser leg. Not his, though, apparently.

He moved around on the makeshift stage like a prizefighter in the opening seconds of a long bout. Cocky, full of energy, ready for a brawl. He was taller than she'd imagined, and much more tightly wrapped. He seemed almost like a nineteenth-century figure to Julia. His voice, higher than George C. Scott's and not nearly as gruff, still carried out over the hundreds of men gathered before him. A sea of black faces, with a solitary moon-white exception here and there. Their eyes all stayed fixed on the general.

"Men, you're the first Negro tankers ever to fight in the American army," he said, his voice booming out. "I would never have asked for you if I didn't think you were good. I will have nothing but the best in my army. I don't care what color you are, as long as you go up there and kill those kraut sons-a-bitches.

"Everyone has their eyes on you, and they're expecting great things from you. Most of all, your people are looking to you—and by that I mean the American people, people of all colors. Don't let them down and damn you, don't let me down!"

"We won't, General!" somebody called out.

"That's the goddamn spirit!" Patton cried back. "Give 'em hell, boys!"

Julia was sure she saw the walls of the giant tent billow out as the assembly roared back. All that muscle mass and testosterone squeezed into a confined space. The heady brew of confidence, tribal bonding, and barely contained bloodlust. She might as well have been on the vehicle deck of the *Kandahar* again. No matter how much you leavened the mix with female personnel, there was something inherently masculine about the business of war. As fucked up and wasteful and pathetic as it was, men secretly loved it. And so did she.

As Patton left the stage to the cheers of the 761st, Prather steered her over in his direction. She was well past her giggling-girl phase, and, having interviewed so many of the top players for the *Times* these last two years, she wasn't at all intimidated by the general. But she wanted to grab a quick interview. He was a sure bet to give her a couple of profanely colorful quotes for the feature she was working up.

Patton seemed to notice her as he was descending the stairs, brushing off the hand of his intelligence chief, a Colonel Black—reminding her of Dan again. He flashed a smile, sizing her up like a dangerous mount, and extended a gloved hand. He had no trouble speaking over the noise of the crowd.

"I've read your work, Duffy. I like it," he growled. "You get close to the fighting man and you tell his story like it is. Prather says you want to ride out with my boys tonight."

"If you're okay with that, sir."

"Don't *sir* me, girlie. I know you don't mean it. And you're a civilian, despite your uniform, which you'll have to get scrubbed if you're going to 'embed' with my army. Can't have any sloppiness. Understand?"

"Uh-huh," she smirked. "I'll be sure to touch up my lip gloss when I'm doing my camouflage paint."

"Excellent!" Patton cried. "Now you come with me, young lady, and I'll make sure Colonel Black here briefs you in on tonight's operation."

"You *are* cleared, aren't you?" Black asked anxiously.

Julia passed over her papers. Black wasn't equipped with a flexipad. Indeed, she'd hardly met anyone in France who was. Even Patton seemed to do without one.

"I'm clear to Top Secret Absolute," she said. "Renewed a month ago."

Patton's intelligence chief studied the paper as they walked through the crush of men, most of whom wanted to press forward and shake the general's hand or pat him on the back. And Julia could see that that old dog was loving it. Black impatiently thrust the clearance forms back at her as they pushed out of the tent and into a starlit night.

Faint flickers of light and a rumble beyond the edge of the world spoke of an engagement somewhere, but nobody paid much attention. The fighting had been constant since the landings.

"Captain Prather said I'd be riding with D Company, General," Julia said. "Don't you think I should be heading over there soon?"

"No," he said somewhat abruptly. "You'll come out with us." When she started to protest he cut in, "No! I don't want to hear a word of it, madam! You won't see anything buttoned up in an armored troop carrier and you'll probably get yourself killed. That's your ass, not mine, of course, but damn it, I want the story of this battle to be told, and I want it told properly."

He stopped and faced her, hands on his hips, one eye almost closed as he scowled at her.

"I meant what I said before. I've read all of your major reports. Read them many times, looking for any insights into the fighting methods you people have brought upon us. Like I said to those men back there, I don't give a *damn* what other people think of you, all I care about is what you can do for my army. And I think you can do us a great deal of good in our never-goddamn-ending fight with the enemy."

"Me, General? Come on now. How can I help you against the Nazis—"

"Not the Nazis, Duffy. Montgomery, woman! Bernard . . . Law . . . Montgomery. Didn't you read any biographies of him? Did you see that movie about Arnhem? I saw it. If that man spent as much time on his job as he did on his goddamn public image, we'd be at the gates of Berlin by now. Which doesn't mean a thing to me, except that he's been gobbling up resources that should have been going to *my* army, to *my* men. And you're going to see to it that we get our fair share in the future." Patton leaned forward until he dominated her personal space, forcing her to stand uncomfortably close to the brim of his steel helmet, lest he think he'd managed to bully her in some way.

"No, you ride out with me. You watch those black boys fight tonight, and you tell the whole goddamn world what a magnificent fucking job they did of pounding the führer's supermen into mincemeat. And they will do a magnificent fucking job, believe you me—and *I* will make sure your story gets run in every newspaper in the free world."

Julia hardly knew what to say.

"I think," she replied at last, in a calm low voice, "that my editor can handle placing the story, and—"

Patton held up a hand, smiling like a wolf. "He probably can. But like I said, *I* will make sure of it."

"You just make sure I get to see what I'm supposed to see," she said, "and I'll take care of the rest."

His smile softened some, becoming marginally less carnivorous.

"All right then," he said. "It's a deal."

He turned to the small group of officers who'd gathered around them.

"Come on, boys. Let's go get Miss Duffy a story."

D-DAY + 25. 28 MAY 1944. 2302 HOURS.
LUFTWAFFE AIRBASE, WIESBADEN.

The airfield was a "masked" facility: two runways painted to look as if they were pockmarked with bomb craters, along with a minimum of buildings aboveground, again looking more like damaged shells than working structures. It had been carefully "neglected" to discourage prying eyes, both human and electronic.

An hour before midnight it was empty of aircraft, except for a couple of burned-out 110s at the end of one runway. Then at the witching hour, it burst into activity. Lines of light briefly flared along the tarmac. Fuel trucks came roaring in from the surrounding countryside as ground crew spilled out of the "abandoned" buildings.

They all peered into the darkness of the eastern sky. After a few minutes somebody called out that he could see the first plane. Everyone stood ready.

They had practiced this at other airfields in Poland, far beyond the reach of even the *Trident*'s sensors. The lead elements of the attack wing would land soon, running on fumes, laden with antitank rockets and bombs. For the next ninety minutes they would work at a feverish pace, refueling a constant relay of ME 262 jet fighters as they massed for a strike on the spearhead of Patton's Third Army in Belgium.

D-DAY + 26. 29 MAY 1944. 0042 HOURS.
BUNKER 13, BERLIN.

For the first time in weeks they had something to look forward to.

The führer was tense, but restrained. His voice had given out a few days earlier and he wasn't able to scream at them anymore, which seemed to have forced him to calm down somewhat.

Himmler, for one, was glad. He had been worried about the führer's mental state. Very few people in the Reich had access to the twenty-first-century archival materials he had seen.

Almost none knew of Adolf Hitler's physical and psychological collapse at the end of the war in *die Andere Zeit,* of his suicide with Eva Braun and the burning of their bodies as the Red Army pillaged the ruins of Berlin. Exposure to such knowledge was almost always fatal, so only a handful of men knew how the last days of Nazi Germany had unfolded.

And nobody but the *Reichsführer-SS* himself was aware of how an "alternative" Heinrich Himmler had been declared a traitor, for contacting Count Folke Bernadotte of Sweden to negotiate a surrender in the West. Anyone with any link to that particular data, discovered in the electronic files of the *Dessaix,* had gone into the ovens—even those who had hacked the files to introduce a "new" history, wherein Himmler died fighting in the streets of Berlin.

Sometimes the fear of discovery kept him awake for days at a time, until his flesh began to crawl with invisible insects and time itself would jump forward in shudders and leaps. Himmler could feel his head swimming, and a wave of nausea would come upon him as he tried to blink the hot grit of sleeplessness from his eyes.

But for the next hour, at least, he had something to think about other than desolation and despair. The Luftwaffe was about to carve a bloodied chunk out of Patton's extended flank. The atmosphere in the map room was subdued, expectant. Nobody spoke above a murmur, perhaps in deference to the führer's lost voice.

"The attack is aloft and proceeding to target," a Luftwaffe colonel announced.

The führer, standing across the table from Himmler, nodded with evident satisfaction. He was in command of this operation, having taken it away from the drug-addled Göring. He had seen to the planning and execution himself. It guaranteed an exceptional level of commitment from all concerned when the supreme leader of the Third Reich suddenly turned up in person, or on the phone, demanding results.

In fact, it wasn't a bad plan, Himmler mused.

Given the oppressive gaze of the *Trident*'s all-seeing sensors, the führer had ordered that most of the preparation take place in Poland, where even the mud woman Halabi could not see. A special air group of 130 advanced jet fighters, E-3 variants on the ME 262, had been given the highest priority. They each loaded out with forty-eighty of the deadly R4M rockets: forty with PB2 antitank warheads, the rest with PB3 antiaircraft shots. Their MK 108 cannons could rip open a Sherman tank with just two hits, and flying from Wiesbaden at top speed they could be over Patton's forces within minutes, while remaining almost fully fueled.

The "masked" airfields were the key. They allowed the attack wing to strike before the Allies' overwhelming air superiority could come into play. Yes, this strategy was likely to succeed, but what then? Even with a great rent torn in the flank of the Allied advance, how was it to be exploited? Every time they moved a force of any significance to engage the enemy, the skies quickly filled with thousands of aircraft—jet fighters, helicopters, medium bombers, Typhoons, Spitfires, Mustangs, and Skyraiders, all of them carrying some hellish mix of explosive cannons, antitank rockets, napalm, and "guided" bombs.

Himmler peered furtively over the rim of his wire-framed glasses and wondered again if the führer really knew what he was doing. The V3 bases were gone, destroyed by the damnable SAS, the scientists kidnapped and spirited away. The *Kriegsmarine* was almost nonexistent, its ships and submarines sunk, its leadership disgraced and executed for their treachery. The finest divisions of the Wehrmacht and the Waffen-SS had been annihilated before they could get within 150 kilometers of the enemy. Now everything turned on the *Kernphysik* Program.

If they could get just one working bomb, it would be enough to force a stalemate.

Himmler desperately wanted to excuse himself from the room so that he might contact Heisenberg yet again, to harangue him about progress. He knew it was not going as well as it should. Every day it seemed that the Allies struck with an almost magical ability to damage the project. He often lay awake at night, feeling the great pressure that now rested squarely on his shoulders to deliver this weapon to the German people, and the people from annihilation. But he could not leave with the first shots in the führer's personal attack about to be fired.

13

"Contacts hostile, Captain. Targets confirmed."

"Designate them for USAAF intercept, Ms. Burchill. Slave to the Intelligence."

"Aye, Captain. Targets designated. Intercept squadrons Thirty-five and Thirty-nine moving to engage. Posh has control."

Captain Karen Halabi thanked her EWAC boss, Lieutenant Burchill, and watched as two squadrons of F-86 Sabers peeled out of the holding pattern they'd been describing over the channel and kicked in the thrust to head off the massed air attack forming up over Luxembourg. Lady Beckham, the *Trident*'s Combat Intelligence, had detected 130 E-type 262s as they entered the edge of her threat bubble, at exactly the point she'd been told to watch for them.

Such a timely warning smacked of a skinjob, one of the Germans from the original Multinational Force who'd been trained up and sent into the Reich as deep-cover agents. Halabi had no idea which of them it might be, but they were doing the good Lord's work today.

The phrase brought her up, just momentarily. That was one of her husband's favorite sayings. She'd picked it up hanging around Mike on her last bit of rec leave in the States. As a lapsed Muslim—well, not that lapsed, because she'd never been that observant—Karen Halabi tended to steer well clear of any biblical or Koranic allusions in her everyday speech. She found it put people on edge. Or it had back in the Old World.

But Mike was an unreconstructed Vatican III Catholic, and

his private conversations were peppered with references to the good Lord, appeals to the good Lord, and occasionally, when things turned to poo, some gutter-mouthed Texan abuse of the good Lord.

Halabi briefly wondered where he was. But she had business in the here and now.

Being the primary command, control, and electronic intelligence node for the Allied invasion of Europe, *Trident* had a huge number of tasks delegated to the quantum processors of her Combat Intelligence. One such job was to guard against the raid now taking shape to the south of General Patton's Third Army. British intelligence had sent through a watching brief ten days ago, ordering that the highest priority be given to early detection and interdiction.

Within an hour of the brief Captain Allan Leroy—the fighter command liaison officer stationed aboard *Trident*—knocked on her door, figuratively speaking, with an air tasking order for six squadrons of F-86 interceptors that would provide a standing combat air patrol. There would be two squadrons permanently on station at any given time.

Halabi was impressed. The Sabers were the latest models, just out of the States, packed with all sorts of design tweaks and mouthwatering mods like AT/AIM-7 Sparrows, first-generation heat seekers, and beam-riding semi-active air-to-air missiles, nose-mounted continuous-wave radar sets, and the new Pratt & Whitney JT3C axial flow turbojets. Those babies could deliver nearly five thousand kilos of thrust, making them almost as fast as the Skyhawks Mike was taking to the Marianas. You didn't put that sort of asset on standby for ten days without a very good reason.

And the eight linked flat panels of her main battlespace display showed her the reason. A hundred and thirty of them, to be exact.

One entire monitor had been given over to the feed from the Nemesis arrays that were focused on the airspace around the approaching Luftwaffe raid. Smaller pop-up windows ran enhanced imagery of the USAAF response and the disposition of ground forces in Belgium. As the *Trident*'s CI vectored the American jets onto their targets, Halabi wrestled with the irrational feeling that she had become something akin to a spectator in the Ladies' Stand at the cricket.

Save for a few suicidal air attacks, the *Trident* hadn't directly engaged an enemy combatant in nearly a year. Having fired off the last of her offensive weapons to repel the German's attempted invasion in 1942, she'd been "reduced" to playing the role of a floating radar station and comm hub. Her ship had been retrofitted with "new" antiship missiles, and a very useful Phalanx Close-In Weapons system to replace her Metal Storm pods and laser packs, but she was also surrounded by the equivalent of her own battle group.

Two Royal Navy carriers and a small armada of battle cruisers, destroyers, and minesweepers attended her every move. A squadron of RAF Sabers maintained a permanent combat air patrol seven thousand meters overhead.

Everyone understood how important the *Trident* remained—not least the Germans, who had expended enormous numbers of men and machines trying to sink her. But Halabi and her largely unchanged 21C crew couldn't help but be stung by the chiding they took from the "real navy," as the 'temps sometimes referred to themselves.

And here they were again, not really fighting, just directing traffic.

"Interceptors closing to range, Captain."

"First missile locks."

"Multiple targets acquired."

"All hostiles now locked."

"Interceptors launching."

Halabi accepted a mug of Earl Grey tea from a young seaman, one of the few 'temps who'd come on board to perform nontechnical duties. "Thank you, Beazley," she said.

On the main battlespace display nearly two hundred white lines reached out from the blue triangles denoting the USAAF interceptors. They sped away from the launch point, tracking swiftly across the screen toward the red triangles of the Luftwaffe's attack group. On screen the German 262s suddenly tried to scatter, their tight formation breaking up into a chaotic swarm of diving, twisting, climbing planes.

"CI reports the Germans have deployed chaff and flares, Captain."

"Thank you, Ms. Burchill. Are they proving significant?"

"Posh calculates that about forty percent of the USAAF salvo appears to have been drawn off-target, ma'am."

But small white circles started to bloom on the monitor as the other missiles, which had not been fooled by the German countermeasures, began to strike home. Just one or two at first, then five or six all at once. Dozens of tiny pixilated flashes marked where a missile had plowed into an exhaust vent, wing, or fuselage and detonated, punching the aircraft out of the sky and its pilot out of existence.

"CI confirms forty-eight kills, Captain."

"Second launch detected."

Dozens more missiles sped away from the blue triangles. Posh counted sixty-eight in total. Again the *Trident*'s Nemesis arrays detected the Luftwaffe pilots' attempts to decoy the AT/AIM-7s, and again they were successful in about 40 percent of cases. But another twenty-six German jets were raked from the sky.

"Third salvo ma'am."

"Thank you, Burchill."

All but five of the surviving attackers were engulfed and destroyed. Halabi watched as the Sabers continued on the same heading for half a minute, suddenly breaking formation as they came within cannon range of the Germans. Less than a minute later every last attacking plane had been scythed down.

The Sabers broke off and made for their base back in northern France, while another two squadrons took up the holding pattern in their place, guarding against any follow-up attack. Halabi sipped at her tea.

"Very good work, everyone," she said. "Mr. Leroy, my compliments to fighter command."

"You betcha, ma'am. That was some fine shootin'."

Halabi nodded quietly, wondering again how Leroy, a Texan just like her husband, had ended up in fighter command, an RAF show. She'd never had a chance to ask him. On most days, anywhere between thirty and forty 'temp liaison staffers were aboard. They came, they went. She'd given up trying to keep them straight in her head.

"Mr. McTeale," she said to her executive officer, "I'll be on the bridge for half an hour, then I'm turning in. Keep my chair warm here, would you?"

"Very good, ma'am," the XO answered in his warm Scottish

brogue. "And congratulations to you, too, Captain. You saved a lot of mams from losing their bairns tonight."

"Traffic control, Mr. McTeale. It's just traffic control."

D-DAY + 26. 29 MAY 1944. 0231 HOURS.
THIRD ARMY MOBILE COMMAND, BELGIUM.

"That must have been it."

Patton's intelligence boss scanned the southern skies with a pair of Starlite binoculars, but there wasn't much to be seen. The weather had closed in, and there was no telling whether the faint flashes came from the air battle Julia had just been told about, or from the sheet lightning that strobe-lit the countryside at irregular intervals.

"Damn shame," Patton said as he looked longingly at his radar-controlled triple-A and SAM half-tracks. "I was looking forward to that."

Julia Duffy rolled her eyes in the dark. These guys took their whole alpha-male routine way too seriously. The last thing you wanted was a bunch of German fast movers getting close enough for you to see the fireworks when they got swatted. They moved *so* fast, there was always a good chance some were going to slip through. She'd happily give that a miss.

For all of the combat she'd covered with the *Times* after the Murdoch takeover back up in twenty-one, she had never seen anything to match the world-ending violence of a big armor clash. Most of her work uptime had seen her embedded with small units of ground fighters, working jungle or mud brick environments in Asia and the Middle East. On those occasions when she had covered large-scale land battles, they tended to be very one-sided affairs, like the battles of Damascus or Aden, with American or British armored divisions rolling over the burned-out wrecks of late-Soviet-era antique tanks.

Patton was using air supremacy to make his campaign as one-sided as possible, but without an Eastern Front to fight on, the Germans had well over a hundred divisions to block the Allied path to Berlin, and they were learning not to mass their armor and artillery out in the open where it could be hammered from above.

Patton leaned over the hood of his jeep, peering at a map covered in a dense tangle of red and blue lines. They'd pulled up on a ridge overlooking the site of a fierce struggle that had taken place an hour earlier between the Black Panthers and what had turned out to be an SS armored regiment.

"Krauts aren't gathering like they used to," he grunted. "They've broken up into these much smaller task groups, some of them with organic air support. It's a lot harder to beat them this way, and a lot less neat."

Julia looked up from the map and scanned the field that stretched away about a kilometer below them. There certainly wasn't anything neat in the aftermath of the battle down there. With her powered goggles she could make out hundreds of torn-up bodies and shattered, burning vehicles. She was glad to have witnessed it from a distance. When the firefight had reached its insane peak, it had looked like some kind of satanic foundry, a place where nothing was created, only destroyed. The crescendo of gunfire, rockets, and clashing armor had only been drowned out by the ear-shredding scream of low-flying aircraft as they ripped overhead to loose whole racks of missiles and hundreds of cannon shells.

Cobra gunships had thudded in and out of the holocaust, hosing down concentrations of German soldiers with miniguns and rocket fire, sometimes dueling with the few Luftwaffe choppers that dared to show up.

Through it all, however, Patton tore across the countryside in his jeep, barking orders at his staff, yelling at radio operators, slapping his hands down on maps, and ordering units to reinforce this battalion or that regiment. In the darkness and violence, he alone seemed to know exactly what he was doing.

Julia did what she could to capture the essence of what was happening where the two armies met, but she kept returning to the figure of the tall, raspy-voiced general consigning some of his men to their doom, and others to glory.

"Do you want to go see your black boys now, Miss Duffy?"

"Sorry?"

She jumped, then looked up, jolted out of her reverie.

Patton pointed down at the field where she had been staring.

"The Seven Sixty-first broke through down there, and they've pushed on to Oostakker, with the Ninetieth Infantry. Those boys made the breach and I'm sending my army through it. I'm proud of 'em, Miss Duffy, they fought like fucking champions. So, you want to follow 'em?"

"Okay," Julia said. "Yeah. Let's go."

Patton's command post consisted of four jeeps and a light armored vehicle that looked like it might have come off the *Kandahar*. But according to Chris Prather, it was only six months old. She'd taken a peek inside, and the electronics were all contemporary.

The small group mounted up, and the jeeps and the LAV bounced down the hillside, through smashed dry-stone walls and over deep furrows dug into the soil by the tracks of the Easy Eight Shermans. Patton's driver, Sergeant Mims, had a bulky pair of night vision goggles, but he'd pushed them up out of the way. Burning tanks and APCs provided more than enough light to navigate the slope. Even Julia took off her Oakleys. They were capable of dealing with the hot spots, but like Mims she found she could see just fine with her own eyes.

As hardened as she was, it was still an overwhelming experience. She wondered how anyone could have survived the maelstrom of high explosives and speeding metal. Dust-off choppers were carrying the first loads of wounded away as medics ran back and forth, providing first aid. The heat coming from so many burning vehicles made the skin on her face feel tight. The screams of the dying sounded no different from what she'd heard before, but Julia had never seen a general hop down from his transport, as Patton did at that moment.

He walked over to a litter, kneeling down and, she was certain, kissing the forehead of the soldier who lay there. Patton's body blocked her view, so she couldn't tell whether the man was a black tanker or a white infantryman, and in the end, what did it matter? With her camera she took in as much as she could of the ruined, burning tanks and the smashed-up bodies of the men who'd fought in them, even though she knew that much of it would be censored outside the Zone. The 'temps were still very touchy about showing their own casualties.

She ducked without thinking as a German Tiger cooked off a hundred yards away, its ammunition bay lighting up and blowing off the turret, which rose about three meters in the air before falling back onto the body of the wrecked vehicle with an almighty clang. Patton didn't even look up. He made his way down a long line of wounded men who were waiting to be choppered back to a MASH, kneeling down and speaking a few words to each, smoothing the hair of one, patting another on the shoulder. She could see now that the wounded men were black *and* white, tankers and infantry.

"Hey, Sergeant," she said, spotting someone she'd met earlier, sitting on the ground and leaning against a stone wall. "Remember me?"

The man tilted his head and squinted in the dark as firelight played over his features. "Sure," he said. "You're Miss Duffy. Captain Prather's reporter. You gonna write about this?"

Julia racked her mind trying to recall his name.

Turley, that was it.

"You bet I am, Sergeant Turley. Are you wounded?"

He shook his head. "No, ma'am. I just lost my tank. We took a whole bunch of RPG rounds. Lost the tracks first, then one punched in through the upper deck. Guy who fired it must have been sitting up in a tree or something."

"Was Lieutenant Robinson in your tank? Jackie Robinson?"

"He was, ma'am. They casevaced him out on the first flight to the aid station. He saved us all, Miss Duffy. Hopped out of the turret with a machine gun. Held off a whole bunch of Germans who were fixing to kill us. Shot most of 'em. Then he ran out of ammo, clubbed a few who got through and tried to climb up, stab him with their bayonets. I guess they'd run out of bullets, too. Or lost their guns. It was confusing, ma'am. I've never been so confused in my life."

"It's okay, Sergeant. Everyone gets confused in combat, all the time. So is Lieutenant Robinson okay?"

Turley gestured helplessly.

"Don't rightly know, ma'am. He got hit twice and jumped off the tank. I got a few of the Germans trying to do him in. And then some white boys come through and cut them down. Three of them was from Georgia. I tell you, Miss Duffy, never in my whole life have I been so happy to see three white boys from Georgia with murder their eyes."

Julia smiled gently. "Do you mind if I quote you on that?"

"No, ma'am. I wish you would."

Turley looked up over her shoulder, and Julia turned to find Patton standing there.

The general dropped to one knee beside her.

"You going to lie there all night, soldier?" he asked.

"No, sir," said Turley. "Soon as you get me a new tank, I'm headed thataway." He nodded in the direction of the advance.

"Good job, son. You get yourself up, go see Captain Mackay over there, and tell him I said to find you a new Sherman. Are you wounded, by the way? Do you need any attention?"

Turley's head and one arm were heavily bandaged, but he pushed himself up off the ground. "I'm fine, General."

"Good man. I'm proud of you, son. You did a great job here tonight."

"Thank you, sir."

As Turley hobbled away to get himself reassigned, Julia saw Patton wipe a tear from his eye. "Absolutely fucking magnificent," he muttered, before seeming to realize that Julia was there. "Come on, Miss Duffy. I won't have my men lying around, and I won't have my correspondents lying around, either. Let's get back to the jeeps. There's a hell of a fight brewing up just along the road."

D-DAY + 26. 29 MAY 1944. 0422 HOURS. BUNKER 13, BERLIN.

The führer had lost his voice, and he'd lost something else, too. Himmler was certain that was why he spoke with such melancholy.

The change had come over him a few hours ago. He'd stormed off in a rage to sleep for a few hours, but returned after only thirty minutes, uncannily subdued. The bunker had come to a halt when he appeared at the doorway. Nobody knew what to say.

The air attack on Patton's flank had been brushed aside. All the hard work and crippling expense that had gone into the plan had counted for nothing. The best planes in the Luftwaffe were gone, and along with them some of the best pilots.

And now the Americans were on the verge of taking the strategic hub at Oostakker.

Himmler's stomach rolled over when he saw the führer reappear. This was going to be very unpleasant. The SS chief stood silently as Field Marshal Gunther von Kluge stepped forward. A sickly green tint colored his face.

The records from the future had revealed von Kluge's disgraceful ineptitude, as he had failed to expose the German plot against Hitler, and Himmler had made use of the information. The field marshal had survived simply because Himmler found it convenient to keep a few of the weaker, more corrupt army officers in his debt. But von Kluge had never fully recovered from his encounter with the SS chief.

Now he stammered his way through a report on the failed air attack, then drew in a deep breath and plunged on.

"After my d-discussion with the commanders in the Belgian sector—those whom I could reach—I . . . I regret to report that, in the face of the enemy's complete c-command of the air, and their omniscient gathering of intelligence, there is no possibility that we will find a strategy to counterbalance their overwhelming capabilities . . . unless we give up the current field of battle.

"De-despite . . . our most intense efforts, the moment draws near when this front, already so heavily strained, will break. And once the enemy reaches open country, an orderly command will hardly be practicable in view of the insufficient mobility of our troops. As a result of the breakthrough by Patton's armored spearhead, the whole Western Front has been ripped open.

"I consider it my duty to bring these conclusions to your notice in good time, *Mein Führer*." With that, he stepped back, and looked like a man prepared to die.

The room was hushed and still. Nobody dared move. Von Kluge was visibly shaking, and when Hitler finally opened his mouth, the field marshal flinched. But the führer merely rubbed at his eyes and spoke in a cracked whisper. He was more rational, more willing to accept the realities, than Himmler had known him to be in months, possibly years.

"If we lose France," Hitler croaked, "we forfeit our key launching point in the U-boat war. In addition, we lose all of the material support we gain from the occupation, including millions of tons of food, and the last tungsten we can hope to get. Still, it is evident—and we must place this at the head of all of our considerations—that it has become impossible to fight a pitched battle in France. We just cannot do it. And yet, we cannot allow Patton to drive his sword toward our heart through Belgium, either.

"We can still manage to regroup our forces, but even then only to a limited extent. Perhaps we should evacuate the coast without further ado, and allow our mobile forces to form reinforced lines that we might defend inflexibly."

His eyes clouded over, and he seemed to go deep into his own mind. When he continued, he almost seemed to be speaking to himself.

"Unfortunately," he continued, "it is also evident that our forces are entirely inadequate to defend even a narrow front. Any further effort in France would be possible only if we could gain superiority in the air, yet we must—no matter how bitter this may be—preserve our new Luftwaffe units *inside* the Reich, employing them only as a very last resort.

"We have lost the missile facilities. We will lose all of the U-boat bases. Our best armor is gone. When and where the last die will be cast, I cannot say."

The führer lifted his eyes from the ground and let his gaze fall on everyone who stood around the map table. They flickered with only the barest reflection of the fire that had once burned in them, but at least it was better than the dead man's gaze Himmler had observed earlier.

Hitler clenched his fists then and said, "Clearly our plan to ambush Patton from the air was betrayed, and this tells me that we have not done enough to root out the traitorous elements exposed by the Emergence. We must do *everything* we can to hunt these spies down, and levy the most severe punishments."

Nobody but the führer dared look at Himmler, but he knew everyone in the room was waiting for his response. He had seized the responsibility for safeguarding the Reich and its leadership against fifth columnists like Rommel and Canaris. He had bathed the state in an ocean of blood to wash away their malign influence. But it had not been enough. He would have to do more. He set his features to demonstrate the steely resolve he would bring to the task, but this was undermined by what the führer said next.

"We must involve *everyone* in Army Group West, conducting this struggle with the utmost fanaticism, and standing firm everywhere. Because mobility, a war of movement, is no longer possible for us. At least in the west. But we have substantial forces securing the border in the east. It is time to review that situation. The Soviets are not yet a threat—they remain greatly weakened by our earlier efforts against them.

"Thus we must temporarily draw down our forces in the east, which are doing *nothing,* to secure our western flank before it becomes impossible to move them at all. We *must* hold the line against the Allies until we possess the weapons necessary to strike back at them."

With that, his eyes bored into Himmler.

"And when do you think that will be, *Herr Reichsführer?*"

14

"It has begun, Comrade Secretary. The Germans are moving at least half their divisions away from the edge of the DMZ. They are heading west."

Joseph Stalin clasped his hands together and showed off a mouthful of yellowed teeth to his assembled cronies: Beria, Foreign Minister Molotov, and Central Committee Secretary Georgi Malenkov.

"Excellent. Just excellent. And so, Beria, do we stand ready?"

The head of the NKVD nodded, though without much enthusiasm. It wasn't that he had misgivings about the operation. No, it was just that Laventry Beria was mindful of any path he walked, checking for dangerous pits along the way. It made him a very calculating individual.

He consulted the flexipad in his hand, although it wasn't really necessary. He was more than familiar with the details of the operation at hand.

"I would never have thought that terrorist criminals could prove so useful," he said. "The trial of the Ukrainians proceeds. Their nationalist guerrillas—along with the Chechens, the Balkars, and Tatars—all remain in open revolt. We have given much publicity to the Red Army's actions in response. This provides cover for the movement of Zhukov's and Konev's forces, although the world remains fixated on Western Europe."

Stalin, playing with his pipe behind his desk in the Little Corner, regarded Beria through eyes as black and unreadable as polished stones.

"But your troops have the situation in hand? We are not about to leap into one battle with another raging at our hindquarters, are we? And these recidivist splitters, they have proven to be much more adaptable than you had imagined, no?"

"Everything is in hand," Beria insisted as a small spasm of terror shuddered through him. "Grozny has been depopulated. The fighting there continues mostly in the countryside. The three nationalist armies of the Ukrainian traitors remain significant forces in context, but they are about to be crushed by the *fifty-four* armies under our command. We have twelve million men ready to fight. Nine thousand tanks. Sixty thousand tubes of artillery and all the special technologies, of course . . . although the numbers are really the concerns of the marshals. I simply state these facts to reassure you that we have nothing to be concerned about."

"And Task Number One?" Stalin asked.

"Is ready," said Beria. "Professor Kurchatov says we shall be able to test-fire a warhead in two days."

"And he anticipates success?"

"He would not dare to mislead me about this. He understands the consequences of miscalculation. And of course, he has been locked away in the *Vanguard Sharashka*, so he knows nothing of the German activities. They did not even factor into his thinking when I spoke with him."

Stalin seemed pleased, and Beria relaxed inwardly. The Soviet leader relit his pipe and began to puff, leaning back and turning the hard wooden chair to part the heavy drapes and peer through the windows at the soft pink-and-orange light of a Russian spring's evening. Beria waited patiently for him to say something.

Molotov and Malenkov kept their own counsel. Nobody in this room really trusted one another. They never had, and the murderous purges of the post-Emergence period had reinforced that base level of paranoia. If Beria could have pulled out a gun, he would have shot both of the others without a moment's thought. But Stalin's Georgian bodyguards would have gunned him down before he could pull back the hammer.

"What of the Americans' Manhattan Project? Do we have any idea of how advanced they are?"

Chagrin distorted Beria's features. He commanded the most fearsome intelligence service in the world, yet he could not answer Stalin's question, as the party boss well knew. He had only asked because of the embarrassment his question would cause.

"We do not know for certain. In the weeks after the Emergence their counterintelligence operations swept up a number of our most useful contacts. It caused some grave problems. But we must assume that they, like us, are well advanced. And of course, they cannot know of *our* progress because they do not know of the *Vanguard*. It will come as a terrible shock to them."

"And to Hitler," Molotov added.

"Most *especially* to that little bastard," Stalin growled, but not without a hint of good humor. "We must ensure that the first bomb does not kill him. I would hate for him to be spared the realization of what is about to happen."

"Again, that is a matter for the air force marshals," Beria said.

Stalin spun his chair slowly around to face them again. "And you, Vyacheslav Mikhaylovich," he said. "You are prepared?"

The foreign minister held up two large brown envelopes. "I have the notes ready to send to the British and American missions," he answered, "along with all the supporting documentation they will require. The sailors and merchantmen we have been holding are already en route to port, if I am not mistaken."

He looked to Beria for confirmation, and received it as a nod. Impounding the Allied convoy PQ 17 two years earlier had been a rash act, although he would never say so to Stalin—or to anyone really, as it would certainly get back to the *Vozhd*. The action had nearly pushed the Allies into declaring war on the Soviet Union, and only the dire strategic situation of 1942 had saved them. The democracies could not afford another enemy.

Beria, who had sent millions to their deaths, had made sure that the Allied personnel were interred under the most humane circumstances possible. A ham-fisted oaf like Malenkov would have liquidated them, but now they provided a perfect sop to the Americans and British, a way to convince them of the Soviet Union's good intentions. They were being trucked back to their ships, which remained at anchor in Murmansk, and would be free to leave on Stalin's say-so.

All that was required was for the leader of the USSR to give the final order, abrogating the cease-fire with Nazi Germany and unleashing the Red Army into Western Europe, as well as upon the Japanese Home Islands. London and Washington would be told within minutes that the Soviet Union was reentering the struggle at their side. They *wouldn't,* however, be informed that by the end of the struggle, the political map of the world would look very different from its outline at the end of the "original" war.

Nevertheless, they could probably work that out for themselves. And since the USSR would be a nuclear power within forty-eight hours, there wasn't much they could do besides offer their lukewarm thanks for the assistance.

Stalin picked up a phone that connected him to Zhukov's headquarters.

"Marshal," he said, "this is Stalin. You will proceed."

D-DAY + 30. 1 JUNE 1944. 1003 HOURS. KORYAK RANGES, FAR EASTERN SIBERIA.

Three months had passed since Major Pavel Ivanov had transmitted any data back to the West. He had to be careful with the data bursts.

Officially he was a free agent, a rogue agent if you got down to it, responsible to no one. He received no instructions from the Multinational Force command or the contemporary Allied intelligence services.

Unofficially two flexipads sat on standby in San Diego and Washington, always powered up and attuned to the ID tag coded into Ivanov's comm-boosted unit. When he sent a compressed data burst into the ether, it would find a Fleetnet node and register on the two pads. The recipients would not acknowledge it, and no messages ever came back from them. That way both Kolhammer and the top British intelligence man in America, William Stephenson, had a deniable back-channel source of information about developments in the Soviet Union.

For two years Ivanov had been transmitting updates on the growing Red Army strength, on his never-ending search for any sign of missing 21C assets like the stealth destroyer HMS *Vanguard,* and on the progress or otherwise of a slew of nationalist resistance movements that had sprung up in the wake of Stalin's separate "peace" with the Nazis. Some of these he had even fostered himself, moving secretly around the country, passing on the fruits of twenty years' counterinsurgency experience in the Russian Federation Special Forces.

The former Spetsnaz officer did have his qualms about what he was doing. The Bolsheviks didn't fuck around, agonizing over their response to "terrorist atrocities." They simply cranked up their own atrocities, on a vastly greater scale. After a train carrying minor party officials was ambushed by Uzbek separatists trained by Ivanov, the NKVD swept through the republic and decimated it, killing 10 percent of the Uzbekistani population. Beria's men had since been back and emptied entire towns, forcing the inhabitants onto trucks and trains and shipping them off to the gulags.

Ivanov had no concerns about the native population of this godforsaken hole. There were no natives left. When his guide, Kicji, took them through the final high pass of the Koryak Ranges at the head of the Kamchatka Peninsula, he had stopped and slowly swept one gnarled hand across the world, grunting in his heavily accented Russian, "All Koryak gone. Only soldiers now. And me." Ivanov had trained a heavy pair of powered binoculars on the spot far off in the haze where Kicji was pointing. They had been standing on a small plateau at least two thousand meters up. The air was as sharp and as clear as he had ever known it to be, although tinged with a sulfurous smell from all the active volcanoes on the peninsula to the south.

He had seen brown haze localized around some sort of huge camp. It was difficult to be sure, due to the distance, but it looked like a prison camp with a heavy industrial component. It was much larger, and generated a lot more aerial pollution than the usual run of camps.

"*Sharashka,*" muttered the guide. "Koryak built it. They are buried inside, with many others."

Ivanov handed the binoculars to his second in command, Lieutenant Vendulka Zamyatin, a female medical officer of the Russian navy who had been working on board HMS *Fearless* at the time of the Transition. She was one of the few survivors from that ship. The pale, good-looking woman they called Vennie played with the controls on the glasses, trying to bring the *Sharashka*—the "special technical prison"—into sharper focus, but without much luck, to judge by her furrowed brow.

"I cannot say, but it looks much bigger than the last one," she commented. "Maybe three times the size of the one in the Urals. It must be significant. Atomics, you think?"

"Maybe," Ivanov said. "Whatever the case, it's too large to attack. I'd guess at a couple of regiments of security, maybe even a division of NKVD, given the extent of the operation."

He turned and smiled at his small band. Kicji, ageless, bitter, looking like a totem carved from the root of a poisoned tree. Vendulka, her beauty marred by a line of scar tissue that ran from just below her left ear and across her face, before tapering off at the corner of her mouth. Sergo the Cossack, who stood six and a half feet tall and seemed to measure a couple of ax handles across the shoulders. And the smooth, dangerous Chechen jihadi Ahmed Khan, emissary of his Caliph, who laid claim to all the lands Ivanov had so recently fought to preserve from the likes of nutters just like them.

"So we won't be kicking in the door," Ivanov said.

Kicji leaned up against an outcropping of smooth black rock. "No need to get in," he said. "There is only one road out to the coast. Every day convoys travel it. Some small, some large. But some with many more guards. These must be important, yes?"

Ivanov shrugged. "Probably."

Kicji rustled around inside a stinking fur vest and pulled out a strip of dried meat, which he began to chew. "There are many places where it is possible to ambush these convoys."

"Not with so few men," Sergo said. "Not even with these." He hefted his new and much-loved assault rifle, a genuine AK-47 with an underslung grenade launcher. Ivanov's gift of more than two hundred Kalashnikovs to Sergo's bandit tribe had secured their loyalty and the man's services.

Kicji gnawed at the jerky, reminding Ivanov of a dog with a treat.

"We can get men from the north. The Chukchi," he said. "Many of them are buried in the *Sharashka,* too. They will fight."

"They're fishermen," Vendulka said. "I served with some on the other side. They are good men, but they know nothing of fighting in the mountains."

Kicji smiled, showing large gaps in his teeth. "Wrong Chukchi," he said. "Those Chukchi are all gone. They lived in villages by the sea. Little buried huts. They couldn't run when the Russians came. All dead now. The *other* Chukchi are reindeer people. They move. Many still died, those on big Russian farms. But some live. They have nothing now, just revenge. They will fight."

Ivanov unwrapped a chocolate bar. He had never met a Chukchi, reindeer man or fisherman. But he knew a little about them. He retained an encyclopedic knowledge of the federation's many ethnic subgroups and their many, many blood feuds. The Chukchi were one of the smaller, more obscure, and infinitely less troublesome populations. As such, they tended to be overlooked. At best, he recalled, they were a shamanistic people, even after decades of Soviet rule and then democratic development. They believed that spirits inhabited the world, and they practiced animal sacrifice to appease those spirits. They had also been enemies of Kicji's people.

"I thought the Chukchi attacked the Koryak," he said. "Drove them from their homes."

"Yes," Kicji answered. "But no more Koryak now. Nobody to remember when I am gone."

With a shake of his head and a minimal rise of the shoulders, he managed a gesture that captured the existential horror and despair of a man who thinks of himself as the last of his kind.

"If Chukchi die, I do not care," he continued, "but they will kill Russians. And I care for killing Russians very much."

Ivanov turned to peer questioningly at the others. The Cossack was sucking slowly at his beard. Ahmed Khan, more prince than guerrilla, regarded the guide like a bad penny. And Zamyatin was staring again at the shrouded prison, a frown digging deep fissures in her forehead.

The Spetsnaz officer finished his chocolate bar and balled up the wrapper, carefully placing it in a deep pocket. He would bury it later, with their other rubbish, when they reached softer ground, or burn it in a lava flow if they passed close to one. The morning was relatively warm, at least ten degrees Celsius. Down on the wide valley floor in the sun it might even get up to twenty or more. A pair of gyrfalcons rode a thermal a few hundred meters away, slate-gray plumage disappearing against the mountain background whenever their spiraling flight path carried them across the face of the range.

He wondered if any of the Uzbeks he'd seen taken away a year ago had ended up here. The Soviets were increasingly using mechanized equipment like tractors and bulldozers. The factories east of the Urals were immense, monstrously so, and they had been running twenty-four hours a day since they'd been built. But he'd heard rumors of this facility since his first days back on home soil, in 1942. It would have been built with slave labor. Hundreds of thousands of workers had probably been needed. Just clearing the forests around the site had to have been the work of an army.

"How long will it take us to reach the Chukchi?" he asked.

Kicji carefully placed the food he had been eating back in a pouch. He scratched at his thin beard. "Moving with care, it will be three days there. Four back—with more men it is slower."

"And how many men can we expect?"

"How many can you arm?"

"Thirty."

In fact, he had arms caches from which he could outfit many more than that, but although he trusted the guide, he wanted to make certain that if Kicji was captured by the NKVD, he could only give up misinformation.

"Thirty we can find," Kicji said. "But we will need to talk to different families. Maybe three or four."

"I understand," Ivanov said. Like many nomads, the Chukchi formed bands held together by familial ties. It probably wouldn't be possible to gather all of the men he needed from one tribe. "Ahmed, Sergo? Are you agreed? We shall raise a party, and take a sizable convoy."

"God willing," the jihadi added.

"As always," Ivanov conceded.

"I agree," Sergo said. "I like it."

"And you, Vendulka?"

The medical officer had remained quiet, as was her wont. Ivanov always asked her opinion last, although hers was the viewpoint that meant the most to him.

"We will have to be quick," she said. "We can jam their communications in the passes, where they would fail anyway. But if they're high-value targets, they will be missed quickly."

"Of course."

Zamyatin raised the glasses to her eyes again. Still frowning. "The haze has cleared a little. Take a look," she said.

Ivanov retrieved the binoculars. He could make out an airfield to the west of the facility. Two small silver planes were coming in to land. "MiGs," he said.

"Rocket planes?" Ahmed Khan asked. "They have rocket planes now?"

"Yes," said Ivanov. "MiG-Fifteens. Jet fighters."

D-DAY + 29. 1 JUNE 1944. 2041 HOURS.
U.S. EMBASSY, MOSCOW.

The Soviet foreign minister, as immaculate as ever in a dark English suit, positively beamed at Averell Harriman. The American ambassador was hurriedly thinking of ways to stall for time, but he didn't need to. Molotov refused to stay for a drink, which was unheard of, begging off with the claim that he had to get to the British mission, as well.

He turned and hurried out the front door, never having penetrated farther than the entrance hall of the embassy. Harriman read through the top-page summary again. It would take hours to trawl though the two-inch-thick sheaf of documents he'd just been handed.

"Well, sir? Is there anything else?" asked his chief military liaison, Colonel Squires.

"Good God, isn't this *enough*? They're back in the war. They're releasing our sailors and ships. And they're attacking Japan, for good measure. You'd better get everyone in, Colonel. We're going to be up all night. I'd best give the Brits an early warning, too. Oh, and I'll need a secure channel to Washington. I'll use the Samsung."

The army officer snapped to attention. "Very good, sir. I'll get Mr. Wilson to call your wife, tell her you'll be late."

"Tell her I won't be home at all tonight," he said grimly.

He had a feeling this was going to be very much like the days after the Allies had bombed the Demidenko center and everyone had sat around on tenterhooks waiting to see whether it would push the Soviets into an open declaration of war on the West. It hadn't—perhaps only because Moscow had denied all along that such a facility even existed. Or perhaps because, as the British argued, it was a chimera designed to draw attention away from other, more important facilities.

Harriman was vaguely aware of an increase in the bustle of activity throughout the embassy, as junior officers and diplomats were roused from their offices or called in from their homes. He walked slowly back to his office, where his secretary already had the British ambassador, Sir Anthony Clark-Kerr, waiting on the telephone. The secure line.

"I just had Molotov over here," Harriman said without preamble. "He's on his way over to you right now. They've declared war on Germany and Japan. They've got twelve million men on the move right now. Stalin wants a summit with the president and Mr. Churchill as soon as possible to discuss 'common goals.'"

"Good grief," Clark-Kerr said. "This is a bit of a turnup for the books. What details do you have?"

Harriman looked at the document Molotov had just delivered. "He's dropped a lot of paper on us. It'll take a few hours to work through it. In fact, we should divide the task, half and half. That'll be much quicker."

"I'll have my intelligence johnnies call yours when we get our package. Divvy up the work, although I'll need to send a preliminary report to London."

"That should be possible. Molotov included a three-page summary as a top sheet. Boiled down, it says two things. The men and ships from PQ Seventeen are being released, and the Soviet Union is now at war with the Axis powers."

"I see," Sir Anthony said. The two-word phrase was heavy with unspoken thoughts. To himself, however, Harriman could not help thinking, *Where in God's name is this going to end?*

D-DAY + 30. 2 JUNE 1944. 0053 HOURS.
NKVD HEADQUARTERS, LUBIANKA, MOSCOW.

Laventry Beria examined his penis. It was hard, and the fish-belly-white flab of his expanding gut threatened to engulf it. As often happened after days of nigh-unbearable stress, he found himself all but overcome by an irresistible surge of sexual energy as soon as he was released from the source of the tension.

He had just spoken to Professor Kurchatov again, and been reassured that the weapon would fire as intended. Initial reports from the Ukraine indicated that the nationalist counter-revolutionary forces had been crushed under the advance of Zhukov's front. That wasn't the primary intention, of course, just a happy side effect of pouring so many tanks and divisions across the western Ukrainian plains. The new weapons, developed under his supervision using information taken from the

Vanguard, were sweeping through the German defenses like a scythe.

All in all, he had done well. Much better than so many others charged with the defense of the Motherland. As he sat alone in his office, the door locked and defended by his bodyguards, colonels Sarkisov and Nadaraia, he rummaged around in his drawer, pushing aside his bloodstained blackjack clubs, numerous pairs of silk stockings, two pairs of panties, and pile of pornographic photographs as he searched for . . .

Ah, here it was. The love letter from Irina, his current favorite among the stable of female swimmers and basketball players he kept to satisfy his appetites. She was a good writer, with a strong clear hand, and a truly amazing ability to recall their Herculean lovemaking in the most exacting gynecological detail. He had his cock in hand and was about to begin when the phone rang.

It was Stalin. Beria had had a separate phone line put in to ensure that he could identify calls from the supreme leader when they came in. A man could die badly in the USSR simply because he didn't answer the phone in time. Beria had authorized a number of such executions himself.

He snatched up the receiver, suddenly fearful that Stalin could tell that the hand holding the phone had been wrapped around his engorged member just moments earlier. Keeping all trace of fear from his voice, he answered as briefly as he could. "Yes, this is Beria."

Half expecting the general secretary to berate him, he was reassured by Stalin's matter-of-fact tone, until he realized what the madman was asking. "I want the bomb tested under battlefield conditions. I've decided it would be a waste of resources to blow it up in Siberia where there are no Germans beyond the gates of our punishment camps. Arrange to drop it on Hitler's Army Group East. Konev tells me they are trying to organize themselves around Lodz."

Completely detumescent now, the lovely Irina all but forgotten, Beria felt an instant headache wrap itself around his temporal lobes. It was like being squeezed in the paws of a giant ape. His mouth opened and closed a few times before words finally came out. "But, I cannot. That is, Kurchatov says—"

"Do not tell me what is possible and what is not. You have boasted often enough about the impossible tasks you have achieved on Projects One and Two. Surely building the bomb was the *major* impossibility. I would have thought dropping it posed no problem at all. It is just a bomb after all, Beria. It is meant to be dropped upon someone, yes? And please do not tell me otherwise, or I shall have you nailed to the thing when it goes off."

"No-no-no," he said, vaguely aware that he was close to babbling. "It is not that . . ." Although in fact he had no idea if the bomb was ready to be used under field conditions. "It is . . . it is just that . . . the effects. Yes! The effects are not like a normal bomb. There is the radiation poisoning. If we drop it near our own armies, we will kill them, as well."

Stalin's voice came through the earpiece, cold and full of menace. "If you drop a bomb near anyone, Beria, you will kill them. So do *not* drop it near them. Use it when Zhukov and Konev are still a safe distance away."

"But the poison remains," he protested. "Possibly even weeks later, it will not be safe to walk through Lodz."

"It is not safe to walk through Lodz *now.* And I did not say to destroy the city. The Germans have built many factories there. I do not want them destroyed. Just emptied for our use, when they have been cleaned of your atomic poisons. Do you understand now, Beria?"

And he did.

"It is a brilliant plan," he gasped.

"Of course," Stalin said. "It was mine. I am not a fool, Beria. I understand this new weapon. Talk to Kurchatov and Zhukov. Consult with the meteorology service. And drop the thing when the wind is blowing west. We shall destroy Army Group East and take Lodz without losing a single Red Army private."

"Indeed we shall, a brilliant, brilliant plan," he agreed.

"Then make sure it works," said Stalin.

15

"Data links verified secure, Admiral. But they're unstable. The relay is patchy and might drop out."

"Thank you, Brooks. You did a good job just getting it through."

Real-time global conferencing was only a happy memory for the surviving members of the Multinational Force. They were a day out of Pearl, still close enough for the *Siranui* to relay the signal back to fleet on Honolulu. From there a daisy chain of the new EC-121 Super Connies fitted out with both AT and salvaged twenty-first comm gear shunted the signal on to the National Command Authority's dedicated ADSL network—a hack job constructed of new coaxial cable and a simple but ingenious hijacking of a portion of the old copper wire telephone network.

Kolhammer sat next to Admiral Ray Spruance in front of a flat-panel display with an attached web-cam. It was like being back at college again. Spruance had cross-decked from the *Enterprise* for the conference, a hookup that included the Joint Chiefs, British ambassador Lord Halifax, and the White House. The screen in Kolhammer's ready room displayed only the conference participants—each in their own window—while a separate screen next to it ran a data package from Hawaii with the latest information from the new European front. He and Spruance managed to view that data before Lieutenant Brooks fully established the precarious link with the United States.

As he scanned the package, Kolhammer's stomach felt as though he'd been force-fed a few pounds of molten lead. The reports were all text-based. There was no multimedia coverage of the Soviet attack, hopefully because no such capacity existed in the USSR, but more likely because they were hiding their true capabilities.

The Communists had hit the soft German eastern flank with a gargantuan assault, supported by some very sophisticated weaponry. The Sovs were back, and they were packing serious heat. Intercepted German signals spoke of jet fighters raking the skies clear of every plane they encountered, of great, lumbering, twin-bladed helicopters bristling with automatic cannons and rocket pods. Whole armies seemed to be outfitted with automatic weapons—doubtless they'd turn out to be AK-47 variants—and shoulder-fired rockets that proved lethal to all but the most heavily armored tanks and vehicles. Probably RPG-2s or even -7s. The speed of the Soviet advance testified to enormous fleets of armored personnel carriers, accompanying thousands of T-34 tanks.

It was like a nightmare from the 1950s.

"Gentlemen, I believe we're ready."

It was Henry Stimson, the secretary of war.

Kolhammer watched the other military officers bring themselves to a higher state of attentiveness. The picture was low res, but even so Roosevelt looked worn out and pinched. Lord Halifax seemed almost gray, and dark smudges stood out under his eyes.

"The latest news we have from Moscow," said Stimson, "is that Konev's Byelorussian front has advanced on Brest, annihilating the Wehrmacht forces stationed at the edge of the Pripet Marshes to guard their DMZ. The Nazis are pouring troops from Poland into Brest and Lodz. Zhukov seems to be maneuvering around Lodz, sending only a fraction of his Ukrainian front to probe the German defenses. Our own intercepts of German signal traffic confirm the broad outlines of the Moscow reports.

"In the east, the Russians have dropped airborne forces onto the southern parts of Sakhalin, the Kuril Islands, and Hokkaido. Three army fronts have moved into Manchukuo, Mengjiang, and the northern parts of Korea. What's left of Japan's Kwantung Army is being destroyed. There are unconfirmed reports from OSS of irregular Soviet forces fighting in northern Indochina. Their eastern forces, at our best estimate, comprise one and a half to two million men, at least five thousand tanks, over thirty thousand artillery pieces, and four thousand aircraft, a small but significant percentage of which appear to be jet-powered. Both their eastern and western armies appear to be equipped with AT weapons and equipment."

Nobody looked directly at Kolhammer, but it was only because they were all staring at the screen in their location where his image was displayed. Being more familiar with teleconferencing, he couldn't miss the way everyone seemed to fix their attention on a single spot in front of them.

At least Spruance didn't turn to stare daggers at him.

"Thank you, Mr. Secretary," Roosevelt said. "Well, gentlemen, I am to meet with Uncle Joe and Mr. Churchill in Tehran. What am I to say? That we don't want Stalin's help?"

Admiral King, the U.S. Navy chief, spoke up before anyone else had a chance. "Pardon my French, Mr. President, but I think we need to tell him to stay the hell out of Western Europe. Once the Red Army gets itself settled in, I don't imagine for a second they'll make any move to leave."

"Anyone else," Roosevelt asked, looking from window to window.

"The admiral is correct," Kolhammer said. "Every foot of ground they take, they will keep, and when the Nazis are done with, they'll come looking for more."

"General Marshall," Roosevelt said, "has your staff made any headway in working out where the Soviet advance is likely to run into ours?"

The image jumped, and the sound crackled in and out, but Kolhammer was able to make out most of what Marshall said.

"It's only a ver . . . rough guess, because . . . on't know the Russian order of . . . their full capabil . . . But given the . . . they've cut through the Germans so far, and the number of divisions we face in . . . rope, you could be looking at a meeting . . . around Bonn. They would most likely also take all of Eastern Europe, Nor . . . Italy, and significant areas of southern France, perhaps penetrating as far . . . Rhône River."

"And this is predicated on the assumption that they don't have any nuclear weapons," Roosevelt said.

"It is, sir. We feel that if . . . had them, they'd have used them."

A cold iron spike of pain began boring slowly into Kolhammer's frontal lobes. If the Communists ended up with most of

Europe and a big piece of Asia, the rest of the twentieth century was going to look *very* different from the one he knew. He heard Roosevelt ask Spruance for his assessment of how much things had changed in the Pacific theater. The admiral explained that initially, at least, it might make things easier, with Yamamoto and Tojo forced to deal with this new threat to their rear. In the medium to long term, however, it meant trouble.

Kolhammer followed the discussion with one part of his mind, but at the same time he couldn't stop himself from wondering how much the president had learned from the alternative history of this war.

It had been accepted for a long time, back in his world, that Stalin had played both the U.S. and British leaders for a couple of rubes at the Big Three conferences. Neither of them had shown any real understanding of the bestial nature of the Communist regime, and they had labored under the naïve assumption that they could do business with Moscow as though it were just another difficult nation. But the USSR under Stalin—and for many years afterward—had been a charnel house every bit as foul as the Third Reich. Its leaders were brutes and criminals with a will to power that even Hobbes would have considered psychotic.

And now, of course, those "brutes" all knew the ultimate fate of their glorious revolution. To Kolhammer the outcome was clear. They had been heading toward this from the moment Manning Pope had opened the wormhole. This war wouldn't be over when Hitler was crushed. It would only end when a Sherman tank burst through the gates of the Kremlin, or a T-34 rolled into the Rose Garden. Assuming the combatants didn't all die in a nuclear exchange first.

He wanted to say all that, but restricted himself, when asked, to explaining what intelligence-gathering assets he could deploy far in advance of Spruance's task force, to determine what—if any—consequences had flowed from Stalin's declaration of war on Japan.

"With midair refueling, we can get AWACs on station in eight or nine hours," he explained. "But they can't stay for long. It's just too far away. Both the *Siranui* and the *Havoc* are outstanding platforms for this sort of work, and lest anyone lack confidence in the former, I'd remind you that she is now staffed entirely by U.S. Navy personnel. However, the *Siranui* is an integral part of this battle group, and losing her is like putting out our eyes.

"The sub, on the other hand, we can live without, and she is a naturally stealthy vessel. Captain Willet is already stationed well in advance of the task force and could be off the Marianas in three days, or the Home Islands in four. This is exactly the sort of work she was originally designed to do. I'd suggest sending her with all dispatch."

"Do we need to talk to Canberra about that?" Stimson asked.

"No, sir," Spruance answered. "They've assigned her to us under her original rules of engagement. For the duration of the operation, the *Havoc* is our asset to deploy as we see fit. She doesn't need to refer back to her national command."

"Good, then," Roosevelt said. "See to it."

"We have other assets we could deploy," Spruance added. "A couple of our destroyers are carrying SEAL and Force Recon teams. They were going to insert to support the landings, but we could probably retask some of them to gather information about the Japanese reaction to these developments."

Roosevelt consulted with his navy and Marine Corps advisers, who agreed it would be a good idea, as long as it didn't significantly detract from the primary mission of the task force.

"Well, gentlemen," the president continued, "I suppose we should prepare ourselves for the worst. What is the phrase your people use, Admiral Kolhammer? The eight-hundred-pound gorilla? I think we need to talk about it. General Marshall, leaving aside the atomic question for now, can we fight and win against the Red Army in Europe?"

Again, Marshall broke up in transmission, but again it hardly mattered. His answer was clear.

"No, sir. We will take sig . . . casualties against the Nazis. We're fight . . . best divisions while Zhukov and Koni . . . their worst. We'll have to resupply . . . Atlantic . . . then the channel. They have a significant advan . . . men and matériel, and while we can't gauge just . . . they've advanced their indust . . . base, it seems obvious that they've used the last two years to . . . least some of their technol . . . to the same level as ours. The Luftwaffe, for . . . is having no better luck . . . their MiGs than they have against our Sabers."

Admiral King, always the most abrasive of the personalities, cut across Marshall when it seemed as if he was finished. "Can we just deal with the other eight-hundred-pound gorilla in the room?"

Roosevelt looked wary, but he nodded. Kolhammer felt a sick feeling forming in his stomach to keep his headache company.

"The Reds didn't come up with the new planes and guns and tanks by cribbing from afar. And they didn't get them from that Demidenko complex they were running with the krauts. That was just a hustle by Ribbentrop and Himmler to keep them on side. I think it's pretty obvious that they've independently laid hands on twenty-first technology and documentation—and possibly even expertise—and they've grabbed quite a bit of it."

He was staring out of the monitor directly at Kolhammer now, having learned the trick of addressing the web-cam rather than the screen image.

"Wouldn't you agree, Admiral Kolhammer?" King concluded.

"I would," he answered without demur.

There was a noticeable shifting among the men on screen. Nobody looked comfortable. He could sense Spruance becoming very still beside him.

"Care to have a guess at which ship you lost?"

The president stepped in before the two men could get started on one of their legendary fights. Although Kolhammer paid due deference to King as the commander in chief of the contemporary U.S. Navy, he was not directly under his command. He answered to Spruance for operational purposes, and ultimately to Roosevelt, but under the Transition Act of 1942 he was permitted to remain within his original chain of command until one year and one day after the cessation of hostilities in both the European and Pacific theaters.

It was a situation that made for some fiery clashes with the aggressive and often unpleasant Admiral King.

"Gentlemen, let's not open another front just yet," Roosevelt cautioned. "Admiral Kolhammer, your thoughts."

"I suspect the Russians may have gotten their paws on the *Vanguard*," he said. "It was a sister ship to Captain Halabi's HMS *Trident*."

He clearly heard a couple of stifled groans coming from speakers.

"In the first months after the Transition, I covertly placed a surveillance team inside the Soviet Union to search for evidence of any Multinational Force assets that might have turned up there, in the same fashion as the *Sutanto* and *Dessaix* were displaced and fell into Japanese hands."

He was aware that Spruance was staring at him, and some of the others looked similarly abashed. Only Roosevelt and, curiously, the British envoy Lord Halifax did not react.

"We couldn't sustain the team in-country for longer than six months before they had to withdraw. During their time in the Soviet Union, they picked up some indications that the Red Army somehow had gained access to twenty-first technology, but nothing conclusive could be found, and there was nothing that couldn't be explained as a result of the Demidenko Project."

Admiral King cut in on him. "So *what*? You bought that crock of shit, and pulled your guys out?"

Kolhammer was about to say that only a few moments ago King had been outraged by the fact of the team being placed in-country at all. Now he was raging because they'd been taken out.

But Roosevelt made the point redundant.

"I'm afraid I ordered Admiral Kolhammer to cease all of his activities within the borders of the USSR," he said. "The situation with Stalin was tenuous, teetering on war really after we hit Demidenko, as you'll all recall. It was my opinion that Admiral Kolhammer's people were in danger of pouring gasoline on the fire. That was a mistake. We could have done with them now."

Nobody said anything in reply. Kolhammer closed his eyes.

Here goes, he thought.

"They're still there," he said. "And still in contact."

He thought the president might have him shot right then and there, so he hurried on with an explanation.

"Major Ivanov and Lieutenant Zamyatin stayed in the USSR, as they were entitled to, since their period of attachment to the Multinational Force had expired. They are operating as free agents now, doing what they can to liberate their country from tyranny.

"It is their right," he insisted as Admiral King snorted volubly on screen. "Major Ivanov was a Special Forces officer back in our world. He was an expert in both combating and fomenting insurgencies. That's exactly what he's been doing, all over the Soviet Union, for eighteen months. Supporting insurgent forces."

Kolhammer let that sink in. The only natural light in his ready room came from two portholes, through which he could see a few wisps of clouds in an otherwise blue sky. A couple of prop-driven planes flew past, a good two or three thousand meters away, while he paused in his delivery. Then he continued.

"There was always going to be a reaction against the central government, when Stalin no longer had the Nazis to unite everyone he'd been tormenting before the war," he explained. "Ivanov has simply been helping that process along. Frankly, I thought it was futile, but it's not my country. At any rate, President Roosevelt ordered me to cease all contact and control, and I did so. However, Major Ivanov has continued to file regular reports. They have been logged by Fleetnet and archived, but no correspondence was entered into.

"We couldn't very well stop him sending the information, after all."

Roosevelt muttered, "I still don't understand why you didn't get on with Hoover, Admiral. You're cut from the same cloth."

Kolhammer tactfully ignored the aside.

"Anyway, Ivanov has been in contact again recently. Fleetnet logged a data burst from him just a few hours ago. He is in the Kamchatka region, and is investigating what the Russians call a *sharashka*. It's effectively a prison, but a gilded one. Not a million miles removed from the Manhattan Project— in principle, if not execution. *Sharashki* are tightly closed R-and-D facilities, some of them as big as cities. Life for the scientists and techies who are effectively imprisoned there is very cushy by Soviet standards. They get comfortable quarters, good food, some minor luxuries. But if they miss a deadline or screw something up, there's a fair chance the NKVD will kill them and send their families to a real gulag."

The president looked more than a little uncomfortable with Kolhammer's uncompromising account of life under Uncle Joe. The other military men, used to dealing in extremes, seemed much less discomfited.

"Major Ivanov has provided us with the locations of three *sharashki* other than the Kamchatka site, and extensive notes on what he was able to find out about each. He hasn't sent much on Kamchatka yet, but I expect that will change soon. The other sites he has logged are a missile range at Novolazarevskaya, a large jet program at Baikonur, and another aviation program near Baikonur that seems to be mainly concerned with helicopter production."

Kolhammer paused to take a breath. He had no idea how anyone would react to his next statement.

"I would strongly suggest that all of these facilities should be targeted for immediate deep-strike missions, if open conflict with the Soviets ensues. The missile base at Novolazarevskaya in particular. If it transpires that they've had two years' access to the *Vanguard,* they will have a very advanced missile program by now. It's quite possible that Stalin will be able to call on ICBM assets—rockets that could reach well into the continental United States. And if he has made any progress on his atomic program . . . well, you don't need me to tell you what a nightmare that would be."

It was evident, even in the little pop-up window, that a few of his colleagues were as furious as they had been in the days after the Transition, when they learned that Kolhammer's ships had destroyed the Pacific Fleet "by accident." He could see that King's face had turned a dangerous shade of red. Marshall was shaking his head, his lips pressed thinly together.

"Major Ivanov has taken some preliminary soil, air, and water samples from around the Kamchatka site, and they have tested positive for low-level radioactive contamination."

He heard Spruance swear softly beside him.

"In addition, Ivanov has sent back some basic imagery of the *Sharashka,* and there are a number of signs that it may be part of the atomic program."

He tapped a string of commands into his keyboard. On the screens at the other end of the link, he and Spruance disappeared. They were replaced by still shots of massive concrete cooling towers. Allowing them a few moments to examine the image, Kolhammer then returned to the video feed from the ready room.

"Major Ivanov intends to secure high-value personnel from within the facility, to question them and confirm its nature."

"How?" Henry Stimson asked.

"He's gonna grab them up and interrogate them as quickly as possible."

"Torture them, you mean," King said.

"No, Admiral. Ivanov has access to a small supply of T-Five. It's a drug we use in hostile debriefing of enemy combatants. It's a lot more effective than kicking them in the kidneys."

"Admiral Kolhammer, what happens if Ivanov gets caught?" Roosevelt asked.

"He won't allow that to happen, sir."

"Oh really."

"No. He won't. I'm afraid that given the nature of his mission, there is very little chance that Ivanov and his companions will escape with their lives. He judges it a sacrifice worth making. And I can assure you, he won't leave traces behind for the Soviets to throw back in your face."

"Admiral, you seem almost eager for this conflict with the Russians," Roosevelt said.

"I have no enthusiasm for it at all, Mr. President. It will be an unholy bloodletting. But in my opinion, it *is* inevitable. The Soviets will not accept their future—the future they found in our records. We'll fight it out in the next few weeks or the next few years, but we will have to fight them. And it's almost certain that Stalin will want that fight to take place now, when he's at his strongest, and before we reach the stage of mutually assured destruction with atomic weapons."

Kolhammer waited for someone—Admiral King, he guessed—to flay him again for having royally fuckcd up their world. He'd built up a thick mass of scar tissue over the past two years of getting flogged on that same point. To his surprise nobody did anything of the sort.

The president, looking unsteady, turned to Lord Halifax. "Mr. Ambassador, what is the position of His Majesty's government concerning the Soviet declaration?"

Kolhammer narrowed his eyes without realizing it. His research on Lord Halifax gave him no confidence in the man. He was a remote, upper-class grandee who was in Washington because Churchill couldn't stand to have him spooking about London. He'd been an appeaser in the 1930s who'd argued that Hitler's territorial ambitions should be accommodated, since they "constituted no serious threat" and even marked the return of the Germany to normality after the trials of the Great War and Versailles. If he'd been born a century later, thought Kolhammer, he'd have been one of those idiots who slapped their foreheads and moaned, "What did we do wrong?" every time some jihadi nutjob blew up a primary school or crashed a super-tanker into a port.

With a long face and a melancholy, almost melodramatic delivery, however, Halifax said, "His Majesty's government has been aware of Major Ivanov's activities, and has been studying his reports for some time now."

That didn't surprise Kolhammer. He knew a Russian-speaking SAS officer had accompanied Ivanov into the Soviet Union.

"It's the opinion of the prime minister and cabinet that war with the Soviet Union is inevitable, and that all preparations must be made to successfully prosecute the conflict as quickly as possible."

"I see," Roosevelt said. He was apparently as taken aback as Kolhammer. "General Marshall, gentlemen, I don't want to fight another war, and I will do all I can to avoid it, but as it will fall to you to prevail in any conflict with Stalin, I must now direct you to begin planning for that eventuality."

Spruance poured himself a second cup of coffee from the pot on the warming stand in Kolhammer's ready room. The task force had moved only a few nautical miles since they'd sat down to take part in the teleconference, but the world had turned itself inside out, again. Maybe one day they'd get used to the feeling, Kolhammer mused.

He finished the dregs of his espresso and stared out a porthole. He could tell from the lazy, heaving motion of the ship and the number of whitecaps out on the deep blue that they were sailing into a weather front. A southerly, if he guessed right.

"Young Kennedy is already a hundred miles out ahead of us," Spruance said. "I intend to chopper a SEAL team out to him, and then send him to drop them on Saipan."

Kolhammer folded his arms and leaned back on the edge of his desk. "Seems a reasonable idea," he agreed. "There's nothing like eyeballing the ground for real. And our drone cover isn't what it used to be."

"No, but we have a larger issue now, don't we?" Spruance said. "If it turns out that Tojo is withdrawing some of his forces from the Marianas to shore up defense of the Home Islands, we have to decide whether or not we'll let him."

"Uh-huh," Kolhammer responded. "My two cents' worth. If the Japanese want to get home, we should let them. It'll mean less resistance for us, and it's going to get bloody taking those islands. More importantly, it'll hold up the Sovs, and believe me, you don't want them getting hold of Japan. I can't think of anything worse.

"You think the Japanese are bad news now, you got no idea. As Commies, they'd be worse than the North Koreans."

Spruance paced the room with hands clasped behind his back. He adjusted his balance to the movement of the ship without apparent thought.

They'd been given no specific orders about how to respond to a Japanese withdrawal from the Marianas. Until they knew better what was happening out there, they'd been ordered to continue as planned. Spruance stopped at a porthole and gazed out over the task force awhile. The invasion fleet that hit Calais had been an awesome sight, even when viewed on screen. But it hadn't been a proper oceangoing armada like this one. This had fewer ships, overall, but to Kolhammer it looked much more powerful.

Spruance turned away from the view. "When we find out exactly what's going on, we will be referring back to Washington," he said, in a tone that made it clear he would brook no argument.

"Of course," Kolhammer agreed. "This is your task force, Admiral, not mine. I'm just here to run my part of it."

"As long as we understand each other then, Admiral. I'm not going to interfere with your tactical decisions. You're playing with technologies and doctrine I've never trained for. But I am not going to make political decisions—and neither are you. If choices of that nature are to be made, they'll be made by the right people, not us."

Kolhammer agreed with as much good grace as he could muster. He liked Spruance, even though he knew the other man found him and his people vexing—to say the least. As long as the Auxiliaries did what was asked of them, though, Spruance had never interfered with their command chain or conducted himself with anything but the most proper of courtesies. Lonesome Jones had only kind thoughts and soft words for him, and that said a lot.

Kolhammer checked his watch. It would be another five

minutes before the Eighty-second's commander arrived. "Any word on when the Sovs will arrive in Washington?"

"No," Spruance answered. "Three or four days at a guess. But you can bet that when they do get there, they'll have an army of liaison officers wanting to swarm all over King and 'coordinate' with our efforts out here."

"Anything to keep us out of the Home Islands," Kolhammer said.

Spruance grunted. He was lost in his thoughts, but the commander of the *Clinton*'s battle group had a good idea of what he was thinking about.

When will we get the bomb?

16

D-DAY + 31. 3 JUNE 1944. 0711 HOURS.
LOS ANGELES.

There had been well over three hundred people at cocktails last night, and dawn found a few of them still lying around on the artificial beach on top of Slim Jim's building. The original owner, a haberdasher who'd gone out of business by refusing to run up any twenty-first designs, had shipped in a couple of tons of sand from Europe and poured it onto the roof around the swimming pool. Slim Jim couldn't understand the guy at all. If he was willing to buy in truckloads of fancy store-bought European sand when there was plenty of free stuff up the road at Santa Monica, why not crib a few pairs of pants from some unborn Euro-queer like Armani? Most of Slim Jim's suits were Armani rip-offs. In fact, if he remembered right, he even owned a chunk of some fashion house back in New York that specialized in re-creating clothes from uptime magazines. Or maybe not. It was hard keeping track of everything he owned nowadays. And anyway he had legions of accountants and lawyers to do that for him, freeing him up for the important business of rooftop beach parties with Hollywood starlets and a select circle of beer buddies.

At that very moment one of his best suds-buds, old Artie Snider, was facedown in the crotch of some B-list starlet from Sammy Goldwyn's stable. He wasn't doing nothing, of course. That'd be a bit fucking déclassé, as Ms. O'Brien woulda put it. Artie had just passed out sometime before sunup and, unable to shift his considerable bulk, the blonde had fallen asleep beneath him. Slim Jim smirked at the twists of fate that spun out of the Transition. He was willing to bet a million bucks that when Snider had his leg shot out from under him by the Japs down in Australia, the big dumb bastard had no idea he'd land flat on his face in some bimbo's twat at a penthouse party in LA.

Slim Jim wrapped a soft, white cotton bathrobe around himself and tried to haul his ass skyward out of the lounger in which he'd crashed. The morning sun had climbed over the highest floors of the unfinished skyscraper across the street, burning through his eyelids to wake him up a few minutes ago. It was now hot enough to give him a bad sunburn if he didn't watch out. He was working on his tan, but it was taking awhile. He had the kind of sallow, moley skin that didn't brown easily. Prison pallor, they called it. Once upon a time anyway. He found people generally fell over themselves to be nice to him these days. Except for those Rockefeller pricks, of course.

Fuck I need a beer.

His head swam unpleasantly as he gained his feet and looked around, taking inventory. Looked like about a dozen girls had stayed over. And maybe half that many fellas. Apart from Artie, he could see a couple of sailors crashed on blow-up mattresses, which bumped against the floating bar like giant bath toys. He didn't really know them, but he always made sure to invite some guys from the forces to his parties. At first Ms. O'Brien had insisted on it as a sort of public relations exercise, but Slim Jim found he got on a lot easier with them than the business types he was forced to mix with anyway. That's how he'd met Snider, at some Kennedy gig or something for crippled war heroes back in New York last year. Old Artie was the very picture of respectability when he was out on government business, but Slim Jim had found him to be a hellcat of a drinker and a skirt chaser, gimpy leg and all, when the pressmen weren't looking. He was a good guy to have around. Sort of reminded him of the old days.

"A pot of coffee, Mr. Davidson?"

"Huh? Oh yeah. Thanks, Albert."

He tried to blink away some of the crust from his eyes, but his butler steadfastly refused to come into focus. Albert was another good guy to have around, but in a completely different way from Artie. Albert, an honest-to-goddamn English butler, was an absolute fucking marvel at turning up exactly when he was needed. Like now, with a pot of strong black coffee and a toasted cheese sandwich.

"Breakfast of champions, big Al. Thanks, buddy."

The tall, gray-haired servant bowed his head slightly. "Of course, sir. Your bath is drawn and your clothes have been set out for the day. A printed schedule is on your desk in your private quarters. Shall I see to the other guests?"

Slim Jim couldn't help sniggering. The "gentleman's gentleman" managed to flick just enough of a spin on the word *guests* to imply they were anything but.

"Get old Artie into bed, if you can, Al. And his girlfriend. You can bundle the rest downstairs to the café for breakfast and then pour 'em into cabs. Put it all on my tab."

"Very good, sir. And Mr. Kennedy's man would like a word with you, too, when you have a moment."

"He still here?" asked Slim Jim. "I didn't take him for such a live wire."

"He has been away and returned, sir. He is waiting for you downstairs in the main conference room."

Slim Jim shook his head. It seemed his whole fucking life was like this now, a never-ending series of meetings with no chance of escape. He rubbed the blurriness from his vision and took a long draw on the mug of coffee that Albert had poured for him. It'd taken a hell of a lot of work convincing the old geezer to let him drink out of a mug instead of some bone china cup-and-saucer arrangement. He'd hoped that maybe he could get in a few hairs of the dog this morning before heading upstate for a surfing lesson. He was really getting into surfing. But he could see that the giant machine known as Slim Jim Enterprises was going to gobble up his entire day all over again.

"Okay, Albert. Did you get . . . uh, what's his name, this Kennedy guy?"

"Mr. Doyle, sir."

"Did you get him some coffee and a roll or something? Can't leave him scratching his ass, I suppose."

"Chef has sent up a tray of fresh pastries and a pot of coffee, sir. Mr. Doyle understands you have been *indisposed*. He is happy to wait."

Slim Jim brayed out a short, sharp laugh. "I'll bet. Okay. Gimme ten, fifteen minutes and I'll be down."

"Very good, sir."

"And don't worry about Snider, I'll see to him myself."

"Yes, sir."

As his butler disappeared inside, looking like some windup figure on a cuckoo clock, Slim Jim drained his coffee and ambled over to the prone form of Artie Snider. He was in uniform, sort of. His pants were down around his ankles, and his shirt had ridden up to expose a growing paunch. A couple of the bimbos were stirring on the far side of the pool. One of them waved lazily and he waved back, smiling as best he could with his hangover. It never hurt to be friendly, even with the little guys. *Especially* with the little guys, in fact. Ms. O'Brien had taught him that, too. The little guys were fighting this war, she always said. They were gonna win it, too. And the world would be theirs. And his, if he kept 'em on his side.

Music suddenly came on, blaring from hidden speakers. Loud enough to wake the hard-core hangers-on. No doubt on Albert's order. Some dumbass uptime song called "Wake Me Up Before You Go-Go." The butler's idea of a joke.

"Hey, Artie," said Slim Jim, toeing his friend on the side of the head, getting a nice feel of the unconscious blonde's thigh while he was at it. "Get up, man. I gotta go, and those war bond assholes are gonna be looking for you soon."

Snider grunted and nuzzled deeper into the starlet's crotch. He didn't look like he was going anywhere quickly. Slim Jim shrugged, walked over to the pool, scooped up a mug of cold water, and returned to pour it all over them. The effect was instantaneous. Snider came awake with a roar, and his companion with a squeal.

"What the fuck?" he cried out, shaking his head like a wet dog.

"Gotta get a move on, buddy. Time's a-wasting. You can crash here if you want, but you got that gig up in Frisco later this morning. You're gonna catch hell if you blow 'em off again."

"Yeah, right," the big man grunted. "Frisco . . . right."

He had some trouble getting to his feet. His knee reconstruction, which wouldn't have even been possible without twenty-first technology and know-how, still wasn't perfect. Slim Jim gave him a helping hand. The reek of sour alcohol on his breath was something to behold.

"You too, darlin'," he said, gently digging his foot into the girl's behind as she rolled over. It was an outstanding behind, after all, and just sitting there, begging to be interfered with. Her bikini top, one of the new teensy-weensy ones, fell off as she got up and she giggled unself-consciously, giving Slim Jim an eyeful and an unspoken invitation.

Dames, he thought. *They never fucking change, no matter what part of town they're from.*

Artie was too far under the weather to notice, and probably wouldn't have cared anyway. They'd shared plenty of women before.

"We ain't gonna surf today, Jimbo?" he asked. "I thought we was gonna have a lesson up the coast? The water's good for me leg, you know."

"We were," shrugged Slim Jim. "But I got this Kennedy asshole downstairs wants a piece of me first. And you got your gig in Frisco. I'll have my guys fly you there and back. You shoulda been there already. We can party tonight."

"Me, too?" asked the girl. *What was her fucking name?*

"Sure, darlin'," said Slim Jim. "Bring some friends. We'll rip it up."

The music had woken everyone by now. Slim Jim could have sworn it was getting louder. It was surely getting more uncomfortable on the "beach" as the sun climbed higher. One of the sailors rolled off his inflatable mattress with a splash and a holler. That awful fucking pop song finished and a new track came on. Crunching guitars and gravel-voiced singer. He recognized it immediately as the Foo Fighters' last single, "Innocence," one of his faves. His flexipad was programmed to wake him with it every morning.

"What is that *noise*?" asked the bimbo.

"That is the unborn genius of Dave Grohl, sweetheart," he informed her. "Have some fucking respect."

"So you figured out which one you're putting into the White House yet?" he joked. "Or is old Joe planning to give all of his boys a turn?"

The Kennedy clan fixer, Mike Doyle, didn't bother to hide his aversion. He didn't like dealing with Slim Jim, and they both knew it. Mrs. Davidson's little boy had spent a good deal of his former life getting the shit kicked out of him one way or another by the likes of Doyle. The guy screamed *ex-cop,* and even though he was now taking his coin from an old bootlegger, it must have galled him something awful to have to deal with somebody like Slim Jim as an equal—or even, let's face it, as a superior. Because in the end, Doyle was just a spear-carrier.

He rolled his shoulders around inside an off-the-rack suit. It was an older contemporary cut, unlike Slim Jim's stylish uptime number, and it pulled tight in all the wrong places as he leaned forward.

"Mr. Kennedy understood that he had a deal with you for your support in this matter, whenever he asked for it. You said you'd back his choice for the primaries with money and votes. What, are you backing out or something? You got your own plans, is that it?"

Slim Jim enjoyed the sensation of being able to say nothing for so long, it became uncomfortable. He enjoyed the view out of his picture windows, the expensive fit-out of the conference room, the acres of polished oak table in front of him.

"Nah," he said at last. "I don't have my own plans. I gave Joe my word, and that's as good as ink on paper. Better, in fact. I got a lawyer who's an absolute fucking wonder at blowing holes in bits of paper. You tell him, when one of the boys is ready to run, I'll do whatever I can to help . . ."

He left the sentence hanging long enough for Doyle to understand more was coming. "But?" said the fixer.

"But," added Slim Jim, "I'm still waiting to hear from him about a little favor that I asked for back in Hyannisport."

"Uh-huh," said Doyle, warily. "And that'd be?"

"The Zone legislation," said Slim Jim. "The sunset clause. Your boss promised me he would help kill it in the House. You make sure he understands that I'm serious. I want that clause nixed. We got a good thing going out here and we don't need the apple cart tipped over by a bunch of know-nothing pinheads trying to wind the clock back. It'd be very bad for business."

Doyle sized him up as though he were still a small-time grifter trying to pass a rubber check.

"That it?" he asked.

"That's it," said Slim Jim.

"Okay then, I'll tell him. Can I get you later today, if he's got an answer?"

Slim Jim shook his head. "Nope," he said. "I'm going for a surf with a buddy. You can call Maria O'Brien and tell her."

17

D-DAY + 32. 4 JUNE 1944. 0852 HOURS.
BERLIN.

He might have expected more panic. The fact that most Berliners appeared to be going about their business may have spoken to something commendable in the German spirit.

On the other hand, Ambassador Oshima thought it more likely that they simply didn't know what had happened. Propaganda Minister Göbbels kept a very tight rein.

All that Oshima had *publicly* read or heard about the fighting in the east was that a poorly coordinated sneak attack on a Wehrmacht regiment at the edge of the Demilitarized Zone had been repulsed, with heavy enemy casualties. Some German newspapers were even speculating that the Ukrainian nationalists might be responsible. There were at least three feuding militias in the Ukraine, and they all had clashed with both Communist and German forces in the last year.

But Oshima knew better.

The Reich's ruling elite was still stunned by the blow Stalin had delivered. They hadn't yet settled upon a response, so no compelling story had been invented to explain away this strategic reversal. As he motored down the Unter den Linden on his way to meet with Himmler, he could not rid himself of the images he had seen of the city of Berlin, ravaged by the Red Army.

He well remembered the Nanking Incident, and it took little effort to imagine the same sort of thing played out here, or at home, once the Bolshevik hordes had arrived at the gates. The ambassador maintained an outward façade of calm, but unless he had good news to send back to Tokyo, he feared what the next few months might bring.

The Red Army would pay a heavy toll for every inch of Japanese soil they defiled, but unlike the blissfully ignorant Berliners, he had seen the raw reports and even some video coverage of the new Eastern Front, and he harbored no misconceptions about the enemy they faced. The Communists had been busy, and most shockingly they had obviously gained access to Emergence technology. They seemed almost as well equipped as the Americans and British, and their armies were much larger. The only way they could be stopped was with an atomic bomb. He hoped Himmler might have word of a breakthrough on that score, because to date the Axis had enjoyed very little success in their atomic endeavors.

As the limousine pulled up at an intersection near the Brandenburg Gate, Oshima watched a couple of SS officers browbeating a fat civilian. It wasn't immediately apparent what crime he had committed, and of course it was entirely possible that the man was only guilty of attracting their attention in the first place. As much as *Reichsführer* Himmler had been a good ally to Imperial Japan, delivering on all of his promises to the letter, the sight of the two black-clad Nazis bullying the terrified Berliner reminded Oshima that his "allies" would just as soon treat him as the subhuman they thought him to be. And that if they did prevail against the Allies and the Communists, their very nature would lead them to seek dominion over the emperor's realm, as well.

A part of him had suspected Himmler of hiding progress on the atomic bomb because he wanted the weapon exclusively for the Reich. But now, with Germany caught between two formidable enemies, it seemed more likely that the *Reichsführer*'s protests and lamentations were genuine. If Hitler had possessed the superweapon, he surely would have used it on Zhukov and Konev. Instead, everything that Oshima heard about the Soviet front led him to believe that an epic disaster was in the making.

His driver apologized for the delay in getting to the Wilhelm-strasse for Oshima's meeting. The RAF had bombed the city the previous night for the first time in weeks, and the roads were still affected, even though the brunt of the raid had fallen a few miles away. A stray stick of bombs had landed on the transport hub of Potsdamer Platz, throwing the central traffic grid into chaos.

Oshima said nothing. He was a world away, in the old wooden streets of Tokyo, remembering his life before this madness. He doubted he would ever see home again.

That last time he had been aboveground for any length of time it was . . .

Well, in fact he couldn't remember. It had been so long, and events had taken such a twisted and evil course since then, that Himmler seemed to have spent most of his waking life shuffling from one dank, stale-smelling underground bunker to another. The touch of morning sun on his face in the brief seconds between climbing out of his Mercedes and hurrying into the nondescript building on a small street running off Wilhelmstrasse had been like a week at a spa in the Alps. If only he could have lingered in the sooty, high-walled courtyard at the back of the building where his car had pulled up. He might have stood there all day, soaking in the warmth and the sweet, soft light. But such an indulgence was not for him. History was bearing on his shoulders, threatening to crush him.

Those foul, creeping, two-faced pigs in Moscow were . . . were . . .

His brain locked up, unable to get past the impacted rage and violation.

This was not supposed to happen. They were supposed to be plowed under by the Aryan race, led by his glorious SS. Instead a horde—a veritable Mongol *horde* of the beasts—was tearing across the steppes, threatening to break into the German heartland and plunge Western civilization into a new dark age. The führer had been so overcome by his anger that he'd suffered some form of seizure and actually passed out in the bunker, stopping in mid-rant and smashing his head on the edge of the table as he collapsed. None of the trembling, whey-faced physicians had been able to revive him. He had simply remained there on the floor, his head resting on the balled-up jacket of a Luftwaffe officer, as grotesque spasms swept over his prostrate form.

Finally Himmler had been unable to stand it any longer, calling for an SS medic to attend. The man had arrived ten minutes later, and unlike the sniveling civilian doctors he had *acted*, getting the führer transferred to a cot in his private chambers and administering a sedative that noticeably calmed the tremors. He had re-dressed the ugly, swollen gash over Hitler's left eye and sternly warned everyone not to disturb him. He had then taken Himmler aside and, in a low worried tone, had explained that it was possible the führer had suffered a stroke and might well be impaired for some time. One arm was lifeless, and the whole right side of his face looked like that of a wax dummy exposed to an excess of heat. It . . . *drooped* was about the best word Himmler could come up with.

At that moment a terrifying loneliness had seized the *Reichsführer*. He felt like a child who loses sight of its parents in a crowd. What if the führer was gone? What if he had been poisoned, or succumbed to the enormous strain of the past month? No one else in the world had to deal with the sort of pressure to which he had been subjected. Nobody else could possibly have withstood the physical and psychic torment like Adolf Hitler.

But what if he was gone?

Himmler had returned to the map room, where a heavy pall still hung, and explained that long hours had caught up with the führer and he had simply passed out, in need of some rest. Yet his endurance was a beacon to all. The SS chief explained then that he would assume administrative responsibilities for the next few hours, until the führer awoke, and told the assembled staff officers that he wasn't going to meddle with their deliberations; they were to dispose of their forces as they saw fit to meet the challenges on both the Eastern and Western fronts.

Then he had excused himself.

Flanked by his bodyguards now, Himmler hastened up the narrow steps into the rear of the building for his meeting with Oshima. The Japanese envoy wasn't due for another half an hour, and it was more than likely that he would be delayed anyway. Once inside, he was confronted with a narrow hallway that

ended in a steel door, which was blocked by two more SS
guards who came rigidly to attention when they saw him. As
Himmler acknowledged their salutes, one of the guards spoke
into a telephone. The door, which resembled a watertight hatch
on a warship, clanked open and Himmler passed through. Bare
concrete stairs led downward on the other side. He descended,
holding tight to the steel handrail. The staircase was steep and
the steps were quite narrow. It would be easy to slip and break
his neck.

Behind him the three-story block presented the façade of a
well-maintained baroque apartment building. Formerly owned
by Jews, it had been converted to office space for use by the SS
after the *Kristallnacht* pogrom. The uniformed Allgemeine-SS
staffers in the aboveground offices were part of a unit charged
with disposing of the worldly goods of Jews such as the former
owners of this building, all of whom had gone into the ovens or
died in forced labor camps.

Deep below street level, however, a series of linked, reinforced-
steel chambers provided safe working space for Himmler when he
needed to be away from the bunkers where most of the activity
took place. While the Waffen-SS played a pivotal role in the war
effort, the greater SS was responsible for much, much more, and
regardless of the demands the armed conflict made upon him the
Reichsführer could not afford to ignore his other duties. He was
still the man responsible for attending to the Final Solution. The
foreign and domestic security and intelligence services reported directly to him. And along with Albert Speer, the armaments minister, he was charged with delivering to the Reich the
ultimate weapon—an atomic bomb.

Unfortunately, he was beginning to doubt that he could.

After an initial period of euphoria and accelerated progress
following the capture of the *Dessaix* and her informational systems, further successes had proved elusive. The Allies were
largely to blame. At times it seemed as if they had devoted entire armies to destroying every facility even remotely connected
with the project. And he had begun to acknowledge, with intense frustration, that he hadn't understood two years ago just
what a Herculean task he had taken on. This project consumed
resources on a scale he hadn't imagined possible.

For once the shelter did not reek of kerosene. They were
plugged into the city's power grid and it was running, despite

the RAF's best efforts. In contrast with the bunker he had just left, *this* one was clean, well lit, uncrowded, and calm. Blond secretaries and square-faced SS men saluted him as he passed through the antechamber into the first of the buried steel tanks. It was at least sixty meters long and twenty across, an open space with dozens of small work pens separated by particle-board dividers. The pens grew larger as they progressed down the body of the tubular structure, until they terminated in two relatively spacious work areas in front of another watertight door. He marched down the room, nodding and smiling to his personal staff, calling a few favored individuals by their first names, stopping to chat briefly with a secretary called Helga who was beginning to show her pregnancy. Her husband had been involved in the doom-struck assault on Calais, and nothing had been heard from him since. Helga was a good German, and she was holding up bravely. Himmler told her he was proud of her forbearance, and said that she must soon rest up and save her strength for the birth. After that, if she wished, he could suggest a number of fine young SS men who were looking for wives.

He dismissed her tears of gratitude and carried on to his private rooms. He feared what would become of women like that if the Bolsheviks ever set foot inside Berlin. He was one of the few people in Germany who'd read anything of the city's fate in the other world. Some extracts from a book called *Armageddon* had been found on the *Dessaix* and translated from French. It made for harrowing reading.

Himmler asked one of the guards to see to a pot of herbal tea as his personal assistant, *Hauptsturmführer* Buhle, presented him with two sets of papers.

"The files have also been loaded onto your computer, *Reichsführer*," Buhle said. "They are the only files on the desktop."

"Thank you," said Himmler, who found the Windows file management system a diabolical confoundment. *And they accuse* me *of crimes against humanity,* he thought as he settled himself in at his desk. *Wilhelm Gates, you are a beast, and your family will pay.*

His tea arrived and he sipped the infusion as he read the latest report by Professor Bothe. The work of the Army Weapons Office was not going well. Bothe complained of shortages and disruptions caused by Allied attacks, and staffing problems that he rather boldly laid at the feet of the Gestapo, which had arrested so many of his best scientists, including Heisenberg, Hahn, and Diebner. The last of his gaseous uranium centrifuges had been destroyed by a British commando raid on the Tirana complex, and at any rate he was running short of the yellow cake supplied by Japan. He did not think it possible that a weapon would be ready within twelve months, let alone a week.

Under other circumstances, Himmler would have punished such insolence with a cold fury. But Professor Bothe was beyond his reach now. A few hours after he had dispatched his report, Bothe had been killed in a Soviet air attack.

There was little point in reading through the rest of the message. Much of it was couched in opaque jargon, and the crucial point was in the first paragraph anyway. There would be no bomb.

Himmler bit down on the sense of despair that was threatening to engulf him. He put the Bothe paper aside and picked up a briefing note from *Gruppenführer* Stangl on the renewed effort to root out fifth columnists, saboteurs, and traitors within the highest offices of the Reich. Normally he skimmed Stangl's briefings. There was rarely anything of note; an admiral here, a general there. But today his eyes bulged as he read the first name on the list.

General Paul Brasch.

Stangl wrote that the Gestapo had been covertly observing Brasch for six months, on suspicion that he had made contact with some enemy agents. One man in particular had been of interest to them, but had evaded capture on a number of occasions. He had been killed in Paris on May 8, just a few streets away from where Brasch had been dining with *Oberstgruppenführer* Oberg. General Brasch had been observed loitering in the area afterward, and approached a number of Wehrmacht personnel who survived a blast they presumed had been triggered by the unnamed spy. He showed great interest in the details of the incident in which the man and many others had perished.

Thus it was decided to pick him up for routine questioning, but when he was approached by two Gestapo men, Brasch had killed one and crippled the other. He was now on the run, somewhere in Paris.

Brasch! Of all people. Could this day get any worse? Brasch

had been intimately involved in some of the most critical research-and-development programs that had grown out of the Emergence. Indeed, he was there from the very first moments, having been sent to Japan on what was first assumed to be a wild goose chase. He had been vetted and vetted again by the SS. His family had been killed in a British bombing raid. The führer had personally decorated him!

It could not be.

As he held the sheaf of paper with a bloodless, shaking hand, however, the *Reichsführer-SS* began to see the outlines of a conspiracy. Brasch's dead son had been T4, a deformed child who would have been put down were it not for his father's prominence. Brasch had enjoyed unrestricted access to the *Sutanto*'s files in Hashirajima and presumably could have learned of the T4 program. But then again, these suspicions had all been voiced early on, and Brasch had been attended for weeks by both covert and overt SS minders. They had never seen any evidence to suggest that he was anything but a patriot.

Himmler pulled out a pad of paper. He began to jot down notes furiously, instructing Stangl to continue the search for Brasch, even if it meant leaving agents behind in Paris to look for him after the city fell to the Allies. Then he scratched out "after" and wrote "*should* the city fall to the Allies." It would not do to be seen as a defeatist.

He further instructed the Gestapo chief to cross-reference with Brasch's work history all major incidents of unexplained sabotage, equipment failure, or even apparent Allied intelligence successes—such as the counterambush of the Luftwaffe raid on Patton's Third Army. His writing grew spiky as his heart beat faster. In a way he hoped this was a misunderstanding. A coincidence. Because if Brasch had sold them out, they were in even worse trouble than he'd thought. The Allies would know details of some of the most sensitive weapons programs in the Third Reich.

They would even have inside information on the broad outlines of the German atomic program.

Oh, this was very, very bad.

18

The crackle and pop of gunfire was a constant across the city, like traffic noise or birdsong in happier times. As the sporadic clashes grew into one long battle, Brasch began to think the French might do themselves more harm in the Liberation than the Germans had done during the Occupation.

He twitched aside the stiff, sun-faded curtain and risked a peek outside. He was hiding, for the moment, in a hotel off the Rue Houdon, although to call it a hotel invested the establishment with more dignity than it really deserved. It was the sort of flophouse where tight-fisted Austrian noncoms or *petit* bureaucrat collaborators might have rented a room by the hour, paying a few francs for a sagging, crusty mattress and an even saggier, crustier companion. The whores were still here, but the trade had dried up, so to speak. The Wehrmacht and the SS seemed to be in general retreat; all that remained were a few thousand of the hardier, dumber Frenchmen who had thrown in their lot with the fascists.

He watched a couple of them who were hiding at the end of the pinched, cobblestone alley that ran between Rue Houdon and the Villa de Guelma, beneath his window. A man and woman, both wearing German helmets but otherwise dressed in civilian clothes. Some sort of fascist militia, he supposed. They nervously checked their weapons and ammunition at a small sandbag barricade. They had just one rifle between them, an 1898 vintage Mauser, but had somehow managed to find a whole box of *Stielhandgranate,* long-handled grenades. The man was sitting on a chair he'd obviously stolen from a nearby café or strip club, his head resting in his hands, his body completely still. The woman, clothed incongruously in a thin cotton dress, odd socks, tennis shoes, and a black bucket helmet, seemed animated by all the energy that had left his body. She held the rifle, checking the load every few minutes, poking her head around the corner into the main street, whipping it back like a frightened deer, and spinning around nervously as though someone had just snuck up behind her. She would start to crouch, then stand bolt upright, back away from the sandbags, then shuffle toward them again. The only sign that her companion was still alive was an occasional shake of the head.

Brasch was sure they would both be dead by the end of the week, if not the day.

The cease-fire among the Resistance, the few functioning elements of the French state, and the German rear guard had frayed as the Allies pushed toward the city. Some fighting had flared as individual units of SS engineers had tried to set off demolition charges at selected sites around the city. The Louvre was a smoking ruin, its artworks looted before the building had been destroyed. Gone, too, the Arc de Triomphe. But attempts to bring down the Eiffel Tower and Notre Dame had failed when the engineers were attacked by an odd alliance of Communist guerrillas and paramilitary gendarmes. Most of the city's police force was on strike, probably working on their excuses for having cooperated so closely with the Germans, and the Communists were in a frenzy of excitement at word of the return of the Soviet Union to the fray. As Brasch had slipped through the city, just ahead of his pursuers, he had seen dozens of posters calling for a workers' uprising in solidarity with the approaching Red Army.

As far as he could tell, most Parisians were only too glad that the Americans and their own Free French forces would arrive long before the Reds.

The whores in the sitting room downstairs swapped rumors concerning the advance, some of them insisting that the Americans were already at the edge of the suburbs. But Brasch knew far more than they did. He could hear the percussion of artillery and heavy bombing in the distance. Probably around Chartres, an hour away. And he'd been able to access Fleetnet via his flexipad for most of the past twenty-four hours. Drones had taken up station above the city, probably in support of Special Forces already inside, some of whom were coming to extract him. He could follow the battle quite closely, and he knew for certain that the Free French First Armored under Leclerc was punching through the last line of defense, and should enter Paris within hours.

His problem was that he might not have hours left. Even though the occupying German troops were almost gone, he'd been chased across half the city by at least six separate squads of Gestapo. They must be desperate to capture him, he reasoned, because the tipping point was fast approaching when the Parisians' fear would give way to a savage hunger for revenge. It would be made all the worse by self-loathing as the French came to terms with the last two years. Time could not be reversed like a vid file. Many had not just served the interests of Nazi Germany but done so with great zeal, especially in the prosecution of the Reich's genocidal Final Solution. There would come a heavy reckoning for that.

"Monsieur Brasch. Monsieur!"

Brasch turned away from his vantage point. The room behind him was dark. The few hours a day of unreliable electricity the city had recently enjoyed were over. The lights had been out for two days now.

Madam Colbert stood in the doorway, her modesty protected only by a moth-eaten bathrobe.

"Do you think it will be long before your friends come?" she asked. "They *will* come won't they? It is just that . . . well . . ."

She trailed off, unable to speak the truth of it. She owed him. He had saved her daughter from rape at the hands of two drunken Wehrmacht men a month earlier. She didn't need to know that he had done so on purpose, to establish a connection with a suitable local and a safe house for the flight he'd always known was coming. As far as Colbert was concerned, he was simply a man on the run from the Boche who had done her a great service.

But he was still a German, and no matter that he needed to hide out while waiting to "defect"—a new word, much in use these days—he remained a German, and so his presence here might bring any number of evil consequences down upon her house.

"It shouldn't be long," he promised her, holding up his flexipad. "I have had word. They are very close. In the next *arrondissement,* in fact. Coming up the Boulevarde Haussman."

Madam Colbert worked the greasy belt of her old bathrobe into a huge Gordian knot. "It is just that I have word, too, monsieur. My lookouts, they tell me there are Germans coming. They are two streets away now. Gestapo. They *must* be looking for you. They are checking all the bordellos in Place Pigalle."

Damn.

Brasch checked the two collaborators again at the end of the alleyway. The man remained stock still, but the woman continued dancing around in her nervous fashion. He could have *sworn* she'd glanced up at his window, then turned her head quickly at the last moment.

He did not want to break cover. He had run out of bolt-holes, and he was *so* close to being safe.

But what good would it serve staying here, if the Gestapo arrived ahead of his extraction team? He could hold them off for a few minutes at best. How long did he have?

Not very long at all, to judge by the sick terror contorting the features of Madam Colbert. He had no faith in her ability to bluff it out. The Gestapo would see through her without even trying.

"You are sure they are Gestapo? Coming this way?" he asked.

"My little pigeons do not lie. They have been dodging the gendarmerie for years. They say it is certain, monsieur. Please. You must go."

Brasch checked the widow again. The woman in the helmet was staring straight at him now, smiling wolfishly.

That sealed it.

He brought his flexipad awake and opened a file stored on the desktop. An encrypted signal pulsed out of the handset, up through the roof, and away into the summer sky. At ten thousand meters it painted the smart-skin arrays of a Big Eye drone on station above the French capital. The drone's Restricted Intelligence recognized the distress beacon from a high-value asset, consulted its daily protocol, and discovered an extraction team five kilometers from the asset, headed in its direction. It alerted both the team and the Combat Intelligence back on its home vessel, HMS *Trident*.

"What is that?" Colbert asked, back in the cramped, musty bedroom.

"A cry for help," Brasch said as he fetched his Luger and checked the load.

"But what shall we do? They will kill us, torture us," Colbert protested.

Brasch took a fat envelope from within his jacket and tossed it across to her. "American dollars," he said. "Close enough to four thousand. I would get your girls out of here, and be quick about it." He paused. "I cannot go any farther. I have to wait here. Go. Quickly."

Confusion, fear, and greed all played across the woman's face. Greed and self-preservation won out. She nodded.

"Thank you, monsieur, and thank you for saving my little Michelle. You are a good German."

Brasch shook his head. "Please don't call me that. Now go, quickly, before it is too late."

Colbert fled, calling out to her girls as she thundered down the hallway. Brasch pushed aside the window curtain again, using the muzzle of his sidearm. The woman was clearly anxious that he not get away. He thought about shooting her but decided against it. It would only speed things up, and he needed all the time—and ammunition—he could get. Downstairs he could hear the squeals and cries of the whores as they exited. He probably had less than five minutes.

It was probably too late.

D-DAY + 33. 5 JUNE 1944. 1351 HOURS.
HMS *TRIDENT*, BAY OF BISCAY.

The radar confirmed reports of a storm system building in the mid-Atlantic. History told them that one of the great storms of the decade was due to touch down on this side of the ocean in a few days, but then history had been an increasingly erratic guide of late, and Captain Karen Halabi didn't fancy hanging around in the comparatively shallow Bay of Biscay with a force-nine gale bearing down on her. It'd be hellish enough in the CI-controlled trimaran, but she feared for the lives of the men—they were all men—on the ships of her escorting force. Some of them would founder for sure.

"Keep me informed, Ms. Novak, and make sure your bulletins go out to group and back to London on Fleetnet. Everyone will want to know what's happening."

"Everybody talks about the weather . . . ," mugged her chief forecaster.

". . . but nobody ever does anything about it," Halabi finished. "Even so, Lieutenant, stay alert. Some of our escorts would roll in a duck pond."

Halabi turned to leave the small office devoted to the ship's Meteorology Division, taking one last look at the radar. On the screen a deep red low-pressure cell was unquestionably forming. She could almost feel the ship beginning to move on the swell in response.

The commander of the *Trident* continued her tour of the decks, stopping in at the air division, the sick bay, and the ops room one after the other. In the latter she found herself among more 'temps than she'd be likely to find anywhere outside the Combat Information Center, where they tended to be observers anyway. In operations, the 'temps ran the show.

An ensign called the room to attention as she entered. The men—again, they were all men—snapped to with commendable promptness, and she bade them to carry on with their work. It was a different matter on shore, but after two years she'd at least established her right to command on this vessel, if no other.

"How goes it, Mr. McTeale?" she asked. Halabi made sure at least one of her senior officers was always on hand in ops, and today she found her XO, the dour Scot, in attendance.

"She goes well, Cap'n," he answered. "Or as well as could be expected."

The others seemed grateful that she'd released them back to their screens and printouts. They were never going to be very comfortable in her presence. She had been to high tea at both Downing Street and the palace, but she'd never once been invited to anything other than briefings and conferences at the Admiralty or any of the clubs favored by the contemporary Royal Navy's ruling elite.

Strangely enough, she frequently got on best with the army's old India hands, especially those who'd had anything to do with the subcontinent's innumerable "princely states," where local potentates ruled on behalf of the British Crown. The Raj veterans seemed to regard her as something akin to a minor warrior princess of some tiny Muslim principality on the Northwest Frontier. At least this meant that they treated her with some civility.

"What do we have on the Soviet advance?" she asked McTeale.

He threw the question to Colonel Charles Hart, one of her favorite Indiamen.

"It's looking rather grim for Jerry, I'd say," Hart explained. "Ivan's got the better part of a Wehrmacht army group trapped in a pocket outside Lodz. The Bolsheviks have detailed off a corps to maintain a siege there, and pressed on through Poland. They're finally hitting stiffer resistance now that they're at the borderlands, but there's just so many of the buggers that the weight of numbers and firepower must tell in the end."

"Thank you, Charlie," she said, her use of the informal noted by a couple of the less approachable 'temps. "How's it affecting German dispositions on the Western Front?"

Before he could answer, her intelligence chief—Lieutenant Commander Howard—appeared at the hatch. "Excuse me, skipper, but best you come see this."

Halabi excused herself with some relief. Visits to the ops room were always a trial.

"What's up?"

"It's one of the HVAs we've been tracking for Baker Street, ma'am. Due for extraction today, but he's got a problem. He's hit the panic button, sent a message saying he's going to get grabbed up by the villains if we don't hurry. I think we might need to reassign some additional drone cover to his sector."

Halabi picked up her pace as they marched down the main passage of the trimaran's portside hull, heading for the Intel Division.

"Is he a skinjob?" she asked.

"No, ma'am. His skin was killed a short while ago. It seems to have ruptured his cover. No, this is an indigenous asset. His jacket says he was supposed to remain in place, but he's been tumbled. We have independent verification of that by sigint. There are eight SS and Gestapo teams that we can confirm looking for him right now. One of them is closing in."

"Eight?" she said. "My word, they *do* want him back. Do we know who he is?"

"Not yet, ma'am. You'll have to authorize opening the jacket and reassigning the drone cover. There's a lot of demand for Big Eye time in France right now."

"Very well, let's have at it, then. Who's our liaison with the 'temps?"

"Nobody on board, ma'am. We're laser-linked back to Baker Street. Ms. Atkins is waiting for you."

"Very good then."

And it was. She got on well with Atkins, another child of two cultures and a woman working at the heart of what was often considered to be a man's world. The intelligence officer for the French section of the Special Operations Executive, she was also assistant to the SOE's chief, Maurice Buckmaster. Halabi swung into the cramped office that served as Lieutenant Commander Howard's domain. Three monitors were live, but two had dimmed their screens, leaving the one on the far left—a video feed—as the primary display.

Halabi smiled when she saw Atkins in the window. "Hello, Vera. A spot of bother, I understand?"

The SOE staffer looked very worried. On every occasion that Halabi had dealt with her, she'd presented herself as a model of Continental refinement and poise. Born in Romania, she'd moved to England with her family in the early 1930s, but returned to the Continent to study languages at the Sorbonne. Her frequently severe demeanor could be softened by a deceptively innocent smile, and she rarely appeared with a hair out of place. This morning, however, she was showing the strain of a night's sleeplessness. Dark half-moons had risen under her eyes.

"Captain Halabi," she said, nodding from the screen. "One of my sources needs immediate protection and extraction. He has lost his controller." Halabi had never known her to use the term *skinjob,* which was considered slightly obscene by the 'temps. "There is an exfiltration team heading toward his location now, but they need more drone coverage. I am requesting authorization and a sysop to control the operation."

Halabi didn't bother nitpicking the details. She trusted Atkins. "Consider it done."

The captain nodded at Howard to begin the process.

"As this is a terminal run, I will need to open his jacket, Miss Atkins. Do you concur?"

"I concur," she answered.

A black file icon turned white on the screen and opened into a separate window. The man staring out at Halabi was a stranger.

"Who is he?"

"Major General Paul Brasch," Atkins said. "Second in charge at the Reich Ministry of Advanced Armaments Research. He is one of our crown jewels, Captain. We need him alive."

D-DAY + 33. 5 JUNE 1944. 1417 HOURS.
PLACE PIGALLE, PARIS.

There was a good chance, thought Harry, that Ronsard might blow the whole thing. Not by taking a potshot at some lingering German outside a requisitioned hotel, but by unloading on one of his own compatriots, most of whom seemed to regard their former overlords with little actual malice. Instead a detached irony defined the Parisian response to the end of the Occupation.

For Harry, this was nothing new. He'd seen more than his fair share of captive cities as they changed hands, and knew that it often took a couple of days for the realization of their freedom to sink in. A certain degree of circumspection was generally prudent.

But as they jogged up the Rue de Clichy, dressed in tatty civilian clothes, past the red windmill of the Moulin Rouge, Ronsard kept up a stream of Gallic profanity aimed at his feckless compatriots for their less-than-delighted response to the end of Nazi rule. They'd been in the city less than twenty-four hours, moving from one safe house to another, waiting for the call from London, and the experience had worn on the Frenchman.

Anjela Claudel was much more sanguine, but then, unlike Ronsard, she had spent most of the past two years in-country and understood the compromises inherent to her own survival. Ronsard had left for England from Dunkirk, and had been there ever since.

"Steady on," Harry cautioned as his companion began to curse at the sight of a local man bartering with a Wehrmacht officer for a sack of what looked like potatoes. They were standing on the steps in front of a small hotel, and at least half a dozen other men and women were languidly watching the exchange. Harry wondered what the Frenchman could possibly have that the German would want at this particular juncture, but human nature was a strange, protean thing; it was entirely possible the man was risking his life for a last-minute splurge on pornography or black-market cigars.

A *Kübelwagen* was idling at the side of the road and obviously intended to make a quick getaway, but the last major convoy had left the city long ago and Harry didn't fancy his chances. Perhaps he'd been ordered by some general—or even a *Reichsmarshall*—to secure whatever it was he was bargaining for.

Harry placed a firm guiding hand in the small of Ronsard's back and gave him a gentle push to keep him hurrying along. A dedicated link to the Big Eye had opened up, feeding threat data and nav aids into the powered sunglasses he was sporting, a pair of retro Ray-Bans that wouldn't look too much out of place. This part of Paris wasn't much different from his own day, and he needed little help in finding his way to the target, but even a few seconds' delay for a wrong turn might mean failure, and London had emphasized in the strongest terms that failure was not an option today. The fact that he and Ronsard had been pulled off the transport for Scotland, and sent into the city without notice or preparation, evidenced not just the urgency of their mission but its unforeseen nature, as well.

There were six of them in the ad hoc extraction team. Harry, Ronsard, Claudel, and three Resistance fighters—a woman called Veronique and two men, Alain and Pietr, whose names he kept confusing. They weren't sprinting down Clichy with their guns drawn. Even now that would attract too much attention. But they were moving at a fast clip, almost running in fact, and while the locals were lightly armed with pistols and a few Mills bombs, Harry and Ronsard were packing Metal Storm VLe 24 handguns and two dozen strips each of ultralight caseless ceramic, close to 860 rounds.

Harry didn't turn off the nav aids that filled so much of his visual field with transparent arrowheads, flashing circles, and red squares. The Resistance crew invariably led him where he was supposed to be, and on the one or two occasions that they hadn't it was only to take a shortcut that the *Trident*'s human sysop and Combat Intelligence were unaware of. As they passed the intersection with the Cité du Midi, a narrow dead-end street lined with much smaller, two- and three-story buildings that seemed to lean over the cobbled roadway, at least eight or nine women burst from the next street along. Dressed for the boudoir, they flew down the Rue de Clichy with their robes and ribbons streaming behind them.

A voice spoke into his earpiece. "*Trident* here, Colonel. Those women just ran out of the target building. Hostiles approaching from the Rue d'Orsel. Estimate two minutes until contact with asset."

"Acknowledged," Harry said, a vibe wire in the frame of his powered glasses picking up his speech and converting it to a quantum signal for relay back to the stealth destroyer. "Right," he said in a much louder voice to the others, "let's go kick some fucking arse."

Still jogging along, they all hauled out weapons and began to run harder.

Harry could hear the first gunshots ahead.

His first shot took the woman in the neck. As the Gestapo approached she'd briefly disappeared around the corner, and when she came back Brasch took it as a sign that the game was on. He aimed at the center of her chest but shot high. He was never that good a marksman. The collaborator spun into the wall as blood sprayed from a severed artery.

Brasch then put two rounds into the broad back of her cohort, who moved for the first time in an hour as the pistol barked. Brasch heard two dull thuds under the Luger's report, then the metal clang of the woman's helmet striking the brick wall. Kinetic energy drove the man into the sandbag revetment, collapsing it into the Rue Houdon. The engineer wondered if he had time to dash down and retrieve a couple of the potato mashers. Those grenades would turn the alleyway into a killing jar.

Then he remembered that he could check. He had access to Fleetnet. He needed only to make the request, and the sysop on the *Trident* would send him a live video feed from the drone above. In response to his signal, they'd told him they had the area under constant surveillance now.

Just as he was about to call the ship, a British voice spoke from his flexipad. "*Trident* here, Herr General. Remain where you are. Hostiles are fifty meters away and closing quickly. Extraction team is two hundred meters to the southwest. Do you copy?"

"Acknowledged."

Brasch moved away from the window frame and into the hallway.

The small screen on his handheld device reformatted with a

top-down view of the streets immediately outside. He could see nine black-clad figures moving quickly; then they stopped momentarily on the Rue Houdon before pressing on with even greater urgency, running toward his building, brandishing automatic weapons. Red triangles shadowed them on the display.

Around the corner he could see six individuals charging around the corner of Clichy and Guelma. A blue circle surrounded one. The leader, perhaps?

He could see that the Gestapo were going to beat them.

19

D-DAY + 33. 5 JUNE 1944. 1341 HOURS.
PLACE PIGALLE, PARIS.

Prince Harry enjoyed more than a passing familiarity with the Rue de Clichy.

In 2007 while at the Royal Military Academy, he'd spent a couple of days' leave in France for the Rugby World Cup. Between matches he and a couple of mates from "Alamein" company at Sandhurst would hit the bars around Montmartre. It was a last taste of freedom before joining the Household Cavalry and, later on, the Special Air Service.

Charging along the beautiful sun-dappled street was a little like running through a V3D memory stick. The war had spared Paris, for the most part, and this area of the old city was almost identical to what he had encountered in his day, architecturally at least. In 1944, of course, there was no sign of the Intifada. Poplar trees still threw their shade onto the narrow footpath, and the length of the street presented an unbroken wall of elegant nineteenth-century apartments and offices, most of them standing between five and six stories high.

Harry pounded down the sidewalk and barged through the scrum of panic-stricken prostitutes, one of them trying to grab at his arm as she cried out something about "Le Boche." The two Resistance men, Alain and Pietr, had pulled ahead of him and were approaching the corner. Ronsard was at his right. Claudel, his left. The other woman, Veronique, was a few feet ahead and carrying what looked like an enormous old Webley pistol in both hands. He had no idea where she'd kept the thing hidden. It looked like a bazooka against her small frame.

The few people on the street were hurrying to get out of their way. Even onlookers on the far side scurried into doorways or made for whatever cover they could find. Gunfire had been a constant and growing background noise throughout Paris for days, but the Place Pigalle had apparently been spared any overt violence until now.

Then a volley of small-arms fire broke out, cutting down Alain and Pietr as they swung into the alleyway. Pietr, a big man, a white Russian émigré, disappeared as momentum carried him forward and out of view, but Alain spun like a child's top and crashed to the ground, his light blue shirt pockmarked with bullet holes and discolored with spreading bloodstains. Harry stopped without thinking and turned, training the muzzle of his weapon back up the street. The German who'd been bartering outside the hotel was standing at the open door of the *Kübelwagen,* his arms full of heavy-looking white sacks. He was too far away for Harry to make out the expression on his face, but he assumed it was one of surprise. The SAS officer keyed up a three-round burst on the 24's selector and linked its laser designator to the targeting chip in his sunglasses.

The German seemed to leap toward him with dizzying swiftness as the Ray-Bans' nano-optics refocused. Now he could see the man's face as though it were just a few feet away. Three small red dots moved in tight, jumpy circles on his chest, just above the sacks. Harry squeezed the trigger and sent three ceramic bullets downrange. The 24 employed a multitube barrel arrangement, with three separate muzzles opening at the mouth of the gun. All three projectiles thus impacted at the same time. They were flechette rounds, engineered to penetrate the target mass and unfold themselves inside, like small tumbleweeds composed of razor wire.

Half of the man's upper torso disintegrated as the kinetic energy flipped him back into the open-topped car.

Harry spun back and ran toward the alleyway. A window

with a top-down view of the contested alley appeared in the lower quadrant of his visual field as the voice of the *Trident*'s sysop spoke in his earpiece.

"Nine hostiles confirmed, Colonel Windsor. Four have entered the building. Five remain outside to guard the exit."

Flashing red triangles marked the position of the Germans in the pop-up window. Two had hunkered down behind a sandbag barricade, in front of which lay a dead man and woman in civilian clothes. Another had taken up position inside a doorway to the building. The last two hugged the wall just around the dogleg corner of the alleyway. They were probably the ones who had killed the Resistance fighters.

Just in front of him Veronique sprinted across the mouth of the back street and pressed herself up against the corner of the building on the other side. A couple of bullets whistled past as she did so. Ronsard and Anjela held position at the corresponding corner on his side. They were all waiting on him, knowing that he could call on any number of views from the Big Eye drone humming far above.

Harry slipped off the Ray-Bans, passing them to Ronsard so he could have a quick look at the drone feed. The Frenchman, who'd trained with the system in Scotland even though he was never likely to have access to his own Combat Optics, nodded and took a look. Then he handed them off to Claudel, who seemed to take a few moments to understand what she was looking at, but she quickly worked it out.

Harry used the brief interlude to remove a strip of ammunition from his handgun, replacing it with another from the breast pocket of the rather threadbare civilian jacket he was wearing. The regiment still had a reasonable supply of reloads for the 24s, having hoarded their own stocks and having benefited from the generosity of Captain Halabi, who'd turned over the contents of the *Trident*'s armory to them. He took the glasses back and fitted them again just as Veronique banged off a few rounds from her antique pistol to keep the Boche in their place.

A clatter of concentrated small-arms fire came from within the building, followed by a hollow boom that shook the whole place and dislodged a sprinkling of masonry dust. His earpiece crackled into life again.

"Major General Brasch requests *immediate* extraction, Colonel."

"All right, all right, tell him to keep his fucking pants on," Harry muttered, more to himself than to the operator back on the stealth destroyer. "Ronsard, give me a couple of seconds' covering fire, then pull right back," he ordered.

The Frenchman opened up, and the others followed suit, even though none had a clear shot: the flat hollow booms of Veronique's Webley; the thinner, much less substantial cap-fire of Claudel's little handgun; and the snarling bark of Ronsard letting rip the short full-auto bursts of another VLe 24.

Harry selected the barrel he'd just reloaded. As the French fighters pivoted away, he calmly stepped up to the corner, raised the weapon in a two-handed grip, and squeezed off half a strip of micronic grenades. They punched out with a slightly softer report than the penetrators he'd fired earlier, exiting the gun with a much lower muzzle velocity. Six of the electronically fired area-clearance rounds smacked into the brick wall at the far end of the alleyway, ricocheted off, and detonated in the middle of the passageway around the dogleg.

The high-explosive lozenges triggered with a roar that surprised the civilians. It sounded as though a barrage of mortar rounds had gone off. Glass shattered up and down the street. Thick clouds of dust came billowing out of the alleyway, and Harry took off again, leading them all in at a sprint. He and Ronsard fetched up at the corner first.

Disembodied limbs and torn, bloodied clothing littered the ground. Harry checked the top-down display in his Ray-Bans. Four of the red triangles had gone out. One was flashing, but he could see through the smoke that it tagged a man who was trying to crawl away, using only one arm. His legs and most of his other arm remained behind. Anjela Claudel put a single shot into the back of his head.

"Gestapo scum," she said. "He should have suffered, but . . ."

A Gallic shrug.

Harry pressed himself up against the wall, which was painted with a sticky organic gruel of flesh and blood. A machine pistol, probably a Schmeisser, started up inside, hammering away in short, irregular bursts. The popgun reply of a small pistol could barely be heard over it.

Harry pulled out his flexipad. "*Trident,* can you get a point-to-point linkup with Brasch?"

"Aye, Colonel. Just a moment. There. Channel three. Audio only."

Harry held up the flexipad like an old-style cell phone. "Brasch. Major General Brasch. Can you hear me? Can you respond? It's Colonel Windsor of the Special Air Service. We're here to extract you."

The German replied in clear, if accented English. He sounded remarkably calm. "Your Highness, a rare privilege. I can talk and shoot, but not well together. I am at the end of the hall on the third floor. I have killed at least two of them with a small directional mine. But two remain and I am outgunned."

"Can you see both?"

"No, just one. The other is probably watching his back. So you must be careful."

Now, there's a statement of the bleeding obvious, Harry thought.

The *Trident*'s sysop broke in on their channel. "Colonel Windsor, we have two other hostile teams closing on your location by foot. The nearest is on the Avenue de Villiers, an estimated ten minutes away. A second team has changed direction and is moving toward you along the Rue du Faubourg St.-Martin. They will arrive in approximately fifteen minutes."

Bugger.

Harry quickly explained the situation to his comrades as the gun battle continued inside.

"Veronique and I will slow down the fascists on de Villiers," Anjela Claudel said when he'd finished. "There is a café there, a favorite of the Communists. We will get help."

There was no arguing with them. The two women simply spun away and took off.

"Right," Harry said. "By the book then, Captain Ronsard."

The Frenchman nodded. Harry spoke into the flexipad again.

"Herr General? We're coming in. Move back from your door and take whatever cover you can."

On the count of three they burst into the building.

Brasch fired off all but two of the bullets left in his clip. He would save those for the Gestapo if they came through the door. Having already upended the heaviest piece of furniture in the room across the doorway—an old, hardwood freestanding closet—he leapt into the small stronghold he'd made in one corner using a small vanity, a cheap writing table, and a stained, poorly sprung mattress. As he dived through the air, his ears were assaulted by an incredible cacophony, ripping bursts of automatic gunfire—much louder and fiercer than the MP40s the secret policemen had been firing at him—splintering wood, and cracking bricks, duller percussive thuds and enormous, bowel-shaking explosions. It was like Belgorod all over again.

Before driving into the unknown building and up three flights of stairs, Harry and Ronsard stripped in penetrators and area clearance. The small entrance hall was a slaughterhouse.

Brasch had rigged up some sort of claymore-type mine and triggered it as the Gestapo had entered. The first two men had taken the full force of the blast and nearly disintegrated. Their remains were embedded in the pitted, ruined hallway walls. The two commandos came in hot, hosing down a narrow arc in front of them with short bursts of tungsten penetrators. Designed to slice through monobonded plate armor, but meeting only plaster, brickwork, and wooden floorboards, they passed through like very small, hyperaccelerated wrecking balls, chewing the old brothel to pieces.

Pounding footsteps on the next landing warned them of somebody's approach. Harry fired a full strip of penetrators into the ceiling, tracing a line along the axis of the corridor on the floor above them. He was rewarded with a strangled shriek, followed by a tremendous thump.

They took the stairs three at a time, their legs working like pistons. Ronsard made the next level first, firing a precautionary three-round burst to clear their way. He needn't have bothered. The German lay in a crumpled heap of black leather trench coat.

"Clearance," Harry called, and Ronsard ducked as the prince pumped two high-explosive rounds up through a gaping hole in the ceiling. Both men hunched over as the pellets triggered with a deafening clap of thunder. Half the ceiling seemed to collapse, and with it came the body of another German.

Hopefully not Brasch.

Harry trained his gun on the body as it crashed to the floor, landing atop a pile of fallen wreckage like a sack of concrete. It didn't move.

"Major General Brasch," he called out. "It's Colonel Windsor. I think we're clear."

He heard grunts and the scrape of something heavy being shifted on the floor above. After a moment the German appeared, peering down through the gaping hole. He was dressed in civilian clothes, but wearing a holster into which he slipped his Luger.

"Your Highness, I hope."

"And Captain Ronsard of the Free French Army," Harry said. "Can you get down, General? Best we don't stuff around too long here. Some more of your former comrades are keen to catch up with you."

In the small pop-up window, Harry could see a gunfight just starting over on the Avenue de Villiers. It looked like a very disorganized affair. Claudel had not had time to set up a proper ambush. She seemed to have found three men to help her, but they were outgunned by the Gestapo, or SS, or whatever they were. The prince's chivalrous nature urged him to tear over there and lend a hand, but a decade and a half of military training won through. The women had effectively offered to sacrifice themselves for the mission, and that meant getting Brasch safely away.

"Trident," he said into the flexipad as Ronsard helped the German clamber down through the ruined ceiling. "I need a route out of here right now."

"Already laid in, Colonel," the sysop replied. "Feeding nav data through now. You'll be heading south, toward the Champs-Elsyées. The second team of hostiles is still three blocks away, but they are moving quickly. Best you get a move on."

A large blue arrow appeared in the heads-up display, although it was a little premature since they were still inside. It pointed at a wall.

Brasch jumped the last, short distance and landed on the pile of plaster and shattered woodwork.

"Right then," Harry said. "Let's scarper."

D-DAY + 33. 5 JUNE 1944. 1454 HOURS.
BERLIN.

It would be time to leave this particular bunker soon. It wasn't wise to linger in any one place too long. The Allies' ability to peer deep into the Reich was almost preternatural, and the

Reichsführer-SS had no desire to be turned into "pink mist," as the Emergence types said.

He was waiting on a report from Paris, after which he would return to Bunker 13 for a few hours to check on the führer's progress before moving to another secure facility for the night. They had all been living like this for too long. It was demeaning, the way the Reich's ruling elite had been reduced to scuttling about like petty criminals. Himmler removed his glasses and used a clean handkerchief to wipe the lenses. There was something about the recycled air in this subterranean hideout that seemed to affect them. He forever had to polish the things if he wanted to see clearly.

Not that there was anything worth seeing, or reading, in the pile of documents covering his desk. It seemed apparent now that Major General Brasch had betrayed them. What a foul, bitter irony given the number of innocent men who'd no doubt died in the purges following the Emergence. Himmler did not regret having taken the sternest measures to root out defeatists and conspirators within their midst. So high were the stakes, it was better that ten innocent men die than one genuine traitor go free. And the men he had killed to correct the false record of his own last days in the other world—well, they, too, had died for the Fatherland.

Given the saboteurs and recidivists discovered all too late within the crew of the *Dessaix,* it was to be expected that the most abominable lies would have been planted about him. He would *never* have worked to undermine the führer. Why, the very idea of it! But of course, he had to remain above suspicion if he was to carry on his work.

A bitter, bitter paradox. Those researchers had done their job, and been punished for it.

Brasch, meanwhile, had sold out his birthright and had been rewarded with promotions, luxuries, and that most rare and precious of indulgences, trust. Himmler wasn't a man given to violent passions, but as he read the reports, he was entirely unable to still the tremors that stole over his whole body as he tried to contain his rage.

As second in command of the Ministry of Advanced Armaments Research and an active participant in its predecessor organizations, Brasch had enjoyed an intimate knowledge and understanding of the country's most important weapons programs   both their strengths and their weaknesses. Now those secrets had been lost to the Allies, and there would be no recovering, not with the Bolshevik horde now descending upon them from the east.

And not with the führer incapacitated as he was.

Yet another dolorous report came from the SS medical officers assigned to Hitler's case. They now theorized that he had suffered an apoplexy that might permanently cripple him. The news was being kept from everyone except Himmler, while he waited to see if the führer recovered, and planned for the possibility that he might not.

His assistant knocked quietly at the door. "It is here, *Herr Reichsführer*. The cryptographic section has just finished decoding the message."

Himmler took the folded piece of paper and dismissed the young officer. They'd had this transmission for three-quarters of an hour already, but because of the *Trident*'s code-breaking computers, all of the most important signals had to be sent using onetime pads. It significantly slowed down exactly those communications that most needed to be sent quickly.

His heart pounding, he unfolded the note and read the first line.

BRASCH HAS ESCAPED.

If it were possible, his hands shook even more violently. A spell of dizziness came over him, and he found it impossible to focus on the rest of the message. Not that it mattered. The details were unimportant. What mattered . . .

"Herr Reichsführer."

Himmler looked up, his head spinning.

His assistant was back, and he was ashen-faced. For a moment the SS leader expected him to announce that the führer had died. But he didn't.

His news was much worse.

20

The flight was entering its sixth hour when the message came through from Moscow. There was a few minutes' delay while the radio operator broke open the sealed envelope containing the one-use code pad and translated the orders.

Proceed to primary target.

A simple message, with the power to change the world.

Kapitän Semyon Gadalov eased the big jet bomber around on its new heading. A flick of the intercom switch, a brief series of orders, and the technicians began to arm the device down in the bomb bay. Suddenly Gadalov wasn't just flying an airplane, he was wielding the most terrible weapon ever invented.

The Carpathian Mountains crawled past to the south—an illusion caused by distance and altitude. They were traveling very quickly—more than a thousand kilometers per hour. It was astonishing, given that just two years ago Gadalov had been flying an Il-4 with about a third of the speed. No matter how many times he went up—and admittedly the Tupolev had only been cleared to fly three months ago—he never failed to be awed by the power of her Mikulin turbojets, the great span of her swept-back wings, or the feeling that he could fly forever. She was a precious jewel, one of only three such craft built so far. Exactly *how* precious was shown by the fighter escort she commanded. Two full squadrons of new MiG-15s had joined up with her just north of Kiev.

The crew were tense but professional. The four of them had trained every day for more than a year, working in mock-ups of the bomber before this one became available. Lieutenant Gologre, his navigator-bombardier, delivered a constant stream of position reports from the glassed-in nose cone. Smedlov, his copilot, obsessively checked the flight instruments, making sure nothing could short-circuit the mission at this stage. And Jerzy, the tail gunner, watched over the technicians as they prepared the bomb, providing a running commentary via the interphone that had been installed specifically for this moment.

At such an altitude it was impossible to make out anything but the most dramatic features of the landscape below. Somewhere down there, the Red Army had crushed one of the rebel Ukrainian militias, but at twelve thousand meters the countryside looked idyllic, a rich quilt of brown-green earth and golden fields unmarked by human folly or ferocity. Small lakes, ponds, and rivers caught the midafternoon sun, throwing starbursts of light out to the curve of the horizon.

It was an unusually beautiful prelude to what he understood would be a day of unmitigated horror.

D-DAY + 33. 5 JUNE 1944. 1633 HOURS. MOSCOW.

Beria, who was trying to keep his consumption of vodka and champagne within limits, could feel the malign energy gathering in the room, like a snake coiling itself for the strike.

Apart from the two diplomats, the twenty men present were all high-level party officials. Survivors, for the moment. The only military officers were messengers who came and went every half hour to mutter into Stalin's ear. In the far corner of the dining room, the British and American ambassadors were trying their best to maintain a dignified façade, turning down as many drinks as they could diplomatically refuse. They looked less than happy, and if Beria had been in a better mood he would have smiled at their discomfort, knowing that by the end of the day their long faces would be positively funereal.

His own face, however, wasn't really beaming, either. Despite the fact that decorum, or the lack of it, demanded that he play the role of toastmaster at these foul, drink-sodden debauches, he hated the fucking things. Despised them, in fact. Only Stalin, the drunken gangster, could truly enjoy himself. And in Beria's opinion the old monster was rapidly losing his grip on his health and sanity under the pressures of the war, the Emergence, and his own bestial appetites.

This party, for instance, had officially begun at lunchtime, when the first bottle of champagne had been uncorked. But all the party magnates, bar Stalin, had arrived still sick and exhausted from the *previous* day's binge. That one had begun, as always, in the early evening, when Stalin declared their business over for the day.

In truth, he did very little business in his office now. The empire was run from his dinner table and private cinema. That was even more galling for the NKVD chief. With the world less than a day away from an epoch-shattering change, the supreme leader of the USSR insisted that his closest advisers join him in his specially constructed theater for a "Tarantino marathon" followed by a "little bite"—which inevitably devolved into a terrible, vomit-flecked orgy lasting six hours or more.

Unfortunately the *Vozhd* had always been a great fan of the cinema, especially American gangster movies and westerns, and with the discovery of the *Vanguard* came access to her electronic library. After being carefully vetted by the NKVD, thousands of hours of movies and television had been released for Stalin's perusal. Almost none had been approved for public viewing, but that didn't mean that the chief himself couldn't watch them.

After all, who could say no to Stalin?

Certainly not Beria. There were any number of files on the *Vanguard* that had been too dangerous to release from NKVD control, including a number of books and articles about Beria himself that had made the secret policeman's head swim when he'd seen them. But they were mostly gone now, deleted along with the unfortunate men who'd found them. The months of nearly paralyzing terror he'd suffered, while covering up evidence of his own less-than-perfect sycophancy at the end of Stalin's life in the future, were but an unpleasant memory. Even so, he found himself subject to random fits of horror at the prospect that anyone might gain access to such information, despite his precautions. He had probably sent two and a half million people to their deaths or into exile based solely on the *Vanguard*'s archives.

Yet who knew what incriminating documents lay in wait in the files of the *Clinton* or the *Trident*? How long could it be before some capitalist spy would try to blackmail him?

One of Stalin's maids, a dumpy Georgian in a plain gray smock and white bib, cleared the plate of aragvi from in front of him. A personal creation of Stalin's, it was a thick stew of mutton, eggplant, tomatoes, potatoes, and black pepper, all of it drowned in a glutinous spicy sauce. Famine stalked the land, with so much of the state's productive capacity given over to crash programs developing new technologies—indeed, whole new industries—but in here there was no such discomfort to be found, judging from the bacchanalian feasts served at Stalin's dacha. When one stupidly valiant servant from the Ministry of Agriculture had written to Stalin about the number of peasant children who were dying of hunger, the man was arrested and shot, though not until he had been shown propaganda films resplendent with imagery of well-fed *kulaks* seated in front of tables groaning with fresh food.

The disturbing thing was, Stalin actually believed that the images were real. Beria knew that, as his body grew more bloated and ravaged by gluttony and alcoholism, the *Vozhd* was losing his mental capacities along with his physical. It was a conclusion he probably would have formed of his own volition, but also confirmed by the uncensored future histories and biographies contained within the British ship's electronic library.

Controlling such information gave him great power, but with it came the risk that Stalin would one day turn on him, deciding he had become a threat. The bowdlerized versions of history he served up were dangerous enough. He had almost wet his pants when he'd had to tell the full Politburo about the collapse of the USSR and its replacement by a gangster-capitalist state. There was no way in hell he was ever going to admit the existence of something like that biography they'd found on the ship—what was it called?—*Stalin: The Court of the Red Tsar*. Even having laid eyes on the cover was tantamount to a death sentence. He had personally burned every page in the book, but not until he'd read it three times, made coded notes of its contents, and then hidden them in a hundred different files, just in case he ever needed to call upon the information.

And now, through his intoxication—which was considerable—he watched the American diplomat Harriman sip at a glass of white wine while Molotov tried to brute him into downing the whole thing in one gulp. Beria knew he should really push himself up, stagger over, and play the bluff Georgian host, insisting that Harriman drink up and taking umbrage when he refused. But he was engorged with food and drink, and he worried that if he moved he would foul himself. Nobody was allowed to leave the table to go to the lavatory unless Stalin said so, and he hadn't called a break in more than two hours.

So instead Beria took another shot of pepper vodka, poured by Nestor Lakoba, the Abkhazian boss, and tried to throw it down manfully. His throat locked and he vomited prodigiously into his own lap, causing great mirth around him. Stalin, sitting at the head of the table as always, roared with laughter.

"You cannot be a true Georgian then, Beria," he snorted. "Look. Our foreign friends are in much better shape than you. Perhaps you are a spy, yes? A plant?"

It could have been a bad moment. Stalin's moods were so changeable, his rages so arbitrary, that such a joke could easily turn into something much more significant. But the NKVD chief was saved by another bout of racking cramps, and he tried to hurl yet more bile into his lap, causing Stalin to dissolve into fits of giggles.

"Here, wash your mouth out with this," he insisted, forcing a half-empty bottle of white wine on Beria. There was no question of demurring. He took the bottle and used it to rinse out the chunks of acid-tasting aragvi while Harriman and the British ambassador Clark-Kerr stared at him with unconcealed disgust.

Well, very soon now, he'd show them.

D-DAY + 33. 5 JUNE 1944. 1708 HOURS.
POLISH AIRSPACE.

Six fighters remained close to the Tupolev, guarding it like sheepdogs. Their comrades had moved ahead to clear the skies above Lodz of any German aircraft, but none had been found. The city's garrison was cut off, bypassed by the Red Army and hunkered down for a long siege. Gadalov knew that a number of divisions from the Far East had been detailed to bottle up the Germans inside, but he tried not to think about them. He'd been assured that the Soviet forces were far enough back from the city to survive the blast and its aftereffects. But he wasn't so sure. The precautions they were taking just in delivering the bomb spoke of something quite extraordinary.

He pulled back on the controls and fed power into the turbojets, taking them into a climb that would top out at the plane's operational ceiling of thirteen thousand meters. Once the bombardier gave the all-clear, the device would be released, but it would deploy three parachutes almost as soon as it fell away, slowing the rate of descent and allowing them to clear the area and record the blast on the banks of equipment back in the fuselage. Gadalov had never questioned any of these precautions during their long period of training. One did not question orders in the Red Army Air Force. But he could ponder their meaning as he lay in his bunk at night, and he had concluded that all of the rumors of a doomsday weapon were probably close to the truth.

The voice of his copilot Smedlov crackled into his earphones. "Ten thousand meters."

The little MiGs kept pace with them, climbing into the sky like silver arrows.

"Goggles," he ordered.

Smedlov fitted his protective eyewear and took the stick while Gadalov adjusted his own. Darkness fell over the bright afternoon world.

"Gologre, have you fitted your eyeglasses?" Smedlov asked.

"Da," came the terse reply.

The navigator-bombardier was obviously concentrating furiously.

"Come three degrees south," Gadalov said, and Smedlov eased the Tu-16 around just a bit as they continued to claw for altitude.

The angle of ascent meant that he'd lost sight of the city. Only Gologre down in the glass bubble could still see the target. It occurred to Gadalov that he would probably never see Lodz again. Gologre would be the last man on earth to see it before it was destroyed.

"Twelve thousand meters."

His arms ached from the strain of controlling the powerful aircraft. He had been grasping the cut-down steering wheel like some stupid peasant with his first motorized tractor, fearful that anything less than an iron grip would allow the monster to get away from him. He tried to relax but found that his heart would not stop pounding.

He forcefully pushed away any thoughts of the people he was about to kill. Originally they'd been briefed to attack an army in the field, but Moscow had changed those orders only a day ago. The intelligence officer who'd delivered the preflight briefing had told them that the fascists had withdrawn most of their troops into the city, and so it would need to be attacked directly.

Again, Gadalov did not question his orders.

But a distant voice whispered to him that he was about to kill thousands of innocent Poles, as well as their German occupiers. With a Herculean effort, he shut down the voice.

"Twelve thousand, five hundred meters."

He could feel the bomber straining for purchase in the thin atmosphere. Leveling off, he found that he could see the city after all, but it was much closer than he imagined.

"Open the bomb bay doors," he ordered.

Smedlov slowly wrenched back the levers, and at once they all felt the aerodynamics change as the great steel shutters groaned open down in the belly of the aircraft. It was a clear day, with the sun dropping gently toward the horizon. In peacetime it would have been quite pleasant down there in Lodz. Gadalov had an uncle who'd worked as a machinist in one of the textile mills before the Great War, and the old man still spoke fondly of the time he'd spent in Poland's second city. Wages were high compared with Russia, and a skilled workman could earn his keep with more than a little left over to spend in the taverns, some of them hundreds of years old, along Piotrkowska Street.

The antiflash goggles allowed Gadalov to view the city even though he was more or less staring into the sun. Apart from a few fires burning here and there, it seemed unremarkable, even quiet. Large swathes of green parkland broke up the gray urban cityscape.

"Coming up on target," Gologre announced.

He was employing the large octagonal marketplace in front of the town hall as his aiming point. Gadalov was wary as they approached, assuming that with such a concentration of German forces inside the city, there would be heavy flak. But apart from one brief line of tracer fire that came twisting up out of what looked like a factory district, there was nothing.

Probably saving ammunition for massed raids.

Gologre's voice crackled through his headset again. "Release point in ten, nine, eight . . ."

Gadalov concentrated furiously on maintaining a steady course. The fighter escorts had all fled by now, as they had practiced so many times. They were alone in the sky above Lodz, their destinies linked with so many thousands of lives below them for just a few more seconds.

". . . three, two, one . . ."

"Bomb released!"

As soon as he felt the tug of separation Gadalov hauled the giant aircraft around and opened the throttles, to put as much distance as possible between themselves and the doomed city. He waited, every muscle singing with tension, for the flash and the shock wave they'd been warned to expect.

Gologre watched as the first atomic bomb to be dropped on a city fell away from the dark womb of the Tupolev Tu-16.

After five seconds three enormous parachutes deployed and slowed its descent to a more measured pace. Lieutenant Gologre had used the latest bombsight to line up on the Lodz town hall, but a light breeze carried the egg-shaped, four-and-a-half-thousand-kilogram load slightly northward. He had been briefed on the effects of the device and knew only too well what he was about to unleash.

The device, modeled on the original Fat Man, was almost cartoonish in appearance, with a swollen body and oversized stabilizing fins. It was so very obviously a bomb that nobody would be foolish enough to stand staring at it as it descended, swinging gently beneath the triple canopy. A small web-cam in the nose sent pictures of the ground back to a mil-grade EMP-hardened flexipad on the Tupolev. Later, bomb damage analysts would be able to replay images of German troops and a handful of Polish civilians fleeing the gardens as the bomb dropped ever so slowly into their midst.

Code-named "Gori," it was an implosion device. In the center of the bulbous casing sat six and a half kilograms of delta-phase plutonium alloy. Some of this had come from the reactors on the British vessel *Vanguard,* but most had been bred in the Kamchatka *Sharashka.* Shaped into a nine-centimeter sphere with a small cavity at its center, the pit—as it was called—was actually composed of two hemispheric halves, separated by a thin golden gasket to prevent premature penetration by shock wave jets that might trigger the bomb's neutron initiator too early. While Beria's researchers had not been able to find blueprints for a bomb in the *Vanguard*'s archives, there was still a wealth of detail about the construction of early atomic weaponry, the sort of thing that the Soviet Union would have had to ferret out with a massive espionage program before the Emergence.

Nearly half of Gori's weight came from its trigger, a high-explosive casing that resembled a giant soccer ball nearly half a meter thick. The hexagonal pieces formed a lens around the plutonium that transformed a convex, expanding shock wave into a concave, converging one.

At six hundred meters off the ground, four radar antennae in Gori's nose determined that it had reached the optimum height for discharge. Bridge-wire detonators fired every panel of the "soccer ball" trigger simultaneously, producing such powerful inward pressure on the plutonium core that it was squeezed into a supercritical condition.

Three effects manifested themselves immediately: blast, heat, and radiation. There was also an electromagnetic pulse, but it had a negligible effect in the primitive environment. Such systems as might have been affected, like those on the Tupolev, had been hardened to withstand the effect.

In the first few milliseconds energy was released in the form of high-intensity X-rays. The steel egg vaporized, and the X-rays expanded into the air above the parkland. Unfortunately for every living organism within the city and its surroundings, the air was not "transparent" to the X-rays, and so their energy was unable to freely propagate. The atmosphere began to heat up, and a ball of expanding plasma formed. Milliseconds after the initial explosion, its temperature could be measured in millions of degrees.

A few milliseconds later, by the time the fireball had grown to about thirty meters in width, it had cooled considerably—to three hundred thousand degrees Celsius, or about fifty times the surface temperature of the sun.

At ground zero the soil boiled and exploded, vaporized, and added its mass to the expanding plasma. So, too, every atom of organic and inorganic matter in the small park. Trees, grass, iron benches, granite flagstones, human beings, birds, insects, everything: it all fueled the atomic furnace. Even a kilometer away, solid stone buildings liquefied as the thermal shock swept over them. Lodz was crowded, and sixty-five thousand souls were consumed by the superhot plasma sphere, but the true destructiveness of Gori was still to be unleashed. A gamma ray pulse and neutron bath added their lethal effects to the light and heat of the small sun that bloomed over the city.

The air surrounding the fireball was massively compressed, then pushed outward. Unlike even the largest chemical explosions, the nuclear blast created a very wide shock wave still thick enough to entirely surround the city's small buildings, crushing them from all sides. The medieval core of Lodz was entirely pulverized.

The impact of the shock wave hitting the ground was akin to the hammer of an old Norse god striking the earth. It set off a vibration that had the same effect as an earthquake as the energy waves spread outward. Near the blast center, with pressures at 200 psi, winds howled at up to two thousand kilometers an hour. These fell away with distance from the blast, but were still strong enough to demolish everything in their path out to ten kilometers.

At a certain point the structural integrity of some objects was such that they did not disintegrate, but rather became missiles, propelled through the air at great speed. Even small, seemingly insignificant objects became lethal at that velocity. But much larger items were also affected. A Tiger tank, for instance, stranded at the intersection of Landowa and Startowa streets for three days because of a lack of fuel, was suddenly on the move again, flying through the air at three hundred kilometers an hour.

Some of the missiles traveled faster than the blast wave, which lost energy as it sped away from ground zero. An SS colonel, standing on the steps of an apartment building on Dabroskiego Street, was killed when a helmet smashed into his head, popping it like a grape underfoot. The destruction did not discriminate. The innocent and the evil were burned, or crushed, or torn apart. Aryan supermen and residents of the Jewish ghetto all died, their ashes drawn up into the towering mushroom-shaped cloud that rose above the city.

D-DAY + 33. 5 JUNE 1944. 1849 HOURS. MOSCOW.

The messenger arrived as Stalin was playing with his much-loved old gramophone, insisting that Molotov and the "gloomy demon" Lev Mekhlis, the political chief of the Red Army, entertain the room with a dance. Beria suspected that the supreme leader had been drinking wine diluted with mineral water for the past few hours. He seemed to be in much better shape than anyone save for Harriman and Clark-Kerr. He scratched the gramophone needle on the old record a couple of times, but Beria doubted whether he himself could have even picked up the disk without smashing it, so inebriated was he.

It wasn't just that Stalin insisted everyone obliterate themselves at these awful parties. Beria also drank to numb his fear that the bomb would not work. There had been no time to test the device after Stalin had ordered that it be used a month ahead of schedule. If it didn't work, there was no question that he would pay. He'd tried to convince Stalin that a test-firing was the only sensible course, but the *Vozhd* had removed his unlit Dunhill pipe and placed it carefully on his desk. That was always a grave warning sign. He had simply stared at Beria until the NKVD chief had started to babble, and double back on his own rhetoric. *Of course, of course the general secretary is right. It will be done, and done immediately, and without fail, and . . .*

Beria shuddered, and felt another spasm of explosive vomiting coming on. At least half of the Communist Party magnates in the room looked in even worse shape than he was. But nobody had passed out. As Khrushchev used to say when he was alive, those who fell asleep at Stalin's table usually met a bad end. And so the debauch rolled on.

Stalin managed to get some scratchy old dance tune playing. Molotov and Mekhlis stumbled around in a grotesque parody of a waltz. The Allied ambassadors could not keep the horror from their faces.

And then, a Red Army messenger appeared at the door.

21

"Sweet mother of God," Kolhammer muttered.

He could hear Spruance's labored breathing beside him. Unlike Kolhammer, he'd never seen an atomic blast, never trained for a nuclear war, and in a way his ignorance protected him.

"Looks like a mess," he said.

"Yeah," Kolhammer grunted. "A hell of a mess."

They stood in front of the banked screens in the main room of the *Clinton*'s Intelligence Division. It looked like a smaller version of the ship's Combat Information Center, though with space given over to desks, cubicles, and a large conference table at one end of the room. At least two dozen men and women worked feverishly at all of these stations, half of them on the data stream now coming out of Europe, while the others remained focused on the task force's advanced surveillance elements as they closed with Yamamoto's forces in the Marianas.

For the moment, however, Kolhammer and Spruance were fully engaged with developments on the other side of the world.

The Soviets had restricted all access to the ruins of Lodz, ostensibly because of the danger of radiation poisoning, although they had been more than accommodating when it came to requests from London and Washington for briefings on the atomic raid. While the Red Army liaison officers who flew into England especially for these meetings would not discuss details of the USSR's atomic program, they were more than happy to provide reams of evidence from Poland about the destructive power unleashed by the workers' state.

"I guess the message is clear enough," Spruance muttered as

footage restarted on the main screen, showing a superfire that had destroyed even more of Lodz than the initial blast.

"Yeah, *Don't fuck with the revolution,*" Kolhammer said. "Jesus, what a shambles. I wonder how close we are to lighting off our first one."

"A lot closer now, I'll wager," Spruance said.

Kolhammer didn't bother to reply. It was a laydown that whatever capacity existed, it would be used to accelerate the Allied atomic program. But it wasn't his business to know about the progress of the Manhattan Project, even though so many of its resources had come from his original Multinational Force. Nearly a thousand personnel from the *Clinton* had been allocated to Groves.

He wasn't completely out of the loop, of course. The decision he'd made two years ago to dispatch Ivanov to the Soviet Union had taken on an entirely new character. Far from being considered "dangerous and stupid"—in the well-chosen words of Admiral King—it was looking like a remarkable act of foresight. Ivanov's little group was about the only card they had to play.

"Admiral Spruance, Admiral Kolhammer, excuse me, sirs. We'll have the link in two minutes."

Both men straightened and turned away from the video display. A young woman, a 'temp, was standing behind them.

"Thank you, Ensign," Spruance said. "We'll be right along."

Kolhammer shook his head as he took one last look at a loop captured by a Big Eye drone that had been moved over Lodz by the *Trident*. The Soviets had protested that, of course, but not too energetically. They were more than happy for the West to see exactly what they were capable of accomplishing.

"Let's go," Spruance said.

They left Intel and walked a short way down the corridor to a comm shack, a much smaller room with three screens, glowing blue and displaying a countdown.

. . . 0056

0055

0054 . . .

Kolhammer and Spruance settled themselves in front of the flat panels as the female ensign checked the videoconferencing connections.

"How long till the *Havoc* gets back to us?" Spruance asked.

"Willet will be on station in about two hours," Kolhammer

said. "She'll deploy drones and start taking the feed immediately. Raw data should arrive in the first burst by thirteen hundred hours. Her intelligence boss will give it a cover note, but we have a lot more analysts than she does, so a full picture will probably be another few hours."

"Until then I suppose we can take the Soviets at their word."

"Yes. If they say they're going to attack the Home Islands, they undoubtedly will."

"Do you think they'll use another atomic bomb?"

Kolhammer shrugged. "We'll know when we know. Lodz might have been their one shot in the locker. Even assuming they grabbed the *Vanguard,* and I think that's a safe assumption now, you can't build a nuclear weapon out of box tops and rubber bands. It's a very difficult task, and it chews up tremendous resources."

"Ten seconds," the ensign announced.

"I hope to God you're right, Admiral," Spruance said. "I wouldn't like to think of old Joe Stalin with a locker full of those things."

"That's why I doubt he has many yet," said Kolhammer. "If he did, he'd have used them on everyone. Including us."

The three blue screens flickered into life, with each displaying a different video window.

"Links verified secure," a sysop announced through the speakers. "Level One encryption." He had a British accent. Probably one of Halabi's people.

In the screen on the far left sat Churchill, Eisenhower, and a clutch of American and British staff officers. They seemed to be in an underground bunker, and Kolhammer assumed it was the war rooms in London, which had been fitted out with some of the *Trident*'s communications gear. In the center screen he found the president and the Joint Chiefs, back in Washington, and on the right-hand display was General MacArthur, beaming in from the South West Pacific Area Command in Brisbane. In the top left-hand corner of each screen a small separate window displayed the local time.

The sound came on with a crackle a few seconds after the video.

"Ladies and gentlemen, welcome." It was President Roosevelt. "By now you'll all have been properly informed about the Soviets' atomic attack on the Germans in Lodz."

Not just the Germans, Kolhammer thought.

"I believe General Eisenhower is going to update us on the situation in Western Europe."

Everyone on screen shifted slightly as they switched their attention to a different screen. Neither he nor Spruance had to, as an experienced operator down in the *Clinton*'s communications center reformatted their display to bring Eisenhower to the middle screen.

"Thank you, Mr. President," the general said before launching into his delivery. "As of six hours ago, the two main German army groups in Western Europe were in total disarray. They were already suffering badly from our coordinated air campaign, but had begun to adapt to that by breaking down into smaller units and moving to enmesh themselves with forward elements of the Allied advance, making it difficult to target large formations for strategic interdiction.

"Following the attack on Lodz, however, such mobile forces as remained intact have begun to redeploy east, back into Germany, leaving comparatively modest blocking forces to delay any pursuit on our part. General Patton's Third Army continues to make deep thrusts into the enemy's northern flank. Patton's lead elements are now threatening the German city of Bonn. In France, Paris has fallen to the Free French Armored Division, but street fighting has broken out among Resistance factions."

Eisenhower paused at this point to look up into the web-cam.

"The French Communist Party has called for a workers' uprising in solidarity with the people of the Soviet Union, and invited the Red Army to help them liberate the French masses. Moscow has denied any such intention, but they also haven't asked their French comrades to lay down their arms. For the moment, the city remains under curfew and Free French forces are attempting to put down the insurgency.

"Fighting in Italy continues, although the Germans have begun to evacuate their forces from Rome as ours approach from the south. Negotiations are under way to declare Rome an open city, though our intelligence sources within the capital indicate that fighting has broken out between Communist cells and the interim administration. The Italian Communists are also calling for the Red Army to move south and liberate them. The

Germans are reinforcing the Gothic Line along the Apennines with some of their troops from the south, but most appear to be headed for Germany."

Eisenhower finished reading from his notes and turned to Churchill, who was sitting beside him. "Mr. Prime Minister?"

The famous voice filled the small communications room where Kolhammer and Spruance sat. "General Eisenhower's briefing runs up to six hours ago, because at that time we received a direct communication from the German foreign minister asking for a cease-fire, as a preliminary step to opening peace negotiations on the Western Front."

Kolhammer heard Spruance curse softly beside him. For his own part, he merely lifted his eyebrows. He'd been expecting something like this. He noted that only Roosevelt and General Marshall seemed to take the news in stride. They'd obviously been briefed before the linkup.

"As significant as this development might be," Churchill continued, "it is just as important that Herr Ribbentrop was acting on the orders of *Reichsführer* Himmler, not Herr Hitler. It appears that some ill fortune may have befallen the Nazi leader, but at this stage we don't know the nature of his situation. We do know, however, what they are offering: a complete cessation of hostilities, withdrawal of all German forces to their 1939 positions, and, most risibly, an alliance against what Foreign Minister Ribbentrop is calling the Bolshevik menace to civilization.

"The Foreign Office has made no reply as of yet."

Roosevelt spoke up again, replacing the British prime minister on the main screen. "Before we deal with these developments, I'd like to ask General MacArthur and Admiral Spruance to quickly bring us up to date on the Pacific theater."

MacArthur nodded inside a pop-up window that suddenly appeared directly in front of Kolhammer.

"I am continuing to consolidate my hold on Java, and to press forward in New Guinea where General Blamey is preparing an attack on Rabaul. I am planning to return to the Philippines in two months, assuming Admiral Spruance gains control of the Marianas."

MacArthur looked like he had a lot more to say, but his audio cut out and a small green light came on atop the middle of the three screens they were watching. Kolhammer worked hard at

keeping his face straight. He could see MacArthur fuming back
in the small pop-up at the edge of the right-hand display.

The word TRANSMITTING flashed on screen in front of them.
Spruance spoke up.

"The Combined Task Force is proceeding as directed to
engage Yamamoto's forces in the Marianas chain. We expect
to be within strike range tomorrow, and have deployed surveillance assets well in advance of our main force. The information we have received back from them indicates that at
least half the ground forces the Japanese had intended to employ in the defense of the Marianas have been or are being
withdrawn to the Home Islands, accompanied by most of the
major surface combatants that Yamamoto had planned to meet
us with. Admiral Kolhammer tells me that the submarine *Havoc*
will be in position off the Home Islands in two hours, and we
should have a data feed from her in about four hours. Until
then we cannot say anything definitive about the size or type
of forces the Soviets appear to have committed to their attack
on Japan."

Spruance shot Kolhammer a questioning glance, but the admiral had nothing to add.

Roosevelt appeared on screen again. "Well, then, let us move
on. Prime Minister Churchill and I have already conferred over
the Nazis' peace offer, and our answer is simple. We reject any
offer other than unconditional surrender. I think we all agree
that, no matter how circumstances may change, it would be
completely unacceptable to leave the Nazis in power, or to remove them but allow their leaders to go unpunished. As long as
they remain, there can be no peace with Germany.

"A military question arises, however, because of the withdrawal of so many German army units to the east. We have to
consider the worst possible circumstances, gentlemen, a war
with the Soviet Union following the fall of the Third Reich. On
this Mr. Churchill and I cannot find common ground. He be-
lieves that we should allow the Germans to withdraw to meet
the Communists on the Eastern Front. Certainly I can understand his point. Anything we do to blunt the advance of the Red
Army can only serve to make easier the job of keeping them
away from Western Europe months or even weeks from now.
But I fear that doing so merely invites Stalin to reinforce his
armies and push all the harder. It also gives him a ready-made

excuse to declare hostilities against us when he has finished with the Germans. Prime Minister?"

Churchill reappeared in the center of the screen. "And I am afraid that I don't believe the Bolsheviks will need an excuse. They are quite obviously coming upon us with full force. The destruction of Lodz had less to do with damaging the Germans than it did with bullying us. I believe we need to prepare for armed conflict with the USSR in the very near future, and, as part of that, any damage we can do to marshals Konev and Zhukov—via the agency of the Wehrmacht—is all to the good.

"I do not propose an alliance with them. I merely suggest that we arrange our strategy to allow those German units to move east. They are not escaping. The Red Army will destroy them, but they will keep Stalin's hordes away from our throats and, of course, avoid those losses we would have sustained in fighting them. This will make us stronger for the conflagration that I believe is now inevitable. Mr. President?"

Kolhammer, like the other military officers, said nothing, although he couldn't help but agree with the British leader. He had warned Roosevelt often enough that this showdown was coming. The Soviets under Stalin were every bit as vile as the Nazis, with their sole redeeming grace being that their ideology didn't adhere to any crazed notions of racial destiny. Nevertheless, their goals were almost identical. Now that Stalin knew the destiny of his beloved revolution and his own reviled place in history, he simply could not—*would* not—accept his fate. It wasn't in his nature, nor that of his regime. He might talk of a grand alliance today, but Kolhammer would lay money on the barrelhead that he fully intended to supplant the Nazis as the masters of Europe.

It wasn't surprising that Churchill saw things in slightly starker terms than the Americans. His little island was probably about to become the front line again. And of course, if the Soviets took Japan, with China falling to Mao, the only powers that mattered in postwar Asia would line up with the Politburo.

He exhaled slowly as Roosevelt spoke again.

"Gentlemen, as I said, this is a political decision, but Mr. Churchill and I now need your advice on prosecuting a war against the Red Army, if that should become necessary. I believe General Marshall has something to say."

Kolhammer drummed his fingers lightly on the desktop, his frustration barely in check.

What about the nukes, he thought.

"Do hop in, General. I'll give you a lift."

Eisenhower felt the prime minister's hand on the small of his back, propelling him gently toward the armored Bentley. He nodded back at his driver to follow them. It was well after midnight in London, with the "dimout" in effect for only the second week. It had proven to be a grave disappointment for the people of London, who had long dreamed of turning their lights on again after five years of blackout conditions. The weak guttering light from a few lonely street lamps merely reinforced how badly the city had fared during the long war. Eisenhower had spent very little time back in the United States since taking over as the supreme commander of Allied Forces in Europe, but each time he came back to England with the impression that he was traveling into a dark age. The comparison with Los Angeles, and the Zone in particular, was especially stark. No blackout was enforced in the San Fernando, where it seemed a whole city had been brought into the world, a fantastic landscape of light and glass that apparently never slept. Privately, he thought it was telling that England seemed little changed by the Transition, whereas America was awash in new fashions and technologies.

"So, General," Churchill said as they settled into the seats. "What did you make of all that?"

It had begun to drizzle outside, and Eisenhower brushed a few droplets of moisture from his overcoat before answering.

"Well, Mr. Prime Minister, like you I guess I'm a bit pessimistic about it all. I don't see this Russian business ending well."

"Of course not," grunted Churchill as the car lurched into motion. The headlights were unhooded now, and twin beams shone forth brilliantly, illuminating the gray scenery through a curtain of light, drifting rain. "I worry that we are in more danger now than we faced after Dunkirk. This is a small island, and just a few atomic bombs would be more than enough to see her utterly destroyed."

"I don't think it will come to that," said Eisenhower, trying for a steady, reassuring tone, even though he felt far from happy. "I think the Russians would understand an atomic attack on London would be met with an overwhelming response."

Churchill, who seemed a lot older these last few weeks, shrugged. "And so we destroy Moscow, St. Petersburg, Kiev or what's left of it . . . and then what. London is gone. And maybe Liverpool or Manchester. Perhaps Paris, too. And I can't imagine Berlin lasting more than another week, or however long it takes Uncle Joe to build another of these infernal devices."

The car ran past a huge bomb site, a couple of acres of old rubble and tumbledown buildings. Trash blew around in the ruins, and it took very little for Eisenhower to imagine the whole city reduced to the same state.

"I think we may have to look at plans for evacuating the population," said Churchill. "There'll be no fighting the enemy on the beaches if the beaches have burned to glass."

D-DAY + 36. 8 JUNE 1944. 1322 HOURS. BERLIN.

"I am sorry, *Mein Führer*. So sorry," the SS leader whispered as he placed the heavy pillow on the gray, lifeless face of Adolf Hitler. He wasn't dead yet, even though he looked it. But the doctors said that was simply a function of the stroke, which had obliterated the part of his brain controlling the multitude of tiny muscles that gave form to a man's features, even when he was asleep. Now there was just slackness, and a terrible vacancy where once one of the great minds of human history had animated this expression. The *Reichsführer* trembled to his very core at the magnitude of the crime he was about to commit. But as a true national socialist, he also understood that sometimes it was necessary to kill for the greater good. And the white light that had bloomed over Lodz only threw that into starker relief.

"I am sorry," Himmler whispered again as he pressed down on the cushion. He thought he felt some resistance, a weak pushing back, and perhaps he heard a muffled whimper, too. One of the führer's legs twitched on the rough camp bed, and he worried that the cot might collapse beneath them. That would somehow have made it all the worse.

One unshod foot thumped against the sweating brick wall with a sick, soft thudding, and he felt a limp hand batting obscenely at his groin, but still he pressed on. It was for the good of the

Fatherland, and for the good of the führer himself. The doctors had assured the *Reichsführer* that there was no chance their beloved leader would recover. His mind was most definitely gone, and Himmler knew that under such circumstances Adolf Hitler would not want to be maintained as a living vegetable.

Reich policies on these matters were quite clear. The T4 program applied in this case, as in all others.

Himmler's vision swirled as he bore down with all his weight. The air in the tiny underground room was hot and stale. It had probably been breathed over and over again. He told himself that the feeble, thrashing form beneath him was not the man he had followed for so long. That man was gone, and had been for days, a victim of this war as surely as any front-line combatant. All that was left of him was this husk, lying on an army cot.

The struggle, such as it was, began to taper off. Gradually, terribly, life ceased. Himmler endured one last weak surge of resistance before he felt the body sag beneath him. It was done.

Hoping for numbness, he instead felt a powerful boiling of conflicted sensation: horror at what he had done, torment at the unknown consequences, relief that he would no longer have to fear exposure concerning his last days in the Other Time. He slumped to the cold concrete floor beside Hitler's body. Breathing heavily, his heart pounding, he turned his head and stared at his surroundings, wondering how so momentous an event could transpire in such a dingy setting. The malarial yellow brickwork. The sagging cot. The chipped ceramic jug into which Himmler had dipped a handkerchief an hour earlier, moistening one corner to dab against the führer's dry, cracked lips.

It was an ignominious end.

There was a furtive tapping at the door. *"Herr Reichsführer?"*

Himmler removed the pillow. His dead leader's eyeballs had bulged obscenely in their sockets, and he shuddered at the confronting image. Brushing them closed with one hand, he called out. "Enter."

Colonel Skorzeny pushed open the heavy metal door with a screeching of poorly oiled hinges. Himmler came up off the floor slowly and awkwardly. His knees hurt, and he had suffered from a stiff and painful back for a couple of weeks. It was all this cramped underground living.

"He is gone," the SS leader said to the newcomer. "He passed away peacefully, without regaining consciousness. We are all alone now."

Skorzeny nodded, staring at the body. Whatever he thought of the situation, it remained hidden behind a heavily scarred face on which nothing seemed to move until he spoke.

"The men are in place."

"Have someone see to the burial detail. It will not be possible to provide full honors because of the bombing, but we must mark this tragedy with all appropriate ceremony. And tell Göbbels to finish his statement for the radio. I will speak to the general staff now."

Skorzeny clicked his heels and nodded, snapping his fingers and calling a couple of storm troopers into the room. Their shocked expressions registered the awful truth when they saw Hitler's corpse on the bed. Himmler admonished them to treat the führer's remains with due respect.

Then, fitting his hat firmly down over his head, he gathered himself and marched out of the room. His bodyguards fell in beside him as he turned into the passage where naked electric bulbs hung at ten-meter intervals and exposed wiring and pipes ran along the ceiling. A detachment of twelve more *SS Sonderaktiontruppen* waited for him at the end of the corridor. They all wore field uniforms and carried submachine guns. Their commander ripped out a salute as Himmler approached, barking at his men to fall in behind their new führer. The crashing of their hobnailed boots sounded incredibly loud in the confined space as they set off after him.

The main operations room was on the next level down. As they approached, officers from all three armed services scrambled to get out of the way. Himmler could see that the two Wehrmacht guards at the entrance to the room had been replaced by his own men. He swept past them, flicking an acknowledgment of their salute back over his shoulder. The atmosphere was already subdued when he entered. SS men had discreetly taken up positions around the room. The assembled generals and admirals hovered over the battle-realm display, where hundreds of little wooden blocks and flags brought imagined order to the chaos of the Western Front.

Himmler pulled up at the edge of the giant map table.

"I am afraid the führer has passed away," he announced solemnly. A few of the women who were present cried out.

"He drew his last breath at thirteen twenty-nine hours. He regained consciousness for a few minutes before the end, and exhorted us all to do our utmost in the defense of the Reich. To that end, and in line with his final wishes, I have assumed the office of chancellor and supreme commander of the armed forces."

He paused, just briefly, in case somebody should wish to chance their luck against him, but the entire room was cowed. Whether it was due to his armed escort or simply by the magnitude of the disaster they faced, he could not tell. It was of no consequence.

All that mattered was decisive action to save his people and their civilization from the peril of Bolshevism. Himmler knew that every soul in this room cried out for strong leadership. It was vital that he provide it, and quickly.

"General Zeitzler," he said, turning his gaze on the army chief of staff. "How stand the armies in the west?"

Zeitzler was holding a single sheaf of paper, and he gave the impression of trying to hide behind it when he replied.

"The Northern Front is in collapse . . . *Mein Führer,*" he replied, somewhat weakly. "Patton's Third Army threatens to break through our final line of resistance. Army Group South is attempting to disengage, but . . . it is difficult. The führer . . . the late führer . . . his instructions to hold France . . ."

Himmler put an end to the excruciating performance with a wave of his hand. He spoke in a reasonable tone, attempting to soothe everyone with the equanimity of his reaction. Having been on the receiving end of Hitler's ungovernable fury more than once, he knew only too well what a double-edged sword it could be. Terror was a marvelous inducement to perform one's duties well, but it also clouded judgment and made it less likely that a leader would hear what he needed to hear, rather than simply being told whatever might avert another episode of explosive rage.

"The führer did not know of the Bolshevik atomic threat," he said, sounding more regretful than anything. "If he had, he would have recognized it for the mortal danger it is."

There was still a great strain in the drawn faces and stiff postures of the men who stood facing him. But as Himmler spoke with—he hoped—great forbearance and composure, some of the more palpable tension began to ease.

"I am afraid the foreign minister had no good news to offer me when I spoke to him an hour ago. The British and Americans have very foolishly rejected our offer to establish a common front against Stalin. If we should fall, they will come to regret that decision. I believe that the very future of civilization will be decided in the next few days. The democracies are corrupt and hopelessly flawed, but beyond certain political matters they are not entirely alien. We share histories and enjoy many cultural meeting points with them. We are Aryan societies, after all."

A few heads nodded here and there.

His SS troops never once relented in their machinelike surveillance of the room, but he felt as if everyone was beginning to relax, ever so slightly, despite the menacing presence of the guards and the press of events. The *Reichsführer-SS*—no, the führer—removed his hat and placed it on the map table in a consciously theatrical gesture. He sketched a thin smile.

"It has never been my way to downplay our setbacks, or to attempt to make more of good news than it deserves—to gild the lily, as the English say."

Another smile. A noticeable relaxation in Zeitzler and the other army staffers.

"There is no point in looking to our own atomic program for salvation. I can tell you now that we are nowhere near close enough to testing a device in the hope that we might use it against the Bolsheviks."

He registered the shock and disappointment on all of the faces, except those of his own men, who remained impressively stone-faced.

"However, we are not entirely defenseless. The Reich Ministry of Advanced Armaments Research isn't the *only* body to have had responsibility for developing the Emergence technologies. Given the exposure of so many traitors within our midst, the late führer and I judged it prudent to quarantine some of the research efforts, keeping them solely within the control of the SS."

Radio receivers crackled in the background, relaying desperate messages from front-line units. Himmler was distantly aware of an air raid somewhere above them, perhaps miles away. It was more an intimation of destruction than anything, a faint rumbling and the slightest of vibrations felt through the soles of his feet.

"We have worked very closely with the Japanese on a few small but now vitally important programs. We do not yet have an atomic warhead capable of battlefield delivery, but we have other weapons, powerful in their own way. General Zeitzler," he said, taking an envelope from his jacket and passing it over to the stunned Wehrmacht officer, "you will coordinate the release of these stocks to our forces on the Eastern Front. Specialist Waffen-SS units will be responsible for deploying the weapons. Your men will need to be inoculated beforehand. Rest assured, they will be perfectly safe. The necessary supplies have been pre-positioned for the most expedient dispatch."

His hand shaking, Zeitzler took the sealed orders.

Himmler raised an inquiring eyebrow, and Zeitzler remembered his position.

"It shall be done immediately, *Mein Führer*."

"Good. Be sure that it is." Himmler pulled himself upright to his full height. He hardened his voice and pitched it to carry to the back of the room. "As terrible as was the weapon that destroyed the garrison at Lodz," he said, "we shall stop the Bolsheviks dead in their tracks. Quite literally. In conjunction with Japan, we have developed a biological weapon, a form of anthrax that can be fired from an artillery shell. We possess a sufficient quantity to seal our eastern borders."

He noted anyone who looked unreasonably horrified by the prospect. If they could not be trusted, then, like *Reichsmarschall* Göring, they might need to be dealt with.

"I will not lie to you," he declared. "We are in desperate straits. As radical and, I admit, as dangerous as our strategy in the east will be, it is only half of the picture. There is still the Western Front to be considered. Zeitzler!"

The army chief of staff came rigidly to attention this time. *"Mein Führer!"*

"I am ordering you to execute Plan Orange. Pull all forces back to the Rhine defenses immediately. Leave such elements there as are necessary to secure that front for two months, and transfer the balance to the east. Release the strategic reserve to join them."

"Yes, *Mein Führer*."

Stillness, then. Nobody moved or said a word.

Himmler allowed himself the briefest of interludes to enjoy the feeling of absolute power that was gathering around him, before the bleak realities of the situation made themselves felt again. There was just one more thing to say.

"We have made mistakes. Myself. All of us. Even our former

leader. We can no longer afford mistakes. I am not a military genius. If any of you have concerns about this plan, I need to hear of them within the next twenty-four hours. The Reich is depending on us. The *world* is depending on us."

A Luftwaffe general, Helmut Lippert, stepped forward nervously. "*Mein Führer. Reichsmarschall* Göring was escorted from here some time ago. Will he be coordinating Luftwaffe deployments for—"

Himmler shook his head. "The only thing Göring will be coordinating is his defense before a people's court. You are now the acting chief of the Luftwaffe, Herr General. Give yourself six hours to prepare a brief for me on what forces you have available to meet the Communists. And I want the truth, Lippert. No matter how unpalatable it may seem."

Himmler allowed a genuine smile to creep across his face for the first time in days. "Blame the bad news on Göring, if you wish. It's probably his fault anyway."

Lippert's rubber-faced anguish was almost too much to bear. "It's a joke, Herr General. You may smile."

The new Luftwaffe chief laughed weakly.

"Excellent," Himmler said. "A cheerful disposition can be worth an entire battalion at the right moment. Is that not so, Lippert?"

"Yes, *Mein Führer*."

22

**D-DAY + 36. 9 JUNE 1944. 0020 HOURS.
HMAS *HAVOC*, SEA OF OKHOTSK.**

It reminded Willet of the Straits of Taiwan, although it probably wasn't as bad as all that. At least she didn't have three Chinese Warbows on her case. And she did have considerably more wiggle room in the waters between Sakhalin and the Kuril Islands.

But the sheer volume of traffic—all of it hostile, as far as she was concerned—was very much like the three weeks she'd spent as a quietly terrified middy on the old *Dechaineux* during the Taiwanese War of Independence. Although the hundreds of Soviet warcraft churning the waters above her were nominally Allied ships, Willet didn't doubt for a moment that they'd turn their weapons on her if she was detected.

"Easy does it, helm," she said softly.

While the *Havoc*'s stealth systems rendered her invisible to the Soviets, she had insisted that they run as silently as if they were sitting off a Chinese port back in twenty-one. Her combat center was still and hushed. Indeed, she could feel the stillness of the boat all around her.

The *Havoc* was unique among the surviving 21C craft in that no 'temps sailed on her. At various times, back in her home waters, she'd hosted visitors from the contemporary Allied navies as well as the occasional politician. But when she loaded up with retrofitted handmade Mark 48 torpedoes and headed out looking for trouble, she always did so with her original crew.

Before the Transition, Willet had prided herself on running a tight but happy outfit. Cut off from their families for six months at a time, the forty-two men and women under her command had become surrogate family members. She wouldn't have imagined they could really be any closer, but she'd been wrong. The Transition had seemingly welded them together forever. There were times when she thought her people were more comfortable on the boat than they were back in the historical theme park of 1940s Sydney. As much as twenty-first-century culture—and a good deal of its antecedent history—had been adopted by the avant-garde crowd and almost everyone under the age of thirty, in a way that merely served to reinforce the sense of isolation they all felt. There was something terribly sad about the 'temp parties she'd attended back on shore, with everyone doing their damnedest to make her feel "at home." You were likely to find yourself talking to a 1940s artist dressed like a 1970s disco bunny, trying with all her might to discuss post-ironic pop culture of the early new millennium. There were a few bars and restaurants owned by uptimers who'd been invalided out of service or simply finished their hitch, and they did a great job of shutting out reality. But stepping out of them at the end of the night was like falling into the wormhole all over again.

Unlike Karen Halabi, with whom she kept in regular contact via data relay, Willet did not suffer overly much from the depredations of pigheaded buffoons. Partly that was because she still worked so closely with Kolhammer's forces. With the immediate threat to Australia having receded, Canberra was happy to attach the submarine to the U.S. Pacific Fleet in the same way that many of the Royal Australian Navy's contemporary vessels served with U.S. forces. And partly, of course, it helped that she was white, good looking, and the end product of a military family stretching back four generations.

She had relatives living now whom she vaguely remembered as wizened old ghosts at the family barbecues when she was a little girl. One of them, who'd died long before she was born, was a brigadier with the Sixth Division. Tom Willet. Like most of his comrades, a citizen-soldier for the duration.

In civilian life Tom was a lawyer to and a good friend of Sir Frank Packer, the owner of a newspaper and magazine empire. He'd taken a shine to his great-grandniece and through the offices of Sir Frank had ensured that her run into the good graces of the local establishment was smooth and hassle-free. She'd like to think that all the Japs she'd killed might count for something, too. But her ghostwritten "Advice from the Future" column in the *Women's Weekly* magazine probably counted for more. And saving the world hadn't really helped Karen Halabi gain entrée to the rarefied circles of the London elite, had it?

Her intel boss, Lieutenant Lohrey, touched her on the arm and nodded to a screen just off to the left of the monitor bank she'd been watching.

Thanks, Amanda, she mouthed silently.

All thoughts of the weird, contrary life she now lived fell away as she leaned forward to peer at the split screen. Willet chewed her lower lip. She heard Lohrey grunt softly beside her. It was like something out of the dark ages, or one of those *1630s* films by Peter Jackson.

"We estimate a million and a half combatants," Lohrey informed her sotto voce.

Willet said nothing. She could hear her own breathing. No keyboards clacked anywhere in the center. Her sysops used touch screens, and such conversation as was necessary was conducted briefly and in low tones.

On the main display cube, above the boat's lifeless holobloc, a CGI schematic of the threat bubble showed them surrounded by Soviet warships. Four Japanese submarines—of the eighteen they'd originally been tracking—still survived. But like her, they were lying doggo. Unlike her, they were undoubtedly waiting for the moment when they might fire off a brace of torpedoes, to do the most damage possible before dying inside of a maelstrom of depth charges and antisubmarine torpedoes and rockets.

The latter two weapons were among the many unpleasant surprises they'd logged since taking up station to secretly observe the battle. The Communist sub killers were primitive by her standards, but far in advance of anything they'd seen the Japanese deploy. It was impossible to tell without actually retrieving one for examination, but as best they could discern through sensor readings, the Soviets had produced large numbers of something like their old SET-53 passive homing torpedoes and a small number of the much more lethal SET-65 active/passive analogs. Even more disturbing than the weapons, however, were the platforms they'd been launched from: dedicated ASW helicopters.

So troubled was she by that development, Willet had ordered Lohrey to devote a primary channel of the Big Eye feed to covering any appearance by the Soviet choppers. One of the main displays carried the continual surveillance, as instructed, and seven split screens were occupied by LLAMPS and infrared vision of hovering, swooping helicopters that looked like the bastard offspring of a Sea King and the old Khrushchev-era Ka-25. Twin-bladed coaxial rotors; a nose-mounted radome structure; towed arrays; a centerline torpedo system; and depth charges fixed to stubby winglets about halfway down the fuselage.

"She's no fuckin' oil painting," her boat chief, Roy Flemming, commented when he saw them for the first time.

"Aye, Chief, but they do the job," Willet replied.

They more than did the job. Most of the Japanese subs never got a shot off.

They were located and destroyed long before the lead elements of the Soviet fleet arrived. The few that survived looked to have done so by lying on the shallow bottom close to shore, surrounded by the wreckage of their sunken comrades. With her Nemesis arrays, Willet knew exactly where they were, even amid the fearsome background noise of the battle overhead.

The Soviets, on the other hand, just seemed to be going through the motions of searching for them now. Having killed the others so quickly in the opening moments, the Russian commanders had probably been lulled into a false sense of security by the clearly demonstrated superiority of their equipment.

The *Havoc*'s captain wondered idly when the remaining Japanese boats would come to life and charge to the surface looking for a quick kill before the inevitable counterstrike took them out of the game. Unlike her, they didn't enjoy the luxuries of remote sensor feeds, or the quantum processing power of an advanced Combat Intelligence. They'd be lashing out in the dark. Literally.

She checked the time hack on the nearest screen. It was twenty minutes after midnight.

The boat's processors were fully engaged filtering the immense intelligence take from the Battle of Okhotsk as it raged through the darkness hours. The Soviets weren't big on emission control, so in addition to the audiovisual coverage coming in from the Big Eye drone, the *Havoc* was also scooping up vast quantities of electronic and signals intelligence. Designed to stalk and strike at the infinitely more capable Chinese navy nearly eight decades hence, the submarine had little trouble accumulating data on her current targets. But with such a small crew, and none of them very well versed in post-Transition Soviet naval technology or tactics, Captain Jane Willet had orders to watch, and nothing more. The Sovs had done so much in secret, there were almost no patches or upgrades to the Nemesis files on them. Willet's people were writing the first ones.

Every two hours Lieutenant Lohrey zapped another compressed, encrypted burst up to the drone, which relayed the package back to an AWACS bird loitering fifteen hundred kilometers to the southeast. From there it went back to the *Clinton,* where Kolhammer and Spruance had dozens of specialists working on the take and joining the very rough dots her Intel Section had mapped out. Even more analysts were on their way from Hawaii.

Willet grimaced as Master Chief Flemming pointed out an especially gruesome scene in one of the smaller windows. A Japanese artillery position was being overrun. The drone gave them a view of the carnage from a virtual height of one hundred meters. What was that line from Shakespeare, she thought.

There's none die well that die in battle . . . The Englishman had been writing about Agincourt, half a millennium ago, but he could just as well have been observing the fight for that gun battery.

From the comparative safety of her hiding place, Jane Willet gave thanks that her life paths had led her to the cool and quiet space of her bridge on the *Havoc,* and not into the middle of the insensate slaughter taking place just over the horizon.

D-DAY + 36. 9 JUNE 1944. 0020 HOURS.
USS *ARMANNO,* PACIFIC AREA OF OPERATIONS.

For the first time since he'd taken command of the USS *Armanno,* Captain John F. Kennedy wished he could trade it for his old PT boat. The *Armanno,* a new *Halsey*-class guided missile destroyer, was a magnificent fighting ship. Unlike his old boat, though, he didn't think she was really meant for this sort of work. He would have felt a lot more comfortable slipping in and out of Japanese-held waters on the much smaller, less conspicuous PT boat. He knew he could have accommodated the six-strong Force Recon team. Even with all their equipment and the rigid-hulled inflatable, he still could have squeezed them in.

But then again, if the nips tumbled them, it'd be a lot easier fighting their way out in the *Armanno.* And of course, Spruance's armada didn't include any torpedo boats.

"Coming up on the release point, skipper."

"Thank you, Mr. Hubbard. XO, give our guests a five-minute warning."

"Aye, Captain."

His executive officer passed on the command via the ship's intercom. Kennedy continued to sweep the sea with his Starlite goggles. He was past marveling at the opalescent view. He knew that down in the ship's CIC, two dozen systems operators were scanning the threat bubble with infinitely more powerful sensors, but his days flitting around behind Japanese lines died hard, and he had lookouts posted all over the ship, just in case some gremlin decided to chew through a golden wire holding all his magical AT gear together. Sonar, radar, active, passive, phased array. It was all good, and he'd never be dumb enough to argue that a Mark 1 Eyeball was better. But as his father used to say, an extra set of peepers on a problem never hurt, did it?

A small meteor shower to the northwest caught his attention, the falling stars appearing as streaks of emerald brilliance in his Starlites. The last time he'd seen anything so beautiful had been up at the family place in Hyannisport back at the end of fall. A cool, crisp night, with the northern stars out in abundance. His father had thrown a party on the last night of his leave, a little going-away soirée. Or that was how they'd sold it to him anyway. When he'd arrived with his date Natalia from upstate New York, the dozens of cars parked along Marchant Avenue spoke of an entirely different purpose. The summer house was full of political types and businessmen. His heart sank as soon as the whole circus caravan swung into view.

He'd tried to convince Ali, as she liked to be called, that they should split before anyone saw them. Head back to the cabin and spend the rest of his leave together there. But she was a sweet girl, and coming from LA she loved a party. They could hear the music drifting down across the lawns as soon as he cut the car engine.

"That sounds like Frank Sinatra," she squealed. "Oh, come on, Jack. We simply must!"

Against his better judgment he gave in to her, and spent the next six hours regretting it as his dad forced him to glad-hand every sweating, drunken idiot in a suit on the East Coast. He died inside every time someone insisted on calling him Mr. President, which was more or less every time anyone spoke to him. He caught sight of Ali's honey-blond hair just once, on the other side of a crowded room, where she was deep in conversation with Sinatra and a rough-headed character who had to be the famous Slim Jim Davidson. He hardly got to speak to his brothers, which in hindsight wasn't such a bad thing, as his dad seemed intent on playing each off against the other. He'd have thought reading the future histories might have dampened the old man's enthusiasm for pushing his sons into public life, but no. Far from it.

Foresight seemed to have fueled a deep, almost unnatural desire in Joe Kennedy to take a stranglehold on fate and choke the living shit out of it. He hadn't been able to rest till he got that Oswald kid away from his mother and into that boarding school in Canada. And poor Joe Jr. still blamed him for getting yanked off the flight line over in England. Man, he'd heard the yelling and the hollering over that one all the way out in Hawaii.

"Hell of thing, ain't it, buddy, having your past come back and bite you on the ass before you even have a chance to fuck it up the first time around?"

"Huh?"

He'd been woolgathering out on the patio, and the man had snuck up on him. The man and the woman, now that he looked.

"Don't worry, Mack, I'm not gonna *Mr. President* you, you poor bastard."

Kennedy found himself feeling genuine relief. He couldn't help being amused by the cheeky, knowing grin on this guy's face, either.

"Well, if you promise you won't whistle 'Hail to the Chief' while you're blowing smoke up my ass," he said, "I won't call for the cops after I check to see if my wallet's still here, *Mr. Davidson.*"

Slim Jim Davidson grinned broadly. "I ain't like that no more, Captain Kennedy. These days I got me a whole bunch of *minions* to do my pickpocketing for me, and on a much grander scale."

"And is this one of them?" Jack asked, nodding to the woman who stood, smiling enigmatically, just behind the famous businessman.

"No," she answered for herself, "Slim Jim and I have had professional dealings in the past, but not like that. I'm a reporter. Julia—"

"Ms. Julia Duffy," he finished for her. "And you're hardly just a reporter, ma'am. You'd probably be as famous as Mr. Davidson here, at a guess. Almost as rich, too."

"Hardly," she snorted.

"Yeah. I'm pretty fucking wealthy," Davidson said with a twinkle in his eye. Kennedy couldn't miss the fact that he was joking *and* being very, very serious at the same time.

"Well, you wouldn't be here if my dad didn't think much of your money," Kennedy smiled.

"But your father couldn't care less about my breeding, right?"

"Not much, no. And you, Ms. Duffy, I've seen a couple of newspaper owners here tonight, but no reporters, other than you. Are you working, or is this just a bit of sightseeing for you?"

She cocked an eyebrow at him, one of the most sexually suggestive gestures he'd ever seen. He suddenly felt a little guilty, although for what reason, he had no idea. He threw a furtive glance over her bare shoulders, looking for Ali.

"Well, I haven't pumped you about your plans for the future, so I guess I must be here for the pleasure of the company," she said.

Kennedy surveyed the other party guests: a close-packed collection of overweight, gin-fueled bores.

"Yeah," he deadpanned. "I can see that'd be it."

Off on the horizon, shooting stars zipped across the sky.

"Cap'n, boat's away, sir."

"Thanks, Chief. Let's hold our position for now."

"Aye."

Kennedy dropped the goggles from his eyes, and with them went the illusion of privacy he'd enjoyed for just a moment or two.

The deck hardly moved beneath his feet, so calm was the sea that night. He could hear the muted putter of the marines' little boat as it carried them away from the bulk of the *Armanno*. They were headed to an island just below the horizon. It had seemed deserted on the first couple of surveillance sweeps a month ago. But as the fleet drew closer to the Marianas, islands that had been beyond the range of Kolhammer's remaining drones came under observation by them for the first time.

And this particular piece of real estate needed checking out.

The water jets were so incredibly quiet compared with an old-fashioned outboard motor that less disciplined troops might have been tempted to ride them much closer in to shore. But Gunnery Sergeant Adam Denny cut the engines at precisely the point his mission specs demanded. All six men in the small, rigid-hulled inflatable slipped lightweight paddles into the warm water and began to stroke for shore. They might well be rowing toward a deserted island, but they proceeded as though they were infiltrating Hirohito's Imperial Palace. Nobody spoke. There was nothing to say at this point. They'd rehearsed this scenario dozens of times back at the Littoral Warfare Training Camp in New Guinea.

The island bobbed very gently up and down in their night vision goggles as they drew closer.

Denny held a three-dimensional model of the atoll in his

head. He'd known this was a special case as soon as he'd been authorized to attend one week of pre-mission prep in the Zone. Traffic between the "old" Marine Corps and its twenty-first off-spring in the San Fernando Valley was surprisingly rare. It was strange, too, until you looked into the politics of it.

Jones's people had some great toys in the Zone. Better even than the AT stuff his Force Recon company had been issued at the start of the year. And *their* stuff was way better than the new gear the rest of the corps was packing nowadays. You'd think everyone would be able to just get along, rather than wasting time and energy that could be more profitably spent killing Japs, but no. Being a simple noncom, Denny wasn't privy to all the backroom bullshit that went on, but he had a good set of eyes in his head, and he could see that of all the services, the corps seemed to be the one resisting hardest any talk of integration with its uptime colleagues. Happy to take the toys and whizbangs like the beautiful M4 carbine he had strapped to his back. Not so happy to play nice with the new guys who'd brought all those things in the first place.

Denny spat a stream of tobacco juice into the sea.

What a buncha fucking baloney.

Did he give a rat's ass if General Jones was as black as a fucking eggplant?

Nope. All he cared about was getting his guys onto this is-land, and off again in one piece with whatever information they might find there. And in his opinion—even though it *was* just the opinion of a lowly noncom—they were that much more likely to get out of this with their asses intact because of the week he'd spent in the Zone, playing with those amazing holobloc machines. Without ever having set foot on the island, he already knew it intimately.

And if there *did* turn out to be Japs hiding there, for sure they woulda built a bunch of stuff like tunnels and bunkers that weren't on the 3-D images he'd examined back in California. Still, he knew all the bays and inlets, the major streams and val-leys, indeed all the topography of the joint, and that'd come in handy for a "greenside" op like this, where they'd have to stay hidden from any hostile forces.

As Denny rhythmically dipped his oar into the water in time with his men, he recalled with real wonder some of the things he'd seen in the Zone. They had three-dimensional images, like the ones he'd seen of his target island, for tens of thousands of other places all over the world. The uptimers had warned him that the imagery might not match up with reality. The Tokyo of *his* day was a hell of a lot different from the Tokyo of the future, for instance. But Denny knew that mountains and rivers and stuff like that didn't move much in just eighty years.

Not in backwaters like this, at any rate.

There'd been some other stuff he'd seen out there, too. Stuff that woulda turned his shit white a few years earlier, before he got into the corps and saw a bit of the world. The little coal-mining town where he grew up didn't run to strip joints or porno houses or "dope cafés." And you never ever saw white folks mixing with anyone other than their own kind. Or ladies walking around with their asses hanging out of such short skirts and their tits bursting out of such tight tops.

He'd really wanted to write his brother about it, but he knew the old man would rip up the letter as soon as he saw it. His dad was a much more formidable censor than the corps. Small-town preachers tended to be a little judgmental and censorious like that.

A slight breeze picked up, bringing with it the unmistakable smell of landfall ahead of them. His nostrils twitched at the stench of rotting vegetation, of smoke, and—he was certain—of cooking.

Denny brought his low-light amplification up to max and scanned the approaching shoreline. Coming in from leeward the surf was low, two feet at most, and its hissing crunch would smother the sound of their final run in. He couldn't see anything unusual until he switched to infrared view, and suddenly two heat blossoms appeared a couple of hundred feet up the headland that dominated this side of the island.

He turned around to face his men and used a series of hand signals to tell them that the island was occupied.

23

In the seconds before the bullet struck her, Julia Duffy relived whole arcs of her life. The field in which she stood, lined up with about thirty or so muddy, ragged GIs, bled into a memory of the field she played in behind her childhood home in Excelsior Springs, outside Kansas City.

She was an only child, but she lived next door to a couple of little girls, aged twelve months on either side of her, and they'd been friends all the way through school. Even when she'd moved to France, and later lived in New York, they kept in contact via e-mail and Christmas cards. Rebecca and Susie had stayed in Missouri. Bec married a cosmetic dentist who kept offices down on the Plaza and out in Johnson County, while her sister snagged the owner of a chain of Krispy Kreme franchises. Apart from her dad, they were the only friends she cared to hold on to after leaving town.

As the German machine gunners primed their weapons she had a flashback so vivid it almost seemed as though she'd not only crossed back through the Transition, but returned to her five-year-old form, as well.

She was having a sleepover at Bec and Susie's place, but not much sleep was happening. At about two in the morning she and Bec had convinced the younger Susie to go in to the girls' parents and ask for a drink. All that yakking under the bedcovers had made them mighty thirsty. Susie had woken her dad, telling him in a singsong voice that she needed a drink. Even though Julia hadn't been there in the bedroom, her memory put her right there next to Susie as her father grunted something about getting a drink from the refrigerator by herself. He probably meant milk, but the girls found a two-liter bottle of Coke in the crisper and, miracle of miracles, managed to unscrew it, pour themselves three glasses full, and continue doing so until it was all gone, without spilling as much as a single drop. They were very proud of themselves.

The caffeine and sugar then kept them awake until sunrise, playing with the sisters' army of Barbies in front of a TV set that was turned down and tuned to a local station running a continual loop of infomercials.

As one of the soldiers next to her began babbling, and crying for his mother, Julia flashed forward to the last moments of her first serious relationship, with a photographer she'd met in college, a narcissist whose self-regard she mistook for sensitivity. They'd dated for three months, an intensely dislocated period in her life when she missed almost every class at school, nearly flunking out before cracking up when this idiot came back from a shoot in the Caribbean to blithely inform her that he'd gotten a Russian swimsuit model pregnant and was going to spend a year or two in Asia figuring out what this meant for him. Neither she nor the model was invited on this epic journey of self-discovery.

Julia recalled in clinical detail how she'd stood at the foot of his carved Thai teak bed and verbally lashed him like a cart driver whipping some home truths into a particularly stupid and stubborn donkey. And how he had remained cool and almost psychopathically self-contained as she fell to pieces, eventually collapsing in a fetal ball at his feet.

He'd stepped over her, sat down at his computer, and begun editing another photo shoot saying sorry, but it was overdue.

These memories came not one after another, but seemingly all at once, as a single massive eruption of recall with past and present fused in a psychic tangle. As the shout of the SS officer in charge of their firing squad—*Feuer!*—reached her ears, she was simultaneously learning to drive in her first car, a twenty-year-old Geo Metro, bargaining for the "morning price" on a sarong in Bali, her first overseas assignment, and attending Mass—her father's funeral—for the last time in her life.

Forrest-fucking-Seymour of the *Des Moines Register and Tribune* was beating her out of first place for the Pulitzer after she'd written eight long pieces in the *Times* destroying Edgar-fucking-Hoover.

She was celebrating her nomination for the prize at the Bayswater.

She was being woken in her apartment by a phone call telling her Hoover was dead by his own hand, copies of her stories by his side, with the word LIES scrawled over them, hundreds of times.

She was double-dating with Rosanna, back when she was first seeing Dan, and Rosie was still thinking about Wally Curtis.

She was on the Brisbane Line in Australia, watching Artie Snider charge up that hill throwing grenades, firing from the hip.

She was partying with Slim Jim, Maria, Sinatra, and Crosby.

She was in Honolulu, fucking John Kennedy a few months after she'd first met him at that party up in Hyannisport and months before she formally split from Dan.

She was shopping for Christmas presents with her daddy at the Excelsior Springs Wal-Mart, the year he'd been laid off from the Ford plant at Claycomo and they'd had to use food stamps to buy frozen Banquet turkey meat in the huge family pack.

She was lying in bed, feeling his tears running down her cheeks as he kissed her good night and told her if she listened real hard she might hear Santa's sleigh bells over the wind howling outside, but warning her that there might not be as many toys in the sack this year.

She was aware of how the birds fell silent in the trees behind them. Of a stone she hadn't had time to remove from her left boot after they'd been captured. Of the smell of somebody's bowels evacuating a few feet away. Of someone in a small voice, imploring his grandma to save him. Of the way the Germans' helmets cast a shadow over their faces, giving them the appearance of human pillboxes. Of a woman's face floating up from the deepest parts of her memories, her mother's face she was sure, even though she'd run off with her boss when Julia was less than two years old, leaving her without even memories. The woman had perversely taken every photo album in the house and burned them the day before.

A small sunburst in the black maw of the machine gun that seemed to be directly pointed at her.

Someone screaming, "No!"

A massive blow to her chest, lifting her feet free of the ground, spinning her over and over, turning her around in midair. The sky, the trees, the muddy grass a blur of bluish green. And the last of her living memories swirling around inside this mosaic as darkness closed in at the edge of her vision. Of Dan, her husband, her dead *ex*-husband, and the day he'd found out that she hadn't had the birth control implants removed as she'd promised. And the look in his eyes when she told him she'd switched on the gene shear, terminating the pregnancy she'd only just discovered, and rendering her barren forever after. Dan fell away from her. And all she could see was his eyes, or perhaps the memory of his eyes, so full of disappointment, pain, betrayal, and the certain knowledge that she had done this on purpose, because it suited her. Without talking to him she had cut off the life they had created together, and the life they were going to lead, the children they would have raised and loved and left to the world.

She had let all that slip away, and let him slip away with it, because in the end she was selfish. She wanted what she wanted for herself, not for them.

As the light went out he disappeared forever. And Julia Duffy cried out, weakly, wretchedly, and so softly that nobody could possibly hear.

"Daddy. Help me."

D-DAY + 37. 9 JUNE 1944. 1151 HOURS.
ARDENNES PLATEAU.

The German front might be in complete collapse, but that didn't make it any safer to be in this part of the world. Captain Chris Prather jumped down from the Sherman and landed on a patch of ground made boggy by the amount of blood that had soaked into the soil. He looked around for a body, but couldn't see one nearby.

"Holy shit," he muttered, barely able to hear himself over the rumble of the tank squadron's idling engines. They'd pulled up at the edge of a clearing near the eastern border of the Ardennes. Nine tanks out of the twenty-two he'd started with, and a company-sized force of the Twenty-ninth Infantry, stitched together from the remains of a battalion that got chopped up crossing the Meuse River.

"They're our guys all right!" a corporal yelled. "Come on."

A couple of medics ran past Prather, hauling their kits, but he doubted they'd be of much use. This was the third execution site they'd come across, and the previous mass graves had been just that. They'd found no survivors.

Prather walked slowly, subdued and even indifferent to what he would find. From the line of bodies it looked like a platoon had bought it. The blue diamond patch, bordered in yellow, on their uniforms marked them as Rangers. He wondered if they'd been tricked by krauts dressed up as Americans. He'd heard rumors of that happening. Most likely, they'd been grabbed up by the SS. Wehrmacht units were beginning to surrender en masse, but as things fell apart Himmler's storm troopers seemed to become even more inhuman in the face of their imminent defeat. The last time he'd had anything like an intelligence briefing, it had stressed the need to be aware of the possibility of poison gas, even germ attacks. Apparently something like that was happening already on the Eastern Front. Although what the hell they were supposed to do about it if the Germans started lobbing shit like that at them, he had no idea.

Neither had the briefers. When asked they'd simply repeated the mantra. *Be Alert.*

Prather plucked a long, clean stalk of grass and began to chew it as he walked. It was a bleak day, with low clouds glowering at him from over the treetops. The dark forest along which they had been skirting loomed to his right. It looked like the sort of place you'd expect to find gremlins and trolls. Ahead of him, the medics were at work, methodically checking each body for signs of life. He didn't—

"Captain! Captain Prather. This one's alive!"

He spat out the stalk and hurried over. He tried to ignore the extraneous details: the promiscuous way in which many of the bodies sprawled over one another, and the thick black knots of flies that seethed around the terrible wounds. One medic continued with the hopeless task of checking the dead, but he was hurrying now as his colleague worked frantically to strip away the webbing and jacket of the critically wounded soldier.

"Hey, shit! This is a woman!"

Prather almost tripped over a leg gone stiff with rigor mortis. His heart leapt into his mouth. He dropped to his knees beside the body. She was covered in mud and gore, almost unrecognizable really, but still he knew it was her. The reporter.

"What the fuck . . . ?"

The medic was having trouble cutting through her battle dress.

"Don't bother," Prather said. "You've hit ballistic plate. There, *under* the jacket, see. You'll just blunt your knife. Quickly, here, pull these tabs."

The plastic material—he forgot the name—came apart with a ripping sound.

The second medic appeared, shook his head quickly to indicate that nobody else had made it, and kneeled down beside them. He joined in the effort, pouring water over her exposed chest to clean away some of the filth. No entry or exit wound, just massive bruising and a deep indentation below the heart. She was breathing, shallow and ragged.

"Quick, check her for bullet wounds," Prather said. "She's wearing twenty-first armor. She might be all right if—"

"Captain," said one of the medics. "They got machine-gunned from fifty yards away. At this range the impact alone would kill—"

"No," he insisted, shaking his head. "This is reactive matrix armor. Nanotube waffle. I've read about it. It can shed enormous loads of kinetic energy. If she hasn't been punctured, she'll need treatment for shock. It could still kill her."

The corpsmen began rifling through the contents of their medical kits. Prather stood back to give them room. He wondered how Julia Duffy had gotten herself into this mess. Last he'd heard, she was supposed to be "embedded" with Patton. She must have struck out again on her own and walked into the shit with these poor bastards.

One of the medics elevated her feet by bundling up a couple of bloodied jackets and using them as pillows. The other checked her pulse and pupils.

A couple of scouts came trotting back from the forest to report. "We got nada, Cap'n. Krauts have gone for good. They left a few signs, though. SS by the looks of things."

"No shit," he said, not bothering to hide his bitterness. He'd liked Duffy. She was a good egg and, from what he'd heard, a hellcat in a fight. He'd read a couple of her pieces, here and there, when he'd found out she was coming to write about them, and he'd thought the style a bit overdone, but in herself she was a real gem. The enlisted men loved her.

Prather levered himself up, his knees creaking painfully. He felt about fifty years old.

How does an old fart like Patton do it?

One of the scouts noticed Duffy's breasts.

"Hey, is that is a dame?"

"Yeah," Prather said. "Good eye. Okay, let's get it done. Tag the site. Call in a medevac for Ms. Duffy. Mark the grid up for War Crimes and Graves registration. Then we'll push on."

He turned away and walked slowly back to his tank. He was looking forward to climbing back inside and embalming himself in the rank stew of diesel fumes, body odors, and mechanical stink. His face was contorted with disgust. It was an expression he recognized on every man he passed.

Fucking Nazis, he thought. "I hope the Reds nuke the fucking lot of 'em."

D-DAY + 37. 9 JUNE 1944. 2134 HOURS.
HMS *TRIDENT*, NORTH SEA.

"One of ours, you say? I didn't think we had any of ours out there at the moment?"

"Aye, Captain. Seems to be a wee stuff-up. She's a civvy. An embedded reporter. Ms. Duffy," explained her XO.

"Julia Duffy?" Halabi asked, raising her eyebrows in surprise. It was deep night outside, and she could see her reflection in the armored glass of the slit windows in the stealth destroyer's bridge.

"Aye, Cap'n. Embedded with the U.S. Seventh Cavalry on D-Day. But she's still listed in Fleetnet as part of the original Multinational Force complement. So she's been sent to us."

Halabi shook her head at the way clerical errors seemed to be the only constant across the multiple realities.

"Do we have the bed space?"

"Aye, ma'am. Three empty cots. No waiting."

"Oh well," the *Trident*'s skipper said, "no harm done then. How is she?"

McTeale checked his flexipad. "Four broken ribs, a small puncture of the left lung. Deep-tissue damage to the upper torso. Apparently she survived an impromptu firing squad. We can patch her up, send her on in a day or two."

"Sweet mother of God," Halabi said as she sipped at a steaming mug of tea. "She's indestructible. Is she conscious? Is she talking to anyone?"

McTeale nodded. "Aye, ma'am. Cursing up a storm, by all reports."

"That'd be right," Halabi said, grinning. "You can look after the shop for a few minutes, Mr. McTeale. I might as well pop downstairs and have a word with our celebrity contestant."

"Very good, ma'am."

Halabi left the bridge and headed across into the starboard hull of the trimaran. The ship was quiet, but not exactly calm. The storms of the last few days had whipped the North Sea into a bit of a washing machine, and her passage through the companionways of the stealth destroyer was a matter of lurching from one handhold to the next. She passed only a few crewmembers, however. Many of her sailors were asleep in their bunks, although the Combat Information Center was fully staffed around the clock, the sysops keeping a constant watch on the feed from the Nemesis arrays. A third of them were monitoring the Eastern Front, and the ship was full of 'temps again, as "experts" in the Soviet military had come aboard to make sense of the data stream pouring in from Poland.

She always felt as if she had unwanted houseguests when the number of 'temps passed a certain point. This lot wasn't too bad. They tended to be of a more academic bent than the usual run of buffoons, and she hadn't been dragged into a pissing contest with any of them so far.

Still, she felt uncomfortable, which was ridiculous, wasn't it, really? It was *her* ship. The crew respected her, and she was doing a great job. In her cabin she had personal letters of thanks from both the king and the prime minister. Her dress uniform was heavy with medals, and the BBC had even had her in as a guest on *Desert Island Discs*. She'd chosen Albinoni's Adagio in G Minor, a Dvořák setting of Te Deum, and a couple of grrrl-power standards like the Donnas' "Fall Behind Me" and Anna B's "Mister Tubbs," before finishing with Jurassic 5 kicking it on "What's Golden." The host, Roy Plomley, was a charming man who was more than chuffed that his little radio program would play on well into the next century—all things being equal. But of course, they weren't.

As pleasant as the interlude with Plomley had been, it was one of the few really enjoyable moments she'd had since coming home. Some days it was hard even to think of England as her home anymore. She had some family here, on her mother's side, but one meeting with them had been more than enough. They'd been horrified at the idea of a "darkie" in the family. Her father's family was somewhere in Pakistan, which wasn't even Pakistan yet, and perhaps never would be. They'd disowned her back up in twenty-one, when she'd left home to join the navy. They thought her a traitor to the faith, and a couple of the nuttier ones had even written to tell her that her life had been forfeited the moment she'd turned her back on Allah.

Dickheads.

They were a large part of the reason she had no faith in anyone but herself, her crew, and her ship. Once she might have added the navy to that list, but although she'd made one or two friends among her contemporary colleagues, they mostly remained aloof and she often had the impression they were just waiting for the immediate crisis of the war to pass, after which they would deal with her, somehow. It was why she'd resolved to leave the service at the end of hostilities, and move to California to join Mike.

She harbored no illusions about the reception she'd find in parts of the United States—in his hometown in the South, for instance. But then again, neither did Mike, and they'd decided to settle in the San Fernando after the war. She'd had a marvelous time there during the all-too-short week of their honeymoon, dining out in twenty-first restaurants, dancing in clubs with proper music, getting some time to themselves up at Kolhammer's place on the lake. She'd loved "slumming it" in downtown LA, which was like stepping into the History Channel, even with the obvious influence of the Zone having wrenched so much of the old city's culture into such weird and wondrous shapes. Even now she often lulled herself to sleep at night with memories of Mike playing his saxophone in a small Latin jazz club in East LA. She felt more at home there, in some low-rent dive on the edge of the barrio, surrounded by zoot-suiters and beats, than she did in London. Frankly, she couldn't wait for the war to end so she'd be done with the place.

The Zone would eventually revert to contemporary control, but that wouldn't be for a few years yet. And by then, they were both sure, the culture of the Valley, of LA and, even of California itself would have changed sufficiently that a woman of mixed parentage married to a white man need not fear the sort of social chill she often felt in London. Mike also hinted in his e-mails that so many companies had now settled in the San Fernando, and were making so much money out of the Special Administrative Zone, that there was a powerful lobby emerging to retain the arrangement as it now stood. It wasn't something they could discuss openly on official channels, but both of them were very hopeful that with such powerful businesses having an interest in maintaining the Zone as a stand-alone entity, there was a very good chance that Congress would fall in line.

The ship climbed up an especially steep wave before pitching over the top and sliding down the reverse slope. Halabi felt the destroyer slam into the trough at the bottom of the abyss and from long experience surmised that they'd just passed through a wave front about 40 percent larger than the chaotic ten-meter seas they had been fighting for a few days. She pitched forward with the momentum.

"Not to worry, ma'am. I'm sure you'll find your sea legs soon enough."

She looked up to find her master chief, Dave Waddington, smiling at her as he hauled himself up the passage by swinging from one grab bar to the next.

"Cheeky fucker," she said, smiling. "How are the kiddies, Dave?"

"Sleeping soundly, for the most part, Captain. Nothing on the threat boards. I'm about to turn in myself. And you?"

Halabi shook her head. She was very fond of Waddington. A better strong right arm she couldn't have hoped for. She also knew, even though he'd never spoken of it, that he'd picked up the fresh pink scar on his jaw in a bar brawl on shore. Defending her honor, according to McTeale. She was going to miss him. She was going to miss them all.

"I've got a few naughty tigers to tuck into bed before I get my head down, Chief. Night-night."

"Cheers, ma'am," he said, nodding as he dragged himself off toward the chiefs' mess.

She'd made it to the infirmary and pushed aside the curtain to

haul herself inside. Three of the six beds were taken, their occupants secured against the movement of the vessel. She recognized Julia Duffy in the nearest cot. She was on a drip and had
a couple of sensors clamped onto her fingers, but otherwise she
just looked tired. *Very* tired. She'd lost weight, too. Halabi assumed her chest would be heavily strapped under the light blue
gown she wore. Julia turned her head slowly when the *Trident*'s
captain entered, and a smile broke slowly over her face, lighting
it up like a sunrise.

"Long time, skipper."

"A very long time. Honolulu, if I recall. That dinner with
Spruance just after we arrived."

Duffy held out a hand and Halabi shook it gently, taking care
not to dislodge any of the sensors. The reporter looked as
though she might have been crying earlier.

"My XO tells me you've been upsetting my sailors with your
potty language, Julia."

The reporter snorted weakly. "As if."

"So how are you doing? I hear you got caught up in some un-
pleasantness."

Duffy shrugged. When she spoke it was in a disconnected
monotone. "I was working with a Ranger squad on deep recon
up near the Ardennes. We got tumbled, got the shit shot out of
us. Then we got captured. They took all my equipment. Cuffed
us. Put us into a truck. Next thing, we're hopping out in some
field full of SS guys, and I've got a bad fucking feeling. Sure
enough, there's about a platoon's worth of American prisoners
there. Long story short, they line us up and cut us down."

Her eyes welled up again.

Halabi took a wadded-up tissue from her pocket and dabbed
away the tears. "Well, they couldn't have taken all your equipment. File tag says you took a bullet on the plating of your body
armor. Saved your life."

Duffy nodded. "Yeah. I was wearing a Bodyglove nanotube
weave. With inserts. I guess the krauts don't recognize quality
when they shoot it."

"Krauts, is it? You sound like a local, Jules."

"Sorry. Going native is kind of an occupational hazard. I've
been smoking Camels and thinking about fucking Betty Grable,
too."

She tried to shift herself up in the bed and winced, turning a little gray in the face. Halabi leaned down and helped settle her against a pillow.

"Thanks," Duffy whispered. She took a few seconds to steady herself before nodding at the engagement and wedding rings Halabi was wearing. "I heard about you and the Texan," she said, smiling weakly. "So what are you calling yourself nowadays? Captain Mrs. Michael Judge?"

"I'd smack you, but I might kill you," Halabi said around a smirk. "But no. I kept my name. It's quite the in-thing now, you know, for a young lady to keep her name. And I'm such a slave to fashion."

Duffy closed her eyes as another wave of pain washed through her. "S'cool," she croaked. "Just gimme a second."

After a few moments she had it back under control again.

"Well, I'm glad for you, Karen. I interviewed your husband once. Out in the Zone. He was a good guy."

"That Texan charm of his does work wonders on the ladies."

Duffy seemed to set herself, like somebody about to lift a heavy weight. "It didn't work out between Dan and me."

"I heard."

"Yeah. It was my fault—"

"Now, Jules, don't—"

"No. It was. He was a great guy and I totally fucked it up with him. Jesus. What a fucking mess I've made." She started to cry again.

Halabi perched on the edge of the bed. Despite the circumstances she appreciated having a contemporary—a true contemporary, not a 'temp—to talk with. She could relax with someone like Duffy in a way that just wasn't possible even with a member of her crew. The closest thing she had to a female friend was Jane Willet on the *Havoc,* all the way off on the other side of the world. And they could only manage a personal e-mail every couple of weeks at best. Sometimes months went by without any contact.

She didn't know Duffy nearly as well. Didn't know her at all, really. They'd shared a pleasant enough evening at dinner a couple of years ago in Hawaii before the *Trident* left for home. Apart from that, she'd followed Duffy's work for the *Times,* and once she'd done an e-mail interview with her for a brief profile in a series on "women warriors." Given the isolation all the uptimers felt, however, that was enough to make them more than just acquaintances. It was a little like meeting a country-man in a strange foreign land.

"Look around, Jules. The whole world's a fucking mess. An even bigger mess in some ways because we turned up. Our personal problems don't really count, measured up against all that, do they? And at any rate, it's not like you haven't achieved anything since you arrived. Your readers love you. And in my opinion, off the record, you did your country a huge favor exposing Hoover the way you did."

Duffy repaid her with a tentative look. It didn't seem to sit comfortably on her face, and Halabi guessed that it was an unfamiliar expression for the reporter.

"You think?" she asked. "I took a lot of shit for that series. People saying I killed him. You had to read some of the fucking hate mail to believe it. I thought whack jobs like that were all a product of talk radio and Fox. Apparently not."

"I hope you don't blame yourself. You didn't put the gun in his mouth, Julia. He did that, and pulled the trigger all on his own. My first commander used to call that sort of thing natural selection at work. As I read it, Hoover's incompetence and sheer lunacy was largely to blame for the trouble the Yanks had catching those bombers who hit New York. If he'd been on the job like he was supposed to . . ."

Duffy's eyelids fluttered with exhaustion and the heavy drug load she was carrying. "You seem very informed," she said with a soft, cracked voice.

"I married an American, remember? A very political American, too, in his off-duty hours. Mike had no time at all for Hoover. Said he was a menace to society. He read every piece you and just about anybody else ever wrote about him. Used to scan them and e-mail them to me. Instead of love letters I'd get these enormous bloody text files with Mike's annotations on the life and crimes of J.-bloody-Edgar."

"Let me guess. He was a blogger, back up in twenty-one?"

Willet smiled. "I think it's what he misses most about the future. Handing around mimeographs just doesn't do it for him."

Duffy chuckled. It was a low, warm sound. "So why'd you two get together. It doesn't sound like he knows how to treat a gal?"

Halabi smiled again. "Mike looks like a hanging judge, if you'll excuse the awful pun, but he's a sweetie at heart. And he came after me. Looked me up when he was in London for some conference. Took me out to dinner. *Showed me off.* You know how with some guys, when you're out with them, you can just tell they're walking ten feet tall because they think they've grabbed the prettiest girl in the room all for themselves."

The corner of Duffy's mouth quirked up in a fair imitation of a grin. "Yeah, I remember."

"Well, that was Mike. Didn't matter where we went. Who we met. He let everyone know that he was *proud* to have me on . . . on his arm."

Halabi realized she was choking up. She felt Julia's hand on her arm. The clamps and wires of the medical sensors made it feel as though a cyborg was trying to comfort her.

"And I'll bet nobody gave him any shit about it, either," Duffy said, her voice becoming a little muddled now.

"No." The *Trident*'s captain shook her head and blinked away a tear. "He's got that whole Clint Eastwood thing going for him. Not once, the whole time I was with him, did I feel like anything other than royalty. Mike has this thing, doesn't matter how much of a butthead somebody is, they just know he's not going to stand for any bullshit."

The soft *peep* of the computer that controlled anesthetic drip, which had accelerated noticeably when Julia sat upright and winced in pain, dialed back a bit. Halabi composed herself and glanced over at an orderly who was checking the other patients, a couple of RAF pilots fished out of the drink with severe burns. They were deeply sedated and made no sound.

Julia seemed to be drifting off to sleep.

"Jules?"

"Still here. Just."

"You should get some sleep."

"Uh-huh. Could I get a drink?"

Halabi checked with the orderly, who indicated that she could have a few sips from the bottle beside her bed. Halabi lifted the tube to her mouth.

"Thanks," Duffy said when she was finished. "And thanks for having me here. It's . . . nice to . . . you know . . . somewhere modern . . . like . . ."

"Like home."

"Yeah. Like home."

24

"So these are from the guys off Kennedy's ship, right?"

"Yes, Admiral. The *Armanno* inserted three teams on these islands here, here, and here."

Kolhammer's eyes flicked over the hologram display of the target area. It had been a long time since he'd seen a holobloc in action, and it felt a little weird. For once he could empathize with the 'temps. The small group of islands floated inside the black cube on a light blue sea. The display wasn't to scale. The landmass had been magnified for the briefing.

Kolhammer, Judge, and the supercarrier's ops staff clustered around the bloc in a chamber just off the *Clinton*'s CIC. The room was dark and uncomfortably chilly. A couple of 'temp liaison officers from the *Enterprise* stood in for Spruance, who was busy with the last-minute details for his own attack plans. Suspended above the ghostly 3-D display, a video cube ran fresh vision from the Force Recon patrol on the southernmost island. The four monitors flickered with images of Japanese troops tending to carefully camouflaged aircraft.

"They look like Nakajima One-One-Fives, or perhaps -Sixes," said the briefing officer, Lieutenant Commander Brenna Montgomery, in her disconcerting *southern-belle-from-New-Jersey* inflection. Montgomery's dad had been—and probably still was—a technical writer for IBM back up in twenty-one, and his job had taken her from central Jersey to Savannah, Georgia, when she was eleven. The move gave her tough-as-nails childhood accent a strangely soothing southern lilt that Kolhammer could happily listen to all day. It reminded him of his wife,

Marie, who'd followed a similar path through life before ending up in Santa Monica, where they'd met and courted.

"Denny's team has estimated that the Japanese had approximately a hundred and fifty of these units on this island alone," she continued. "Klobas and Whittington report at least another hundred spread evenly across the other two islands, where there seems to have been less time to prepare facilities."

Montgomery checked her flexipad.

"Looking at the stats from the original time line, given numbers like that you'd expect about thirty-five of the *kamikazes* to get through a contemporary air defense net. We have no way of knowing what the AT mods will do to those numbers. But we do know that eighty percent of the ships struck by aircraft of this type were sunk. They generally load out with three hundred fifty kilos of high explosive for the one-way trip, so that's not surprising."

Kolhammer asked a sysop to pull the view in closer on the main island. The computer-generated image swelled to fill the entire block. It was much more rudimentary than he remembered from before the Transition, but that was to be expected, given the relative lack of imaging power they now had to call upon. It was less photo-realistic, too, and something more like a cut-scene illustration from an old Xbox game. The task group commander pointed at a couple of dark circles at the base of the major feature of the island, a two-hundred-meter-tall hill at the eastern end.

"How long till Denny can give us some of idea of what they've got stashed in there?" he asked.

Lieutenant Commander Montgomery didn't need to check her own briefing notes. She nodded at a flashing blue triangle halfway up the elevation. "They've been trying to gain access for eight hours now, Admiral. But a frontal approach is a no-go. Drone surveillance indicates there are a couple of ventilation shafts that might work out, but the island is thick with enemy troops, sir, and there's no way we can extract our guys if the brown stuff hits the fan. The Japanese make 'em, and they're dead meat on a stick. Sir."

Kolhammer folded his arms and let his chin sink onto his chest. He looked very unhappy.

Mike Judge spoke up from the other side of the bloc. "I'm guessing that great minds think alike, Admiral. To me, that looks like a hell of a lot of engineering work for something as lame as a Nakajima One-One-Five. Even a hundred and fifty of them. You want my five cents' worth, Yamamoto's got some evil jack-in-the-box just waiting to pop out of those holes and make us jump."

"Uh-huh," Kolhammer grunted. "Could be. Ms. Montgomery, what's the latest vicious gossip on the Japanese, uh, *tokkotai*? Is that the right term?"

"Yes, sir. From *tokubetsu kogeki tai*, or special attack units. Captain Willet sent a burst from the *Havoc* a few hours ago, a report about a couple of midget submarines, probably *Kairyu*-class analogs, that blew themselves up under a Russian—*sorry, a Soviet*—troop carrier off Sakhalin Island. She's also logged one large wave of Nakajima One-One-Fives, which flew up out of Hokkaido, probably from Hakodate, and threw themselves onto a couple of Soviet divisions. Caught them in a choke point. Damn near wiped them out, too. But that's it, so far."

"What about rocket bombs? *Ohkas,* or whatever they called them last time," Kolhammer asked. "Any chatter about them yet?"

"No, sir," Montgomery answered. "Quiet as a mouse. A bit like that Sherlock Holmes story. The one where the dog *didn't* bark. Makes you wonder, if you're so inclined."

Captain Mike Judge leaned over the holobloc, examining the island like a three-dollar bill. "You could fit a lot more on that island than the Nakajimas Denny's counted. And they're all out in the open, well, sorta. They're all under that netting in those sunken pits. Does make a man wonder, what's the point of driving so many big goddamn holes into that mountain if you ain't got jack worth hiding down there."

Kolhammer nodded. "I agree. Brenna, I'd like to put a request through to Admiral Spruance to have Denny's recon patrol penetrate the inner perimeter of that mountain facility, *whatever the cost.*"

"Sir," she replied in a clipped voice. If so ordered, the men were almost certainly going to die.

Kolhammer looked even more unhappy than he had a few minutes earlier.

"I wish I had some of Lonesome's guys in there," he muttered.

D-DAY + 38. 10 JUNE 1944. 1136 HOURS.
USS *KANDAHAR*, PACIFIC AREA OF OPERATIONS.

The message—a simple e-mail—had been sent anonymously, and Jones hadn't thought to look at it until it was too late.

Three months after the congressional hearings into the second sneak attack on Pearl Harbor had concluded that the Japanese had received *some* assistance from unknown members of the crew of the *Dessaix,* a 'bot cleaning out his message stacks found the unopened note from his brother-in-law, Sublieutenant Philippe Danton. Monique's little brother, whom he'd met only once, at the wedding, had been named as a possible collaborator in the Japanese attack, and perhaps even a saboteur. A few fragmentary signals between the *Dessaix* and Yamamoto's fleet, picked up before the Japanese had reestablished emission control, implied that one of the Frenchmen on board had turned on his erstwhile comrades after disrupting the missile strike, and Jones had known, down in his bones, that it had to be Philippe.

Such evidence as was available all pointed to his involvement in thwarting Hidaka's attack. But still the committee had returned an open verdict, saying that nothing could be settled until after the war, when the enemy's own records might be inspected. It had taken all of Jones's moral strength not to see that as insult directed at him. God only knew there were plenty of people who were more than happy to characterize it as a strike against his own reliability.

Now, as he sat in his small cabin on the *Kandahar,* finalizing his personal affairs in preparation for what promised to be a terrible slaughter, a couple of lines of text floated on the small screen in front of him, threatening to unbalance the frail equilibrium he had sought to achieve between his personal ill feelings about the 'temps—or some of them, anyway—and his loyalty to and love of the corps and the country he had served all of his adult life.

My Dearest Brother
    I hope you get this message, for I do not think we shall ever meet again. You will know by now that my ship has arrived here, but we were captured by the Germans during our incapacity after the Emergence . . .

Jones frowned at the word, but having materialized in the Atlantic and been taken prisoner, Philippe would have used the Axis terminology without thinking. He read on.

I have little time. I am watched so closely by the Nazis I could not send this message before now, and even now I cannot send it directly. I have encrypted a pulse to go out with the launch of the missiles on Hawaii. I can only pray it finds a Fleetnet node somewhere and eventually finds you. I have done what I can to impair the fascists' plans but I fear it is not enough. There is no more time. When they discover what I have done my life will be forfeit, but I shall do what I can before the end. I do not know if you will ever see Monique again but if you do, please make her understand that I did not dishonor my family or the Republic. Vive la France. And good-bye, brother.

Philippe

Stony-faced, keeping the tightest rein on his emotions, the commander of the Eighty-second Marine Expeditionary Brigade opened two encrypted files that were attached to the mail. In the first he found a list of names: the crew of the *Dessaix* and brief notes explaining the fate of each man after their capture. At a glance it looked like most had been tortured and killed by the Gestapo for refusing to cooperate. A few, like Philippe—with the consent of their CO, Captain Goscinny— had pretended to work with the Germans in order to have a chance at sabotaging the vessel. Only his brother-in-law had survived long enough to sail into the Pacific.

In a separate section, Philippe named a handful of crewmembers who had genuinely gone over to the enemy.

The second file was a technical log of all the actions carried out by Philippe and the other saboteurs. It was mostly beyond Jones's understanding, but it seemed impressively long. It made him wonder what might have happened *without* their interference.

Poor kid, he thought. It must have turned pretty fucking ugly on that boat when Hidaka realized what had gone down. He sent a quiet prayer to his brother-in-law before closing the e-mail and its attachments.

He hadn't even realized Philippe was on the *Dessaix* until a couple of boxheads from 'temp Naval Intelligence turned up in the Zone to ask him about it. There was nothing to be done now but send a copy of the message to Kolhammer and Spruance, with a letter asking that they make sure it got back to the relevant authorities in Washington and London, where the French government-in-exile still had its headquarters.

But then, after a moment's consideration, he opened his address file and pulled up an address for Julia Duffy. She'd written some good stuff about that business with Margie Francois sanctioning those camp guards in the Philippines. And she'd gone into Hawaii with the battalion when they took it back from the Japanese. She was a good embed. She could be trusted, and she wasn't beholden to the chain of command. Not like the admirals.

General J. Lonesome Jones knew he could trust Kolhammer and Spruance. But the guys above them?

As if.

After all, look what had happened when Francois came to him with that DNA match on Anderson and Miyazaki's killer. They'd taken it to Kolhammer, who'd taken it right up the chain, and he'd been assured at every step that it'd be dealt with.

The bottom line? Two years on and the murdering prick was not only walking free but living off the fat of the land.

Jones grunted in disgust.

He knew that Kolhammer had made the case his personal jihad, but he also knew that in the end it hadn't counted for anything. The 'temps weren't about to have one of their heroes perp-walked, not on this one.

There's no way the thing would have been so completely smothered if the victims hadn't been a *nigger* and a *Jap.* Well, there might be nothing he could to do for them, but at least he could prevent Monique's little brother from swinging in the breeze.

And with that thought, he hit the SEND button.

D-DAY + 38. 10 JUNE 1944. 1422 HOURS.
USS *HILLARY CLINTON*, PACIFIC AREA
OF OPERATIONS.

"Holy shit," Kolhammer said.

He'd just sat down in his stateroom to a late lunch of stale ham sandwiches and a cup of coffee when he read the e-mail from Jones.

"What's up?" asked Mike Judge, who was also taking a ten-minute break, the only downtime they'd get for the rest of the day.

Kolhammer shook his head and sniffed.

"Lonesome was cleaning out his accounts and he found an old note he'd missed. Here. Have a look."

The touch screen was too big to swivel, forcing Judge to walk around the desk in the admiral's office.

"Yeah. Okay. Holy shit is about right," he said after scanning the message.

"He copied it to Julia Duffy at the *Times,* as well," Kolhammer noted with more than a little chagrin.

"I saw. Do you blame him, though? It's a personal letter. Sort of. And he took a lot of shit over Danton. Probably figures there'd be someone somewhere wanted to hush this up, for whatever reason. Politics, you know."

"Yeah. I know."

Kolhammer chewed joylessly on the sandwich. Unlike Mike Judge, he knew that Jones was probably thinking of something more than his brother-in-law's reputation, and by extension his own. Besides Jones, of all the uptimers, only he and Margie Francois knew about the DNA match that related back to the murders on Oahu, just after they'd arrived. Of the 'temps, Nimitz knew, because Kolhammer had taken it to him, demanding justice.

But Nimitz was dead. Before he'd died, though, he'd extracted from Kolhammer a promise that the admiral would deal with this through channels. Kolhammer had no idea how far Nimitz had taken it, but right now the case was still sitting, undisturbed, in Washington. In his darkest moments he had considered opening a file in the Quiet Room back in the Zone, but signing off a sanction on an American citizen without the benefit of a trial was a step too far.

"I think I'd better call him," Kolhammer said, shaking himself out of his reverie.

D-DAY + 38. 10 JUNE 1944. 1429 HOURS.
USS *KANDAHAR,* PACIFIC AREA OF OPERATIONS.

"It's got nothing to do with that rapist motherfucker," Jones said.

"I wouldn't hold it against you if it did," Kolhammer replied.

Mike Judge had left him to it, carrying away the remains of their so-called lunch. Kolhammer hadn't dicked around when he'd called the marine officer, asking him why he'd thought it necessary to cut the press in on the Danton e-mail.

"She's not just press, she's one of my original embeds. I *trust* her."

"And not me?"

"That's unfair, Admiral. You're tied down by politics. Marge Francois got a clean match on his blood and semen. As good as a needle in the arm, where we came from. And you couldn't do a damn thing about it. That file is sitting in somebody's bottom drawer back in Washington, stamped TOO FUCKING HARD, and meanwhile he's rolling around the country copping blow jobs from movie stars."

Kolhammer kept himself still, stifling the urge to drum his fingers on the desktop where Jones could see and hear his frustration via the video link.

"You might want to recall, Lonesome, that Ms. Duffy was a big part of creating the guy."

Jones nodded on screen. "And she'd send him to Hell in a goddamn New York minute if she knew about that match."

Kolhammer couldn't argue with that. He knew Duffy well enough after two years to be able to understand her on a professional, if not personal, level. He doubted that even Dan Black had really known what went on deep inside her heart. He leaned back and showed Jones his open palms, conceding the other man's point.

"Lonesome, it was a personal communication. Granted, it was about military concerns—but I'll stand behind your decision to release it. It's not like you sent her the attachments, after all."

"No, it's not. And thank you."

Kolhammer shook his head.

"You don't have to thank me. You have a right to expect my support, and you haven't always had it when you needed it, the last few years."

It was Jones's turn to shake his head. "You've had your own battles to fight, Admiral. That shitty business with Hoover and his pet congressmen. The Zone. The Old Navy. I haven't been looking for you to get my back because I knew you had a full-time job watching your own."

Jones's image loomed in the monitor as he leaned toward the camera.

"Just so as we're clear. I don't blame you for the Anderson-Miyazaki thing, either. I know you went to the mat. It was almost like they were using it as a lesson."

"What d'you mean?"

"Do you really want to go there?"

"Probably not, but go on."

"I don't think the little prick was alone. Our War Crimes people said there was evidence of at least four attackers. And as big as he is now, I don't think he could have avoided the payback unless he had someone protecting him. We don't even know how he came to cross paths with Anderson and Miyazaki. There was a curfew, if you remember. And that drunken asshole they assigned to the case was like a fucking caricature of a bad cop. He was never gonna make it happen. You want my opinion, someone let the 'temps smack a few of our guys down. Make sure we understood who the big dogs were.

"I don't think they meant for things to get outta hand like they did, but that cracker asshole was a ticking time bomb. They were probably hoping he'd get himself killed by the Japs, and his buddies with him. But true or not, none of this will ever be tested, because it's such a septic mess now it's gotta be buried so deep nobody can ever dig it up."

"Jesus, Lonesome. You should have written for television or something. You really believe all that?"

Jones threw his hands up. "What I believe is irrelevant, isn't it?"

Kolhammer opened his mouth to say that no, it wasn't, but he couldn't.

"Okay, look," he said instead. "On your brother-in-law, I've already sent a heads-up to Spruance and Pearl, insisting that Danton's message goes onto the record. Even if you hadn't sent it on to Duffy, I would have had it released in the Zone. So it is going to happen, one way or another."

Jones nodded brusquely.

Kolhammer continued. "On this other stuff, I don't know. There *will* be consequences. I can't say what, exactly, but you're probably right in thinking that somebody wanted us to understand our place in the world, at least as far the investigation went. Making any headway on that case was like pushing wet sand uphill. And I promise you that when I get back, if I don't get some satisfaction, I'm gonna nuke the fucking hill. And if that gets us nowhere, then there's always the Room.

"Okay?"

A shadow of a smile passed across the marine's features. "Okay."

"Now," said Kolhammer. "Last I recall, we were supposed to be at war or something. How's that going on your end?"

25

D-DAY + 39. 11 JUNE 1944. 0012 HOURS.
HIJMS *YAMATO*, PACIFIC AREA OF OPERATIONS.

Long before the Kuril Islands appeared over the horizon, Yamamoto could see evidence of the firestorm raging around them. The first signs of the titanic battle became obvious as the Combined Fleet steamed up past the southern reaches of Hokkaido. The new Siemens radarscopes picked up faint returns from the waves of *tokkotai* streaming north to throw themselves on the Bolshevik invaders.

Standing on the bridge of the mighty *Yamato,* peering into a deep obsidian darkness that seemed to flicker with the intimation of a great storm, he felt like a boy creeping along the edge of a volcano in which lived unknowable numbers of demons and monsters.

He was going to his doom, of that at least he was certain. Of nothing else but that.

It was the third time he had sortied from Hashirajima at the head of the fleet, and only on the first occasion had he done so with anything approaching a sense of confidence—or rather hubris. That was now what he thought of his mental state before the accursed miracle at Midway.

The attack on Hawaii, which had gone surprisingly well,

thanks to Hidaka and the *Dessaix,* had nonetheless occasioned in the grand admiral a crisis of faith. It had been an entirely negative gambit. He'd known then that he had no hope of defeating the Allies. Even before the emergence of Kolhammer's barbarians, the strategic weight of this struggle lay with the industrialized democracies. Hawaii was taken to buy time, and nothing more.

Time that had proved to be worthless.

Yamamoto steadied himself by laying a hand against the cool metal of a bulkhead as dizziness threatened to sweep his legs out from underneath him. There would be no German atomic bomb. No Japanese revenge for Hiroshima and Nagasaki—although to be pedantic about it, those events hadn't yet happened. Even if the Communists had not stabbed them in the back, he doubted they could have held out against the so-called free world. The Americans and British were fanatics, not warriors as he understood the term. They would not rest until their enemies lay charred and dead, in the ruins of a hundred incinerated cities.

"A message, Admiral."

Yamamoto took the scrap of paper from the earnest young lieutenant. Three seaplanes had gone missing on patrol southeast of the Marianas. They had not reported anything untoward in their last scheduled updates, but their sudden vanishing spoke volumes. Kolhammer and Spruance were moving in.

Yamamoto could not help but feel disappointment that what would surely be his last action would not be against them. He had prepared as well as any man could, given the disparity in the two forces. The battle for the Marianas would probably have ended with the Stars and Stripes flying over the islands, but he was certain that if he had been able to deploy his defenses as he'd planned, he would have struck a heavy, perhaps even a crippling, blow against the old foe.

Instead he was creeping north at the head of a much-reduced Combined Fleet, a force about a third of its original size, to spend himself in a desperate lunge against the emperor's newest enemies, the godless hordes of Joseph Stalin. He wished he'd never heard of Kolhammer or the Emergence. It would have been better to perish as he was meant to, shot down in 1943. Even defeat and occupation as they had originally played out would have been preferable to enslavement under the Russians, as now seemed to be the fate of Nippon.

He was aware of the grim mood on the bridge of the battle-ship. There was none of the elation or anticipation of victory he remembered from Midway or Hawaii. How could there be, when he had such limited resources with which to gamble? He had only three carriers under his command, and one of them, the *Nagano,* was a converted cruiser with nothing but *tokkotai* aboard. Once they were launched, she would revert to a simple support role, her offensive capacity entirely used up.

He caught himself shaking his head. There would be no *Kassen Kantai* with the U.S. Navy, no last great decisive battle. His life and the lives of his men would be spent in a hopeless, unplanned stand against an enemy of whom they knew little, other than the fact that he enjoyed a vast superiority in men and matériel.

Yamamoto flexed his injured left hand, which ached with phantom pain. He had lost two fingers fighting against this same adversary almost four decades earlier, at the Battle of Tsushima. That engagement had been a stunning victory over an old, corrupt European regime.

It had heralded a new world.

He feared that this next battle against the Russians would do exactly the same, but with infinitely darker consequences for his countrymen.

D-DAY + 39. 11 JUNE 1944. 0232 HOURS.
HMAS *HAVOC*, PACIFIC AREA OF OPERATIONS.

"Captain? You'd best come see this."

Jane Willet tried to blink the crust of sleep from her eyes, but it was too thick, forcing her to rub away the residue that had accumulated in just a few hours. Not surprising really. She'd been so tired when she turned in that her eyes had been stinging and watery even as she lay her head on the pillow. And stim supplements were just a happy memory.

"S'up," she croaked at her intelligence boss, Lieutenant Lohrey. "Trouble?"

"As usual."

Willet hadn't changed for bed. She'd known she was only ever going to get her head down for a short time, anyway. Shrugging her gray coveralls back on over her shoulders, she accepted a cup of tea from Lohrey.

"Cheers," she said as she sipped at the steaming mug. "So don't let me die wondering, Amanda."

"Looks like the Marianas gig is off," Lohrey said. "We've got a major Japanese force at the edge of the threat bubble, heading toward the Sovs at full clip."

That got her attention.

Everyone had been wondering what the Japanese would do, faced with a two-front attack. There'd been little evidence of any ground units being moved from the Marianas, but until now the question of the imperial fleet had remained open. Willet sucked down a mouthful of the painfully hot black tea. It completed the job of waking her up.

"Okay. Bring me up to speed."

The two women squeezed out of her cabin, heading for the Combat Center a short distance away as Lohrey filled her in on the latest.

"All organized resistance on Kunashir and Shikotan appears to be finished. We're picking up evidence of isolated small-unit clashes there, but nothing of greater significance. Red Army engineers have already begun extending airstrips and repairing the port facilities at Yuzhno-Kurilsk.

"The Hokkaido landings are a bloody mess, but the Japanese just don't have the forces in depth to hold out. The mass *kamikaze* raids are really fucking with the Sovs, though, focusing on their landing ships, which are banged up pretty badly. Admiral Yumashev is gonna have some explaining to do."

They entered the sub's control center and Willet nodded to her executive officer, Lieutenant Commander Grey. A quick glance at a nav screen told her they hadn't moved from their new station, thirty miles to the southwest of Kunashir, the southernmost island in the Kuril chain. The Sea of Okhotsk had grown too crowded for comfort, and Willet had ordered the boat back out into the northern Pacific. Now, it seemed, they were lying directly in the path of what was left of Yamamoto's fleet.

"I hear we have company," she said to her XO. Having removed themselves from right under the keels of the Soviet armada, it was no longer necessary to maintain silent running. In fact, they probably hadn't really needed to earlier, but Willet had insisted anyway. Better safe than sorry.

Conrad Grey nodded. "We've got a Big Eye moving south to

cover them, ma'am. No visual yet, but the bird's arrays have locked on and they're showing a task force of forty-nine ships, including at least eleven major surface combatants. We're also picking up indications of some comparatively advanced radar equipment, probably of German origin. The new Siemens sets, if I had to take a punt."

Willet handed the empty mug to a sailor as she reached the battlespace display at the center of her bridge. Three of the sub's four drones were airborne and feeding data back to the *Havoc*. At a safe remove from the hostilities, she was able to lurk just beneath the surface to take the signals live. One large screen ran a vision of the Soviet fleet in the waters off Hokkaido—the northernmost of Japan's main islands—and the southern Kurils. Another featured low-light-amplified pictures of the ground fighting on Hokkaido. But it was a third that claimed her attention, a flatscreen full of computer-generated imagery, representing the approach of Yamamoto's Combined Fleet.

"How long before we get a visual?"

"Twenty minutes, max," Grey responded. "That Big Eye is running down. We can't move her much farther south or we won't get her back."

"Okay," said Willet. "Here's a Pepsi Challenge. Do we sink them or not?"

Lieutenant Lohrey remained poker-faced.

Her XO smiled mischievously. "That's why you make the big bucks, Captain. Those calls are way beyond my pay grade."

"Amanda?"

The intelligence boss shrugged. "You really want my opinion, Captain—let 'em at each other. I think we all know where this bullshit with the Sovs is leading. Yamamoto kills a bunch of these clowns now, just means we won't have to fight them a few weeks down the road."

"You're such a cynic, Amanda."

"Generational ennui, ma'am. Comes from cleaning up after the boomers and those lazy Gen-X fuckers."

"Don't look at me like that, Lieutenant. They ran out of letters for my generation. And for what it's worth, I think you're right.

"So here's my plan. We're going to sit on our arses and do precisely nothing, Generation-X-style. We'll just watch this movie nice and quietly. We'll rip and burn all the data we can get. And in the unlikely event that any of the Japanese survive and turn around to head for Kolhammer and Spruance, *then* we'll kick the shitter out of them. Concur?"

"Sounds groovy," Lohrey said.

"XO?"

"As I said, skipper, that's why you get the big bucks."

"Actually, it's pounds nowadays. And not that many of them. All-righty, then, let's get ready. Prep the last drone. I want full-spectrum coverage of this toga party."

D-DAY + 39. 11 JUNE 1944. 0342 HOURS. HIJMS *YAMATO*, PACIFIC AREA OF OPERATIONS.

"The *tokkotai* are ready, Admiral. They await your orders."

Grand Admiral Isoroku Yamamoto stood at the blast windows, hands clasped behind his back, as immovable as Mount Fuji. He could see the outline of the *Nagano* against the faintest hint of approaching dawn. She stood out from the other two surviving flattops because of the radical tilt of her flight deck, designed to fling the Type 44 *Ohkas* up into the sky at a twenty-degree angle. The piloted rocket bombs were a marvelous engineering feat, yet also an indictment of Japanese science and industry and, beyond that, of Japanese society. While this iteration of the original powered rocket bomb was a vast improvement on the primitive efforts mustered by the navy at the end of the original war, it was still a crude attempt to compete with much more advanced technologies now pouring out of factories in America.

He sighed quietly.

No *American* fliers would be asked to turn themselves into living warheads. Their country was already producing missiles that relied on inanimate circuitry to guide them to their targets. Nothing as wondrous as the rockets and death rays—*lasers,* he corrected himself—that had arrived with Kolhammer. But still a great leap beyond what he had to call upon.

"Admiral?"

Yamamoto half turned toward the timid voice. "Tell them to launch," he muttered.

The junior officer snapped to and barked out an acknowledgment. Behind Yamamoto a small surge of activity swept over the men on the bridge as they moved to play their part in the next act of this long, strange war. Orders spread outward, bringing the crew of the *Yamato* to general quarters, and from there out to the Combined Fleet, where they had the same effect.

On battleships, cruisers, and destroyers men ran to their guns, boots hammering on steel plate, curses and barked commands ringing off the bulkheads. On the fleet carriers *Shinano* and *Hiyo* flight crews prepared waves of old-fashioned dive-bombers and torpedo planes. Down in the hangars the last of the nation's elite fighter pilots awaited the command that would send them aloft to fly combat air patrol over the fleet. A heavy counterattack was expected when the Bolsheviks realized that a new threat had arisen on their southern flank. What form that Soviet attack would take—whether jet planes, or missiles, or something less exotic—nobody could know.

In a few moments Yamamoto would have to make his way down to the plotting room to control the battle from the nerve center of the mighty ship. Not that there was much to control. Unlike his ill-starred plans for Midway, the arrangements for this encounter were the acme of brutal simplicity.

The flight deck of the *Nagano* suddenly blazed into brilliant life as the first of the Ishikawajima Ne-20 turbojets powering Vice Admiral Onishi's pride and joy fired up. Yamamoto lifted a pair of binoculars to his eyes. The sea was quite calm, and the immense mass of the *Yamato* made for an easy ride. The *Nagano* leapt toward him in the twinned circles of the looking glasses. The wind was favorable, and the makeshift carrier was already pointed in the general direction of the Soviet armada, about 150 kilometers away on the far side of the volcanic Kurils and the northeastern quarter of Hokkaido.

Yamamoto prayed that the intervening landmass would hide him from the quarry until the proper time. The fact that no enemy aircraft appeared to be streaking toward them already was a good sign. The Russians were most likely concerned with the next wave of prop-driven *tokkotai,* which had hitherto always approached from Sapporo, on the far side of Hokkaido.

On the *Nagano* jets of white-blue flame threw back the predawn darkness. It was both awesome and terrible, the power he was about to unleash and the sacrifice he was asking of the young men who had willingly turned themselves into his sword.

The first fiery lance shot down the length of the ship's deck. Yamamoto released a pent-up breath as it climbed away. He would never see the long, cigar-shaped plane again. It had a range of only 225 kilometers, enough to carry its payload of nearly fourteen thousand kilos of tri-nitroaminol explosive into the heart of the Soviet fleet, and no farther. The rudimentary ailerons, flaps, and stubby little wings did not provide for anything beyond the most basic maneuverability. The pilots would fly low, straight, and level for most of the distance before plunging their aircraft onto the decks of a targeted vessel at more than a thousand kilometers an hour.

All of the pilots were volunteers, mostly from the liberal arts faculties of the country's universities. They had been trained to seek out American capital ships, concentrating on carriers, large troop transports, and any vessels sporting an unusual number of radar domes or antennae, on the assumption that these latter might be some retro-engineered version of the command and control vessels called Nemesis cruisers. There had been no time to retrain for a different opponent, so the *Ohkas* were flying off with the same instructions.

Yamamoto could only hope it would work.

D-DAY + 39. 11 JUNE 1944. 0346 HOURS.
HMAS *HAVOC*, PACIFIC AREA OF OPERATIONS.

"What the *hell* is that?"

"Not sure, ma'am. But it looks nasty."

Lieutenant Lohrey interrogated the touch screen in front of her, pulling in tight on a view of the odd-looking Japanese carrier. Its runway appeared to have been fashioned into a ramp, a little like the last generation of British and French carriers used back up in the twenty-first. To Willet's eye it was obviously a kludge, but the planes roaring down it were not. Somebody had invested a shitload of time and money in *them*.

She leaned over Lohrey's shoulder, anxious for a quick verdict, but it was her old boat chief, Roy Flemming, who provided the answer.

"It looks like a Yokosuka MXY-series special weapon, skipper. The Japs called 'em *Ohkas,* or Cherry Blossoms. Our guys knew them as *Baka*. Crazy bombs."

While he spoke, Lohrey worked quickly, bringing up all of

the files she had on the subject. She knew Master Chief Flemming well enough to trust his call. Back home he probably had a basement full of scale models of the things. And if she didn't move quickly, he'd start lecturing on them.

"Okay. Got 'em," announced the intelligence officer. "In the original time line, the *Ohka, Baka,* or whatever was produced by the First Naval Air Technical Arsenal, located in Yokosuka. Hence the name. They first appeared in combat on March twenty-first, nineteen forty-five, when fifteen Betty Bombers, carrying piloted rocket bombs attacked Task Group Five-Eight-Point-One. Or they tried to anyway. They got chopped by the air screen about a hundred klicks out before the Bettys could release."

"So they started out as air-launched cruise missiles, with a *kamikaze* pilot to guide them in?" Willet said.

"Yup."

"And now?"

"Looks like the Japanese have been working some mods," she answered. The intelligence officer pulled up half a dozen still shots of the sleek, jet-powered aircraft they had spotted on the deck of the carrier. "The first versions of the *Ohka* ran off a solid fuel and had a range of about fifty-eight kilometers. Later on they switched to thermojets, and then, at the very end, to a turbojet tagged the Ne-Twenty and made by Ishikawajima-Harima Heavy Industries. They picked up range and speed, and there were plans for carrier-launched versions and even land-based models."

Willet's craggy, tattooed boat chief leaned in over the workstation with the two female officers. "If you don't mind me, Captain, Ms. Lohrey?"

"Go ahead, Roy," Willet said.

The master chief dialed up the maximum magnification on one of the stills, and they waited while rendering software cleaned up the image. Flemming narrowed his eyes to gun slits and sucked at his teeth. Willet suppressed a smile. All he needed to complete the scene was a big piece of straw between those teeth. He grunted and mumbled to himself, chewed at his lip, and scratched his thinning hair.

"This is no good, skipper. We've all been wondering why we haven't seen any Japanese jet planes, like the German Two Sixty-twos. This is why, I reckon. They poured all the money into these things. Ms. Lohrey will be able to check the archive but as I recall, first time around they didn't make more than a handful of the later-series MXYs. Looks here like they've got a hundred or so, just on this one ship. And they're independent. Don't need a bomber to launch them. That makes them much trickier for the 'temps to deal with. Originally most of them were destroyed in transit before they launched. With these babies, Yamamoto's got himself an over-the-horizon strike capability. The Russians are gonna get swarmed by these things. It'll be like a mini-Taiwan."

Willet, who had been leaning forward, straightened up and stretched her back muscles. "The Soviets had a pretty good air defense net over that fleet of theirs," she said. "Nothing too flash, but it does the job, in context."

Flemming nodded at the screen. "But these things are out of context, Captain. We've been watching them shoot down old prop-driven box kites. These *Ohkas* are cruise missiles, whichever way you want to cut it."

Willet gave her intel boss a querying glance. "Amanda?"

"I'm with the chief, boss. I think the Sovs are gonna get it in the neck."

Willet shrugged. "Oh well. Shit happens. I can see that worried look in your eyes, though, Chief. So fret not. I'm one step ahead of you. Amanda, cut this into a data package for Kolhammer and Spruance. Immediate flash traffic via Fleetnet. This is probably what's waiting for them in the Marianas if that goes ahead. Chief, you said the Japanese originally worked on a land-based variant on this thing."

"More'n that, Captain. They had blueprints for hiding these things in mountain caves—they were gonna shoot 'em out of the cliffs at the Yanks when they got close enough. Probably woulda done some real mischief."

"Probably will, you mean."

"Yeah. I do."

Willet nodded. All around her the crew in the submarine's Combat Center maintained their vigil on the fighting. Dozens of screens ran with lowlight and infrared coverage of the battle-space. The result was an eerie scene.

On Hokkaido at least half a million men tore at each other across a sixty-five-kilometer front. In the waters offshore, the Soviet invasion fleet seemed unchallenged. Destroyers and light cruisers steamed up near the coastline to lend gunnery support to their comrades who were pushing inland. Overhead at least two dozen Russian fighters maintained a combat air patrol over the ships at all times.

"How long?" Willet asked.

"Not long at all," Lohrey answered. "Those things are really moving."

She nodded at a large screen to her right.

The *Havoc*'s Combat Intelligence had a fix on eighty-two rocket bombs screaming toward the Soviets in a long stream. Apparently there was no forming up into squadrons for the attack. The *Ohkas* just took off and made for the enemy at top speed.

"Amanda, as Captain Judge would say, *git-r-done.*"

D-DAY + 39. 11 JUNE 1944. 0351 HOURS.
PACIFIC AREA OF OPERATIONS.

As he sped toward his death, Corporal Chuji Asami could not shake the image of the girl, Reiko, who had tormented him so with her cat. Asami had always hated cats. It was only natural, having been born in the Year of the Mouse.

Around him the world had contracted to the cramped cockpit of the rocket bomb. The roar of the engine was so powerful, the tremors of the airframe so violent, that he felt as though he was trapped at the very center of an earthquake. Asami gripped the flight stick so tightly that his arms ached, and he tried to concentrate on following the long line of exhaust plumes that stretched out in front of the bubble canopy, like a string of shooting stars. But he seemed fated to face the end of his life pursued by the memory of Reiko, giggling as she chased him around the little noodle house in Chiran Town, holding her cat up like an evil charm.

Was it *his* fault that he couldn't stand to be in the same room as the filthy animal? Could he help it if his face contorted and his flesh crawled at the very sight of the beast? How many times had he complained to Torihamasan? But his friends in the squadron thought it a great joke, and they encouraged the girl in her endeavors, roaring with laughter when Asami fell off his stool in his haste to escape the little troll and her pet. It was only natural that the girl's parents would not discipline her, given the joy she brought to the Thunder Gods with her antics.

That's what they were known as now. The Thunder Gods. Meteors screaming toward destruction. His friends. His leader, Lieutenant Uemura.

That would be Uemura, up ahead. One, two, three, *four* exhaust plumes. He was much older than the rest of the squadron. Twenty-five to Asami's seventeen. A graduate of Rikkyo University, and a father, while most of the men did not even have girlfriends. Asami's heart swelled with memories of how diligently the lieutenant had trained them, how he had looked after them as though they were his own family. He was a kind man, unusually so. He had taken all of his charges to one last meal at Torihama's noodle house before they left Chiran for the fleet base at Hashirajima.

Uemura had produced a barrel of junmai-shu sake from somewhere—a rare treat in these hard times—and among them they had sipped to the last draft. Asami had been so drunk, he had not been able to change the records on the phonograph. And of course Reiki had waited until he was almost incapable of fleeing before suddenly leaping at him from the shadows with the cat in her hand. Such a shock had he received that he bumped his head on a low beam trying to get away. He could feel the gash rubbing against his goggles even now.

Everyone had roared with laughter, but Lieutenant Uemura had picked him up off the floor and shooed the cat away.

"A mouse you may be, Corporal Asami," he'd said, laughing, "but soon the little mouse will terrify a great elephant. Yes?"

"Yes!" Asami had agreed, nodding his head so vigorously that a few drops of blood flew from the graze he had given himself.

"Then drink up, little mouse! You have earned it."

The roar of his friends that night echoed still beneath the roar of his engines. Below, and away to the west, a low moon threw a curving scimitar of flickering light across the waters. Ahead of them, the volcanic peaks of the lower Kurils glowed a dim ruby red. To the east a new dawn hovered on the cusp of the world.

Asami wondered if Uemura was thinking of his family.

Masahisa Uemura's heart ached. The lieutenant had fixed a small doll to his dashboard where he could see it easily. It belonged to his little daughter, Motoko, who had played with it in her crib, and it bore the marks of having been chewed and sucked and handled roughly by her. He intended to focus only on the doll as he plunged his rocket plane into the enemy. That moment, the ending of his life, could not be far away now.

As they approached the volcanic range that shielded them from the Russians his stomach felt like it was trying to rise up into his mouth. The *Ohka*'s airframe shuddered as it plowed into weird, contrary masses of air. He'd struck pockets of turbulence and thickness and strange, empty spaces that were less than nothing. The fiery peaks rushed toward him at an insane rate.

Life rushed away just as quickly. The life he would have led raising little Motoko. Her life, which he would never know, but for which he was about to die.

He craned around as far as could in the restricted confines of his flying coffin. As far as he could tell the men remained in position behind him. He felt better, thinking about that. They were good boys. The bravest of the brave, and he hoped he had trained them well. They were all that stood between the Japanese people, the emperor, and annihilation at the hands of the Communists. He was sure they would do their duty. If only he could be certain that it would mean anything—that the admiral's gambit would pay off. After all, this was not the mission they had trained for.

As he swept through the gap between Kunashir and Iturup islands he caught his first glimpse of the invasion fleet: a dozen or more vessels anchored offshore, their running lights blinking in the gloom. With their speed it seemed they would be past the enemy's lead elements well before he could respond, and indeed, the Communists fell behind him before he observed any reaction on their part. It was probable, however, that the last of the *Ohkas* would fly into a barrage from those ships as the crews realized an attack was under way.

Uemura wrested the plane around on a new heading, taking her a few degrees to the northwest, where the bulk of the Soviet armada lay ahead. He had a very short time left to spend in the same world as his wife and beloved daughter now. A quick check of his wings told him that the guidance lights were functioning properly. His men would be watching closely, trusting in him to lead them toward the quarry. They had been assigned the task of the striking at one of the two "helicopter carriers"

identified as potential command centers for the invaders. Little
was known of how the Soviet air defenses might perform
against them, but hopes were high. They could not be anywhere
near as advanced as the Americans or the Emergence barbarians.

Some of the Thunder Gods should get through.

To the left of his cockpit the northern shores of Hokkaido
ripped past. He took a moment to savor the view. Soon he
would have no time, and everything would pass in a blur. He
sent his daughter a last prayer, reciting the lines of the letter he
had left for her.

Motoko, you often looked and smiled at my face. You slept
in my arms, and we took baths together. When you grow up
and want to know about me, ask your mother and Aunt
Kayo. I gave you your name, hoping you would be a gentle,
tenderhearted, and caring person. I wish you happiness
when you grow up and hope you become a splendid bride,
and even though I die without you knowing me, you must
never feel sad.

As the sun's first rays poured over the horizon, he chanced a
brief gesture, taking one hand off the control stick to stroke the
small doll his daughter had played with and enjoyed so much.

When you grow up and want to meet me, pray deeply, and
surely your father's face will show itself within your heart.
You must not think of yourself as a child without a father.
I will always protect you as I do right now.

And then, it was time.
The enemy ships had appeared in the distance before them.

26

The smell of something like bratwurst awoke him.

"Sorry, guv'nor, but it's sausage sangers for you this morning. Bit of a blow on, you see. No sit-down feed this morning."

"Was ist los?" he asked in his own language, before remembering where he was. "Sorry. What do you mean?"

The English sailor passed him a sausage wrapped in a piece of white bread. Brasch had to brace himself against a bulkhead so as not to go tumbling out of his bunk and onto the floor.

"See what I mean, guv. Got some big seas today. Had to nuke this up for you. Couldn't use the fryer. Brought some coffee, too. Black, two sugars."

As he shook the cobwebs from his head, Brasch thought he understood. They were in the middle of a storm, or at least a rough passage of water, so the galley could not operate as normal. It was good to know that these people hadn't mastered everything. He nodded his thanks as he took the "sanger" and the plastic squeeze bottle with his coffee. The sailor tipped him an informal salute and waited until the ship rolled in the right direction to take him out of the small cabin. Brasch noted that a new guard had come on duty while he'd been asleep.

He checked his watch. He had slept for twelve hours. Exhaustion had caught up with him. Not just the physical and mental strain of his escape, but something more. A release of some sort. For two years he had expected to die in a Gestapo cell. His one respite from the gnawing terror had been the knowledge that his family was safe, somewhere in Canada. He had not been conscious of the effort involved in suppressing his fears for the future of his wife and boy, but it had been enormous.

Now, with the very real possibility that he might not just see them again, but that they might live out a normal life, uncontaminated by the poison of the Nazis . . . well, it was almost too much to bear. Brasch felt giddy, as though teetering on a precipice, which in a way he was. Fate was about to spill him into an entirely new life. Just as it had when he'd survived that day at Belgorod, and been sent east to investigate the arrival of the *Sutanto*. The ship from the future.

He ate the sandwich in three bites, amazed at how the small patch on his inner wrist had quelled his usual seasickness. A few sucks on the coffee bottle revived him even further. The ship's cook brewed an excellent espresso. When he was finished, he swung his feet down and climbed into his boots. The British had given him new clothes, a comfortable civilian outfit. It was odd to think that he would never wear a uniform again. They had relieved him of his flexipad and sidearm, which was to be expected. Otherwise, apart from the guard on his door, he'd been treated with rare civility.

"Excuse me, sir."

Brasch looked up from doing his laces. The guard had put his head inside.

"When you're ready, General. The captain would like a chat, sir."

Brasch nodded as he finished. Steadying himself, he waited for a sympathetic movement of the ship and used it to propel himself upward with at least some control. He had no idea how these nautical types put up with this rubbish. The *Sutanto* had been even worse.

The ship plowed into the base of a steep wave and began to climb. Forcing him to haul himself out of his cabin and into the companionway, where he found an additional guard waiting for him. Whenever he moved about the ship he always had at least two overseers, but they were unfailingly polite, even deferential, as far as it went.

The three men struggled along the corridor, flexing their knees as the deck shifted beneath them. About thirty meters down they climbed to a lower deck and doubled back, ending up somewhere beneath his cabin. Brasch swung in through the door as indicated and found himself in a darkened room, with a handful of Allied personnel gathered around a bank of large, glowing computer screens. Brasch had never made it aboard the

Dessaix while it was being stripped, but he imagined it must have looked something like this. As advanced as the *Sutanto* had appeared to him at first, this vessel was obviously a great deal more sophisticated. The British had not been very forthcoming in answering his questions about it, though.

The *Trident*'s commander, the half-caste woman Halabi, was waiting for him with Prince Harry and a small group of men and women, none of whom he recognized.

"Good morning, Herr General," Halabi said. "I'm glad to see you got your head up. I take it the Promatil patch is working."

"Yes," he answered. "It is working very well indeed, thank you, Captain. Is there something I can help you with? I thought I was supposed to be transferring to land today."

Halabi, who seemed to have no trouble maintaining her balance in the difficult conditions, waved a hand at one of the screens. "My colleagues wanted your input on a few questions, if you wouldn't mind."

Brasch shrugged. "I imagine I'll be doing nothing but answering questions for a long time to come."

"I'm afraid so." She pointed to a distinguished-looking man seated at the table, wearing a British army uniform. "Colonel Hart."

The officer smiled unsteadily at Brasch. He was having a hard time with the violent movement. "Herr General. Young Harry's been telling us of your adventures in Paris. Sounds like a smashing time."

Brasch returned the smile uncertainly. "Like most adventures, it was best experienced in the telling, rather than the execution."

"Marvelous," Colonel Hart said. "Now, if I might. Would you mind awfully telling us if you chaps had any plans for using germ bombs, or poison gas?"

The abrupt change in topic caught him somewhat off-guard, and he had to search for an answer. It wasn't that he wanted to hide anything. Rather, it was that he didn't want to appear to be doing so.

"I didn't work on any such projects myself," he said at last. "It wasn't my specialty. But I understand Himmler did have a special projects section of the SS investigating such weapons. When it became apparent that the atomic program might not deliver quickly enough, he was quite desperate to find an alternative. Why? Has someone used such a weapon?"

"Not on us," Hart replied, before moving aside to give Brasch an unrestricted view of the large computer screen behind him.

Captain Halabi spoke up as he did so. "These images were captured by one of our drones a few hours ago," she explained. "To my people, this looks like a bio-weapon."

Brasch looked on with creeping horror as a movie played in a window on the screen. Shells burst among what he assumed to be Soviet troops. A few near the detonation were knocked down by the blast. Then within seconds their comrades had also dropped, their bodies racked by violent seizures. The small room remained in silence while the footage played. At the end of it, Brasch released a deep breath.

"I see. And how much of this . . . gas, I suppose . . . how much has been used?"

Prince Harry spoke up, his usually jolly personality held in check. "It's impossible to say with accuracy, but we think at least five SS artillery regiments have been equipped with the stuff."

"Only SS?"

"Yes. No Wehrmacht units, so far."

Brasch gripped the back of a chair as the ship took another wild ride through a canyon of seawater. "And tell me, does the effect persist? Are they using it as a—"

"As an area denial weapon?" Harry finished for him. "Yes. It appears so, which is why we wanted to know if you knew anything of this program. Nerve agents that do not easily disperse tend to come from what we call the V-series. They wouldn't have been synthesized for another seven or eight years yet. This doesn't look like the sarin or tabun Hitler began making at the start of the war."

Brasch's lighter mood evaporated, replaced by a dark melancholy that felt all too familiar from his time on the Eastern Front. So inured to surprise had he become since the Emergence— indeed, since his survival at Belgorod—that for a moment part of his mind seemed to float free, to detach itself from his body with a slight tug and hover just above the clutch of military men and women gathered here. Two days earlier, had any of these people chanced to cross his path, they would surely have tried to kill him.

The disconnected moment collapsed in on itself abruptly as Captain Halabi pressed a hand to her ear and began to speak to someone he could not see. Brasch assumed she enjoyed some sort of communications link, perhaps even embedded in her body, of which he was ignorant. There had been no guided tour of the *Trident* for him, but what little he had seen bespoke a level of technological advancement that was *still* almost incomprehensible.

"Excuse me," she said, and Brasch was fascinated to see that they all deferred to this small, colored woman as easily as they might have to Eisenhower himself. "We have more data feeding through on the laser links. Live coverage this time."

Halabi then said something in a hushed tone to the machine operator sitting at the console around which they were gathered. The young woman—another *schwarzer,* although much darker in skin tone than the captain—began to dance her fingers across the screen in front of her. Brasch watched in fascination as items on the display seemed to follow her touch, some collapsing, some inflating to display new windows in which he could see some sort of movie that was running, this time in full color. The woman occasionally dropped her hands to a keyboard and ripped out quick bursts of typing, doubtless entering some command that required more than the brush of a fingertip on a monitor.

"My Intelligence Division informs me that the Soviets are trying to push a division through a valley just here." She pointed at a topographic map on one of the screens. "We'd best watch this down in the CIC, but . . ."

She favored Brasch with a level stare.

"Herr General. It is not my usual policy to allow enemy combatants into the heart of my ship. But Colonel Windsor and your controllers in London assure me that you can be trusted."

Brasch bowed slightly in the direction of the warrior-prince, but Halabi wasn't finished.

"I can be trusted, too, Herr General. I can be trusted to have you thrown over the side in heavy chains if you give me even the slightest reason to doubt you."

"I would expect no less, *Kapitän.* You have quite a fierce reputation in the Reich. Göbbels calls you the black widow, but the men of the *Kriegsmarine* prefer the Black Widowmaker," Brasch said with a wry curve of the lips. He saw Prince Harry smile and heard a couple of the English officers snigger.

Halabi merely cocked a very cool eyebrow. "Well then, if you wish to see your family again, you will behave yourself."

"Of course."

"Mr. Waddington!"

"Yes, ma'am."

Brasch jumped slightly at the strength and proximity of the voice behind him. He hadn't realized that anybody was standing there, but turning slightly he found a slab-shouldered, hard-faced man holding a black device of some sort down near the small of his back.

"Chief, stay close to our guest. If you have to, taser him."

"Yes, ma'am," the man called Waddington replied, with an evil glint in his eye.

"Right, then, follow me ladies and gentlemen," Halabi said, and they began to file out.

Prince Harry hung back and fell in beside the German.

"She is quite the dictator, yes?" Brasch said.

"Liberated women." Harry shrugged. "What's a bloke to do?"

In a different part of the ship, Julia Duffy awoke to find herself dreaming—or at least she thought she was dreaming for a few seconds of free fall before she realized that Captain Marcel Ronsard was indeed standing, somewhat awkwardly, by the side of her bed.

"Holy shit," she said.

Ronsard shrugged. "Not the welcome I was hoping for, but it will have to do. And how are you, *mon cherie*?"

"Well, for one thing," she said, pushing herself up in the bed, which moved to compensate at least partly for the pitch and yaw of the ship, "I'm not your fucking *cherie*. But I guess I'm glad to see a friendly face. A little surprised, though. What the fuck are you doing here?"

Ronsard unloaded another Gallic shrug on her. "You know I cannot say. You, however, I have heard all about. If you did not want to join me in Scotland, you had only to say so, you silly girl. There was no need to run away with Patton to end our affair."

"Asshole." She smiled. "You hear I almost got waxed?"

"They told me," he said, the levity disappearing from his voice. "They said the fascists tried to murder you, along with some GIs."

Duffy sighed, feeling ragged and all too fragile.

"They killed all those boys," she said, shaking her head. "Woulda killed me, too, but I was so covered in mud and crap by that stage they didn't see that I was wearing matrix armor. I don't think they even realized I was a chick. And the boys kept it quiet, God bless 'em. It was kind of a rush job. Not up to the usual efficient SS standards when it comes to atrocities. Himmler is gonna be pissed."

She found a relatively comfortable position and settled into the pillows. "So if you can't tell me where you've been, can you at least say where you're going?"

"Back to Scotland, like I told you. I was delayed in France by a broken heart."

She chuckled, and then winced at the pain. "Jesus, Ronsard, you'll fucking kill me where the Nazis failed."

Julia felt the ship climb up a precipitous wall of water, hover in the air, and come crashing down on the other side with an almighty hollow *boom*. In her specially constructed bed she was hardly troubled, but Ronsard had some difficulty keeping to his feet.

"You wanna hop in with me?" she asked.

"Well, I—"

"I don't mean in that way, Filthy Pierre. I couldn't put out at the moment if my life depended on it."

Ronsard gingerly hopped up on the bed, making sure not to squash her. "So, you are on your way to hospital back in England then?" he said. "And I could come down from Scotland, perhaps, when you are well enough to, what was it, get the leg over?"

Duffy patted him on one leg. "Nice thought, but I'm going back to France."

"You cannot be serious, surely?"

"I am, and don't call me Shirley . . . sorry, old joke."

He looked confused and for a sad, terrible moment she was reminded of Dan. Looking back on their relationship, he'd sported the same poleaxed expression more often than not.

Okay, that was a little unfair. Dan had been in love with her, truly, madly, and deeply, as the saying went. And he'd had that thing Halabi spoke about, that self-satisfied look all men get when they think their woman is the finest piece of ass in the room. He was a great guy, but in the end he just got confused.

Confused about why he loved her. Confused about why she

couldn't be what he wanted. Why she couldn't give any more than she was willing to give. And why that was so little compared with what he'd come to expect of a woman. Most painfully she remembered the complete and utter incomprehension contorting his poor, sad, beautiful face when he discovered that she had aborted their child and sterilized herself.

Compared with that, Ronsard's bemusement was minor.

"Don't bother, Marcel," she said. "I'm from another world. You'll never understand."

He held up a hand in protest. *"Non,"* he said, and she detected a deep sadness behind his martial façade. "I think I understand only too well. You forget I have been at war, too, *cherie.* I was with a woman recently who made a decision that she had to leave and run toward danger. She felt she had no choice."

"And did she?"

"Have a choice. No. And did she go? Yes, she did. And now she is dead, which is why I am able to sit here talking with my beautiful American from another world."

He reached out and stroked away a lock of hair that had fallen in front of her eyes. It was a tender gesture.

"Was she a lover?" Duffy asked, surprised to find out that she cared about the answer, but not so much one way or the other. A strange feeling.

"No. A comrade."

"I'm sorry."

"Such is war, no?"

"I suppose so."

Ronsard took her hand, and they sat in silence for a minute.

If he'd seen this room two years ago, he'd have known that Hitler was doomed.

Stepping into the CIC of the *Trident* was akin to passing into another world. The merest glance at the giant video wall that dominated the hexagonal space was enough to explain why the Allies had seemed almost omniscient at times. In effect, they were. There were too many individual display units for Brasch to be able to count, but all he needed to see was the eight networked monitors that took up three sides of the room. As he stood in front of them, they seemed to enclose him, providing a view of the entire European theater that was godlike. The dcnsity of information available was beyond his ability to interpret.

He assumed that the two or three dozen operators working quietly but briskly at the stations had trained for years before they even set foot in this place. The Continent was buried under hundreds of data tags and miniature video windows, which were themselves in constant flux as one controller or another called up some particular piece of information. As an engineer he could appreciatc the complexity and the decades of development that must lie beneath such a system. So mesmerizing was the effect that he was almost tumbled to the floor when the ship dipped and rolled dramatically on the storm-tossed sea.

"Are you all right, General Brasch?"

It was Halabi, the captain. She had taken his arm with a surprisingly strong grip to save him from the indignity of a fall.

"I was just thinking that if the high command had really understood the danger of this ship, they would have devoted the entire resources of the Reich to its destruction," he said.

"Well, then, best we keep it our little secret. Mr. Howard?"

A dark-haired man pointed a flexipad at the main display, inflating two windows from a couple of tiny data tags that were hovering over the Oder River on the German border with Poland. Brasch was instantly drawn by the movement, but forced himself to take in as much of the wider picture as hc could.

It appeared, as far as he could tell, that both the Eastern and Western fronts seemed to be rapidly contracting toward the Fatherland. Fourteen, maybe fifteen Wehrmacht divisions in the Balkans werc moving north. Dozens of divisions he knew to be in western Germany were now to be found heading east, or had already arrived there. The situation across Western Europe looked chaotic in the extreme. Indeed, there was no front, as such. It seemed to have collapsed in the face of the Allied assault, which was but a fraction of the size of the Soviet attack.

There could be only one explanation. Berlin was throwing everything into a defensive line to keep the Bolsheviks out, and allowing the Americans and British to advance practically at will. It was impossible to tell for sure, because of the complexity of the display. But the use of little electronic flags, just like the wood-and-paper markers on an old-fashioned map table, allowed him to get a rough idea of what was happening.

It meant the end of the Reich, one way or another.

"General Brasch, if you wouldn't mind?"

"Excuse me," he muttered to Captain Halabi. "I am sorry. It is just so . . . so overwhelming."

"The *Dessaix* had a CIC very similar to this one."

"I never saw it," he conceded, struck by the incongruity of the situation. Although he had been one of the most trusted men in the Reich, he still hadn't been considered a safe bet by the SS, which jealously guarded all access to the Emergence technologies. Here, though, the demands of the situation and a word from Prince Harry meant that he found himself in the beating heart of the Allied war effort.

"The top left-hand screen, Herr General, if you wouldn't mind."

He refocused his attention on the appropriate display. Two windows were active. One displayed a Waffen-SS artillery unit busily servicing a battery of 88s; the other, what had to be Soviet infantry. Subsidiary windows leapt out of the second window, resolving themselves into close-ups with quite amazing clarity. It was as though he were hovering a few dozen meters off the ground.

"A penal battalion," he said with distaste.

The British all turned in his direction.

"Why do you say that, sir?" asked the dark-haired man. Mr. Howard, if Brasch recalled correctly.

Brasch nodded at the close-up screen. "Observe. Only one man in three has a weapon. They are making no attempt at concealment. They simply move into the contaminated area and . . . well, you can see."

They could. The Soviets ran forward, only to stumble and collapse. Many regained their feet for a few moments, only to fall again. Almost none made it up a third time. They seemed to be afflicted with fits and dementia. Grotesque spasms twisted their bodies into fantastic shapes.

"I am afraid I am unfamiliar with effects of this nerve weapon," he admitted. "I do not think there is much I can help you with. Other than to confirm that, yes, I know Himmler's men were working on such projects."

"Could you sit down with some chaps in London and work out what industrial capacities the Reich might have diverted to this project?" the army officer called Hart asked of him.

Brasch shrugged. "With the ministry files I sent you, and some help, yes, I could make an estimate."

"Good," Halabi said. "As soon as the weather permits, we'll get you on a chopper. Thank you, General Brasch. Your country will thank you one day, too."

Brasch looked at the red tide pushing toward Germany's eastern border. He wasn't sure his country would exist in a few weeks.

"I find it hard to imagine the führer would allow withdrawal on either front," he said, genuinely perplexed at the story told by the giant electronic display.

"Oh, didn't anyone tell you yet?" Halabi asked. "The führer is dead."

27

D-DAY + 38. 11 JUNE 1944. 0833 HOURS.
RIVER ODER, THE EASTERN FRONT.

Lieutenant Filomenko clutched the Tokarev pistol so tightly he thought the grip might leave a scar on his palm that would last for the rest of his life. Not that he expected to live much past the next few minutes.

As an officer in a Soviet penal battalion, he had a very short life span anyway. He'd been attached to this particular "forward unit" for one month, when all of its other leaders had been killed in the advance through the Ukraine and across the Polish plains. The rules were straightforward. Survive the month, and he could "retire" back to a rifle company, his four weeks of service counting sixfold when it came to calculating his army pension.

At that he almost laughed. Climbing through piles of corpses torn asunder by German artillery, how could the prospect of old age be anything but a cruel joke.

"Move your fucking asses," he screamed at his men, firing off a couple of rounds from the handgun to encourage them forward. It was hard to think of them as "his men," though. These were the walking dead. Criminals. Traitors. Cowards. The very bottom of the barrel.

Wearing blue tunics and black caps they ran forward, shoulder-to-shoulder, only the most trustworthy of them actually armed with imperial-era Mosin-Nagant rifles. Like Filomenko they would shoot down any who wavered. Many of them had no boots. Others had fashioned crude footwear from rags and even sheets of tree bark. If by some miracle they survived the poisoned ground, the swim across the Oder under heavy fire, and the scramble up the far bank, most of them would have to throw themselves onto the fascists with only their bare hands and their teeth to use as weapons.

Filomenko didn't expect to get that far. Hopping quickly over the mounds of his slaughtered comrades, he recited a silent prayer. To be caught even whispering it would mean permanent exile to a penal battalion.

That thought brought forth another ironic chuckle.

"Hail Mary full of grace . . ."

The field sloped gently down toward the river. The ground in between was thick with the dead, but already he could tell the difference between the smashed and shattered remains through which he was currently forced to move—a Stygian field of severed limbs, shredded torsos, and spilled viscera—and the eerily peaceful scene that lay ahead. The soft ground was largely undisturbed, but was carpeted with hundreds of bodies, all of them twisted into hideous contortions. Filomenko expected to taste or smell something besides burned earth and scorched remains, but other than the usual stench of a battlefield, there was nothing.

Perhaps the poison had cleared.

". . . the Lord is with thee . . ."

He had time enough to wonder why the Germans weren't firing at them, and he noticed how dry his mouth had become. He was used to that, of course. Before a big push he routinely instructed his men to carry extra canteens. Although admittedly had hadn't bothered with these animals.

"Blessed art thou among women . . ."

Oh no.

He saw the first man go down about thirty meters in front of him.

"Keep going, keep going," he roared. "Speed is your only hope. *Push through.*"

He squeezed off a couple of shots in the air just above the bobbing heads of the front rank.

"And blessed is the fruit of thy womb, Jesus . . ."

The men pressed on, many of them screaming a guttural war cry. As Filomenko cleared the last of the bodies destroyed by artillery, he fumbled at his hip for a water flask. He was thirstier than he had ever known.

He blinked away tears and snuffled up a runny nose. Still moving forward, he tried to raise the flask to his lips but missed, hitting himself in the cheekbone.

"Holy Mary mother of God . . ."

The front ranks were down now. Tangled up with the arms and legs of the men who had gone before, and died.

It was no use. They would not get through.

Another soldier in another army might have turned back. But not a Russian. One of the convicts turned around and jerkily attempted to retrace his steps. Filomenko shot him in the face.

"Forward! *Forward!*"

A dizzying wave of nausea enveloped him, and his chest felt so tight he thought he might be having a heart attack. It felt as if he'd run thirty kilometers, not the two and a half they had just covered. His legs buckled at the knees and he fell forward, landing with a bone-jarring thump next to a man who was shrieking and gurgling, clawing at his own eyes.

Filomenko's bowels evacuated, massively and violently. He vomited with such force that surely he must have ejected a part of his own stomach. Great spasms began to convulse his body, and he found himself facedown, thrashing involuntarily, sucking up clods of dirt.

"Pray for us sinners now and at the hour of our death . . ."

Lieutenant Filomenko wanted to cry out. But he couldn't.

D-DAY + 38. 11 JUNE 1944. 1108 HOURS.
THE KREMLIN, MOSCOW.

It wasn't a simple thing to make an atomic bomb. Not a simple thing at all. If only the *Vozhd* would realize that.

Beria had a piercing headache and was sick with worry precisely because Stalin refused to accept this fact. The general secretary sat across the desk from him, regarding the NKVD chief with a cold, implacable stare. It was a look as empty of human feeling as the expression on a bronze statue. Indeed, any sculptor who produced such a likeness would probably be shot. None of the other men in the room gave him the slightest hint of sympathy.

"I have been pushing and pushing, Comrade General Secretary," Beria protested. "I even had a couple of laggards and their families removed from the program and transferred to a punishment camp, just to encourage the rest."

"Really?" Stalin said. His expression didn't change. No one else dared speak.

Beria was about to reiterate how stern and uncompromising he had been in pursuit of the business of state, but something in Stalin's tone stopped him.

The supreme leader of the Soviet Union spoke again in a chillingly flat manner.

"Perhaps you should not have done that, Laventry Pavlovich. Your methods have been somewhat crude, yes? If you had not been so heavy-handed with those few British sailors who survived the Emergence, perhaps we would not be having this unpleasant conversation. Perhaps we would be toasting the victory of the workers in Berlin. Or London. Or Washington."

This was intolerable! Stalin accusing *him* of being crude!

Beria was only too aware that every eye in the conference room was now resting on him. The chill in Stalin's gaze was repeated a dozen times around the table as the other members of the *Stavka,* the supreme Soviet war council, weighed the risk of incurring his wrath should he survive this meeting.

Clearly they found his chances wanting. The military officers remained stone-faced, but he could see all too well the shameful joy in the eyes of the civilian ministers, especially Malenkov. That fat freak was practically wetting himself with suppressed mirth.

Standing in his place at the table, struggling to control the tremors that wanted to turn him inside out, Beria fought for his life.

"Comrade General Secretary, it was necessary to adopt the harshest measures with the captives. If I might be allowed to remind you, they attempted to destroy their own ship when apprised of its situation. And there was no way for us to know that they possessed the inserted devices that allowed them to withstand so much pain. Indeed, we did not even know we were killing them! Our methods seemed to yield few results until it was too late."

Stalin did not shout. He didn't respond at all. He played with his empty pipe, which Beria knew from long experience was infinitely more worrying.

Finally he spoke. "And the last of them, the Negro woman. You knew about *her* inserts. Did you not?"

"Yes, we knew," he cried. "And we tried to remove them. I have written authorization from you, approving the procedure. Nevertheless, it was no easy thing to dig such a device out of a woman's spine. Little wonder that she died on the table."

"For which you jailed the doctors, if I remember correctly," Stalin replied. "They failed and they were punished."

"*You* failed. So?"

A grin slithered across Malenkov's ugly face, like an eel, but Beria concentrated on bargaining with the *Vozhd*. "The bomb we dropped on Lodz did not fail. It wiped the city from the map and sent the Germans into full retreat toward the Oder."

"Yes. And where are the follow-up attacks?" Stalin asked. "I was assured that we would pave the way to Berlin with these weapons."

"And we shall. We shall," he declared, using a cuff to wipe away the sweat that was leaking from the top of his head, plastering down what was left of his hair. It was a warm summer's day outside, but the heavy purple drapes in the room remained drawn, on his own recommendation. He had read about sound guns that could be pointed at a window to pick up the conversations being conducted within. Presumably the heavy drapes would act as a baffle.

"*How* shall we?" Stalin asked. "How shall we press the advantage, when you tell us you cannot deliver the weapons?"

"That is not what I am saying," Beria replied. "We have three more warheads under construction right now, as we speak. But these are not gasoline bombs. They are horribly complicated devices. One slip and the entire facility could be destroyed. And where would we be then? At the mercy of Churchill, who wants to use his own bombs on us. At the mercy of Truman, soon enough, who has proven in the other world that he will act with utter ruthlessness, when the occasion calls for it.

"We already know that the Allies are planning war with the Soviet Union. They will not allow history to take its course. If we strike, and our assault is a failure, they will sense weakness and they will act. Have no doubt about it. They . . . will . . . *act*.

"We must have enough warheads to smash the Nazis with one blow, *and* to hold what gains we make in the next few weeks." With that he stopped and glanced around the room to see if his words had had any effect.

He couldn't believe it. They were actually listening. Stalin's frozen glare had thawed, just slightly, as a hint of real interest entered his expression.

Beria, desperate to save his hide, summoned all his energies.

"The struggle against the fascists will not be the end of this war, comrades. Do we want the imperialists, the bankers and merchants, back in this room a hundred years from now? Because that is exactly what will happen if we miscalculate. We know the Allies are not capable of absorbing punishment of the sort we have endured. Can they live with ten million, twenty million dead? Can they shrug off thirty million bodies and continue to fight? No! We know they cannot. They are weak and squeamish about the true nature of conflict. They are not *meant* to succeed.

"But they will succeed, through pure chance, if we do not execute our next moves perfectly. The shock of Lodz has paralyzed them—for a moment. Another single warhead will not frighten them. But three, or four, or five delivered in one mighty blow? That will be too much for them to endure. They will collapse before us."

As he paused to draw breath, Marshal Timoshenko, the defense minister, interrupted. "Comrade, you sound as if you are already making war on the Allies. But we are not at war with them. We fight the Nazis."

"For now. For *now*!" Beria replied, exasperated. "But only for now. I am not talking about an atomic strike against the Allies, Marshal. They will have their own bomb program, and if we hit them they will strike back at us. But a coordinated atomic assault on the Germans, a wall of atomic fire along the Oder, to open the way for Konev and Zhukov, *that* will stun the Allies, paralyzing them with fear."

He turned back to Stalin, whom he noted was filling his pipe.

"We have always understood that the ends of this war are political, not military," Beria said, more calmly now. "The destruction of the Wehrmacht is a precondition for final victory, but it is not the victory itself. How many times have you yourself said that, Comrade General Secretary?"

Stalin shrugged, but a grin tugged at the corners of his mouth. His arbitrary nature could be fatal, but it might save a man's life, too.

Beria was still sweating, but it was with excitement now, as he sensed his escape. Perhaps even victory. The sour odor of panic was abating, just a little.

Malenkov looked ill again.

"Kurchatov has thousands of technicians working on production at the *Vanguard* site. Thousands more are racing to stay abreast of him at Kamchatka. I cannot say that he will have four or five warheads available at the stroke of three this afternoon. But he assures me we are close. Very close."

Stalin leaned back and lit his pipe. Puffing on it, he raised a thick cloud of gray, acrid smoke. "Marshal Timoshenko," he said, pointing the stem at his defense minister. "Do you need Beria's bombs to break through at the Oder? What latest news have you from there?"

The cavalryman's bald head shone in the lamplight. His hooded, slightly Asiatic eyes remained dark pools. He had been surpassed in Stalin's affection by Zhukov, but he remained a formidable figure. The purges of the late 1930s and the post-Emergence period had come nowhere near him. Nothing in the electronic files incriminated him, and Beria had to admit that he had done sterling work mechanizing the Red Army in preparation for its return to combat. When he spoke he betrayed no fear of the secret policeman. All the more reason for Beria to be wary of him.

"Zhukov reports that the Nazis are increasingly using the nerve agent to seal their eastern borders. At first we thought it was simply gas, but the British and Americans have relayed to us their suspicions that some Emergence weapon is more likely. It is being delivered by artillery shell and aircraft, and once contaminated, a piece of ground remains impassable for an indeterminate length of time."

Beria leapt on the possible weakness. "Well, perhaps you

could devote yourself to determining how long that might be, Marshal."

Timoshenko's lips curled back from his teeth. "We are doing just that, Comrade Beria. At the moment we have no good news to report. The entire northern advance, more than six million men, has been held up as we search for a way through. While we waste time, the Germans are reinforcing with divisions stripped from the west."

The foreign minister, Molotov, spoke up. "I have been in constant contact with the British and Americans via their embassies, but I cannot gauge whether they are letting the Germans in front of them escape because they are incompetent, or because they wish us to do their fighting for them."

"No," Stalin said. "They wish us to do their dying for them. Churchill thinks like us in many ways. He does not have our power, but he sees the same basic truths. This war is no longer about defeating Germany. It is about dismembering the carcass of Europe. I do not think we can expect much relief from them. Marshal Timoshenko, they have not yet come to our aid in the Pacific, have they?"

Timoshenko shook his head and looked over at the people's commissar of the navy, Admiral Kuznetsov, a relatively young man in this group of aging party members.

Beria felt confident enough in the change of dynamics to quietly take his seat again. It felt like slipping into a hideout.

"The Americans have made no move toward cooperating with us," Kuznetsov responded. "In fact, they seem to have ceased offensive operations around the Japanese Home Islands. There has been no indication of any Allied submarine activity in the last forty-eight hours. It is almost as though they have decided to leave the Japanese alone."

"Good," Stalin said. "Then we shall take the islands from under their noses. The postwar correlation of forces in the Pacific will be much more amenable that way."

His gaze fell on Beria again.

"Do not imagine that you have escaped my wrath, Laventry Pavlovich. I want my bombs, and I want them yesterday. Do you understand?"

"Yes," he said in return, and his voice cracked somewhat. "Yes, Comrade General Secretary."

"And now," Stalin said, "let's have some soup, shall we?"

Beria's heart sank. He still had too much work to do.

"Oh, not you, Beria," the *Vozhd* said. "You are excused. Get the hell out of here and go do your job for a change. No soup for you."

D-DAY + 39. 12 JUNE 1944. 0006 HOURS.
KORYAK RANGES, FAR EASTERN SIBERIA.

In the week and a half they had been away, there had been a noticeable increase in traffic around the giant *Sharashka*.

Just before they had left, Ivanov had watched two silver MiG-15s come in to land at the airfield a few miles to the west of the facility. Now it looked as if an entire fighter wing was based there. Lumbering transport planes—C-47 knockoffs by the looks of them—glided in and out almost constantly during the daylight hours. Ivanov checked the time hack in his night vision goggles.

Just after midnight.

Of the forty-three fighters who were hunkered down on the ridgeline above the road that snaked all the way down to the Communists' research base, only he and Vennie were equipped with NVG. The others in his tiny band—Sergo the Cossack, Ahmed Khan, and Kicji their guide—made do with whatever vision nature gave them. As did the three dozen or so guerrillas they'd brought back from the Chukchi lands that lay to the north.

Ivanov was impressed with the reindeer herders. They moved through the mountains like snow leopards, and he had no doubt of their hunger for vengeance against the Bolsheviks who had all but wiped out their tribesmen. They had been eager recruits even before Ivanov had supplied them with British-made Kalashnikovs.

The Russian Spetsnaz officer wormed his way up the hard rocky surface and into a small, natural bowl-shaped depression. He pulled up his goggles and used a pair of LampVision binoculars. The approaching convoy was still a few minutes away, with more than a few switchbacks to negotiate before it would reach the ambush point. He handed the glasses to Vendulka, and after a moment's observation she passed them onto Khan and Sergo. The two men had stayed behind when Ivanov journeyed north looking for allies. They had been watching the newly built road, recording vehicle activity.

Ivanov was convinced something pivotal was happening. Even in his own time, the Kamchatka Oblast was an isolated backwater. The provincial capital, Petropavlovsk-Kamchatskiy, a small industrial and scientific center on Avacha Bay, was entirely surrounded by volcanic mountains and could not be reached by road. Indeed, even by 2021, no roads ran into Kamchatka.

So this two-lane highway hacked out of the rock and leading up from the *Sharashka* had to be significant. He had no trouble imagining that thousands of lives had been lost in its construction. Sergo and Khan hadn't been able to follow the road to its destination, but they had observed enough traffic to insist there was a better than even chance that high-value targets would be passing through the ravine between midnight and 0200 hours.

Ivanov checked the position of the convoy again. It was hidden now behind a series of switchbacks, but he could tell from the way the glow of headlights leaked upward that they were close enough. He nodded to Kicji, holding up three fingers. The wizened guide slipped away to tell the leaders of the Chukchi that they were three minutes away.

"Sergo. Be ready. Remember, I take the lead vehicle. You take the last one."

Wrapped in a dusty cloak, the huge Cossack was a green-tinged rock monster in the LampVision goggles. He nodded once . . .

"I take the rear."

. . . then moved away to a presighted firing position twenty meters downslope. Ahmed Khan, carrying three reloads, followed him.

Ivanov uncapped his own tube and plugged the missile sensors into his goggles. A targeting grid sprang up in front of him. He heard Vendulka shoo away a couple of Chukchi fighters who had crept up to watch him use the wonder weapon.

"Flames," she hissed, pointing at the back of the tube. "Move away or die." That did it.

Ivanov settled into as comfortable a position as possible, crouching down ready to raise himself up. The opalescent glow of approaching headlights grew stronger on the sheer sides of the ravine below, and his goggles began to adjust to the changing conditions. A thin green line of light, invisible to the naked eye, reached out from the launcher. An Israeli-designed B600, it was accurate out to nine hundred meters, and he was firing from a range of only two hundred. Sergo had the harder shot, but Ivanov had learned that the Cossack, trained as a young boy to fire from horseback, had a much better aim than him. He'd turned the second launcher over to him without any qualms. His only regret was the small number of rockets they had left. After this engagement there would be no more.

On the other hand, I really don't expect to survive this oper-ation, so what does it matter?

The LampVision goggles dialed back to minimum amplifica-tion as the lead vehicle rounded the last corner below. It was an eight-wheeled armored personnel carrier, very much like an old BMP, but without the tracks. An identical carrier followed be-hind it. Ivanov had a good minute or so to examine the vehicle, setting his goggles to record. If these things were going to roll over Western Europe, any intelligence on them would be use-ful.

The grinding rumble of the armored vehicles was joined by the grunt of heavy trucks shifting through gears as they negoti-ated the slope. He counted three of them before another BMP appeared at the convoy's tail end.

Raising himself up on one knee, he powered up the launch system and placed the laser point on the upper deck of his tar-get just in front of the turret. The main armament appeared to be a small cannon and a rocket that rested on a rail directly above it. Probably something like the original Sagger missile. He wondered if it was wire-guided.

A chime in his ear alerted him to target lock. Waiting a few seconds to ensure that the last vehicle in the convoy had entered the killing box, he breathed out, and fired.

The high-explosive multipurpose missile ignited and leapt away on a bright cone of fire. Reactive optics in the LampVi-sion system damped down the searing white light to protect Ivanov from temporary blindness. The soft lime green of artifi-cial illumination returned as the warhead sped away.

In his peripheral vision he saw Sergo's rocket lancing down-range at the same time. They hit almost simultaneously. The HEMP rounds featured a "crush switch" in the nose of the rocket, which determined in the microseconds after impact that it had struck a relatively hard surface. Rather than detonating im-mediately, the weapon's processor chips delayed any reaction momentarily, allowing the warhead to penetrate its target, at which point it went off with a spectacular explosion that caused his night vision system to dim down for nearly two seconds.

He heard the cries of Chukchi, guttural and triumphant as they opened up on the convoy from both sides of the road. Vendulka slammed another rocket into the launcher and slapped him on the shoulder. "Clear!"

The targeting grid came up again, and he laid the designator on the second BMP, which had lurched to a halt. Its turret traversed wildly, seeking someone—anyone—at whom the gunner could fire.

BOOM.

They got off a shot, but the crew was firing blind. Ivanov pulled the trigger on the B600 as a single shell crashed into the slope two hundred meters to his left. Chunks of shattered rock and pebbles rained down around him. The second missile took off with a *whoosh* and speared into the troop carrier's upper deck, with identical results. A massive flash and the thunder crack of detonation.

"To the rear," Vendulka cried, fitting home the last rocket. "Airburst!"

As his optics came back online, Ivanov laid his sights on half a dozen infantrymen who'd spilled out of the BMP before he could hit it. Some had been knocked to the ground by the blast, but others were running to the trucks, shouting and trying to organize a counterattack. Automatic fire from the slopes lashed at the length of the stalled convoy. Ivanov readjusted his aim, choosing a canvas-topped truck. He pressed the selector for ANTI-PERSONNEL and the last of his missiles snaked away.

It burst directly over the truck, spraying the ground with white phosphorous and hundreds of pieces of shrapnel. The screams of the wounded echoed through the valley as superhot beads of the incendiary chemical burned into them.

Discarding the launcher he picked up his assault rifle, an AK-47 clone identical to the ones carried by the other fighters. He squeezed off a round with a thick, flat *crack!* It went high, and he adjusted his aim before methodically picking off any uniformed personnel he could see below. Where the Chukchi poured in torrents of fire, the veteran special operator nailed each of his victims with one or two shots.

The volume of return fire quickly died away, and he called out to Kicji. "Let's go."

The last of the Koryak yelled out a few words in some impenetrable northern dialect, repeated almost immediately by other voices up and down the valley. Suddenly the slopes were alive with guerrillas, throwing themselves downward onto the remnants of the escort.

"Prisoners. We need prisoners," Ivanov called out before jumping up to join them.

He and Vendulka half ran, half fell down the steep incline. The footing was treacherous, and two or three times he was forced to let himself drop onto his ass and slide part of the way. Here and there single shots, or short bursts of automatic gunfire, rang out. As he made the shoulder of the road he checked the time hack in his goggles. It was a quarter past midnight.

"Ahmed, Sergo," he called out. "Quickly. We need prisoners before any response force gets here. *Move,* before the Chukchi kill them all."

He and Vendulka ran for the second truck, which remained relatively unscathed. As they dashed forward, leaping the bodies of the fallen, he noted that troops wore NKVD uniforms, not Red Army. It made him feel a little better about the slaughter.

"Ivanov, over here."

It was Sergo. The Cossack was pulling a man wearing civilian clothing out of the back of the truck. The prisoner howled in pain. One arm looked as though it had been struck by a bullet. He appeared to have two elbow joints, with the second one in the middle of his forearm.

"Go," he said to Vendulka. The medical specialist ran forward, pulling a canvas bag full of supplies off her back.

Meanwhile Ivanov slowed down and looked to the night sky. The heavens were alive with cold, hard diamond points of light. He took off his goggles. He didn't need them. The fires from the burning trucks and armored personnel carriers provided more than adequate light to see the Chukchi stripping the bodies and occasionally killing a surviving NKVD man.

"Kicji," he called out, "tell them to spare any officers they find. We need to interrogate them."

The old Koryak guide shrugged. "They will not like that. They came here to kill Russians."

"Oh, for fuck's sake . . . then tell them to spare the officers because I want to torture them," he said, barely containing his impatience to be away.

"Ah, *that* they will like," Kicji said.

Ivanov inserted a fresh magazine into his weapon as Ahmed Khan dropped down from the back of one truck.

"Five civilians," Khan said. "Three dead. One wounded. One simply shitting himself."

"Gather them up and let's get going," Ivanov said. "We won't have long."

They had chosen the ambush site because the Bolsheviks' radios would be unlikely to work well in the folds of the mountains. Lord knew he'd had the same trouble in Afghanistan more than once.

But you could never be certain of anything. They needed to get to the hideout and start questioning the prisoners as soon as possible.

28

D-DAY + 39. 12 JUNE 1944. 0354 HOURS.
MOSKVA, SEA OF OKHOTSK.

The fleet carrier *Moskva* was the pride of the Soviet navy, although Admiral Yumashev would be prouder when he commanded a ship that was truly the product of Soviet labor and ingenuity. The *Moskva* was merely a copy of a British carrier that had been impounded at Murmansk for two years, and a rough copy at that.

Hastily built in the new shipyards at Vladivostok, she lacked even the rudimentary comforts of her British model, and *that* ship had been positively Spartan by the standards of the *Vanguard*. The commander of the Soviet Pacific Fleet had enjoyed a single tour of the Emergence ship, and been amazed—not just by her perverse situation, sticking out of the tundra in the Siberian wilderness, but also by the level of comfort the crew had enjoyed before the Emergence had killed most of them.

Or that was the story anyway. Yumashev knew better than to ask questions about their fate.

Sitting in his chair in the center of the *Moskva*'s bridge, surveying the fleet in the dim red glow of the surrounding volcanoes in the Kuril chain, Yumashev could only wonder what sort of power might be his to command in ten or fifteen years' time. The Pacific Fleet had grown from next to nothing at the start of the war into a mighty force, as the Japanese had discovered to their chagrin. It was amazing what could be achieved when the virtually limitless resources of the workers' state were applied without regard to any consideration other than success. Even so Yumashev was well aware of the fleet's shortcomings.

He sipped at a glass of hot sweet black tea, and worried about the things that could go wrong. He wasn't so much concerned about the Japanese as he was with the potential for an unwanted contact with the Allied forces. The intelligence reports he'd seen, of the force Spruance had assembled to take the Marianas, was the stuff of nightmares. Multiple carrier battle groups, swarms of guided missile frigates and destroyers, staggering tonnages of capital ships—all of them equipped with what the Americans quite rightly called Advanced Technology.

And of course, at the heart of it, Kolhammer's rebuilt task force. The *Clinton*. The *Kandahar*. The *Siranui*. And the dozen or more vessels specially constructed for their so-called Auxiliary Forces in Los Angeles and San Diego. Yumashev had read the reports. The firepower contained within that one group— just a subset of Raymond Spruance's armada—would be enough to shatter Yumashev's entire fleet within a matter of minutes.

Even putting aside the magical powers of the "Nemesis" radars, the quantum processors, and the inhuman Combat Intelligence that could control every aspect of a battle, Yumashev had no doubt that the *comparatively* primitive electronics systems that had become standard equipment on the U.S. Navy's contemporary vessels would be years beyond the systems on his own ships. He wasn't complaining, mind you. His ships had proved more than adequate against the Japanese. Without the new radar sets he would have taken much worse damage at the hands of the *kamikaze* maniacs. And he *had* taken a terrific pounding in the first few assaults.

They were winning, though, and—

"Admiral. An alert, sir. Fast-moving planes approaching from the south."

"The south?" he replied. "But there is . . . never mind. Bring the fleet to general quarters and prepare to receive the enemy."

Horns and Klaxons blared. Bells rang and men shouted orders as Yumashev searched the southern skies for the danger. He saw them almost right away, and his heart began hammering painfully.

Coming over the jagged ranges of the southernmost Kuril Islands he could see dense clumps of bright white stars. They grew in size and number as he watched.

A single line of tracer fire reached up from a ship on picket duty. Then another and another. As he watched, fascinated and horrified, one of the shining comets fell away from the cluster and dived into the little destroyer. A massive fireball consumed the source of the tracer fire, which ended instantly.

All around him, voluble but tightly controlled chaos ruled as his men reacted to the attack. Without needing to say a word himself, he heard orders shouted to vector the combat air patrol onto the incoming raiders. Another voice issued commands that brought the full weight of the fleet's antiaircraft artillery to bear. Technical officers relayed information from the ship's electronic sensors as it became available.

"A hundred-plus hostiles . . ."

"No surface combatants . . ."

"No subsurface threats . . ."

"Incoming airspeed estimated at one thousand kilometers per hour . . ."

Yumashev's brows climbed skyward at that.

One thousand kilometers an hour!

This was no ordinary *kamikaze* attack out of Sapporo. These were jet-powered planes. Perhaps even rockets.

For a terrible second he wondered if the Allies had decided to strike directly at him. They couldn't be happy at the prospect of Japan falling under Soviet control, and in the last twelve months the Pacific Fleet had prepared any number of scenarios involving combat with the Americans. The results always went badly.

But as soon as the thought occurred to him, he dismissed it. From his own studies he knew that when Kolhammer struck, the target rarely had a chance to respond, or even to take evasive action. For all of the surprise of this attack, he still had a chance to fight back. Yamamoto had not enjoyed the same luxury when the missiles from the *Havoc* caught elements of his fleet in Hashirajima, just two years ago. By all accounts the Japanese had had no idea what was happening as they died.

For that reason alone he suspected he wasn't fighting Spruance, or Kolhammer. No, he was certain this was the Japanese grand admiral.

Yamamoto.

"So, my friend," he said quietly to himself. "You did not go south after all."

It was, all things considered, a beautiful sight.

As the lower Kurils fell away behind the *Ohka,* Lieutenant Masahisa Uemura took the briefest of moments to appreciate the vista that stretched out before him. One enemy ship was already ablaze, struck amidships shortly after it opened fire on them. Engulfed from stem to stern in flames, it slipped beneath his wings.

Before him the Sea of Okhotsk was congested with ships large and small, none of them moving at any great speed. A few gun flashes lit the surface of the waters, giving him a chance to get a fix on his prey, a large flattop vessel in the center of the flotilla. Then the twinkling of small-caliber gunfire and the flare of the big-bore guns spread across the Russian fleet, lighting up the world in front of him.

As scared as the pilot was—and he was *very* scared—a part of him felt strangely detached. It was the part that caused him to smile sadly and to stroke his daughter's doll with one gloved, trembling finger—but only ever so briefly. He had to keep both hands on the stick to avoid a catastrophic loss of control, so close to the end.

The roar of the engine seemed much louder, and every vibration of the airframe shook him to his core. His mouth was dry and he wished that he could have just one last sip of water.

Antiaircraft shells began to burst around him, buffeting his plane with great violence. Two close explosions shook his daughter's doll loose from where he had fixed it on the console.

"No!" he cried.

It seemed a much worse thing than his approaching death. Uemura did a quick calculation. The target vessel was now lit up by dozens of guns throwing a storm of metal into the air in front of him. He was about thirty seconds from impact.

He cursed, gripped the control stick with all the strength in his right hand, and leaned forward to grope around as best he could for Motoko's doll. He felt the plane veer down and gave a tug on the stick.

A quick glance over the dashboard.

The Russian ship was getting much closer, and growing ever larger.

He grunted in frustration, almost crying.

Then he had it in his hand, and a beatific smile spilled across his face as he raised the doll to his cheek. It was like being kissed good-bye by his daughter.

Lieutenant Uemura gripped the controls in both hands again. He pushed the nose down toward his objective. Motoko's little doll crushed up against the stick.

The carrier was rushing at him.

An insane velocity.

No time for—

The voices of his officers bellowing orders down the chain of command betrayed an edge of real panic as the *kamikaze* swarm raced toward them. The enemy was coming in at much greater speeds than in the previous attacks. Almost three times as quickly.

The Stormoviks of the combat air patrol had closed quickly with them, only to find themselves firing at empty space as the rocket planes swept past. Admiral Yumashev cursed his lack of jet fighters, but there simply hadn't been time to develop a carrier version of the MiG-15. It hadn't been done in the world on the other side of the Emergence, either, forcing the Soviet navy to crib from the British carrier planes they had impounded as part of convoy PQ 17. Hence the striking similarities between his Stormoviks and the British Sea Hurricane.

The predawn gloom was banished entirely as every gun in his fleet opened up. The head of the flying column had already begun to spread out, however, with dozens of rocket-propelled bombs peeling away to throw themselves onto their victims. The noise was head splitting, with hundreds of cannons and machine guns pounding away, all of it laid over the scream of the Japanese engines.

One, two, three of the attackers detonated in midair. But dozens more speared through the burning debris.

"Steam, I need steam," someone called out.

Yumashev's eyes bulged as four of the flying demons drove themselves down into the body of the *Moskva*'s sister ship, *Kiev*. His heart sank into his boots as the carrier died within a cyclone of high explosives. Any hope that her great mass might absorb the damage was forlorn. The first three blooms of fire swallowed her up just before the fourth and last attacker dived in and blew the entire ship to pieces with a roar that he felt inside his chest from over a kilometer and a half away.

Yumashev opened his mouth to tell the fire control officer to coordinate a fleetwide defense of the capital ships, but it was too late. The words died at the back of his throat as he saw five of the Japanese rocket bombs heading directly for him.

He had time enough to register that the planes appeared to be painted white before the first one—now just a streak, a blur across his visual field—stabbed down into the flight deck directly in front of the carrier's island.

D-DAY + 39. 11 JUNE 1944. 0402 HOURS.
HMAS *HAVOC*, PACIFIC AREA OF OPERATIONS.

"Holy shit!" Willet said.

"Yeah, there's nothin' like a good piece of hickory," Master Chief Flemming muttered.

"Sorry, Chief?"

"Gratuitous classic reference, ma'am."

Willet shook off a confused look and turned back to the main display, where the second of Yumashev's two flattops had disappeared within a catastrophic series of blasts.

"Analysis, Amanda, as soon as poss'."

"How about 'better them than us,' Captain?" Lieutenant Lohrey answered.

"You can do better," Willet replied before addressing the crew of the sub's Combat Center. "C'mon. Heads down and bums up, people. Every pixel, every pulse, every stray scrap of data. I want it all, and I want it yesterday. We've got to get this away on Fleetnet at the first opportunity."

Normally hushed, the *Havoc*'s control room hummed with chatter as the first images of the titanic clash in the Sea of Okhotsk came in from the Big Eye drones lurking at twenty-five thousand meters above the Soviet host. Willet chewed a stick of peppermint gum and tried to take it all in.

The boat's Combat Intelligence was way ahead of her, assigning individual data tags to all the Soviet combatants down to the smallest motorboat and numbering each of the Japanese attackers for after-action study. Within the quantum arrays, separate channels were established to track the history of each combatant; autonomous software agents had already begun to crawl over the data like programmed spiders, spinning intricate webs of potential meaning around the rapidly accumulating information load.

More than two hundred kilometers away from the action, resting safely deep below the surface, the *Havoc* plugged into the battle via a thin tendril of nanonically engineered optical fiber. It trailed up and away from her conning tower to a small receiver pod bobbing on the wavelets 180 meters above. Skin sensors probed the threat bubble directly around the submarine out to a distance of ninety klicks. Willet's defensive sysops maintained an obsessive-compulsive watch for any potential foes.

At the moment they had nothing on the boards but one very old and noisy submarine, probably a Mitsubishi, sixty-four thousand meters to the southwest. It was completely oblivious to their presence.

Also unnoticed were the *Havoc*'s drones, two of them over the Soviets and one keeping station above the remnants of Yamamoto's Combined Fleet. The lightweight plasteel disks, seventy-five centimeters in diameter, were powered by phosphoric acid fuel cells and packed with hundreds of different sensors in the outer ring, which surrounded the power plant and a monobonded carbon fan. Anyone standing just beneath one of those disks would see what looked exactly like a big eye— hence the name.

Bejeweled with multiple micronic lenses, a drone was more like the segmented eye of an insect. Only 40 percent of its internal mass was given over to visual systems, however. Most of the weight—such as it was—came from the suite of arrays originally designed to vacuum up electronic intelligence from a twenty-first-century battlespace.

As panicky radio transmissions arced among Yumashev's vessels, the combat air patrol, and the Soviet ground forces on Hokkaido, the *Havoc*'s Big Eye drones listened in, recording everything. When the antiaircraft cruiser *Belgorod* powered up fire control radar, the drone's electromagnetic sensor suite went active, locking in on the Soviet ship's arrays to generate a full-spectrum profile of the systems' performance.

The column of Japanese *Ohkas* had completely broken down into dozens of constituent parts. As Willet and her officer looked on, the Soviet Pacific Fleet was reduced to a handful of destroyers and smaller boats. Time and again elongated white streaks punched into lumbering ironclad ships, always with devastating results. The Soviet fighters, prop-driven relics that looked like a straight clone of the old British Sea Hurricane, were left floundering.

The volume of the triple A fell away and—she glanced up to check the clock running in the top right-hand corner of the main screen—after three minutes it was done. No Japanese planes survived.

"CI has the prelims, Captain," Lieutenant Lohrey announced. "Seventy-three percent of the attackers got through. Eighty-nine percent of those targets that were struck were destroyed, although they seem to have allotted at least four missiles to each of the larger vessels. Five, in the case of the flattops."

"They weren't missiles, Amanda," Willet corrected her. "They were men."

"Sorry, Captain. Force of habit."

Willet moved a little farther down the control room, where Yamamoto's task force was moving toward the tip of Hokkaido. Their progress looked quite stately, even serene, but the grand admiral probably had pedal to the metal.

"What's happening back at the Death Star, Chewie?"

A heavily bearded sysop pointed at a window displaying one of the Japanese carriers. Touching the tip of his finger to an icon, a small magnifying glass, he pulled in to a virtual height of 150 meters above her decks. "They're prepping for a conventional attack, Captain. Zeros. Torpedo bombers. Nothing exciting."

"Unless you're on the receiving end," Chief Flemming said.

"Captain Willet," another sysop called out. "Long-range Nemesis scan has another airborne attack forming up out of

Sapporo. No visuals, but the returns look like Nakajima One-One-Fives and -Sixes."

"Probably going in to finish off the job," Willet said. "Okay. Amanda, you've got some work to do. And I've got a call to make."

D-DAY + 39. 12 JUNE 1944. 0522 HOURS.
USS *HILLARY CLINTON*, PACIFIC AREA
OF OPERATIONS.

Kolhammer ate his breakfast in front of the big screen in operations. At least a dozen officers crowded in around him to watch the Battle of Okhotsk. He finished his toasted muffin and coffee just as the second *tokkotai* wave arrived over the remains of the Soviet fleet.

The slower-moving Nakajimas were nowhere near as successful as their colleagues in the *Okha* attack had been. But it didn't matter. The sea was already littered with burning debris and floating corpses. After the second wave broke over the survivors, only four destroyers remained afloat. It was a stunning reversal. Admiral Spruance, who'd cross-decked from the *Enterprise* half an hour ago, stood nursing his own cup of coffee and shaking his head.

"I suppose this is what they had planned for us," he mused.

"Have planned," Kolhammer said. "I'll lay money on the barrelhead that they've stashed away a whole bunch of those *Okhas* on the islands. Land basing would give them some real throw weight, too. Sovs got hit with, what, just over a hundred or so? We could be looking at three, four, five times that number. Who knows, could be even more. They haven't invested in a jet fighter program like the Germans. It's all gone into this madness."

"Madness it may be," Spruance said, "but it worked. The Russians don't have any strategic depth in their Pacific assets. You're looking at everything they had right there."

He nodded at the screen.

Kolhammer brushed crumbs off his fingers. On screen six Nakajimas converged on one Soviet destroyer. He shrugged. "They did a hell of a job throwing that much together," he said. "The Reds didn't have a navy worth the name five years ago. They still don't. Or not anymore, anyway. But think about what it must have cost them in men and materials just to put that task force together. We've got to get some recon birds over Vladivostok. I'm betting we'll see some real changes there."

"I don't see how they could have done it on their own so quickly," Spruance said.

"You're thinking like a liberal. The Sovs wouldn't blanch at killing two, three million slave laborers to build dockyards and the ships to fill 'em, in the time they had. And I'll bet they've got a lot more twenty-first-century tech than the Nazis or Yamamoto ever let them see during the cease-fire."

Deep shadows pooled under Spruance's eyes, giving his face a hollow, haunted look. "So you're convinced they got your ship. The *Vanguard*."

"Without a doubt. It would explain what they've been doing on their vacation, where all those wonderful toys they've been using against Hitler came from. And it would have given them a big head start building that task force Yamamoto just cleaned up. The electromagnetic signals Willet picked up are pretty backward, even compared with our AT stuff. But they were well ahead of where you'd expect them to be at this point. Unless they've been cherry-picking something like the *Vanguard*.

"It can't have been Demidenko. Himmler purposely set that up as a waste of resources. They were never going to let Stalin have a look at the good stuff. Question is, what now? Willet has firing solutions on the Japanese. Does she take them down?"

"We're going to need to refer this back to Washington," Spruance said, shaking his head. "Normally there would be no question, but . . ."

He trailed off.

"But," Kolhammer finished for him, "if we take out Yamamoto, what's to stop Uncle Joe from raising the Red Star over Tokyo a few weeks down the track. I dunno. Maybe he doesn't have the power projection capability?"

"Maybe," Spruance echoed. "But if he does, we end up dealing with a Communist Japan."

"Yeah," Kolhammer grunted. "Bottom line, we need to know what's on those islands up ahead of us."

29

It was relatively safe in this part of the jungle. As safe as it could get on an island full of Japanese soldiers guarding a secret facility on which hung the fate of their empire.

Denny's patrol had hunkered down about three-quarters of the way up the large limestone hill that dominated the island. Hastings, his communications specialist, insisted on calling it a mountain, but then Hastings hailed from Kansas, so you could push a small pile of dirt up with the toe of your boot and he was liable to go christening it Mount Something-Or-Other.

Hastings didn't seem to be dwelling much on the topography at the moment, though. He was busy taking down the thin wire antennae he'd strung between a couple of trees. He wasn't grumbling as he did it—he was too well trained, and they were way too deep in the shit for that. But Denny could tell from the awkward stiffness of his movements that he was pissed off.

Hell, they were all pissed off. That last message they'd gotten might as well have been a death warrant.

They'd been told to penetrate the subterranean facility and report back *today,* at all costs. In other words, do it now, or die trying.

He lay on the spongy floor of the jungle, hundreds of ants and weird unidentifiable bugs crawling over him, and examined the map. They were hiding on a small boggy plateau, no more than fifteen feet long and half that wide, on the heavily forested southern slopes of Mount Something-Or-Other, looking down over the coastal plain where the Japanese had built and then disguised a runway and sunken bunker complex. The last two nights they'd probed the edges of an airfield that was well hidden beneath camouflage that went *way* beyond a bit of netting and palm fronds.

Mobile garden beds on giant wheels covered the length of the runway. The aircraft were assembled in vast dugouts covered in yet more living vegetation. A keen gardener himself before the war, Denny would have loved a chance to inspect the setup without having to worry about getting run through with a bayonet, but he'd had to settle for a perilous inspection, from a short distance, in the dead of night. It was nonetheless an impressive piece of work.

Impressive, too, was the excavation that had obviously been carried out to enlarge a natural cave system at the base of Mount Something-Or-Other. But a close inspection there had proved impossible. A platoon of Japanese marines was on guard just back inside the mouth of the main entrance, twenty-four hours a day. They very rarely ventured outside, and they never left the post unless relieved by another, equally dedicated bunch of nips.

It was infuriating was what it was.

And now they'd been told to go in anyway.

"This'll be that fucking Kolhammer, you know," Corporal Barbaro muttered into Denny's ear. "Those fucking marines of his, they were pissed about us getting—"

"Stow it, Tony," Denny said. "Let just get the job done."

Barbaro shut up, but his face said it all. The others pulled in close as Denny smoothed out the map.

"I figure our best chance is to go in through one of those air shafts they drilled. They cut 'em outta the limestone, so it's not gonna be like banging around inside a metal pipe. If we're real careful, we keep the noise down, chances are we can get in and out."

Chances, bullshit, Denny thought. If he'd really believed the shafts were an option, they'd have used them a day ago. He had no idea whether the things were even navigable. The nearest one, about four hundred yards away, opened out into a rough circle about two and a half feet in diameter. But they might taper down to a fraction of that. Whoever went in might have to negotiate a vertical drop of a hundred feet or more. The hand-holds would probably be nonexistent.

But orders were orders, and they had to try to get inside.

At all costs.

Barbaro was probably right. Talk was that Kolhammer's marines, those Eighty-second guys, were pissed as hell that they were being held back from the important jobs because nobody would trust them. They were always bragging about the "special" operations "their" outfit was supposed to have done, even though most of the guys in that unit had never seen combat. In fact, most of 'em were 'temps who'd transferred in. Maybe some of the original Eighty-second guys mighta done something worth bragging about, back up in their own war. They'd sure as hell kicked some ass when they'd helped retake Hawaii. But they were outnumbered about three to one by all the Johnny-come-lately types who'd filled out the two extra battalions the Eighty-second had put on.

So who knew? Maybe they *were* being sent on some kind of suicide mission, just because somebody in Jones's brigade had been bragging that *his* guys coulda done it, and so some two-star asshole up Denny's chain of command goes, *Yeah, well, my guys could beat your guys into those caves any fuckin' day*.

In Denny's experience with the military, that was exactly the sort of shit that got guys like him killed all the fucking time.

"Right," he said, "the clock's ticking on this one, so we have to move out in daylight. Barbaro, you're taking point. Hastings, you be ready to set up as soon we get there. Even if they tumble us while we're inside, we gotta get word back to the fleet what we find. Everyone understand?"

They did.

They were dead men.

The five marines moved as quickly as they dared. The jungle was both a help and hindrance. It provided the best possible cover: the underbrush was so dense that a man a few yards away could remain undetected, as long as he had good camouflage and knew how to keep his ass still.

Of course that meant they could easily run into some Jap who knew his business, too, except that Denny was betting they weren't setting up ambushes on an island they thought they owned. The Japs patrolled, and they were good at it. But his guys were better. Part of the reason they were better, though, was because they were careful—or had been, at least. Now it was *to hell with caution, we gotta haul ass*.

Where they might have taken four hours to cover the ground to the air-shaft, he gave 'em two. It was still slow going, but to Denny it felt rushed.

Barbaro was his best guy on point. For an Italian city kid he was a natural in the jungle, and he adjusted to the increased tempo a lot better than Denny. The other men in his patrol, privates Stan Sanewski, Pete Hastings, and Gwynne Davis, had all done a year of jungle warfare training in northern Australia, and had spent the last six months spooking around the highlands of New Guinea, sharpening their edge against the remaining enemy forces down there.

Denny had come to understand something that Barbaro seemed to know instinctively. The jungle was neutral. It wasn't your friend, or your enemy. It was just there and you had to deal with it, same as the Japs did. They had learned that the island was crisscrossed by paths, some of them wide enough for three men to walk down shoulder-to-shoulder. But although one ran right past the airshaft, Barbaro kept them off the track, something the instructors had emphasized in the training center Down Under.

The double-canopy jungle reached out for them with thorny creepers, gnarled roots, and stinging vines. The steep floor was a boggy mulch of rotting vegetation, crawling with snakes and centipedes. It threatened to give way in small localized mudslides at random intervals.

Once, they had to stop and wait while a twelve-man enemy patrol moved along the nearby path, just yards away. The terrain had forced them closer and closer to the track, which looped back on itself a couple of times as it descended. Barbaro waited until they could confirm that the Japanese had made it all the way down to the coastal plain. They had just moved off again when Pete Hastings hand-signed . . .

Stop.

Denny frowned, turning on the marine with a pissed-off expression. Hastings was pointing at something on the scarp above them, but glancing up there Denny couldn't make out anything through the curtain of fat pandanus leaves and dense lianas. He showed Hastings his open palms and shrugged as if to say, *So what?*

The marine pointed up in the direction of the rock face again and silently mouthed, *Look.*

Denny had no idea what he was supposed to be looking at. Palm fronds, creaking tree trunks, thick stands of bamboo, a mess of creepers, all of them swaying in the breeze. He was about to tell Hastings to knock it off when the gray rock face *moved.* He shook his head like a kid seeing a magic trick for the first time.

The palm trees swayed again and he distinctly saw the supposedly solid gray rock flex in and out a couple of inches.

Goddamn, he thought.

The news from home was the best tonic Lieutenant Yukio's men could have hoped for. There had been no official announcement of the grand admiral's stunning counterstroke off Hokkaido, just as there had been no official announcement of the Russian attack on the Home Islands in the first place. But rumors traveled fast, even all the way down here, and as Yukio toured the eastern hangar from which he would begin his last flight in a matter of days, he noticed that the men went about their work with just a bit more snap in their steps and steel in their spines.

The treachery of the Communists, the technology of the Americans—in the end none of it was proof against the warrior spirit of the Nipponese fighting man. The *gaijin* went on with a lot of rubbish about loving life, but in the end they simply feared death and eschewed sacrifice. They were weak, and they would fail.

Yukio walked down the line of waiting *Ohkas,* stopping every now and then to share a word with a ground crew chief or one of the other pilots, some of whom had also quite obviously heard of news from Okhotsk. It was amazing how just a glimmer of hope could change a man's whole outlook. Yukio had been assiduously tending to the men's morale, as was his duty. And for the most part they had remained steadfast in the face of their approaching deaths. But now he could sense a real eagerness to launch themselves at the enemy. Everyone here knew that their sacrifice could make a real difference, and that was all they needed to dedicate themselves anew.

As he passed a rocket plane with its cowling open and three technicians messing about inside, he noticed a small sheet of paper by a toolbox at their feet. Someone had inscribed a few lines of poetry that seemed to sum up the feelings of everyone on the island.

> *Little clear streams rustle*
> *Down through the mountain rocks*
> *And finally let the battleship*
> *Float on the sea.*

Tiny drops of water they might be, as individuals, but together they would be a mighty flood sweeping their enemies away. One of the techs looked over his shoulder, his face lighting up as he recognized Sekio.

"A fine day for a walk, Lieutenant," quipped Onada, the oldest and most experienced of the crew chiefs on the island. "So sunny, and such a fresh mild breeze."

Yukio snorted at the joke. They were buried beneath millions of tons of rock. The cavernous space smelled of oil, rubber, chemicals, and body odor. And none of the ground technicians had felt the sun on his face for weeks.

"A fine day, indeed, Chief Onada. A fine day for it." He smiled in reply. "No sign of our German comrades, then?"

"They are working in the southern cave this morning, Lieutenant. I cannot say I miss them. A surly bunch, those Germans. And only too happy to give the impression that they think themselves better than the emperor himself."

Yukio made a helpless, accepting gesture. "What are we to do about it, Chief? We wouldn't be here without their help."

Onada pish-poshed the very idea with a grunt and the wave of a thick-fingered, oil-stained hand. A true nationalist, he simply would not hear of it. "Tinkerers and copycats, that's all they are," he insisted. "Anyone can copy the design for a rocket if they have the blueprint. But only a truly creative culture would devise a use for such things in the way that we have. And—"

The lieutenant essayed a dampening gesture with both hands. "You do not need to convince me, Chief Onada. I agree with you. But now I must continue my inspection. Has anyone checked the tunnels this morning?"

"Bah! You worry needlessly. *Here* is this morning's real work," Onada said, patting the dull white nose cone of the *Ohka*.

"Then I shall do it myself," Yukio said. "I know you think it a waste of time, but what would happen if falling rocks blocked a launch rail, hmm? This whole base might be blown into the sky like Krakatoa. So I will check."

He set off again, purposely striding toward the sheer rock wall at the end of the cavern. It was clear at the moment, but come launch day it would be a maze of cranes and gantries as the Cherry Blossoms were moved into place for takeoff.

It really wouldn't do not to check the tunnels every day. They were effectively nothing less than the barrel of a gun out of which he and his men would fly at the Americans like human bullets, hopefully with the same success their comrades had enjoyed against the Bolsheviks.

And just like a good soldier, Yukio felt the need to clean and check his gun every day. So he headed for the closest of the steel ladders that led up to three circular openings about ten meters off the floor of the cave.

Looks like an old mine shaft or something, Denny thought.

The tunnel was obviously man-made. It was too regular to be a natural formation. A rough oval shape, it was much wider than it was tall. Chisel blows had disfigured the soft limestone walls, and two small rails ran downslope toward a much larger cavern beyond the tunnel mouth. It was well lit down there, and, he could see and hear that it was full of men and machinery.

Japs.

Denny's heart hammered at the inside of his rib cage as he slowly inched downward, with Barbaro just behind him. What the hell the Japs were doing, he had no idea, but the rails had to be significant.

He breathed slowly and deeply, trying to calm himself as they moved closer to the enemy. The tunnel was gloomy, but he worried about being spotted anyway. Only he and Barbaro had entered; the others were waiting for them back in the jungle, beyond the large canvas sheet that obscured the mouth of the cave.

It had been painted to match the surrounding rock face, with small plants stitched into the fabric—a cheap but effective disguise. He wondered how much work had gone into the facility.

How much of the cave system was natural and how much carved out by men? Slave laborers, if he knew the Japs.

Yukio's boots sang on the iron rungs as he climbed. The ladder was thin, and the drop to the floor of the cave would be nasty.

He kept his eyes focused on his hands as he climbed. It probably wasn't necessary to inspect the launch tunnels every day, and it certainly wasn't part of his duty, but he had made it his responsibility anyway. What if the American suddenly appeared on the horizon without warning? He'd heard sailors talk of invisible American ships, cloaked by some device from the future that had allowed them to sneak in among the Combined Fleet at Hashirajima and sink so many vessels.

Sailors were notorious for the stories they made up, but there could be no doubt that the Allied navies enjoyed remarkable advantages in technology. It was a proven fact some of their new ships and planes baffled the radar sets that Japan had bought from the Reich, and the very act of turning on the radar seemed to act as a beacon, attracting swarms of rockets and bombs when the *gaijin* were about.

Given all that, he thought as he neared the top of the ladder leading up to the launch tube, it was only prudent to make sure that they were ready to get away at a moment's notice. Literally. And he'd meant what he said to Onada. If an *Ohka* struck an obstacle on the rails, it could be disastrous, perhaps even destroying the entire base in an explosion that set off a chain reaction among the dozens of *Ohkas* lined up for launch.

So he would check the launch tunnels for any problems, obstructions—anything that might interfere at the last minute. And he'd do so every day, if no one else would.

Reaching the top of the ladder, he poked his head over the rim.

Denny and Barbaro were almost at the end of the tunnel, carefully inching forward along the floor. It was a precarious business. The slope was steep; crawling down it, Denny felt as though they might slip forward and tumble over the edge into the midst of the enemy.

About eight feet from the opening, he could already see that they'd struck pay dirt. The huge cavern was crowded with the

Japanese flying bombs he'd been tasked to locate. *Ohkas,* if he remembered right. These things looked just like them. The wings were a little swept back, and they looked bigger than he'd expected, but they had to be the jet-powered *kamikaze* planes everyone had been expecting.

A quick radio call, and this nest of vipers would be somebody else's problem. He was just about to turn around and start the climb back when a head popped up over the edge, and he found himself staring into the startled eyes of an enemy soldier.

"Fuck," Barbaro hissed.

The Jap screamed something out in his own language. Everyone on the floor of the cavern froze and stared up in their direction.

Then all hell broke loose.

Americans!

Yukio almost tumbled back off the ladder, he was so surprised.

"Americans!" he screamed. "Americans in the launch tunnels!"

He reached for his holster, scrambling for a gun, cursing as he remembered that he wasn't wearing it. It was forbidden to carry sidearms in the caverns. An accidental discharge might set off a calamitous explosion.

The faces of the enemy registered shock and fear.

He almost slid down the ladder, but stopped himself at the last moment. A cringing, animalistic response welled up in him, urging him to flee.

But screaming his *kiai* instead, he vaulted up the last couple of rungs.

Denny shot the guy in the face. One round from his .45 took off the top of the Jap's head and sent the corpse cartwheeling backward into space.

The sound broke a spell that had hung over the tableau, and instantly the room below them was seething with enraged nips.

"Get back to the others," he shouted at Barbaro, unslinging his carbine and flipping the selector to full auto. He squeezed off a long burst that cut down a couple of the enemy running toward him. "Get word back to fleet. They gotta knock this place down. Bomb it to fucking rubble."

"But—"

"Just fucking *go*. I'll be right behind you."

Barbaro took off up the steep incline, tripping once on the rail and cursing.

Denny cringed, expecting a hail of return fire, but none came.

He flipped his selector back to single shots and started picking off targets.

He just had to give the others a few precious minutes to get the word back to fleet.

30

D-DAY + 39. 12 JUNE 1944. 1446 HOURS.
USS *HILLARY CLINTON*, PACIFIC AREA
OF OPERATIONS.

The recording ended abruptly with a clatter of gunfire and the harsh, staccato sounds of someone shouting in Japanese. The admiral nodded at the sysop to close the file. The CIC staffer shut it down with a few key clicks and awaited further instructions.

Kolhammer's expression didn't betray in any way the feelings he had about the transmission. A comm screen deployed from the ceiling of the *Clinton*'s Combat Information Center, dropping in front of him and revealing a somber-looking Ray Spruance.

"I don't think there's any doubt that they're gone, Admiral," Kolhammer said. "And given the data Willet sent through from Okhotsk, we'll be coming within range of those things very soon. I have a Skyhawk flight fitted out with bunker busters, ready to roll on your say-so."

If he expected a fight from Spruance, he didn't get one. The temps really had hardened up in the last two years. In some ways they seemed even more inured to suffering than folks had been in his own time. Less of a victim culture, he supposed.

Last he'd heard, at least eighty thousand Frenchmen and women had died in the preparatory air strike over Calais. You couldn't pull shit like that back up in the twenty-first without most of the media and half of Congress demanding that you be indicted as a war criminal. Or a Nazi, he thought with yet another spasm of twisted irony. That was always a fave, whenever people at home were exposed to the actual brutality of warfare. Out would come the tar and the feathers and the hand-painted NAZI sign to hang around somebody's neck.

Somebody like him.

But Spruance remained focused on the big picture, no matter how grim-faced he was at having to listen to the destruction of Sergeant Denny's patrol. They had to assume that the other Force Recon units inserted on two nearby islands had been compromised, as well. Yet they couldn't allow that to distract them.

"I agree, Admiral Kolhammer," Spruance said. "Launch your planes."

In the short walk out to her Skyhawk, Flight Lieutenant Anna Torres began to leak sweat. The air temperature was hovering over forty degrees Celsius, but down on the *Clinton*'s flight deck it seemed to be about half again as much. The roar of jet engines, the heavy traffic in personnel and equipment, the reflected heat scorching off the composite decking—it all created a very uncomfortable environment. She didn't envy her chief as he readied the stepladder just beneath the cockpit. He must have been broiling inside his coveralls and powered helmet.

Torres gave him a thumbs-up as she strapped in and the bubble canopy slid down into place. She could have sworn there were about twice as many people watching from whatever vantage points they could grab as she ran through preflight. That was only to be expected. Although the A-4s had been flying off the *Clinton* for a few months now, this was their true baptism of fire. Slung beneath her fuselage on the centerline hard point she had a laser-guided sixteen-hundred-kilo GBU-20. A bunker buster that could chew through five meters of reinforced concrete before detonating. She was also carrying a couple of thermobaric glide bombs, two under each wing, and four hundred rounds of 20mm cannon ammo.

She was sitting at the controls of one of the most advanced

operational fighter aircraft in the world. A couple of the Big Hill's original Raptors were still functional, but they were back in California, in the Zone, and probably in about a million pieces, being studied by a team of aeronautical engineers. One of them had been hers. Nicknamed Condi, after her daughter, whom she missed every single day. The marines were still flying Super Harriers off the *Kandahar,* but they were being held back as a strategic shield for the task force. So she and her fliers were the spear point of the free world today.

She checked her electronics systems: her heads-up display, the link to the AWACS bird that was already aloft, and the link to the *Clinton*'s Combat Intelligence, Little Bill. All good to go. Torres fed power into the turbojet, which cycled up into a screaming roar. She set herself.

The catapult fired and slammed her back into the padded ejector seat. The outside world blurred past as she shot down the runway and lifted off into clear space. For just a few seconds everything was clean and uncomplicated. She had a canopy of blue sky, dusted with fairy floss, the sort of day when once upon a time she would have taken her daughter down to the park, to just lie on the grass looking for shapes in the clouds. For that brief moment there was no war, no Transition, no madness and dislocation and the aching fucking loneliness of knowing that she was never going to see her child again.

And then she banked around to the northwest and the world rolled back into view. The Combined Task Force filled up the wide bowl of the sea beneath her wings, a vast armada carving white arrowheads across the Pacific. Her own ship, the *Clinton,* stood out because of her size. Fully twice as large as the next biggest flattop, she launched one plane after another into the sky. All of them A-4 Skyhawks like hers, the distinctive delta wings standing out as iron-gray triangles against the deep blue.

She formed up with her squadron, and in turn they fell in behind the E-2D Hawkeye that would control their mission.

After settling in for the flight, Torres called up the V3D map on her HUD, showing the target. The quality was abysmal compared with what she'd been accustomed to back in the twenty-first, but that was to be expected without satellites or full-spectrum drone coverage. Most of the image was computer-generated and didn't come anywhere near photo-realistic, but it'd just have to do.

The principal terrain features should all be easily recognizable—
she hoped—and her primary target was easy enough to spot,
some sort of launch silo drilled into the side of a six-
hundred-meter-tall hill that dominated the southern end of
the island.

For eight months now she'd been training on the Skyhawk,
getting ready for just this kind of mission. The novelty of flying a genuine museum piece had long since worn off, and she
very much missed her old F-22. It was a hell of a lot more
comfy, for one thing. The climate control in this plane sucked.
If they'd just let her have her old baby, she could have nailed
the job herself and been back in time for an afternoon nap. But
it was going to be a long time before a working squadron got its
hands on a Raptor again.

A text message from the Hawkeye came up on her HUD via
laser link. The AWACS plane was about to roll into a holding
pattern, allowing it to stay a safe distance from the objective.
Six A-4s configured for air superiority broke off to take up
watch over that rare and precious bird.

Torres checked the mission data in the bottom left-hand corner and saw that an in-flight refueler had just lifted off from the
Clinton—it would be there to meet them on the way home. She
keyed in a query and found that a mixed crew was driving the
tanker. Originals and AF 'temps.

Not so long ago she'd have had uneasy feelings about that,
but the 'temps were learning, and those who put their hands up
to join the Auxiliary Forces tended to be especially motivated.
It was as if they had something to prove—both to the uptimers
and to their former colleagues. Besides, who the hell wanted to
fly old Corsairs or Mustangs or even an F-86 when they could
be driving something like this baby? Primitive as it was.

At least three-quarters of the pilots in her squadron were
'temps now, what with so many of the original *Clinton* air
group being sent back stateside into the labs and lecture halls.
Torres had been spared by the luck of the draw—*somebody* had
to stay behind and teach these clueless newbies how to handle
the fast movers.

It'd been a tentative business at first. The looks on some of
her pilots' faces the first time she'd stepped into the briefing
room on the *Clinton*—Jesus, what a fucking nightmare. Nobody
had been fool enough to diss her, or even look sideways at her.

They'd had that particular brand of piss and vinegar whupped out of them back in the Zone, at Andersonville.

That's where it became obvious pretty quickly who wasn't going to be able to make the adjustment, answering to women or people of color. A surprising number of those assholes had turned up, thinking they still had the run of the joint, but none lasted very long.

So Torres only had to deal with the 'temps who made it through that winnowing-out process, for which she was endlessly grateful. Even then, there was a cultural brick wall that separated 'temp from uptimer, and she probably butted up against it at least a dozen times a day.

Sometimes it was meaningless things, like a joke they didn't get, or some cultural reference she slipped into conversation without thought. Like referring to the squadron as the Scooby Gang, or responding to the news that the *Clinton*'s battle group would be fighting under 'temp control with the timeless Kent Brockman quote, "And I for one welcome our new overlords."

Torres sighed. She really missed home.

The mood in the CIC was hushed, and even a little tense.

Or maybe that was putting it too strongly. Most of the men and women in here were Big Hill originals. Some had even fought with Kolhammer off Taiwan and North Korea. So they probably weren't particularly anxious. More likely they were just stretched taut by returning to major combat for the first time in the retrofitted supercarrier.

In all of the sea trials and war games off San Diego they'd adjusted with alacrity to the new mix of technology and personnel on board. The old girl wasn't half the ship she'd once been, but she was still the biggest, meanest piece of floating iron on the face of *this* particular world. And while a good deal of her electronic architecture had been stripped out and left back in the States, very little had changed in the CIC. Between her organic intelligence assets like the Advanced Hawkeyes and the Nemesis arrays of the *Siranui,* Kolhammer knew he was riding with the king.

Or maybe the queen, in this case.

The main battlespace display was almost entirely devoted to the A-4 raid on the island where Denny's patrol had discovered Yamamoto's nasty little secret. The fighter-bombers were beginning their payload run and would deliver in less than two minutes. So far no radar had painted them, and the Hawkeye was picking up nothing in the way of signals traffic. Kolhammer's only real concern was how the new snap-on laser guidance kits would perform. They weren't anywhere near as accurate as the precision-guided munitions he was used to, but then they were a quantum leap ahead of anything that had been deployed by the 'temps so far. As Mike Judge said, they were "probably good enough for government work."

In the short time he had until the strike went in, Kolhammer had been watching a data package from Jane Willet's sub, the *Havoc*. She was still lurking off the southern Kurils, with three drones at high altitude above the engagement between Yamamoto and their putative allies, the Soviets. And they were feeding her some scarifying footage.

In all his years in the service, Kolhammer had never fought a naval battle at close quarters. Even Taiwan had been contested from well over the horizon. The only experience he had of closing directly with an enemy was in warding off suicide attackers using speedboats.

On one of the panels of the main display, however, he could see Soviet and Japanese ships pounding at each other from just a few miles away. And the Sovs were having a very tough time of it. All their major combatants had been sunk or heavily damaged in the surprise attack by the jet-powered *tokkotai*.

By the time Yamamoto's Combined Fleet came pouring through the channels of the lower Kuril Islands, they were opposed by a handful of crippled destroyers, or maybe even corvettes. The Japanese probably could have finished them off with conventional air strikes, but for some reason Yamamoto wanted to get in close with his guns. Perhaps he knew it was the last chance he'd ever have to fight like that.

"Ten seconds from release, Admiral."

"Thank you," Kolhammer replied, switching his attention back to his own onscreen battle.

There was no drone coverage of the target. Torres and her guys were doing this the old-fashioned way. Consequently he had to be content with watching a CGI projection of the unfolding attack. It was all very primitive, but he knew that over on the *Enterprise,* Spruance and his staff were taking the same images in their refitted CIC and probably feeling like they were there in the cockpit. Everything was relative.

Lieutenant Torres's voice, clipped and slightly distorted, came over the speaker system. "I have the target. No triple A. No radar locks. Releasing payload."

The GBU-20 detached and fell away, beginning a long glide toward the side of the small mountain. The Skyhawk seemed to bounce upward after it let go of the sixteen-hundred-kilo weight.

Torres heard both of her wingmen release as she brought the A-4 around and powered up the laser designator. The pod was new, the product of a collaboration between a San Fernando–based start-up company called Combat Optics and a Bell Telephone subsidiary set up within the Zone to exploit the parent company's future intellectual properties. The two directors of Combat Optics were 21C senior chief petty officers whose enlistments had expired about two months after the Transition. With a total of fifty years' experience between them in the care and feeding of precision-guided munitions, they returned to civilian life and went straight to the downtown offices of O'Brien and Associates with a proposal to set up Combat Optics and go hunting for federal government contracts. The company was now publicly listed, employing two thousand people, and was worth well over half a billion dollars. Its main line of business was producing strap-on laser guidance kits for dumb iron bombs, designator pods, and night vision equipment.

The system Combat Optics had settled on was a variant on the early Paveway bomb series—for which a relatively new contemporary company known as Texas Instruments was being paid a 5 percent royalty in a deal hammered out by Maria O'Brien. The early Paveways had the benefit of being simple, rugged, and well within the capability of local industry to manufacture, given engineering guidance by the principles of Combat Optics.

So as Lieutenant Anna Torres hauled her Skyhawk jet fighter around, the designator pod lit up and threw a beam of coherent light down onto the cliff face where the Force Recon team had discovered the launch tubes. Torres laid her "sparkle" on a point chosen by the *Clinton*'s Combat Intelligence as the most likely location for the opening of the shaft, given the data provided by Denny's patrol before they were wiped out.

Three Penetrators whistled down through the humid tropical air. Pop-out fins adjusted the flight path to keep the wobbling ordnance on course. For Torres, who was used to fire-and-forget systems, it was a nerve-racking business trying to fly the jet, hold the laser on target, and maintain enough situational awareness to avoid a midair collision.

A voice crackled in her headset. "We got flak."

"We're on it," another replied.

She heard a few distant booms and tried to ignore them. Suppressing ground fire wasn't her department. She had to hold the target . . .

. . . hold the target . . .

. . . hold the target . . .

Three blurs flashed across the low-res black-and-white screen she was using to guide the bomb in. Two large puffs of smoke and a single smaller one marked the impact point.

Then, a split second later, the side of the mountain blew out.

The footage from the mission recon bird—an A-4 fitted out with 21C battle-cams, a small lattice memory cache, and an old digital transmitter—arrived on screen in the *Clinton*'s CIC via relay from the Hawkeye a few minutes later. Kolhammer could hear cheering outside the CIC where the vision was playing on screens throughout the ship. The reaction in the Combat Center was subdued by comparison, more of a buzz than an outbreak of whoopin' and hollerin'.

It was immediately clear that the bombing run had been a success: the replay showed massive secondary explosions being set off in the wake of the primary blast. Damage analysts on both the *Clinton* and the *Enterprise* were already picking the footage apart, but Kolhammer didn't need to know much more. Half the mountain had blown out. Other scenes ran on multiple screens: strings of high-explosive warheads dropping into what looked like raw jungle, only to detonate, setting off further explosions that bespoke the presence of fuel, ammunition, and more planes—the "half-buried" bunkers Denny had identified.

On two smaller, flatter islands the *Clinton*'s second and third Skyhawk squadrons hammered away at more facilities. On one atoll, another Force Recon team called in and adjusted the strikes from a hiding point. The third unit had called in that they were under attack from Japanese ground forces, and nothing had been heard from them since.

"*Enterprise* reports they're launching now, Admiral."

"Thank you," Kolhammer said.

The islands were now in range of the older, prop-driven attack planes like Spruance's Skyraiders. Where the A-4s had gone in with precision strikes, the Skyraiders were simply tasked with smashing flat anything left standing.

"Extraction flights lifting off the *Kandahar,* sir."

Kolhammer grunted in acknowledgment. Maybe Lonesome's guys could grab up that last 'temp unit. If they couldn't, nobody else could.

31

D-DAY + 39. 12 JUNE 1944. 2310 HOURS.
HIJMS *YAMATO,* SEA OF OKHOTSK.

Admiral Isoroku Yamamoto paused, eyes closed, to breathe in the delicate scent of the tea. There was little to distract him from the brief moment of stolen pleasure. The bridge of his flagship was quiet and orderly as the helmsman held station at the center of the fleet lying off Hokkaido.

The giant battleship scarcely moved on the light southeasterly swell that rolled away to break softly upon the shore of the large island miles off to port. His surviving carriers rode the same gentle motion of the sea around her. A flight of Zeros, rare radar-equipped night fighters, climbed slowly into the west to patrol the starlit skies above the ruins of the Russian armada.

Yamato's sister ship, *Musashi,* was silhouetted by a quarter moon that bathed the enormous battle wagon in a soft, silver glow. The rest of the Combined Fleet's big gun platforms—the *Kongo, Nagato,* and *Yamashiro*—were out of his line of sight, but the evidence of their work lay all around. Soviet naval power had been smashed by the warrior spirit of the Thunder Gods.

A score of destroyers churned up the waters, alert to the possibility that even one American or Russian submarine might sneak in among the resting giants on a suicide mission. As Yamamoto admired the sight and raised the thin porcelain cup again to his lips, he could only marvel at the fates that had placed him here.

When the general staff had dispatched him to attack the Americans in their lair at Pearl Harbor, so long ago, he had considered it madness. There was no way to strike at the barbarians' production centers, and he knew it would only be a matter of time before the weight of America's industrial base was brought to bear against his country.

Even then he had underestimated his enemy's ability to recover—and later, to exploit the windfall of the Emergence. Many of his colleagues *still* blamed the time travelers for all the evils that had befallen them since mid-1942.

But Yamamoto knew better. It wasn't the *Siranui* or the *Clinton* or even that damnable submarine the *Havoc* that was to blame for the eclipse of Japan. The blame lay squarely with Japan herself. Where were *her* guided missile destroyers? Where were *her* antisubmarine helicopters?

Or jet fighters, or hovercraft? The Americans and their allies had responded to the Emergence with much greater speed and flexibility and even more ruthlessness than anybody in the empire or the Third Reich. This wasn't merely a facet of their industrial capacity. There was something in the way they viewed the world, something about how they approached war itself, that made them infinitely more daunting an opponent than even he had suspected.

No, they were not weak and corrupt, as they had appeared to be all through the 1930s. When finally aroused, they had proven utterly formidable, and they made war without remorse or honor. Their bombers had burned half of Germany to ash and bones, and would soon do the same thing to Japan. Their soldiers, sailors, and airmen had fought just as valiantly as his own, and increasingly they did so with weapons he knew would be completely beyond the capability of his own countrymen to produce.

They were going to win, of that there could be no doubt. The admiral finished his tea and passed the cup to an orderly, who silently bore it away. He wished to sit quietly, for just a minute longer, admiring the vista of the fleet that stretched out around him. To watch the moon's rays caressing the barrels of the *Yamato*'s guns. It was a fine and stirring sight. If only it could be an omen, of a bright future beyond war's end.

For the end was close now.

Had there been another path he might have taken? Some decision made—or not made—that might have changed everything?

Perhaps. Perhaps not. Above all else, Admiral Isoroku Yamamoto was a warrior, and no matter what he would have prosecuted this conflict to the last, even if the cause was hopeless. But that did not free him of regrets. He no longer entertained the hope that Japan would survive this conflict in anything like her current form.

Too many mothers grieved, he knew. Too many fathers faced the end of their lives without a proper heir. Too many of his own had been committed to the deep. How many more, he wondered, had yet to die?

And to what end? Was his country fated to be enslaved by the godless Stalinists? Would it be better to surrender to the Americans, to throw themselves on the mercy of people they had attacked without warning, and fought without pity? Would Roosevelt and his allies even *accept* an unconditional surrender at this point? The Australian prime minister seemed interested in nothing less than the annihilation of the Japanese people, which was understandable, given the numbers of his own citizens who had been murdered by General Homma's forces. And Roosevelt had pledged to levy the most terrible of punishments on Nippon for the actions of Hidaka and his men in Hawaii. Less temperate voices in the United States had even called for the entirety of the Home Islands to burn inside an atomic firestorm, leaving nothing but fused glass from the northernmost tip of Hokkaido to the southern shores of Kyushu.

It was the sort of thing he might expect of Adolf Hitler. Yamamoto scowled at the thought of the führer, whom he had met twice, and whom he had regarded as little more than a sentient beast. He was convinced that even if they had triumphed over the Allies, it would only have been a precursor to yet another global war. There was madness in the hearts of the Nazis, and they would never be satisfied with a world that was not completely remade in their own image. Could there be any question that Hitler, or Himmler, or whoever came after them, would have turned on their erstwhile partners in the end?

None at all, in his mind.

Yamamoto realized with an irritated frown that his mood had soured even further at the thought of the hideous little German and his warlord cabal. It might be time to get on with the work of the day—another grinding series of planning meetings to shore up the defenses of the Home Islands against the coming storm. There would be no time now to return to the Marianas.

They would fall.

He levered himself to his feet just as a young sublieutenant called out. "We have an incoming air strike from Vladivostok at the edge of our radar field, Admiral. MiG-Fifteens."

Yamamoto sighed inwardly. "Have the fleet withdraw beyond Kunashir, and prepare to receive the attack," he replied. "Thus we will be at the very edge of their combat range when they arrive. Coordinate the air defense net from here, and launch the rest of our night fighters in twenty minutes at—" He checked the clock. "—twenty-three thirty hours."

"Yes, sir," the young officer barked.

If nothing else, the men's morale was high, which was only to be expected. They had fought a great battle against a superior foe, and had comprehensively bested him. The situation on Hokkaido itself was not nearly so clear-cut, however. The Soviets still had significant forces intact, and although they were now cut off from reinforcement, they were going to be very difficult to defeat.

Already the defense of the Home Islands had been thrown into disarray by the Communists' surprise attack. Yamamoto wasn't supposed to be here. He was supposed to be protecting the Marianas. Some of the army divisions now fighting on Hokkaido were supposed to be preparing for the defense of Guam.

The wreckage of the Soviet Pacific Fleet was an apt metaphor for his own personal feelings, Yamamoto realized. As the *Yamato* made steam for the waters of the northwest Pacific, it left behind a sea of bobbing, burning flotsam. His men had achieved something akin to a miracle here, yet the grand admiral felt burned out and cast adrift. He wondered whether anyone would even remember the feats performed today by the Imperial Japanese Navy, in the Battle of Okhotsk.

Probably not, if the Bolsheviks prevailed.

Perhaps, if the Allies won.

A lieutenant appeared at his elbow with a folded piece of paper. "A message, sir. From Admiral Onishi."

Yamamoto took the note and read it in silence. His face remained a stone mask, but inside, as he absorbed the information the communiqué contained, he felt as though he were in free fall. Tumbling end over end toward oblivion.

No, there would be no repeat of the success of the *Ohka* raid. Onishi had just sent word, coded via a onetime pad.

Spruance and Kolhammer had destroyed the hidden bases from which his special attack forces would have struck at them.

The Marianas lay open and defenseless.

D-DAY + 40. 13 JUNE 1944. 0314 HOURS. HMAS *HAVOC*, PACIFIC AREA OF OPERATIONS.

"Firing solutions laid in, Captain. We have four target locks. *Yamato, Musashi,* and two unidentified cruisers."

"Thank you, weapons. Keep 'em locked up, but hold fire for now."

Jane Willet stood with her arms folded, staring at the flat-panel display on which she could see at least nine major surface combatants. Two were burning brightly amidships, hours after the Soviet air attack out of Vladivostok, but it remained to be seen whether the damage they'd taken was fatal. The *Havoc*'s CI had drawn light blue boxes around them. No sense wasting a perfectly good torpedo on a dying ship.

Flashing red target boxes lay around four of their sister ships. Two of them were behemoths—the battleships *Yamato* and *Musashi.* Two were flattops.

More likely than not Grand Admiral Isoroku Yamamoto sailed on the *Yamato.* Was he on the bridge right now? There . . . in the lower left-hand corner of the screen? She could pick it out quite easily in both infrared and LLAMPs mode.

A couple of years ago she would have been able to put a hypersonic combat mace through the blast windows and drop it into his lap from six hundred klicks away. If she wanted to take him down this morning, though, things would have to get a lot more intimate. The *Havoc*'s retrofitted ADCAP torpedoes only had a range of six thousand meters. She'd have to go in under the destroyer screen to launch.

It wasn't a particularly daunting prospect, really. Most likely, the Japanese wouldn't even know she was there until the warheads went off.

Sitting thirty-five kilometers away, stalking her prey via the Big Eye drones hovering far above the enemy, Willet rubbed at her hot, tired eyes and weighed the options. The Japanese had done reasonably well at beating off the MiG-15s that had shown up a few hours back. According to the Big Eye sensors, they had controlled their fire using a fleetwide radar system similar to the Siemens models the Germans had been deploying with their triple-A batteries.

But for now the question was, what was she going to do?

The last of Japan's heavy hitters were sitting squarely within her crosshairs. As weakened as she felt without her original armory to call on, she still had more than enough firepower to rip the heart out of the Imperial Japanese Navy, or what was left of it.

Whether or not it would be wise to do so was another matter.

Willet stared at the screen where the enemy ships appeared to be heading south again. A few feet to the left was another display, wherein the land battle for Hokkaido continued. The Soviets had stopped their advance and appeared to be digging in, awaiting resupply that would now probably never come—certainly not by sea, anyway. Did the Sovs have the capacity to build an air bridge to the island?

Nobody knew.

Nobody knew much at all about their capabilities. That the Soviets had built up their Pacific fleet over the last two years came as no surprise to anyone. The *extent* to which they had done so, however, came as a shock. As did the MiGs, the missile boats, the electronics systems. And the biggie, of course—that fucking nuke they'd busted on Lodz. What other nasty little surprises lay in store? With no intel coverage coming out of the USSR, she couldn't say.

But while the full extent of Stalin's capabilities might remain obscure, his intentions were not. Not to anyone with access to even a modest historical archive.

"Comm," she said, "better dial up Fleetnet. See if you can get Spruance and Kolhammer for me. I think I'm gonna kick this one upstairs."

"Excuse me, sir. You're needed online."

Kolhammer had been dreaming, pleasantly, of his wife. Marie had traveled to Germany to meet him when he flew into Ramstein, after his stint as the UN administrator in Chechnya. They'd flown straight out to Italy and enjoyed four wonderful weeks together in Rome, staying in a small *penzione* off Piazza Navona.

He'd been dreaming of a café where they'd had a late breakfast every morning in the local style. A coffee, a pastry, and a look around. Kolhammer awoke from the memory, lying fully clothed on the couch in his quarters. He hadn't even made it into bed.

"Coffee, sir. NATO standard."

"Thanks, Paterson," he rasped, his voice thick with sleep. "Online you said?"

"On the screen at your desk, sir. Captain Willet and Admiral Spruance."

"Okay. How long did I nap?"

"Hour and a half, sir."

He dragged himself up and over to his desk. Marie was smiling out of the photo he always kept there, and in his disoriented, half-waking state, he thought for just a moment that when he was finished he might be able to sneak down to the café with her.

Damn.

The image of the Australian submariner and another of his task force commanders brought him back to reality with an unpleasant tug. "You'll have to excuse me," he said. "I was stacking a few Z's."

"Me, too," Spruance grunted.

"My apologies, gentlemen," said Captain Willet, who looked disconcertingly wide awake, "but you need to be in on this. I'm trailing the Japanese Combined Fleet, away from the Kurils. They're withdrawing south after finishing off the last of Yumashev's guys. I have target locks on a couple of carriers and Yamamoto's big gunboats. The *Yamato* and *Musashi*. I have enough warshots to take them down, and probably to sort out the rest of his capital ships, too. But . . ."

In the window on Kolhammer's fifty-eight-centimeter flat-screen, Jane Willet shrugged and raised her hands.

He flicked a quick glance across at Spruance, trying to read his expression. The admiral still looked tired, and vaguely pissed off.

"So what's the question?" Spruance asked. "You don't need permission to fire on the enemy, Captain Willet. We only have one rule of engagement. Destroy them. In the absence of further directions from Washington—or in your case Canberra—I don't see the dilemma. Just do your duty and sink them."

With her eyes Willet flashed an unspoken plea at Kolhammer.

"I don't know that we should be so hasty, Admiral," he said. "As I recall, nobody thought Soviet occupation of Japan was a good idea. If Captain Willet takes these guys down, the odds are that we'll have to deal with a Communist-controlled Japan before long."

He could see that Spruance wasn't happy. His mouth was pressed into a thin, straight line, and he bit down on his frustration. "I know you think differently of the Japs, Admiral Kolhammer. But we are still at war with them. They *are* trying to kill us. They did invade Hawaii, and slaughter tens of thousands of innocent people. If we let them wriggle off the hook and God forbid they get hold of an atomic weapon, they won't hesitate to use it. So I say again, in the absence of different orders, we have no decision to make. We have only our duties to perform, and that means sinking those ships."

Kolhammer refused to give up easily. "Under normal circumstances that would be undeniable," he said. "But I can assure you that the Politburo won't be doing business as normal for the next few weeks. This isn't just a military struggle to them—it's a political one, and they are maneuvering their military forces for political effect. Hokkaido is part of that."

He leaned forward and looked directly into the minicam on the top of his monitor.

"Admiral. If those red bastards get in there, we'll have the devil's own job getting them out. We're not just talking about the next couple of weeks. This is about the next hundred years. Perhaps even the next thousand. Yes, we are at war with Japan. Yes, there will have to be a heavy reckoning for what they've done. But we are also in the early stages of an even longer war with international Communism, and Captain Willet is right to question whether or not the demands of the first conflict supersede those of the second.

"I do not believe she should fire on Yamamoto unless he poses a clear, present, and significant danger to our Allied Forces."

Out of the corner of his eye Kolhammer noticed that Willet nodded brusquely. Spruance, on the other hand, looked as if he'd been handed a two-headed dog.

"But by the logic of your own argument, Admiral Kolhammer, the very mission we are engaged in should be called off altogether. You are effectively saying that the Japs should be given a free pass to keep the Soviets out of their Home Islands. The end point to *that* line of thinking is that we make a separate peace with them. That we do not attack or degrade their military infrastructure, or their productive capacity. That we do not punish them for their crimes, and instead we rearm them and support them in any conflict they may have with our *allies* in Russia."

Kolhammer maintained as neutral a façade as he could with so little sleep and such a short fuse burning on his temper. "No, that is not what I'm proposing at all. I'm just saying that any attack on Yamamoto *at this stage* would be precipitate and unwise. This is a political question, and I think it needs to be resolved on a political level."

Spruance shook his head. "We can't hold fire out here, waiting on some sort of gabfest to decide whether or not being at war with someone means shooting at them. We—"

"Excuse me, gentlemen."

It was Jane Willet. She looked especially disconcerted.

"My comm officer tells me that she has just picked up a transmission from a flexipad on one of the ships we've been trailing. It's a message for Admiral Kolhammer. An e-mail from Yamamoto."

32

There was only one advantage to the sickening reverses of the last few days. Stalin was no longer in a mood to party all night, thus sparing everyone the ordeal of his orgiastic benders.

Nevertheless he was still a creature of the night, and the business of the Soviet state was almost entirely conducted after the fall of darkness. For Beria, this was akin to a blessed release. He had moved mountains—literally in some cases—to deliver the weapons the *Vozhd* had demanded. He could hardly be blamed, could he, if after two years of Herculean effort involving the labor of ten million workers, there was an extra day or two to wait?

Oh yes, he could.

Stalin was the master of finding blame where none existed. Beria himself was something of a savant at the practice. If he had failed, he would be facing a gruesome end in one of his own cells. But as he seated himself at the long table in the Politburo meeting room, Beria felt the giddy, light-headed joy of knowing that his life would go on.

Not everyone there that early morning could be so confident.

Well, at least there was no drinking.

Stalin could be such an animal when the alcohol flowed. His moods were entirely arbitrary, and you never knew from one minute to the next whether you would see the dawn. Beria was convinced that if he hadn't been excused from that nightly debauch, two days earlier, he wouldn't have been able to drive the project through to fruition. So he probably owed Hitler and Tojo a favor.

Or Himmler and Tojo, rather, if that was how the dice had

fallen. Nobody could be certain what was happening in Berlin at the moment. It was always so when empires died. The same air of madness had preceded the end days of the Russian monarchy.

Anyway, fuck them all.

He was going to live, and the Soviet state was going to prevail. Not just over her immediate enemies, but over her *original* foes as well. The capitalist democracies.

He took a cold, reptilian pleasure in letting his gaze fall on every man in the room who had reveled in his discomfiture of the previous weeks. For Malenkov he reserved a particularly chilling gaze and was rewarded when the oafish swine flitted his porcine eyes away anxiously. Beria could imagine the dread Malenkov was experiencing, as if the cold finger of a dead man had been laid at the base of the spine, making the heart lurch and the balls contract upward.

Stalin strode in, looking disheveled and gaunt. Scraps of paper fell from the pockets of the uniform the marshal had affected ever since the fascists had attacked in 1941. Nobody dared meet his gaze. Even Beria thought it wise to examine the folder that lay on the table in front of him.

He had one small item of bad news: a partisan attack on a convoy in Kamchatka that had killed a number of middle-ranking researchers. But such things were unfortunately commonplace across all of the republics. More importantly, he had good news from Project One. Given the extra time and a touch more encouragement from the NKVD, Professor Kurchatov's team had succeeded beyond expectations.

It was a happy day for Laventry Beria.

By way of contrast, the defense minister and navy chief looked physically ill. As well they should. Okhotsk had been a disaster of the first order. Yumashev had assured them all that he possessed the resources to carry out the invasion and protect the beachhead. Now he was dead, luckily for him, and Kuznetsov would be forced to deliver the report, but Soviet maritime power, and its prestige in the East, had been comprehensively fucked. When Beria thought of the resources that had gone into the building program at Vladivostok—the millions of men and the staggering sums that had been spent so profligately to create a modern Pacific fleet, virtually from nothing—it was a disgrace. If just a fraction of those funds and a few hundred thousand of the laborers had been devoted to his projects, then he would not have had to suffer through the fear he had endured.

"So, Admiral Kuznetsov," Stalin said as he seated himself at the head of the table. "Tell me exactly how you failed."

Stalin's voice was quite low, almost inaudible. Beria noticed a few of the others straining forward to make out his exact words.

The man for whom they were intended had no difficulty understanding their import, however. He blanched a sort of gray-green shade and began to babble about some sort of secret Japanese terror weapons, and possible interference by the Americans, possibly even by Kolhammer himself.

While he spoke, Stalin used his fingertips to trace patterns on the polished wooden surface of the conference table. His pipe lay in front of him, but he never moved to fill it, or to light it.

"All of our intelligence spoke of Yamamoto moving south to engage the Americans at the Marianas," Kuznetsov said. "Our liaison staff in Washington and London confirmed the same. The Americans *expected* to meet him. They told us they were moving to engage him decisively. And these rocket bombs. These suicide attacks. Nobody had seen the like before—"

"Rubbish!" Stalin shouted, smashing an open palm down onto the table so hard that a few drops of water sloshed out of Beria's glass a good three meters away. "The Japanese have been using *kamikaze* attacks for months!"

"But not with these sorts of planes," Kuznetsov pleaded. "They were like the missiles we heard of, the ones that smashed the Americans at Midway. They were so fast, and since they were being piloted they were able to adjust course to avoid flak and to pick and choose their targets. If Spruance had encountered them without warning, the result would have been the same."

"Ah, but there you are wrong, aren't you, *Admiral*," Stalin said. "Because we now find out that Spruance *has* encountered them, and completely neutralized the threat. Something of which you have proven yourself incapable."

"But . . . no, I did not—"

The supreme leader of the Soviet Union cut him off by slamming his hand into the table again, this time in a closed fist. "Enough! I have had enough excuses. Timoshenko, do you bring me excuses about the Western Front? Beria, what about you?"

Beria did not want to let the defense minister escape by the agency of his success. He stared the man down.

"We are stalled at the Oder," Marshal Timoshenko said. "The fascists have created an impenetrable boundary with these nerve weapons. But in Southern Europe we progress. Our forces have overrun Romania, Bulgaria, Hungary, Yugoslavia, and Albania. They have entered Greece and northern Italy, the southern regions of Austria, and fresh air assault divisions are being readied to jump into southern France. I can guarantee that within two weeks Vichy France will be ours. The Allies will hold the northern half of the country. I foresee a border that stretches probably from Belfort to La Rochelle. Italy will be cut off entirely. Switzerland can be neutralized."

Timoshenko's delivery had been forceful and confident. Beria was grudgingly impressed. The man had somehow made a virtue of failure. For the inability to break through at the Oder was surely failure of the worst sort.

Stalin, however, seemed mollified.

"And Project One," he said, turning to Beria. "I hope you have something positive to report. Have you finished the two bombs?"

The NKVD chief couldn't help himself. He smiled.

"No. I have finished three."

D-DAY + 40. 13 JUNE 1944. 0629 HOURS. KORYAK RANGES, FAR EASTERN SIBERIA.

The T5 was wearing off, but they had everything they needed to know.

Ivanov finished writing up his report for the compressed data burst. The glow of his flexipad was the main source of the light in the fetid-smelling cave where they crouched. A couple of whale oil candles flickered farther down the narrow tunnel, filling the cramped space with dark smoke and a pungent aroma.

"What will we do with them?" Vendulka asked.

Ivanov shut down the flexipad's word processor and dropped the file into a dispatch tray. Internal software agents began to encrypt and compact the long file, which comprised about five gigs of text, audio, and video images.

He regarded the unconscious scientists with professional reserve. As was normal with interrogations carried out through the use of the T5 drug, he had accumulated a great number of irrelevant facts: details concerning their families, their hometowns, the menu at the *Sharashka* canteen where they ate. All of it useless.

It did humanize them, however. They were no longer simply ciphers to be decoded. The younger one, Anatoly, was recently married. His mother and father had died of starvation during the collectivist period of the 1930s. His wife was pregnant. He hated the cabbage soup.

The older one, Viktor, who had been injured in the ambush, had a secret stash of forbidden literature in his laboratory. He had a wife and five children, all of them grown. Three had died in the first year of the war. He *liked* the cabbage soup, as long as there was enough pepper to spice it up.

"Kill them," Ivanov said.

Vendulka grimaced.

"We cannot take them with us," he said, refusing to allow her response to sway him. "We were lucky to get this far. If we want to get out with our skins intact, we have to move fast and light. Just the five of us."

"And the Chukchi?" she asked.

"They came to fight the Bolsheviks." He shrugged. "They don't want to run away, and they think we are cowards for doing so. They will stay and delay the pursuers."

His flexipad beeped. The file was ready for transfer. He held it like a talisman.

"They understand that we need to get this message out. That it will hurt the Stalinists if we do. That is enough for them."

Vendulka was clearly unconvinced. She was a medical officer, and it wasn't within her nature to snuff out a life for the reason of simple convenience. Ivanov appreciated that part of her character. Even with all the shit they'd been through to survive the last two years, she had never become like him. A simple killer.

He looked at the scientists.

"Best you leave now, Vennie. They will not suffer."

Her eyes implored him to walk a different path, but he held her gaze without remorse. They lived because they had been careful.

If Stalin or Beria found out they were behind so many of the rebellions that had flared up across the Soviet Union, he would think nothing of assigning a million men to hunt them down. It was only because they remained invisible that any of them still drew breath.

He didn't need to explain it to her. She wasn't naïve, or willfully stupid. It was just that Vendulka Zemyatin had somehow maintained feelings for her fellow man, while Ivanov had not. It probably had more to do with the lives they had led on the other side of the Transition. Hers had been relatively clean and uncomplicated. His had been spent fighting the worst sort of scum.

After Beslan he had never been the same.

Vendulka sighed and removed herself.

The scientists were still in a drug-addled stupor. They would not suffer, as he had promised.

Ivanov took a small metal case from his backpack. He removed two syrettes of letha-barb and in turn jabbed each man in the neck. The life ran out of them like air leaking from an old tire.

The Spetsnaz commando gathered up the rest of his gear and hurried back out toward the entrance of the cave. He had to crouch to avoid hitting his head on the low ceiling. A couple of clumps of bloodied scalp and hair attested to others who had not been so careful.

The sun was up, pouring over the rugged peaks of the Koryak Ranges. Kicji was waiting for him, chewing on a strip of smoked reindeer meat. He offered a piece to Ivanov, along with a bladder full of soju, a Korean rice wine.

"Thanks," he said. It would do for breakfast. Probably for lunch, as well. "Any sign of the Bolsheviks?"

He could hear the distant whine of jets and the mushy, dampened thud of rotor blades. The sounds were distorted as they echoed around inside the myriad gorges and defiles of the mountains.

Kicji nodded, pointing to the northwest. "Three valleys over. Some of the Chukchi are fighting to draw them away."

Ivanov nodded. He was surprised, though. He hadn't arranged a diversion. Kicji had seemed to read his mind. For a wizened old man who looked like an evil charm that had fallen off a witch doctor's wand, he was sharp.

"The Chukchi decided this among themselves. Ten men stay behind. The rest might get away."

Ivanov mulled it over. He inhaled deeply, enjoying the taste of clean air in his nostrils. "They understand that they cannot come with us?"

Kicji snorted. "They do not want to. They called you the blunderers. They say your footfall would bring down the side of a volcano, it is so heavy."

"Fine." Ivanov shrugged. "We will separate this morning, then. After I have sent my message."

Kicji nodded, and left to inform the Chukchi. They were so well hidden in crevices, under hanging rocks, and inside the caves that riddled these mountains, Ivanov could not keep track of them. Good. It meant the NKVD would have the same problem.

His own team, Vennie, Sergo, and Ahmed Khan, had huddled down to share some food and drink before the day's march.

Ivanov quickly unpacked his comm gear, setting up the pulse unit and its dish on a small collapsible tripod. He jacked in the flexipad and set the program to transmit an encrypted signal on wide-area datacast. The burst would travel outward in an arc for five thousand kilometers. He had no idea whether it would pass over a Fleetnet node, but he had to assume that Kolhammer had moved some assets into the area to take the feed.

To be certain, he would repeat the process whenever possible until he received verification that the signal had been intercepted. It was a ham-fisted, inefficient method of communicating such important intelligence, but without satellite cover they had no choice.

D-DAY + 40. 13 JUNE 1944. 0629 HOURS. THE KREMLIN, MOSCOW.

So pleased was the *Vozhd* that he ordered breakfast served in the conference room. Even Admiral Kuznetsov looked more relaxed. It seemed that, today at least, he would benefit from Stalin's capricious moods.

The main table was littered with official papers and dossiers, with plates of half-eaten food, pots of coffee, and bottles of champagne. Beria used a glass spoon to scoop dollops of Beluga caviar onto hot buttered black bread. Stalin threw grapes and hunks of cheese down the table.

"It is a great day, Comrades. A great day," he declared. "Today we change history. Today the correlation of forces shifts back into alignment. I knew. I knew—did I not tell you?—that there was a mechanical inevitability about all of this. We may not understand the physics yet, but the laws of dialectical materialism would not allow the revolution to fail. And so, as antihistorical pressures built up, they ruptured history itself, delivering us the means to . . ."

Beria tuned him out. The old fool was talking nonsense again.

The NKVD boss well remembered the shock and fear that lived on Stalin's face in the first days after the Emergence. They all expected Nazi storm troopers to burst through the gates of the Kremlin in some sort of invincible supertank, firing death rays and wonder rockets. Stalin had claimed that the Emergence was a product of an unstable history on the other side of the event, but it was all so much eyewash.

As information had trickled in, Beria had been briefed by his best scientists about the experiment that had been conducted by the madman called Pope. About what he had been attempting to do, and the theory behind it. He had tried to explain it to the *Vozhd* and the rest of the war cabinet, but had backpedaled when it became obvious that Stalin needed an explanation for why all of his statues would have been pulled down.

For Stalin it was simple. History was wrong.

And since history was subject to determinist laws, just like an apple falling from a tree, it had corrected itself. Now the workers' revolution would proceed as nature intended.

A couple of Red Army guards appeared pushing one of the electronic boards retrieved from the *Vanguard.* A nervous technician followed them.

"Excellent. *Excellent.* Bring it in," Stalin roared. "Turn it on, man. Quickly," he continued. "We have the business of state to carry out."

Beria chased the last of his caviar around the bottom of the bowl while the shaking apparatchik attempted to do as he'd been ordered. When the dull white screen winked into life, you would have thought he'd just given birth. The technician handed Stalin a small black, handheld device and attempted to instruct him on its use. The general secretary tossed it back at him.

"You do it," he instructed.

How fortunate for the poor bastard, Beria thought. *Stalin has enough trouble making an old gramophone play.* It wouldn't be worth one's life to embarrass him with a complicated piece of equipment like this.

After a few seconds' fiddling with the remote control, a map of the world appeared.

"Marvelous," Stalin said. "Can you—what is the correct word—*define* Berlin and Tokyo? Make them flash or something?"

He could.

"Good. *Very* good," Stalin said. He was positively beaming. "Marshal Timoshenko, can you see those two cities?"

The defense minister nodded, unsure what this was about.

"And if necessary, do you have a bomber that could reach them?"

Timoshenko appeared to think it over. "The Tu-Sixteen could easily make it to Berlin and back, if we staged the flight out of a Polish base," he conceded. "Tokyo would be more difficult. It could certainly be reached from Vladivostok. But the return trip is too far."

"But the pilots could reach the Japanese capital?"

"Oh yes."

"Then if you wish to purge yourself of blame for the disaster at Okhotsk, you will take the bombs that Laventry Pavlovich has made, and you will drop them. Two on Berlin, and one on Tokyo. And then you will do whatever is necessary to break through at the Oder and to relieve your forces on Hokkaido.

"Do you understand? Whatever the cost, you will pay it."

33

"Whatever the price, gentlemen, Do you understand?"

Each of the Joint Chiefs nodded, Army Air Force commander General Hap Arnold the most emphatically.

"All right. Thank you, then. General Groves, you have preparations to make."

The general thanked the president and excused himself, accepting the plaudits of the chiefs as he departed with rare humility.

While he was waiting for Groves to leave, Roosevelt rolled a pencil between his fingers, a poor substitute for the cigarettes he had given up. He no longer suffered from the physical cravings — the tiny insert in his arm had taken care of those. But he still found himself longing for the familiar ceremony of smoking, the soothing effect of the ritual itself. At times like these it was almost impossible to resist the urge to just go through the motions. He was going to write a long letter to Truman, who was campaigning in Iowa at the moment, telling him exactly what he thought of the tobacco companies and what should be done about them. Assuming Harry won in November.

"You have admirals Spruance and Kolhammer via audio relay," an aide told him.

"Put them on the speaker box," Roosevelt instructed him. "Everyone needs to be in on this. Lord Halifax, you should stay, too. His Majesty's government will have a say in this matter."

The British ambassador smiled and brushed some cookie crumbs from his lap with his one good hand.

The speaker set on the president's desk crackled before settling back into a sibilant hiss.

"Admiral Spruance, can you hear me?" Roosevelt said.

"Yes, sir," came the slightly distorted reply. "I'm sorry for the lack of a video link, Mr. President. We're too far out. I have Admiral Kolhammer with me."

Kolhammer's voice crackled out of the box. "Mr. President."

"And I have the Joint Chiefs and the British ambassador with me," Roosevelt responded. "Now, tell us about this message from Yamamoto."

It was Kolhammer who answered.

"The *Havoc* picked up a wide-area datacast a few hours ago, Mr. President. A few hours after the Soviet Pacific Fleet was destroyed. It was a personal message from Admiral Yamamoto to myself, seeking to make contact to discuss the possibility of a cease-fire, prior to the immediate withdrawal of all Japanese forces to the Home Islands."

Every man in the room reacted. Admiral King, the U.S. Navy chief, cursed volubly. Lord Halifax raised his eyebrows theatrically. Hap Arnold snorted and General Marshall, the chairman of the Joint Chiefs, shook his head in amazement. Roosevelt, whose whole life had been spent cutting one deal after another, merely bobbed his head up and down.

"I see," he replied. "And what details do we have of this offer? Is Yamamoto acting on his own? Can he deliver the rest of his general staff? Does he think this is a way to avoid reparations, and trials for war crimes? Will the Japanese submit to occupation?"

It was a hot and brutally humid summer day outside the Oval Office. Hardly a leaf stirred in the still, heavy conditions. Roosevelt wondered what time it was in Kolhammer's part of the world as he waited for the slightly delayed response.

"On the last matter, Mr. President," Kolhammer replied, "I would hazard a guess that the Japanese would be only too willing to submit to occupation by our forces, if only to avoid a Soviet takeover."

"And you think that's a good idea, I suppose," Admiral King interjected. He and Kolhammer had a famously antagonistic relationship. Butting into the middle of a conversation between Kolhammer and the president was well within his character.

Roosevelt was glad when the other man didn't bite.

"I have no opinion either way," Kolhammer responded. "This is a political decision. That's why we're calling it in."

Roosevelt could hardly suppress the grin that wanted to break out and run wild on his face. Phillip Kolhammer was just about the most political commander he knew. Even Douglas MacArthur was shaded into a distant second place by the man's Machiavellian machinations. He was just damn lucky that Eleanor had taken such a shine to him.

The president had to wonder what the man was playing at.

"Is the *Havoc* in contact with the Japanese fleet?" he asked. "I understand she was supposed to be shadowing them. Is that correct?"

"Yes, sir," Spruance answered. "Captain Willet is stalking the Combined Fleet and reports that she has independent target locks on their carriers and largest gunships, the *Musashi* and *Yamato*."

"Then why are they still floating?" Admiral King asked, nearly shouting to make his voice heard from across the room.

Inevitably, Kolhammer fielded that question. "Captain Willet exercised her best judgment, Admiral. And in her judgment it was an open question as to whether or not our goals were served by destroying the major impediment to a Communist takeover of Japan."

"Our *goals* are to defeat the Japanese and the Nazis," King barked back. "Look it up in your history books, Admiral. I'm sure it's in there somewhere."

"That's enough," Roosevelt said. He threw an almost pleading look at George Marshall. "General. What's your feeling about this matter? I must confess, my initial reaction is to say *damn it all* and send them to the bottom."

Marshall was sitting with what looked like painful formality in a Chesterfield armchair, and he didn't waste time mulling the question. "As I understand it, the Soviets' ability to project power in that theater has been dramatically constrained by their losses off Hokkaido. Even if the *Havoc* were to cripple the Japanese now, it wouldn't necessarily mean that Stalin was free to walk into the place and take over. Look at our own projections for an invasion of the Home Islands. Without using atomic weapons, you're talking about millions of men and hundreds of thousands of casualties."

"But the Russians have atomic weapons, General," Roosevelt said.

"I don't believe they have many," Marshall replied. "If they did, we would have seen them by now. It's even possible, if you agree with Admiral Kolhammer, to imagine them bombing *us* if they thought they could get away with it. How many bombs would *that* take? How many cities would we be willing to lose, just to hold out against Communist demands? How many would your people trade for their freedom, Mr. Ambassador?

"I doubt Stalin has the capacity to launch more than another three or four atomic strikes at the moment. Assuming he wants to concentrate his efforts on Europe, that means a largely conventional campaign to take Japan. And as I said, all of his sealift and naval air capability was destroyed by Yamamoto. So I guess I come down on the side of Admiral King. Sink them."

Roosevelt surveyed the room. Hap Arnold nodded. King did so vigorously.

"Mr. Ambassador?"

"I'm afraid the PM would want to make this call himself—"

"For chrissakes, we can't ring London every time a sub captain wants to put a torpedo into a Jap," protested King, who had almost no time for his British allies.

Lord Halifax, a sickly man with a withered left arm that ended in a stump, smiled wanly. "I do not propose to ask any such thing of you, Admiral. I was merely pointing out that Prime Minister Churchill would doubtless prefer that you heard his opinion, rather than mine, or even my best guess at what his thinking might be. It is an operational matter, in the end."

"Excuse me."

It was Kolhammer's voice again, sounding strained, which was to be expected since the argument was running against him.

"It *is* an operational matter," he agreed, "but it will have broad political consequences. *Historical* consequences. I cannot emphasize this strongly enough. You cannot allow the Soviets to gain control of Japan. They have overrun China already, apart from areas where the Nationalists are holding out. They have pushed deep into Afghanistan, within artillery range of India's Northwest Frontier, last time that I checked. They have advance forces in northern Indochina and Korea. They are going to enslave four-fifths of the world by the time they are finished.

"This war is not about the last four years, not anymore. It is about the next hundred. Possibly the next five hundred. I'm sorry that I appear to be the only one with this opinion, but I am going to put it out there, and put it strongly. *And* I want it recorded that I disagree in the strongest terms with any decision to reject Yamamoto's offer without even investigating the terms. Mr. President, this is Yalta on a global scale."

Roosevelt prickled at the reference to Yalta. When the first "future histories" had been published, he'd taken real damage over something he hadn't even done. At what point in his life in *this* world had he consigned Eastern Europe to Communist dictatorship? Kolhammer could be insufferable at times like this.

"Admiral Spruance," he said brusquely. "You will order Captain Willet to sink those ships."

Kolhammer tried to speak again. "Mr. President—"

"I have made up my mind, Admiral. Now, if there is nothing else."

To Roosevelt's surprise, there was.

Spruance spoke. "About the same time Captain Willet intercepted the Yamamoto datacast, she also received one from Major Ivanov, the Russian officer who arrived with Admiral Kolhammer and who is, uh, operating within the Soviet Union of his accord."

Roosevelt could feel high color in his cheeks, and he was certain his blood pressure surged. He'd already had it out with Kolhammer over this one, and it was galling in the extreme to find himself in a position where he was forced to concede the utility of having Ivanov in the USSR.

"Go on, Admiral *Spruance,*" he said, trying to keep the aggravation out of his tone.

"Well, Admiral Kolhammer is better informed than I, Mr. President, as he's had time for a full briefing from his Intelligence Division—"

That'd be right, Roosevelt thought.

"—but as he explained it to me, Major Ivanov has confirmed the existence of a Multinational Force ship, the *Vanguard,* within the USSR, and the existence of a large nuclear facility in eastern Siberia, in which the Soviets constructed the weapon used over Lodz. He has provided the location, some surveillance images, and a good deal of technical data obtained from a number of Russian scientists who worked at the facility."

"And where are those scientists now?" Roosevelt asked.

"They're dead, sir," answered Kolhammer bluntly. "Major Ivanov terminated them."

A great weariness threatened to steal over the president. What was the French word for existential despair? He felt it more and more often whenever he contemplated a world remade in the image of people like Kolhammer. There were some days when he couldn't wait to be free of it all.

Aloud, he said, "Well, my decision stands. Captain Willet is to close with the enemy and destroy them."

D-DAY + 40. 14 JUNE 1944. 2340 HOURS.
USS *HILLARY CLINTON*, PACIFIC AREA
OF OPERATIONS.

Death Cab for Cutie's "Crooked Teeth" poured from the speakers in Kolhammer's cabin. The admiral swirled the ice-filled glass of Coke, sipped, and stared at the flexipad on his desk as the Cuties sang about making a horrible call.

There was nothing he could do. Willet had her orders and she would obey them without question, regardless of her own personal misgivings. He looked at his watch. She was probably launching her first salvo right now.

He leaned over and picked up the flexipad. A small icon, an open envelope, marked the e-mail message from Yamamoto.

Another icon designated Ivanov's file. His eyes flicked over at the door to his room like the tip of a rawhide whip. There was one chance that he might yet influence events. He and Willet had talked their way around it after the audio hookup with Washington, convincing Spruance that the *Havoc* should only take down those ships that provided a clear and immediate threat to Allied vessels.

It left one possibility open.

He didn't stop to consider the consequences.

Opening Ivanov's message, he quickly excised the location of the Siberian *Sharashka* and copied in a few details about the facility's purpose.

He checked the SEND and HARD-DELETE boxes at the top of the message. The pad linked to the *Clinton*'s Nemesis arrays and pulsed outward. Microseconds later a software agent cannibalized that portion of the pad's lattice memory that held any trace of the e-mail. Then it ate itself as the music played on, assuring him that there had been nothing there all along.

Kolhammer turned off the pad, finished the Coke, and stood up. It was time to get back to the bridge.

D-DAY + 40. 14 JUNE 1944. 2340 HOURS.
HMAS *HAVOC*, PACIFIC AREA OF OPERATIONS.

The *Woomera*-class submarine slipped through the warm bath of the Pacific like an assassin's blade. It never came closer than sixty meters to the surface, but a thin cable trailed from a recessed slot at the rear of its conning tower and ran all the way up to the surface, where it maintained a constant link to a Big Eye drone that was maintaining its position above the center of the Japanese fleet.

"Target lock verified, Captain."

"Thank you, weapons," Willet said, never taking her eyes off the screen in which the Japanese ships steamed south. "You may fire."

The sub's offensive sysop ran her fingers down a line of icons. A hundred and twenty meters forward of the Combat Center, eight torpedo tube doors slid open and an impossibly complicated waltz began, with the *Havoc*'s Combat Intelligence tracking its prey via the link to the drone, then passing the position fix data down to the seeker heads in the retrofitted torpedoes.

One after another they launched, leaping from the tubes and accelerating away. They were driven by hydrazine monopropellent rocket engines, and trailed guidance wires back to their mother ship.

Standing behind her chief weapons officer, Willet watched with unspoken misgivings as the flashing blue triangles crawled across the flatscreen toward software-generated representations of their intended victims.

The sysop and the Combat Intelligence controlled the Mark 48s until they reached three thousand meters—the limit of their guidance wires. Well before then, however, passive/active seeker heads had acquired the acoustic profiles of four ships. *Yamato, Musashi,* and the fleet carriers *Shinano* and *Hiyo.* Since it had no offensive capability left, she had decided to ignore for now the converted *kamikaze* carrier, the *Nagano.* Willet had a limited number of torpedoes and agreed with Admiral

Kolhammer that they should be reserved for the functioning carriers and gun platforms.

Her boat chief Roy Flemming appeared at her side. "I hope this turns out to be for the best, Chief," she said.

Flemming gently clamped one of his meaty paws on her shoulder—he was the only person on the boat she would allow to take such a liberty. They had served together for a long time, and he was as much a favorite uncle as anything else.

"Don't worry yourself overly, skipper. Remember what these bastards did at home, and in Hawaii. Some people are just in desperate need of being killed."

The blue triangles separated from the thin black lines representing their guidance wires.

"Seekers active. Targets still locked, Captain."

"Thank you, weapons . . ." She caught Flemming glancing at her apprehensively. "I know Chief, I know. I've got no sympathy for them. Kill 'em all, I say. Still, I just wonder if we're gonna be back up here in a few years' time, facing off with the People's Democratic Republic of Nippon because of this."

"If that's the case, we'll just have to kick their arse, won't we."

"CI indicates one minute till impact."

D-DAY + 40. 14 JUNE 1944. 2341 HOURS.
HIJMS *YAMAMOTO*, PACIFIC AREA OF OPERATIONS.

He hadn't really thought much would come of it. It had been a moment's foolishness. Madness really. He couldn't expect the enemy to treat with him after the savageries of the last four years. Even Admiral Kolhammer, an outsider, and a man he had studied—as far as it was possible—in the finest detail. Even he could not be expected to step outside of the rigid demands of military command, to act independently. Not for something as fundamental as this.

Yet Grand Admiral Isoroku Yamamoto kept dipping his good hand into the pocket where he kept his personal flexipad, furtively checking to see if he had received a reply. He hadn't cleared the contact with the general staff. Had not mentioned it to anyone beyond the Emperor, in fact. He had reached out to Kolhammer, unofficially, man-to-man, in the desperate hope that he might be able to avert the cataclysm he was certain was now inevitable.

He had no way of knowing whether or not the message had even gone through.

He leaned forward now and placed both hands on the edge of the map table in the *Yamato*'s operations room, surveying the abysmal situation. The Americans were estimated to be close to launching their strike on the Marianas. He had no idea what the Soviets were going to do about Hokkaido. He didn't even know if they had committed all their naval forces to the failed mission. The army was in general retreat throughout the Dutch East Indies, or had been bypassed completely by MacArthur's land forces.

The operations staff moved quietly around him, nobody daring to speak. Would they now head south to the Marianas, to face certain defeat against Spruance and Kolhammer? Or did they need to remain here, ghosting about the Home Islands, as insurance against another Soviet thrust? And what possible help would they be when Stalin sent planes with nuclear bombs, to avenge his humiliation in Okhotsk?

His mind was a blur as he tried to keep all of these questions suspended in his imagination, hoping that some brilliant stratagem, some unforeseen correlation of events and actions might suggest itself to him.

His flexipad buzzed and he almost dropped it as he tried to haul the device out of his pocket with his crippled, shaking hand.

It was Kolhammer.

It had to be.

Yamamoto stared at the screen where a message was indeed waiting for him. But it made no sense. The message title read: SOVIET A-BOMB FACILITY.

Before he could open the file two gigantic explosions rang throughout the body of the Japanese flagship. Yamamoto was flung into the low metal ceiling, breaking his shoulder and cracking a cheekbone, and he slammed back down and smashed his face on the edge of the map table.

D-DAY + 40. 14 JUNE 1944. 2344 HOURS.
HMAS *HAVOC*, PACIFIC AREA OF OPERATIONS.

"Good work, Ms. Wilkins."

"Thank you, ma'am. Second salvo away."

Willet felt the submarine shudder with the energy of the launch as another eight heavy torpedoes spat out of the tubes and began their terminal runs. She was no longer concerned with watching their progress, though. The boat's Combat Intelligence had set the firing sequence, and the Nemesis processors had tracked the initial launch to the point of impact. Diagnostic software agents poring over the data feedback detected a few glitches with the guidance mechanisms, but nothing lying outside an acceptable margin of error.

Every warhead had detonated as intended, a few meters under the keel of its target. The results were spectacular.

On the main display, which was running real-time vision in high-definition color from a virtual height of two thousand meters, it looked as though the ADCAP war shots had broken the backs of the two carriers. Willet distinctly saw them lift a good few feet clear of the water amidships, while the bow and stern merely tilted back up toward the fatal rupture.

"Like snapping a twig," Lieutenant Lohrey said.

CPO Flemming pointed at the two battleships. Their greater mass had absorbed the kinetic blows with more success, but they were still badly damaged. "More like a big fucking log for those two," the chief muttered.

"Mmmh," Willet responded absently. "Weapons. Override the CI and designate both *Musashi* and *Yamato* for another two hits."

"Aye, ma'am."

"Captain. We have four destroyers heading in our direction. Throwing depth charges."

"Thank you, Mr. Knox. Attack profile?"

Her chief defensive sysop took a moment to consider the pattern of the destroyers' movements and weapons launches.

"They don't know where we are, ma'am. They're making a guess based on the placement of our shots. They're pretty good, actually. But it's still only a guess."

"Okay. Helm, take us down to two hundred meters. We'll make our away around to the far side of the target group and launch our next sequence from there."

The first depth charges went off, but they were a long way distant, like the thunder of a late-summer storm you know from experience will pass by without harm.

D-DAY + 40. 14 JUNE 1944. 2348 HOURS.
HIJMS *YAMATO*, PACIFIC AREA OF OPERATIONS.

That damn woman, again.

An entire division of the Imperial Japanese Navy had devoted itself to the study of Captain Jane Willet and her submarine the *Havoc*. Yamamoto had ordered it after her attack on the anchorage at Hashirajima had gutted the Combined Fleet. As soon as he heard that a submarine had crept in and crippled him again, he knew.

Willet.

The torpedoes had struck like the twin hammers of a vengeful god, their power great enough to wrench seventy thousand tons of iron plating and armor out of shape. Already the deck had begun to list to starboard. It was only slight, but it was noticeable, and it was increasing.

Pandemonium had broken out on the lower decks. Not panic as such, but a rushing, half-desperate haste to respond to a new crisis that was clearly greater than anything the ship and her crew had yet been required to face. Men came up hard against each other in the companionways as they hurried to their stations. A drum solo of deep-seated explosions shook the ship again.

"You must hurry, Admiral."

The young officer, a sublieutenant, took him by the arm.

Yamamoto slowly and deliberately removed his hand.

"No, Lieutenant. *You* must hurry. This is most important. Take this," he said, holding out the flexipad. "You see the information on the screen. The location there. Latitude and longitude."

The youngster, who looked as though he'd never had to scrape a razor across his chin, nodded. His eyes were bulging.

"Do you have a pencil and a notepad? Give it here, boy. Take this note to the radio room. And make sure this message gets back to Hashirajima. These coordinates. This information. And my instructions. Understand?"

The lieutenant nodded. Clearly he was more fearful of failing the grand admiral than of drowning, if the ship went down.

"Go then. Go! Do not fail."

The young man saluted and took off running up the slanted deck.

Do not fail, thought Yamamoto. *What a bitter irony it is that such a thing should be my last order.*

D-DAY + 40. 14 JUNE 1944. 2352 HOURS.
HMAS *HAVOC,* PACIFIC AREA OF OPERATIONS.

The third and fourth torpedoes exploded under the *Yamato*'s keel with spectacular effect.

The previous strike had fatally wounded the giant, fracturing her spine beyond hope of repair. When the following shots arrived they detonated, as before, a few meters under the keel. The pressure wave again lifted the monster battleship partly out of the water, and as it came down, the actual explosion ripped into her damaged innards. With a tearing screech, she split and a sixty-five-meter-long section of the stern tilted ninety degrees, lifting her screws clear of the water.

Willet watched dispassionately as the section quickly knifed down into the depths. The greater bulk of the dying vessel was still afloat, but surely not for much longer. Hundreds of men swarmed over the upper decks and threw themselves into the churning waters.

Similar scenes repeated themselves throughout the Japanese fleet, which was now in complete disarray. Both of the conventional carriers had already gone down. The *Musashi,* like her sister ship, had been cleaved in two. Six heavy cruisers were in their final throes.

"Captain, that converted carrier, the *Ohka* ferry, is boogying to the south. I can get a target lock in just a few minutes."

"Thank you, weapons. Just hold on a second. Mr. Knox. What do you have on your threat boards?"

"The destroyers still haven't found us, ma'am. But there are about a dozen of them, throwing depth charges everywhere. It's a bit like flying over Baghdad or Damascus, with everyone shooting into the air. Somebody might get lucky."

Willet made a show of weighing her options. "All right, then. I think we've earned our pay for today. Helm, let's blow this Popsicle stand. Wouldn't do to get nailed by a random shot."

"Aye, ma'am," the helmsman replied.

But Willet wasn't really paying attention. She was watching the *Nagano* slip away.

34

The last B-52 ever built rolled off the Boeing assembly line in 1962, thirty years before Caro Llewellyn was born. They were still kicking ass sixty years later, when she was flying Raptors off the Big Hill for a living. The air force had been intending to keep them in service until 2050, at which point the youngest of the airframes would be coming up on ninety years old. Of course, being a navy flier, that meant shit to her.

Or it had until Manning Pope had opened a can of wormholes and dragged Caro's sorry carcass all the way back to 1942. Now, sitting in the pilot's seat of a brand-new B-52 Stratofortress waiting for clearance to open the throttles and get the hell out of Dodge, or out of Alamogordo Air Field at any rate, she shifted uncomfortably in her new Army Air Force flight suit and tried not think about the Escher-print metaphysical detour her life had taken that day off East Timor. A year ago she'd been transferred without consultation into the newly formed Strategic Air Command, given the temporary rank of colonel in the Army Air Force, and dropped into the middle of the New Mexico desert. And these undeniably weird contortions in her personal fate were all of infinitely less consequence than the mission she was about to lead: the dropping of three atomic bombs on Nazi Germany.

New Mexico had been a real head spin. There were a lot of uptimers stationed out there. Nearly a thousand at her reckoning, which gave them some say in determining the culture of the place, but only some. There were thousands more 'temps, and nearly as many of them were civilians as military. It felt very different from the Zone, where she'd been working on the

A-4 program, but it was also a world away from the rest of the country.

"You're clear to roll, Colonel. Good luck."

The voice in her earphones was female, an air traffic controller at the main tower. From the clipped, correct tones Llewellyn took her to be a 'temp, but you could never tell. Some said they could. The uptime vocabulary was generally given to more interesting profanity and was littered with the detritus of a great deal of as-yet-unrealized mass culture. But even if you took those surface elements away, there was something deeper still that separated them, an innate slackness or mental drawl of some sort that some linguists insisted on identifying in the speech patterns of everyone who'd arrived from the next century.

Colonel Llewellyn shrugged inwardly as she pushed the throttles forward to feed more power into the eight massive underwing engines. It beggared belief, the money and manpower Uncle Sam must have poured into the task of just building those behemoths. And if you let your mind expand from there, thinking about the effort involved in retroactively constructing the giant bombers, or a rough facsimile of them, and beyond that again to the Herculean labor of the Manhattan Project itself . . . well, it was enough to make your head spin.

As the plane lurched forward, the tips of its wings visibly flexed up and down. She was aware of the crew around her, performing the last of their preflight routines. She was more distantly aware of the other bombers in her squadron as they built up thrust and began to roll off the parking apron toward the long concrete runway, which was already beginning to shimmer in the morning sun. She briefly waved to the small crowd of observers gathered by the control tower and on the raked gravel garden beds in front of the airfield's small cluster of administrative buildings. General Groves was certain to be over there somewhere. He'd spoken personally to all of the aircrews just over an hour ago, wishing them good luck and commending their actions to history. Some of the top civilians had also been present in the briefing room. She'd shaken hands with professors Teller and Oliphant, and shared a few moments with Oppenheimer himself, who seemed to be darkly amused by the squadron's motto: "We are become death, the destroyers of worlds."

It had seemed like a great joke at the time. Now, as she wrestled the Big Ugly Fat Fucker down the specially constructed runway, the mordant humor was lost on her. She knew, intellectually, that there weren't yet enough atomic bombs in existence to destroy the world, but as the scream of the jets cycled up into a painful shriek, Colonel Caro Llewellyn could not help but feel that she was about to start a nuclear war.

D-DAY + 41. 13 JUNE 1944. 1415 HOURS (LOCAL TIME). BERLIN.

It was over. He could feel it down in his meat. The Thousand-Year Reich was dying. Some part of Berlin was almost constantly in flames now. On those few occasions he ventured aboveground for more than a few minutes he never failed to spot hundreds of Allied bombers and fighters somewhere over the city. Right now, as he waited in the small courtyard of the SS safe house, penned in on all sides by high brick walls, he could tell that another raid was somewhere overhead. Possibly a bit to the north, hitting the rail junctions again. Even underground there was no escaping the destruction. In his deepest bunkers he could still feel the impact of thousands of bombs as they systemically pounded the old city to rubble and ash. Nor was Berlin the only target. With the Luftwaffe all but annihilated, every production and population center in the Fatherland was coming under relentless attack. He had no doubt that the fat criminal Churchill was behind that. He was a pig of a man and was obviously going to incinerate hundreds of thousands of innocents just so he could face his voters next year with proof of the vengeance he'd extracted for the Blitz. What a pleasure it would have been hauling him before a people's court.

That would never happen now, however. They were well and truly into the end of days. The brave start he'd made with the high command, calling for a full and realistic assessment of their situation, had done nothing but convince everyone that said situation was hopeless. The *Kriegsmarine* lay at the bottom of the ocean. The Luftwaffe was a ghost force compared with its former glory. And the army was in disarray everywhere but on the Russian front. The certain knowledge of what would happen if the Communists broke into the heartland seemed to be stiffening the resolve out there; that, the doomsday weapons, and all the men and resources stripped from the battle against the Anglo-Americans. They couldn't be certain, of course, but his Wehrmacht generals even suspected that Churchill and Roosevelt had ordered their forces to allow significant numbers of German troops to move east. Given their utter mastery of the skies and a preternatural ability to know exactly where and when to strike, there could be no other explanation. They were going to bleed his country white in the same way they had allowed the USSR to soak up so much punishment in the Other Time.

And they accused *him* of war crimes?

He craned his neck and sniffed at a freshening breeze that somehow managed to penetrate the well in which he stood. He could smell the acrid traces of destruction on the air, but not much besides. His SS bodyguards trailed him everywhere in the small, cramped yard. It was ridiculous really. He could only move about ten meters in any one direction, but they shadowed him anyway. He checked his watch. Twenty past two. It would be time for his daily strategic briefing in an hour. They would have to move off soon, although the pointlessness of it all was beginning to wear him down. If it were not for the fact that he still had a duty to the Reich and his race, he would have made good his escape by now. Some already had, as the chaos and panic that followed the Soviet atomic strike had made it impossible to keep track of people. It was telling that he had done nothing to capture these defeatists and make an example of them. There was just no time, and resources were too scarce.

He wondered if that was a lesson they could have learned earlier. Might the Reich have had a chance had the führer died a year ago?

Well, there was nothing to be gained by such maudlin fancies.

All he could do was try to save some of the German people from enslavement and genocide at the hands of the Bolsheviks. The Reich was in general collapse on all sides. The Western Front was more an idea than a reality. In the east the Communist horde was being held at bay only by the profligate use of chemical weapons, which would probably poison the earth for so long that it could no longer be considered part of Greater Germany. It really was no-man's-land now. To the south two of Stalin's airborne armies had leapt into southern France and were driving toward the Atlantic. Perhaps they would crash into the Allies at some point and a new war would begin. But again, what did it matter? Heinrich Himmler knew that by then, it would be too late for him and his people.

He rubbed at the stubbled beard that was itching so much in the hot sun. It might help, if and when he tried to make good his escape to South Africa, but he doubted it. The Boer Emergency Council had offered him covert sanctuary, but what would the British do when this war was over? He doubted they would allow their former colony to be governed by the new regime. It looked too much like his own. And even if the Allies lost interest in pursuing him, the Jews never would. What a cruel joke history had played on him. He well remembered his horror at reading the electronic archives from the *Sutanto*, and their revelation of a world without the Reich, a world in which a Jewish state was a—what did they call it?—a superpower. And now it seemed inevitable that that perverse result was going to come about anyway, despite his best efforts. The *SD-Ausland* had just this morning sent him a report of fighting in Jerusalem between Arabs and "Israelis," as the hook-nosed scum now insisted on calling themselves. It was not going well for the Arabs.

"*Mein Führer,* the car is ready."

Himmler acknowledged his bodyguard with a nod. It was a pity to be heading back to the bunker. He had spent so little time in the sun and fresh air during the last weeks that even a few minutes stolen in the open air were like a month at a spa. He replaced his hat, straightened his cuffs, and strode across the small garden to the armored Mercedes, wondering if he would ever return to this particular building.

D-DAY + 41. 13 JUNE 1944. 1546 HOURS (LOCAL TIME). IN FLIGHT.

Far beneath them to the south a convoy was tracking eastward, crawling across the Atlantic on the cusp of the horizon. Llewellyn gave them a cursory glance as the last of the jet fuel poured down the hose from the in-flight refueler. She tapped her copilot, Major Vallon Davies, on the arm.

"I think I forgot my wallet, Val," she said. "Can you pay for this tank? I'll get the next one."

She heard Davies's snort of laughter through the headset.

A chime sounded, alerting them to the end of the fuel transfer. The drogue disengaged with a loud clunk, a few spots of JP-8 hitting the windscreen before disappearing. The tanker, a newly built analog of the old KC-135, banked away to top up the other two bombers in the flight. It was another custom-built system, designed especially for Strategic Air Command. Infight refueling had become a common practice with all Western air forces, but converted DC-3s were the standard workhorse. The 135, known locally as a "Whale," was smaller and less powerful than its uptime progenitor. And as best she knew there were only three of them in existence. But it was still a long way ahead of the nearest competition.

Llewellyn watched it maneuvering into place for its next customer.

"Okay, boys," she announced through the intercom. "Let's go make some history."

D-DAY + 41. 13 JUNE 1944. 2150 HOURS (LOCAL TIME). HMS *TRIDENT*, NORTH SEA.

"Thanks for letting me watch this, Karen."

Julia spoke in a low voice that carried no farther than the captain of the stealth destroyer, who was standing right next to her in the chilly blue cave of the ship's Combat Information Center.

Halabi smiled, briefly. "General Patton is not the only one who understands the power of publicity."

She took her eyes off the main display and turned them directly on Duffy.

"I would have let you come up here anyway, Jules. Old school tie and all that. But in fact I had orders from Downing Street. First, just to keep you on board, and then to make sure you got an A-reserve seat. I suppose the PM wants everyone to remember that England had her own role to play at the death."

Julia nodded slowly. Quick movements sent spasms of pain down her neck into her back. She was safely strapped into a chair in the old satellite warfare bay. She wasn't allowed to shoot any video images in the CIC, and anyway the SS death squad back in the Ardennes had taken her flexipad and Sonycam. So for now she'd gone back to basics, writing shorthand notes with pen and paper. Halabi had promised her access to Fleetnet later on to file a report.

It was hard to believe she was watching this happen.

The eight linked flat panels of the main display were still largely given over to theaterwide coverage of the European battlespace, which now reached as far east as the Ukraine. But one screen was devoted to tracking the progress of the B-52 flight out of New Mexico. That was a hell of a shock right there, the idea of those monsters climbing back into the air again. In a way it was almost reassuring. They were such a part of her life back up in twenty-one that it was like hearing of an old friend from the future who'd suddenly popped into existence in the next room. Granted, there were only six planes, and she wondered how many of them were carrying atomic weapons. Perhaps all of them, perhaps only one. That information had not yet been released. But it was great to know they were back. They'd saved her ass more than once back home, and now, who knew? Maybe they were going to save the world.

Not much was happening at the moment, however. Dozens of tags indicated the presence of long-range fighter escorts. Sabers, according to Halabi. They were scheduled to top up their tanks in forty minutes, the last time they'd refuel before reaching Germany.

Julia had already filled pages of her notebook with color detail of the ship, the crew, the mix of 'temps and uptimers who were standing watch over this epochal moment. Both she and Halabi had lived long enough in the next century to see two Western cities reduced to atomic slag heaps, but she found herself anxious and increasingly restless as the moment drew near in this reality.

"Any misgivings?" she asked Halabi.

"Are you going to quote me?"

"Only if you want me to."

The captain of the *Trident* stared at the big screen for a moment. The business of war went on without pause. Sysops constantly scanned the threat bubble around the destroyer's battle group. Intelligence officers analyzed the vast flow of data from ship sensors, drones, Nemesis arrays, and 'temp assets. Junior officers came and went, whispering urgent messages into the ears of their masters before carrying off replies whence they had come. On the battlespace display flashing black tags tracked the lead elements of the Soviet air assault into southern France, and the progress of Free French and U.S. armor rushing down to "link up" with them—in reality, to block them from any further encroachment. Many more data hacks crept over the western reaches of Germany as Patton and Montgomery raced each other toward Berlin. Three screens were entirely concerned with monitoring the stalled Russian advance on the Eastern Front, one of them showing new and ever more gruesome video coverage of the chemical warfare raging there.

It was all so horribly enthralling that Julia was a little surprised when Halabi spoke up again. She'd been lost in her own thoughts. She raised her pen inquiringly, and the commander of the *Trident* nodded.

"I have been fighting for nearly twenty years," said Halabi. "And I have taken many lives. I have burned men alive in their aircraft. I have drowned them by sinking their boats and ships. Some I have crushed at the bottom of the sea. Others have been atomized by the weapons I fired at them. I never once hesitated to take their lives, whether they wore a uniform or not. If they intended harm toward my crew, my ship, or the realm we protect, their lives were forfeit . . ."

Julia had some trouble keeping up with her. It had been a long time since she'd been forced to take shorthand, and she wasn't very comfortable in her bandages and strapping. Halabi seemed to sense her struggling and paused for a moment. Some of the men and women nearby were looking on, trying not to be too obvious about it, but failing. Karen Halabi waited until the reporter had stopped scribbling and then spoke again.

"Of course, not everyone I killed was armed. Not everyone had evil intentions. Some were innocents. And I can only imagine the ocean of blood on my hands. How many thousands have I killed by directing bombers onto their cities and towns? I have no idea. None at all. But the dead are many. And tonight, in a few hours, I will add to that toll. I regret that. When I allow myself to think about it, about babies burned in their mothers' arms, about children irradiated and dying over the course of days and weeks, I feel physically ill. Tonight I will help to kill hundreds of thousands of people, old and young, innocent and guilty. I will not sort them, I will just kill them one and all. And I will regret that through all of my days. But it is my duty. War is an unmitigated evil, and so tonight I will do great evil. But I will do it hoping that something even worse is brought to an end because of it."

Julia looked up from her notepad and expected to find a tear tracking down Halabi's cheek. But there was none. Her eyes were hard and clear and utterly devoid of sorrow.

D-DAY + 41. 13 JUNE 1944. 2310 HOURS (LOCAL TIME). OVER BERLIN.

They came in on a heading determined by the quantum arrays of HMS *Trident,* their progress tracked by two of the stealth destroyer's Big Eye drones.

"One minute to release, Colonel Llewellyn."

Well, that was a surprise.

The voice of the air controller on the British trimaran was American. A Texan to be sure. Llewellyn could only wonder how he'd ended up there.

"Warheads armed."

"The Sabers have reached a safe distance, Colonel."

She grunted. The fighters had to put a lot of space between themselves and the blast, lest they get swatted from the sky like bugs.

"Looks like we're on our own, boys. Let's light 'em up."

She tried to keep her tone light, but the enormity of what they were about to do could not be denied. The German capital was blacked out, but was everywhere lit by fire. Pathfinders had ringed the center of the metropolis with incendiaries. Not that she needed it, with the *Trident* guiding her in. But if that link failed for whatever reason, it was good to know that they could still find the target with their own eyes.

"Twenty seconds to release."

Llewellyn held the giant bomber steady at its operational ceiling of fifteen thousand meters. It took a surprising amount of physical strength to control a B-52, and she'd had to put a lot of extra time in at the gym. Her arms looked much bigger than they had been a year ago. German flak arced up out of the conflagration below, long golden lines of fire seeming to leap away from the open furnace over which they flew. Shells burst harmlessly far below her. The decoy planes had not been needed. There were no German fighters aloft.

The bomb bay door whirred open.

"*Trident* has us dead on course," her navigator reported.

"Ten seconds."

"All systems check out green."

"Eight, seven, six . . ."

How many people slept beneath her wings tonight? How many were good? And how many evil? Would God protect the virtuous and the meek?

"Three, two, one. *Release.*"

No. God would not.

D-DAY + 41. 13 JUNE 1944. 2310 HOURS (LOCAL TIME). BERLIN.

It was a quiet night, as far as these things went nowadays. The RAF and their American cousins seemed to be giving the citizens of Berlin a brief rest from the terrors of all night bombing. A medium-sized raid had dropped incendiaries a short time ago but the Allies had not followed up like they had at Dresden.

Riding in the back of his Mercedes, feverish with lack of sleep, Himmler had no doubt they were already thinking of the next war, against Stalin. By way of contrast he could only contemplate the end of this war, which was surely days away. Or weeks at best. The briefing had not gone well. His instructions to speak the truth had liberated the high command to be completely frank about the utter impossibility of effecting any kind of reverse to the Reich's military situation. One by one, his generals explained why defeat was inevitable. He had not screamed at them. He had not accused them of defeatism or threatened anyone with execution for bearing unwanted news. He had ordered all the nonexistent units in Western Europe removed from the map table, a task that could have been accomplished with one dramatic sweep of his hand. Instead General Zeitzler had plucked the little wooden blocks off one by one. There was nothing left between them and the Allies in the west.

Why had they not listened to his offer? Why had they been so stupid in the face of the obvious? Now they would have to face the Bolsheviks alone, having done their utmost to cripple the best defense Western civilization had against the subhuman armies massing at the gates of Europe.

As his limousine motored slowly down Unter den Linden the last führer imagined the city occupied by enemy troops. It was all too easy to envision on the dark canvas of a blackout, punctured by the eldritch light of an incendiary blaze a few blocks away. The streets here, once teeming with life, were empty save for a few fire crews rushing to their work. He could not help but see them filled with Slavic berserkers mad with plunder and rape.

His feelings surged between despair and a sort of frenetic psychosis, a desire to throw himself into the last lines of defense, even while knowing that the only hope was that Berlin would fall to Montgomery or Patton before the arrival of the Red Army.

He looked at the small scrap of paper crumpled in his left hand. A piece of history, no less. His order to the high command—issued at the end of the dismal meeting an hour ago, and effective immediately—to cease all hostilities in the west and to allow the Americans and their allies unimpeded access to the Fatherland.

Churchill and Roosevelt might not have accepted his offer of an alliance, but they would not be able to ignore an unconditional surrender.

He smiled wanly.

It was a masterstroke really. He was going to make *them* responsible for the defense of Germany, and beyond that of civilization itself. If he weren't so exhausted he could have laughed. When one stared defeat and annihilation in the face and accepted them, it clarified everything.

He could not win, but he could save his *Volk*.

Not that he would be around to see it, of course. Would he spend the rest of his life in hiding? Or would he be dragged before some sham court to . . .

The question was redundant.

At eighteen minutes past the hour three spheres of brilliant white light bloomed overhead, and Heinrich Himmler, Berlin, and the Third Reich all passed into history.

35

Before speaking into the microphone on his desk, the president of the United States of America coughed lightly to clear his throat. The Oval Office was crowded. His press people had tried to convince him to do this broadcast from the dedicated studio that had been built in the previous year, but Roosevelt had insisted. There were three cameras in the office, recording the event for posterity, and when Americans watched this speech hundreds of years from now, he didn't want them to see him hunched into a sound booth in the basement of the building.

The Joint Chiefs of Staff were seated in the lounge chairs looking somewhat uncomfortable, as were the secretary of war, the secretary of state, the Speaker of the House, and the British ambassador. His wife was perched on another chair near the door. The cameras were all twenty-first technology, and it would be at least a day before the images they captured would be telerecorded onto film for national distribution to the various news services. The microphone in front of him, however, was the same one he had been speaking into for years. He'd never been comfortable with the teeny-weeny clip-on things the uptimers made him wear.

A producer counted down for him. "Mr. President, we're on in three, two, one . . ."

Roosevelt leaned forward just fractionally and addressed himself to the millions of his fellow citizens who would be gathered around their radios, listening at home, in their workplaces, in coffee shops or train stations, on ships, and in the field around the world.

"My fellow Americans," he began. "At eighteen minutes

after cleven o'clock local time last night, our planes dropped three atomic bombs on the capital of Nazi Germany. Berlin has been destroyed, and the heart of our enemy torn out. All organized German forces in Western Europe have laid down their arms. They continue to fight in the east, and on our best information to date they will do so until the Red Army observes a cease-fire. I call on our allies in Moscow to do just that and to avoid any further wasteful destruction."

He paused for a full second, emphasizing the import of his last statement—and the next.

"The three bombs detonated over Germany last night were not the only atomic weapons in our arsenal. We have *many* more and we now have the means to deliver them *anywhere* on earth. I say to the Japanese war cabinet, you have only two choices. Surrender immediately and unconditionally or I will order the United States Army Air Force to begin reducing your cities, until there is nothing left of your nation and its ancient culture."

Roosevelt turned the page of his speech. A technical person had offered him an electronic version on one of those teleprompter things, but he felt much more comfortable reading from a real document. And of course, it would become part of the national archive in a way that an electrical document never could. Not in his mind, anyway.

"There will be no escape from justice for those responsible for starting this war," he continued. "Or for those who have committed crimes in its prosecution. But your people do not need to share in that punishment. The invasion of your Home Islands for which you are preparing will not come. No American soldier will set foot there while we remain at war. There is now no reason for them to do so. Lay down your arms, and we will come peacefully, to help you rebuild and to take your place in the community of civilized nations. Resist us and you will be destroyed. There will be no glory, no honor in such resistance. Only the most abject folly. Your warrior spirit will count for nothing inside the fireball of an atomic explosion. Such human or spiritual considerations are irrelevant. You have twenty-four hours to reply."

Again, he allowed a small pause to add gravity to his words. The faces of the military men in the room were somber, and largely unreadable. Henry Stimson, his secretary of war, was nodding grimly, but with noticeable enthusiasm. It was Stimson who had argued strongly—and in the end, effectively—for delaying their first atomic strike until they had a sufficient store of weapons to launch equally devastating follow-up strikes and, just as important, enough planes to deliver them as far as Moscow if need be. It was the only way to dissuade the Soviet Union from any misadventures. Truth was, Roosevelt could have ordered the destruction of Berlin at any time in the last three months, and he knew that years from now there were going to be historians damning him for not having done so. If he had been planning to run in the next election, there would doubtless have been some dunderheads who accused him of letting Americans die needlessly while he built up a stockpile of A-bombs that could have saved their lives.

But in his heart, Franklin Delano Roosevelt knew that they did not die needlessly. Stimson was right. With no knowledge of how far any Communist atomic program had advanced, there was no alternative to building a deterrent that was immediately available and credible. When Lodz had disappeared inside a mushroom cloud, that debate had ended.

In the brief moment while he drew his breath he glanced over to his wife, who smiled at him with such understanding and kindness that it nearly broke his heart. He pressed on.

"And finally to you, my fellow citizens of this great republic, and to our friends and allies throughout the free world, I can only say, thank you. In our history books it is presidents, prime ministers, and generals who are credited with winning wars, but those books are wrong. It is you, all of you, who have worked and fought and sacrificed so much these last years, to whom victory belongs. Unfortunately I cannot promise you that peace is with us just yet. I cannot force our enemies to see reason if they are intent on blinding themselves to it. But I can promise you that we will not spend one life more than necessary to bring them to account. And if that means burning them from the face of the planet, then so be it.

"Thank you for listening, and good-bye."

He held the blank gaze of the middle camera lens until the producer signaled that they were done. It was a weird unnatural thing, sitting there with a silly grin on your face, and not something he saw himself ever growing used to. Harry S was welcome to it.

Polite applause broke out among the civilians as he relaxed.

"Well, do you think they'll get the message, Henry?" he asked Stimson.

"Who, Mr. President? The Japanese or the Russians?"

"Both of them."

D-DAY + 42. 14 JUNE 1944. 1705 HOURS.
THE KREMLIN, MOSCOW.

"You! You are responsible. This is your fault!"

Beria could feel his bowels turning loose and watery as Stalin pounded the table and shouted at him in front of the whole Politburo. The fact that they were meeting at such an unusual hour was evidence enough of a crisis. Stalin's dark, knitted brows, and the pipe lying broken on the empty table in front of him, confirmed the worst. He was in a killing fury of such unbridled intensity that nobody dared speak, or even look sideways at the object of his anger, lest the supreme leader of the workers' state suddenly transfer his wrath. Even Malenkov kept his eyes studiously downcast, and he could always be counted on to revel in any misfortune that befell Laventry Beria.

"But I am not responsible for the Americans' atomic program," the NKVD chief protested. "I am responsible for our own, and that has delivered more than I was asked."

"Three bombs!" thundered Stalin. "Three puny little bombs to their, what, dozens? Hundreds? Does anybody have any idea? Any idea at all? No! And these planes they have flown from the middle of their deserts to the middle of Germany. What do we know about them? How many do they have? Can we shoot them down? Or does the *Rodina* now lie open before them like some drunken washerwoman with her ankles up around her ears? Nothing! You know nothing!"

Beria had to protest that. His life depended on it. "But we do know about these planes. They are called B-52s. Stratofortresses. They fly at over a thousand kilometers an hour, not much more than our Tupolevs. Perhaps even less. At best they have a maximum range of thirteen thousand kilometers, not much more than our bombers. We have always assumed they would build these things, and they have. It is not a surprise at all!"

Stalin hammered the desk with his fist, once, making a water jug jump two centimeters off the polished walnut surface. "You looked very fucking surprised when the Americans sent over a copy of Roosevelt's speech. And anyone can read a computer file. I do not want to be quoted old Wikipedia articles about this new bomber. I want to know how many they have. How many they can produce. And how many atomic bombs they can put on them this very day."

Mercifully, Stalin allowed his fearsome gaze to widen, encompassing the entire Politburo.

"I want to know if we can beat them now. Timoshenko, what say you?"

The Soviet defense minister, the formidable peasant warrior from the Ukraine, jutted his chin upward. He at least would not be cowed. "If they have no more bombs, yes. We can roll over them. If they have three to five, a parity of atomic force with us, it will still be possible. But if Roosevelt is speaking truthfully and they have 'many' more bombs, even double or triple our number, we cannot hope to prevail."

The *Vozhd* turned his malign glare back toward Beria. "And does the NKVD have even the slightest idea of what remains in their atomic arsenal?"

Beria's heart, already racing, lurched in his chest. Keeping his voice as calm as possible, he spoke quietly but forcefully. "We have all known that the reactionaries gained a great intelligence gift, the value of hindsight, from the libraries of Kolhammer's ships. Dozens of our operations were instantly compromised. Our British networks with few exceptions were wrenched out root and branch. We lost our best sources who could have answered that question, and we have known that for years."

Fear was giving his argument some impetus now. He had managed to stop gulping and stammering, and a sense of genuine indignation animated his speech.

"But we can still use our brains. Look at the Berlin raid. Three warheads used on one target, completely annihilating it. They would not have been so wasteful if they had no other weapons. And this demand of Roosevelt's, that the Japanese surrender and submit to immediate occupation or face the systematic destruction of their cities. It is meant for us as much as them. But it cannot be a bluff because if a day passes and they cannot deliver on the ultimatum, we will know them to be lying.

No. I suspect they have enough bombs to destroy at least three or four major Japanese cities, with still enough in reserve to employ on the battlefield against us if they have to."

Timoshenko nodded his shaven head, lending Beria some unexpected support. "That is logical, Comrade General Secretary. The three bombs that hit Berlin convince me. It would be madness to have wasted them so if they did not have more. Yes, it sends a message to us. But I cannot see it as a bluff."

Stalin appeared to hang on the edge of a precipice. He could have gone one way or another; exploding again, or taking the answer in calmly and reasonably. To Beria's great relief, reason won out.

"So why, if they had so many bombs, did they wait until now to use them? They could have annihilated the fascists with one big raid."

"And that would have left an empty Europe at our feet," said Beria. "They needed forces on the ground to contest that ground with us. Plus, they have no stomach for anything that gets too hard. Would we send six million men to fight in a radioactive battlefield? Of course, if it meant victory. Would they? No. They could not. They are beholden to their bourgeois classes. They simply cannot act with our freedom. Plus, we must remember first principles. They are *capitalists*. To destroy a host of French and German cities is to destroy a vast storehouse of capital that they would otherwise seize for their own use. Like Timoshenko, I do not think they are bluffing. I believe they have many more atomic warheads."

Stalin drummed his fingers on the table. "It is a poor correlation of forces we face—"

Beria was bold enough now to interrupt him. "But it is not, Comrade Secretary. We control so much more of Europe than we did at the end of the war in the Other Time. Our forces are largely unopposed in China and much of continental Asia. We have the men in place to demand a division of Japan. If we can consolidate our hold over these gains, we will control much of the world in five years. An excellent correlation of forces."

The spymaster risked a glance around the long table. He quickly surmised that well over half the assembled ministers and military officers were in agreement with him. Others, like Malenkov, maintained a studied neutrality.

"Timoshenko," said Stalin, "I want the truth. Can Zhukov

and Konev break through the German defenses where they have deployed their chemical weapons?"

The defense minister shook his head. "Not without using our atomics. And once they have gone, we will stand naked before the Americans. We need those weapons to stop them from attacking us. We know that Churchill and some American generals are in favor of doing just that. And Kolhammer has spoken openly of the need to do away with us."

At the mention of the infamous naval commander a ripple of anger and disgust traveled around the table. Beria had a whole section of his intelligence services devoted to the top commanders of the former Multinational Force, but by far the greatest number of analysts was assigned to Kolhammer. His every public utterance, and some of his private ones, was studied with great intensity. More than once Foreign Minister Molotov had called on the U.S. ambassador to protest yet another insulting and dangerous statement by the commandant of the Special Administrative Zone. It was infuriating, the way he was allowed to run wild. He was worse even than MacArthur or Patton.

Before Stalin could speak again, there was a knock on the huge double doors that sealed them into the committee room. An NKVD colonel appeared, seeking permission to enter. Stalin nodded, and he hurried over to Beria. Bending forward and whispering into his ear. As he listened, the spymaster's balls contracted right into his body. His throat tightened with fear. He had to pour a glass of ice water with a shaking hand to compose himself before relaying the message.

"Well?" growled Stalin. "Good news, I hope."

"I . . . I'm sorry, Comrade General Secretary," said Beria. "No. It is not good news. A Japanese carrier has launched over a hundred suicide planes at the Kamchatka facility. Our MiGs shot down most of them. But nine made it through. Three of them dived into the reactor building. It has been destroyed. Most of the facility has been destroyed."

For once, Stalin surprised him. Rather than exploding he simply shook his head, like a man who has just seen a dancing two-headed dog. "But how? How did they get near enough? Was the navy not patrolling those waters? Timoshenko?"

The defense minister looked aghast. "Most of our modern ships were deployed to the Kuril campaign. But we did leave some advanced destroyers in place."

"Not enough," said Beria. "They're gone, too."

"It must be the Americans," said Molotov, the foreign minister. "They must have had a hand in this. Just as they let the fascists escape from Western Europe, they have let this Japanese carrier escape. They must have. How else would Yamamoto have known where to strike?"

Beria turned back to Stalin with the greatest reluctance, expecting to find those cold, dark eyes on him, blaming him. But the Soviet leader was lost, deep in thought. Silence descended on the room for a long time. Laventry Beria peeked out of a window, where the heavy drapes had come apart a few inches, allowing him a view of what appeared to be a glorious late-afternoon sky.

"I have decided," said Stalin.

D-DAY + 43. 15 JUNE 1944. 0749 HOURS.
IN-FLIGHT, SEA OF JAPAN.

The Red Army Air Force did not run to the luxury of in-flight refueling, but with a range of seventy-two hundred kilometers, the short hop from Vladivostok to Japan would not stretch the capabilities of the Tu-16. It was a stretch for *Kapitän* Gadalov and his crew, however. They had flown the length of the USSR, through eleven time zones, stopping to refuel three times. That had been a cautionary measure, but one the men had appreciated, as it allowed them to disembark for an hour to stretch their legs and breathe some fresh air.

The coast of the *Rodina* slipped away behind them. The squadron leader of the fighter escorts waved to them as the morning sun glinted off the bubble canopy of his MiG-15. He, too, had flown across the vast expanse of the republic but, with a much more limited range, had set off two days earlier and been forced to land for refueling more than a dozen times. It would have been easier to use one of the squadrons based out here in the east, but Moscow insisted on using the same personnel and equipment as in the original raid on Lodz.

Gadalov did not mind. It was an honor to serve the people and workers of the Soviet state, and to be chosen twice for such a mission was a rare distinction. He had been lavishly fêted since Lodz. His pension had been increased to the level of a general's, and his family had been moved out of their cramped apartment in Kiev into a dacha that had once belonged to a Romanov prince. A true believer in the revolution, however, he was happier simply to have served his comrades and, as everyone said privately, to have sent a warning to the capitalist West: they should not imagine the Soviet Union was going to disappear anytime soon.

"Two hours to go, precisely," announced Lieutenant Gologre, his navigator-bombardier.

Gadalov acknowledged the update.

If he had any regrets about what he was about to do, they were simply that these bombs would not be dropped on the Nazis. As much as the Japs needed punishing for what they'd done to the Pacific fleet, he reserved a dark little corner of his heart for the so-called master race. He could only hope that he would soon be back over the skies of Germany with another bomb bay full of nuclear fire.

D-DAY + 43. 15 JUNE 1944. 0922 HOURS. TOKYO.

The grounds of the Imperial Palace were always beautiful, but Emperor Hirohito particularly enjoyed them at this time of year. It was not as picturesque as during the cherry blossom festival in April, of course. But there was something exquisite in the warm stillness of the morning in summer. It was as if time itself were suspended while the day hovered on the edge of creation. Hirohito thought anything might be possible. His people might be saved. His throne delivered from the threat of the godless Communists and arrogant Yankees. Why, Prime Minister Tojo had sent word this very morning of another stunning victory over the Bolsheviks somewhere in their northeastern territories. An attack by the navy on some secret atomic facility. As long as the empire could still reach out to strike and cripple the enemy like that, there was hope. Even with Admiral Yamamoto dead and the Combined Fleet gone, there must be hope. He had personally approved of Yamamoto's approach to the Emergence barbarian Kolhammer. The admiral had thought him the most likely of their enemies to see reason, and that had not changed.

But had Kolhammer responded to the message?

If he had not had time, might he still do so, before it was too late to stop the Communists?

The emperor paused on a small wooden bridge to listen to the trickle of water and the trilling of a night heron, up well past its bedtime.

He died listening to birdsong as a small, brilliant sun bloomed overhead.

D-DAY + 43. 15 JUNE 1944. 1153 HOURS.
HMAS *HAVOC*, SEA OF OKHOTSK.

"Target lock, skipper."

"Thank you, weapons. On my mark—"

"Begging your pardon, Captain, but you may need to see this."

Captain Jane Willet felt a brief flicker of irritation, but suppressed it immediately. Her crew were well trained, and would not interrupt her without good reason. She stepped away from the offensive systems bay and raised an eyebrow at her duty comm officer.

"Yes, Mr. McKinney?"

"Flash traffic on Fleetnet, ma'am. Immediate cessation of hostilities in the Pacific. All units to hold position, further orders to follow in an hour."

Before she could say anything, more text scrolled across the screen in front of her young officer. She saw his eyes go wide, just for a moment. The Combat Center of the submarine was already hushed and taut as they prepared to put a torpedo into the *Nagano*, but she was aware that the tension suddenly seemed to ratchet up a few notches for everyone on duty.

"Tokyo has been confirmed destroyed by an atomic strike of Soviet origin. Japanese national command has shifted to Hashirajima Naval Base, with Admiral Moshiro Hosogaya acting as chief of the Imperial general headquarters. He has formally contacted Admiral Spruance to offer an unconditional surrender."

"Bugger me," said Roy Flemming, her boat chief. "They nuked Tokyo for Kamchatka, eh? Mad bastards."

Willet eyed the defenseless carrier steaming southward on the huge flatscreen to her left. There were no planes spotted on its flight deck. It had carried nothing but jet-powered *Ohkas,* and every one of them had been launched at the Soviet nuclear site. Farther up the body of the submarine a smaller screen played video of the three Soviet destroyers she'd been forced to sink to allow the *Nagano* to carry out its mission. Before they reached port her IT boss would scrub away every quantum flicker of evidence linking the Australian submarine to their demise; the contemporary government would never be informed.

There was one loose end left, however. The *Nagano* itself. While her crew remained unaware of the guardian angel that had shepherded them north, the ship could still not be allowed to return home. After-action analysis of her mission would reveal a very large question mark over how she'd have survived the hazardous, high-speed run to deliver her suicide planes.

"I suppose if I were Lord Nelson, I would just put a telescope to my blind eye and pretend I hadn't seen anything," said Willet.

"But you're not, are you, ma'am?" said Flemming.

"Nope. Weapons, still got a target lock?"

"On six tubes, ma'am. Programmed for simultaneous impact."

"Very good. Fire them all. Now."

The weapons sysop swept his fingers across a touch screen, lighting up six icons, before thumbing a final command. The sub vibrated slightly as all the warshots left their tubes at the same time.

"Why do you think they lit Tokyo?" asked Flemming as they waited for the kill.

She shrugged. "Temporary madness. Show of strength. Vengeance for Okhotsk. Who knows with the Sovs? They're a bunch of fucking Klingons, those guys."

The ADCAP torpedoes closed the gap to their prey quickly. A drone at sixty-five hundred meters followed the *Nagano* in LLAMPS vision, and the ship's Combat Intelligence provided a simulated display of the attack on another screen. Less than a minute after launch all six warheads simultaneously struck the refitted *kamikaze* transporter deep below the waterline, detonating with such force that the vessel completely disintegrated.

"Good shooting, everyone," said Willet. "Now what do we have on the threat boards?"

"Nothing immediate," her executive officer reported.

Willet sighed, feeling tired and hollow.

"Okay, that's good. We'll need to linger a little while and ensure there are no survivors."

D-DAY + 44. 16 JUNE 1944. 0633 HOURS.
USS *HILLARY CLINTON*, PACIFIC AREA
OF OPERATIONS.

The picture of his wife was real, not a quantum image on a thin-
screen. Protected by a small sheet of glass, housed in a simple
dark wooden frame, Marie Kolhammer smiled out at her husband from across the gulf of time. She was sitting at a garden
table on the back deck of their house in Santa Monica, a light
lunch of bread, cheese, and fruit laid out in front of her. A half-
filled glass of white wine in her hand. He had taken the snap the
last time he'd been home, just before leaving for the Timor deployment.

Admiral Phillip Kolhammer wondered where his wife was
now. The idea of another world, of his world, remained strong
with him. Shortly after he'd arrived here he'd spoken with Albert Einstein, who'd assured him that in a way his wife was
closer to him than the shirt on his back. The idea kept him from
going mad with grief.

Many of his colleagues had adapted to their new lives in the
past. Some, like Mike Judge and Karen Halabi, had found companions from among the thousands of men and women who'd
come through Manning Pope's wormhole. Others had partnered
up with locals, and as with all relationships some had worked
and some hadn't. That was just the way of things. He would be
nothing like that, however. Kolhammer kissed the image of his
wife before rubbing the impression of his lips off the glass with
a shirt cuff and replacing the old-fashioned photograph on his
desk. He and Marie had often discussed what would happen if
one of them was lost to the other, and in all of their discussions
it had been implicit that she would be the one left behind. They
had joked about it gently. Him saying that he was too wrinkled
and salty and goddamn rough-headed to attract another woman
foolish enough to marry him. While Marie had always insisted
there could not be a more "difficult" woman than her in any of
the continental states. They had known that whatever happened,
there could be no others for them.

A deep breath, held for too long, escaped him.

"Oh darlin', I do miss you . . . ," he said softly.

His PA, Lieutenant Liao, appeared in the doorway, coughing discreetly. "General Jones is here, Admiral."

"Thanks, Willy, send him through."

The commander of the Eighty-second stepped past the lieutenant into Kolhammer's day cabin, saluting and standing at attention. Kolhammer waved him in and bid him to sit down on the old brown couch across from his desk.

"Well, Lonesome, are you disappointed?"

Jones let the formality run out of his posture. They were old friends now. "Disappointed at what, Admiral? Not getting killed? Not getting my boys and girls killed? No. Of course not. Some of the youngsters are pissed as hell. But they'll get over it. I'm already proud of them. And as we both know, there'll be time and opportunity enough for getting killed in the future."

"Oh yeah," said Kolhammer. "There'll be plenty of that."

He stood up and made his way over to a side table. A small plate of cookies sat next to a gurgling coffeepot. A new one, just out of the States.

"Would you like a brew, Lonesome? We've got ten minutes before the meeting?"

"Sure. And one of those little choc-chip motherfuckers wouldn't go astray, either."

Kolhammer smiled as he poured two mugs and handed one, with the plate, to the big marine. "You hear the Sovs have signed up to the cease-fire?"

"Heard on the way over," said Jones. "Guess they figure they were checked for now."

"They'll be back," said Kolhammer. "For my money, that's why they nuked Tokyo. They're preparing the ground. If they couldn't have the city themselves, they figured they'd give us the ashes."

"They nuked Tokyo because of Kamchatka," said Jones. "Getting even. Sending a message."

"That, too," the admiral agreed. "Seems just about everyone with a nuke seems to be sending a message these days. Might be an idea if they all took a breather, don't you think, before there's nobody left to get the goddamn message."

Jones dunked a cookie and sipped from his coffee mug. "You think Roosevelt's gonna let them have half of Japan?"

Kolhammer shrugged.

"He's going to have a hell of a time telling them no, unless he plans on flash-frying a whole bunch of their cities before they have a chance to hit back."

"He doesn't strike me as the type," said Jones. "He's no Hillary."

"No," agreed Kolhammer. "He's not."

They sat in a companionable silence for a few moments, each man alone with his thoughts. Kolhammer was trying to weave some sense of what might happen from everything that had gone wrong. It was not a happy prospect. You'd have thought that knowing how things *would* have turned out, folks might have been some way along the track to figuring out how they *should* have turned out. But no. People seemed to have an infinite capacity for willful ignorance. It wasn't just the Soviets running wild over half the world, or civil wars in places like Palestine and South Africa. It was back home, too. Things would never come to a shooting war there, but you could see there were some hard days coming as the country tried to digest its future.

"What d'you think you'll do?"

"Huh? Sorry." Lonesome's question had caught him off-guard.

"When we get back. Will you stay in the service? Or go private."

Kolhammer's answer was delayed by the muted roar of an A-4 ripping down the flight deck not far above their heads. It was a question he'd given some thought to, but without coming to any conclusions yet.

"I don't know," he said. "Things will change when peace breaks out. The sunset clause will start ticking, for one thing. But people will feel a lot freer to air their differences and to act on them, too. The Zone, the Valley, or whatever you want to call it, is going to be at the center of that. I feel I should be there one way or another. What about you?"

Jones surprised him with his answer. "I'll be staying in the corps. I think Truman will get the job come November, and he'll desegregate the forces. Then the real work will begin."

"You wouldn't be working under our system anymore, Lonesome. You'd be in their world. They'll take your brigade from you, for starters. You know that, don't you?"

The general nodded. "I do. But because it *is* going to happen, like you, I feel the need to be there. Besides, I don't think we're done fighting. Not by a long way."

Kolhammer nodded his agreement.

The task force was still steaming eastward but it had turned north, away from the Marianas, after detaching a smaller force to accept the Japanese surrender there. Everything was up in the air. He assumed they'd be occupying the Japanese Home Islands, at least in the short term, but that hadn't been confirmed yet. Nobody even knew how those islands were going to be divided among the winners. It was a fair assumption that Tokyo was going to end up in the American and Australian sector, though. On the Asian mainland China was still convulsed in war, with the Soviets and Mao's Communists allied against the Nationalist government. Sheer mass was going to tell in that battle, he was certain. Indeed, Uncle Joe's minions had been busy all over. They were fighting in Korea, Indochina, Afghanistan, and Persia. Not to mention the huge bites they'd taken out of Eastern *and* Western Europe.

"Yeah, there'll be some fighting yet," said Kolhammer.

Lieutenant Liao appeared at the door again. "Excuse me, sir," he said. "But we've just received a priority encrypted data burst from Captain Willet on the *Havoc.* Your eyes only. It's on your desktop now."

He thanked his assistant and clicked on the flashing icon.

Jones took another cookie while he waited.

"Hmm," said Kolhammer. "That's a shame."

"Can you say what?"

"Captain Willet caught up with the *Nagano,* that *kamikaze* transport, and sank her. But she regrets to inform us that it was after the cessation of hostilities. The cease-fire orders didn't get through in time."

"She pick up any survivors?" asked Jones.

"There were none," said Kolhammer, pointedly.

The marine shrugged.

"Fortunes of war, Admiral."

"I suppose so," said Kolhammer.

EPILOGUE

f she squinted into the bright morning light and concentrated on the northern headland, where developers hadn't gained the upper hand back in twenty-one, it was almost possible for Jane Willet to imagine she was home again. Bondi Beach remained the same deep, south-facing bay. That would never change. The biscuit-colored cliffs looked just as they had when she'd last left *her* Sydney, the beautiful, conflicted, and utterly self-obsessed meta-city of 2021. Standing in the fresh air on the flying bridge of the *Havoc*'s conning tower, she could see the old art deco apartment she'd rented for a year when studying for her postgrad degree at Sydney Uni, except that here it was a "new" building, standing out rather starkly on the raw, scraped-looking heights of Ben Buckler. The third story had not yet been added and two modern houses that had stood beside it in her memory were gone, replaced by fibro cottages. Goats roamed freely over what would one day be the links of the North Bondi golf course.

"Fancy a drink at the RSL, Chief?" she asked.

Roy Flemming didn't take the binoculars from his eyes. "They haven't built it yet, skipper. Just a big sand dune there at the moment."

The great, black cigar-shaped hull of the most powerful submarine in the world passed smoothly through the cold blue waters of the Pacific as they drew nearer to the end of their long voyage. There was almost no swell to speak of today, no lines of whitecapped breakers rolling in toward the golden crescent of the beach. Her beach. That was fine by Willet. It'd make for a much smoother passage through the Heads.

"Not much of a welcome home, is it?" mused Lieutenant Lohrey, her intelligence boss.

"Not much," Willet agreed.

There were only a few sailboats out on the deep, and no RAN vessels or officials to greet them.

"We *are* having a reception at town hall tomorrow, remember," the captain offered a little weakly.

"Whacko," said Flemming.

"Spiffing," Lohrey agreed in the same monotone.

Willet smiled thinly and muttered, "Wankers."

They passed the cliffs at Vaucluse in companionable silence, watching as the lighthouse drew up, then slipped behind them. Soon enough they were turning to port for the run in to Sydney Harbor, and as Willet was afforded a better look inside the vast anchorage, her heart began to beat harder. A real smile broke out, lighting up her face.

The entire harbor was choked with flotillas of sailcraft and warships. A dozen ferries, all of them crowded with cheering and waving spectators, were drawn up in the waters off Manly Pier. Tugboats pumped huge white geysers from their fire hoses, high into the sky, forming rainbows as the winter sunlight refracted through the falling spray. Horns began to blare. Whistles shrieked and tooted. And Willet could feel in her chest the roar of what had to be a million voices raised in acclamation of their return. She wanted to speak but a lump in her throat prevented any words from coming. She swallowed and tried again, beaming as she turned to Lohrey. "Amanda, you'd better make sure the crew can see this on shipnet. They're gonna be pissed if they miss it."

The *Havoc*'s intelligence chief sported a rather sheepish grin. "Already taken care of, skipper."

Willet narrowed her eyes in suspicion. "You knew? You knew this was waiting for us and you didn't say anything?"

Lohrey showed her a pair of open, honest palms. "Orders from the PM, ma'am. Mr. Curtin was adamant that this was to be a *surprise* party. He's waiting for us at Woolloomooloo along with an honor guard, our families, such as they are, and a couple of hundred freeloading dignitaries."

Willet's curse was lost in the roar of six RAAF jet fighters sweeping overhead, waggling their wings and trailing green and gold smoke, a nice uptime touch. A battery at the North Head artillery school commenced a twenty-one-gun salute.

The captain of His Majesty's Australian Ship *Havoc* saw almost none of it as tears dissolved the scene into a swirling miasma of color. She felt Roy Flemming's hard, leathery hand slap her once on the back.

"Good job, skipper. Good fucking job."

7 AUGUST, 1944.
CANADA.

Paul Brasch stepped lightly out of the jeep and thanked the driver before collecting his duffel bag. Night was falling on the small lakeside village; one bright star had already appeared in the east, a single point of light in a burned orange sky. Without the wind of the jeep's passage, he became aware of a rich stew of unfamiliar scents and the chaotic overture of birdsong and insect calls.

The village, a tiny hamlet that serviced the local salmon-fishing industry, was a good mile around the curve of the lake. He caught the briefest hint of singing and a piano playing as the breeze changed direction for a moment. And then it was gone again, and he was left alone at the end of the long gravel roadway down to the waterfront cabin.

The sound of the jeep's engine faded away, and he began to walk. With each step he found his throat growing tighter, and his eyes bleary with the first tears he had shed in an age. He walked slowly, taking in the magnificent view and the quiet peace that surrounded him, hoping to compose himself before meeting his wife and son. He had no idea whether they would stay here in this obscure part of Canada, no idea what the rest of their lives would bring. He had money enough to give them a new life anywhere in the free world, but perhaps, for the next little while, they might just sit quietly here by the edge of this lake and wonder at the miracle that had delivered them from evil.

Brasch was imagining long fishing trips with little Manny, and the first night he would spend in bed with his wife, when a small, piping voice brought his head up with a start.

"Papa! Papa!"

It was Manfred and Willie, both of them running up the path toward him, arms out, their cheeks red and wet with tears of joy. But there was something wrong with the boy's face and his voice. Brasch experienced a second of free-floating panic and then realized what was so different. Manny's voice was clear and his mouth a perfect O as he ran toward his long-lost daddy. The cleft palate with which he'd been born—the small deformity that would inevitably have seen him fed into the ovens of the Reich at some point—was gone. Fixed by surgery, he supposed.

But gone. Gone forever.

"Papa! Papa!"

Paul Brasch, the good German, dropped his duffel bag and ran toward them.

7 AUGUST 1944.
LOS ANGELES, CALIFORNIA.

"So when are you starting work, ma'am."

Mohr's voice was a raspy bellow in her ear. It had to be, or she would never have heard him over the roar of the nightclub.

"Please, Eddie!" she yelled back. "Would you knock it off with the *ma'am-and-skipper* routine. We're not on the quarter-deck and I'm not even a captain anymore. Karen will be fine."

The big chief petty officer smiled and winked. "Right you are, ma'am. Karen it is, then, skipper."

His face glistened with sweat, and stage lighting glinted off his scalp beneath the short back and sides. Karen Halabi rolled her eyes, but she, too, was smiling. She was free. She was alive. She was a little bit drunk. And she was married to the greatest guy in the world who was, at that very moment, up on stage, playing his beloved electric guitar in public for the first time in three years. Mike was a little rusty, but like everyone in the Palomino Club he was also drunk and happy and well beyond caring whether his version of "Smoke on the Water" paid sufficient homage to the original. The guys in his garage band were all uptimers and they were just loving the chance to play some old-school rock and roll for the heaving crowd of Zoners and Angelinos who gathered at the Palomino four nights a week to dance along to some kickin' tunes.

"So, you didn't answer my question . . . Karen. When d'you start?"

Halabi finished her beer and signaled an overworked bartender for two more as Mike and the boys started in on their version of "Smells Like Teen Spirit."

"Next Monday morning," she shouted back at Mohr. "So

Mike and I have a few days left yet. He has an extra week's leave, so he's going to be getting the house set up, making my dinner, ironing my shirts. All the old-fashioned corporate-wife stuff."

Eddie Mohr, the master chief of the USS *Hillary Clinton,* grinned like an old fox at the henhouse door. "Will he now?"

Halabi punched him on the arm. "And you won't be teasing him about it either, *Chief.* I've got a good housebroken man up there on that stage, and he's going to stay broken. Understand?"

The beers arrived and Karen paid for them with her Combat Optics credit card. The guys at CO had insisted she take it as soon as she signed her employment contract. As senior vice president in charge of R&D she enjoyed a generous personal expense account over and above her corporate allowance. The combined sum of the two was appreciably more than her husband pulled in as a U.S. Navy captain, and the sign-on bonus had been generous enough to pay cash for their beachfront house in San Diego. It wasn't in-Zone, but she'd found to her delight that the U.S. West Coast felt a lot more like her sort of place than she could have hoped for back in the UK. Probably something to do with being in the New World.

The crowd roared as Mike plucked out the first notes of "Louie Louie."

Eddie Mohr charged his glass and shouted, "To the future."

Karen Halabi sloshed beer over her arm and his shirt as they clinked glasses, but she figured *What the hell?*

"To the past," she cried back.

7 AUGUST 1944.
SANDRINGHAM HOUSE, NORFOLK, ENGLAND.

It had taken quite some time for Harry to get used to his being so much older than his grandmother. Princess Elizabeth had been a very young sixteen when he'd arrived, and if anything Harry had been more nervous about their first meeting than she. After all, he had loved her all his life, but he had known her as the aged monarch of another era. Here she was a smooth-faced teenager and he was the increasingly aged one. At least it felt like that some mornings. He really was getting too fucking old to be jumping out of planes and into punch-ups with the likes of Otto Skorzeny.

He rolled the shoulder where the SS colonel had plunged in a bayonet as Harry strangled him to death in a cellar in Magdeburg. They were walking through the southern reaches of the estate, and it was unseasonably chilly.

"It's a lovely day, don't you think, Harry?"

"It is, Granny. It's good to be alive."

The princess had dissolved into giggles the first time he'd called her that, and Harry had blushed beet red, but as Elizabeth had laughed and laughed, until tears began to stream from her eyes, an embarrassed chuckle had escaped her grandson. It turned into a genuine full-bellied laugh, and soon they were both rolling around on the floor of the great hall at Sandringham, under the unblinking gaze of a stuffed baboon that Harry remembered fondly from his own childhood.

Now, strolling the grounds, Harry called her Granny without a second thought. It had become his pet name for her, and she had settled into a close, comfortable relationship with him that was more akin to that between siblings than anything else.

They walked a little behind the rest of the shooting party of about thirty, including the king and queen mother. Elizabeth was unarmed, but Harry cradled a beautifully handcrafted shotgun. They were after a pheasant for the dinner table that evening.

"He's a bit scared of you, you know," she said.

"Who?"

"Philip, silly. My *husband*."

Harry smiled. "You haven't married him yet, you know, Granny. You haven't even had a real date."

She may have blushed then, or perhaps it was simply her skin's response to the chill of the morning.

"Oh you. You're awful."

Harry sucked in a draft of stinging-cold air. "Am not," he replied.

7 AUGUST 1944.
SAVANNAH, GEORGIA.

"Thanks, but not for me, Vern."

"Your loss, Phil. From what I hear, these things are gonna be banned one day."

Phillip Kolhammer leaned back in the rocker on the porch of the slumping old homestead and shook his head.

"No. I don't think you're going to see a revolution in Cuba now, Vern. Without Castro or Guevara to lead it, it might have happened. But all that aid money flowing in there now is tied up mighty tightly with all sorts of strings. Things are gonna be different there at least. But don't let that stop you enjoying your stogie."

"It surely won't."

"No. Nothing ever stops Vernon enjoying himself," said Louisa Cuttler as she stirred a tall glass of iced tea. "I've been clipping him stories about how those things are going to kill him, and do you think he'll listen? No. Not for a million dollars will he listen . . ."

The lilt of her voice reminded Kolhammer of Marie so much, it hurt. But it was a sweet pain, and much softer than it had been when he'd first sought out her maternal grandparents. There was so much of Marie in Louisa's eyes and voice that he could close his own eyes, rocking gently back and forth on the tired gray boards of the porch, and it was almost as if his wife were with him again. Like Einstein had said, she was *this* close.

He'd never met Vernon and Louise Cuttler back up in his own day. They had both passed on by the time he'd met Marie. But they'd raised her after her own parents died in a car crash, and his wife had loved them with a childlike devotion, even as a grown woman.

"That was a wonderful dinner," said Kolhammer. "I can't thank you folks enough for taking me into your home and . . ."

"Now, Phil," Louisa insisted. "Don't you go getting yourself all choked up. You're family and that's the end of it. I know things are . . . well, a little strange . . . And our granddaughter as you knew her will never be born in this world. But the good Lord knows her soul, and I know He will send that soul to us in some form at some time of His own choosing. That may be of no ease to your suffering, but you should never doubt that you have a home here with us, and with all our family. You'll always be welcome."

Kolhammer rocked forward and picked another beer out of the icebox lying on the floor between Vern and him. An owl hooted somewhere in the dark beyond the mosquito netting, and cicadas began to screech.

"I really want you to know how much I appreciate it," he said. "I cannot imagine I'll ever get back to see Marie again, but

I know she's out there somewhere and I know she remains the only woman for me in this or any other world."

Vernon nodded, his lips turned down at the corners. Louisa smiled, but it was the sort of sad, encouraging smile you offered to someone trying to bear up under great pain.

"We would understand it if you met someone else," she said. "You're a good man, Phillip. Any woman would be lucky to have you."

"Well, there won't be any other women," said Kolhammer. "But it's good of you to say that. And it's good of you to have me here. Not everyone would have been so welcoming. I'm not . . . uhm. Well, not everyone likes me. And that's only going to get worse in the future."

"Oh, you can't listen to them know-nothin' peckerheads," said Vern.

"Vernon!" his wife scolded.

"Well, that's what they are," said Vernon. He leaned forward to grab himself another drink. "Listen, Phil, you gotta do what you think is right. That's all God ever asks of a man. Not everyone's gonna agree with you. Hell, sometimes even *I* won't agree with you." Vern winked at him over the foaming neck of the beer bottle. "That's when you'll know you're wrong, by the way."

Kolhammer snorted. "I'll keep it in mind."

"Do you think you're going to run for office soon?" asked Louisa.

Kolhammer took a long draw on the icy-cold beer. Moths batted up against the porch netting, and a dog began to bark in the distance.

"I don't know," he answered truthfully. "I really don't know."

7 AUGUST 1944
NEW YORK CITY.

It took the concierge three trips to haul up all of the mail Julia had accumulated while she was away. It sat in a big pile on the massive table in the center of the kitchen in her open-plan apartment. Constructed of wooden beams salvaged from a warehouse slated for demolition, it was at least ten meters long, and inset every two meters with sunken ice buckets for holding bottles of wine and champagne. Two of these had filled up with letters and parcels, and a great mound of mail lay between them. Julia simply couldn't face the idea of sorting through it all. It was late, coming up on midnight, and she had been to a war correspondents' dinner in the Oak Room at the Algonquin.

She was almost fully recovered from her injuries but found herself getting tired easily. That had started when Dan had died and had been getting worse ever since. She missed him and Rosie and even geeky little Curtis more than she could have imagined. Some days the pain was like a hole where her heart should have been. She took a jug of ice water from the fridge, a new model Kelvinator that aped the looks, if not the performance, of the double-door Jenn-Air back in her apartment in 21C New York. It seemed that no matter how much money and energy she invested in trying to create a fortress of uptime solitude in here—and she had invested *shitloads*—the contemporary world always had some way of sneaking back in.

She was heading for the bedroom, glass of water in hand, ready to flake out for about twenty-four hours, when her eyes fell on a package from her lawyer in California. Maria O'Brien had moved out to the Valley when her firm's headquarters had been completed, and they talked only infrequently at the moment. Julia had given her a check-signing authority for her investment account; all she really needed to do was sit back and watch it grow exponentially. Two years ago that would have been enough to keep her entirely happy. Now, as long as the money was always there, she was largely disinterested in the actual math.

Still, at least it wasn't hate mail—or even worse, fan mail.

She grabbed the parcel on her way past. It might be dull enough to lull her off to sleep.

Julia had a long hot shower, followed by a short cold one. It'd been a stinking night outside, and she had the contemporary air-conditioning cranked up high. It was an AT Carrier model meant to chill a restaurant much bigger than her place. Domestic A/C hadn't really taken off yet. Stepping out of the cold shower into the frigid dehumidified air felt like an insane luxury after the steam-press heat of the streets.

Wrapping a silk kimono around herself, Julia walked to her bedroom, her legs aching in anticipation of her collapsing onto the mattress. She ripped open the parcel and tipped out another sealed package and a handwritten note. It was from Maria.

Hey Jules,
    This was sent to you c/o the office out here. Our security guys checked it. No boom-boom. But it's marked confidential, so that's all I can tell you. Call me if you need a hand.

Best,
Maria

The note was dated for the previous day. Frowning, she checked the outer parcel and saw that it had no postage marks. It'd been hand-delivered via the front desk while she was out at the dinner.

Julia opened the inner parcel and spilled the contents out onto her sheets. A photograph came down next to her pillow, and she was more than a little surprised to see Artie Snider's mug grinning up at her. She grinned back. She hadn't seen the big palooka in ages. Not since he'd turned up at that Kennedy gig with Slim Jim Davidson. What a fucking night that'd been . . .

She wondered if there was a letter from JFK somewhere in that mail mountain out in her kitchen. She hadn't seem him in ages, either, and he'd hopefully be getting home soon. Maybe she should call him, like he'd said.

Curious now, she turned to the other documents, instantly recognizing a DNA graphic and wondering what the hell this was about. Less than two minutes later she knew: with her head spinning and her stomach lurching, she rushed over to the toilet bowl in her en-suite bathroom to vomit.

Snider, the war hero she'd help create, was the killer, or at least one of the killers of Daytona Anderson and Maseo Miyazaki.

He hadn't been tried, of course, but the documentation was damning.

Where the hell had it come from?

And then, asking the question, it became clear.

From her lawyer. Maria O'Brien. The West Coast Quiet Room controller.

With shaking hands, sniffing to clear her blocked nose, she read the note again.

Call me if you need a hand.

Julia Duffy, the Quiet Room agent, opened the drawer of a bedside table and retrieved a flexipad. Rosanna's old Samsung.

She powered up and walked unsteadily over to the phone, removing the jack and hooking the Samsung into the phone network via a plug-in adaptor. Keying in a code on the touchpad, she waited while software agents negotiated their path through the old copper wire network to a black server somewhere in LA. As the pad logged in, security software at both ends engaged and began an elaborate verification procedure.

After a long wait, a chime told her she had a message.

Unable to stop herself she looked back over her shoulder. The apartment was empty, as she had known, rationally, it had to be.

Julia opened the message. A vid-mail that would hard-delete after she had watched it. It was O'Brien.

"Sorry, babe," she said. "I have something for you, for a change. Snider, as you've gathered. He's unfinished business. We can't officially sanction him, of course. But you can do your thing with the data I've sent through. Good luck. I'll see you for lunch next time you're in town."

The screen folded in on itself and the pad beeped three times to let her know the file had been erased at a quantum level.

All the fatigue that had threatened to drag her low vanished as she began to sort through the papers.

She had already hardened her heart to the task ahead.

As much as she had liked Snider, there was no chance of her turning this one down. They were in a war here. Not a shooting war, exactly. Not like the one that had just ended, or the next one that seemed to be coming on them like a fast-moving hurricane front. But a war nonetheless.

In his own dim way Snider had probably known that. Sifting through the papers, it seemed obvious he hadn't acted alone—that he'd probably been under orders of some sort. She began to arrange the pieces of the puzzle on her bed.

He wasn't an enemy combatant. He couldn't be sanctioned.

But he could be destroyed as a man in front of the world. Left with nothing but his shame and humiliation. An effective Sanction 5, if not an official one. And in her experience these things tended to end the same way anyhow.

They certainly had with Hoover, her last Quiet Room target.

Julia Duffy unplugged her flexipad and hooked up the phone

again. She placed a call to the night editor. He answered on the second ring.

"Hey, David. It's me, Duffy," she said.

"Hello, Julia. I thought you were at the big dinner tonight. What's up?"

"Same old same old, Dave. I've got a story we need to run. Nobody's going to like it, but we need to run with it anyway, okay?"

The editor sounded unsure. "Well, it's too late for tomorrow's issue, Julia, we—"

"Don't worry. I don't need tomorrow. I probably won't file for about two weeks. I'm going to have a lot of research to do. I just need you to write me up as being out on a job tomorrow, okay?"

"Okay. Where are you going?"

"The Zone."

ACKNOWLEDGMENTS

The usual suspects did their usual above-and-beyond routine, God bless 'em. Cate Paterson and Brianne Tunnecliffe in Sydney, with Steve Saffel and Keith Clayton in New York, all helped turn my pile of beer-stained scribbles into a real book. A couple of last-minute arrivals were Jim Minz at Del Rey and the redoubtable Steven Francis Murphy of Kansas City, who ran a soldier's eye over the first draft and reminded me, among other things, that you can't fire RPGs at a target only five feet away. These people make me look good, and I owe them.

I also owe my blog homies at Cheeseburger Gothic (http://birmo.journalspace.com) for providing an excellent sounding board for crazy ideas, bitch sessions, Pepsi Challenges, and general ranting.

You'll notice this book is dedicated to my old neighbors Rose and Angus, who stepped up to the line again and again when the deadline tsunami loomed, helping out with child minding and free food.

And as always, last thanks are due to Jane, Anna, and Thomas, who put up with a lot from the crazy man in the basement.

Read on for a sneak peak at
John Birmingham's next novel,

ONE DAY

Published by Del Rey Books

The killer awoke, surrounded by strangers. An IV line dripped clear fluid through a long, thick needle punched into the back of her right hand. Surgical tape held the silver spike in place and tugged at the fine blond hairs growing there. The strangers— they're all women, she thought dully—leaned in, their faces knotted with anxiety, apparently for her. But she stared instead at her hands as they lay in her lap on a thin brown blanket. They looked strong, even masculine. She turned them over, examining them. The nails were cut short. Calluses disfigured her knuckles, the heels of both palms, and the sides of her hands, from the base of both little fingers down to her wrists. The more she stared, the more unsettled she became. Like the women gathered around her bed, those hands were completely alien to her. She had no idea who she was.

"Cathy? Are you all right?"

"Nurse!" somebody called out. And then, "Doctor!"

The strangers, all five of them, seemed to launch themselves at her bed and she felt herself tense up, but they simply wanted to comfort her.

"Doctor. She's awake."

She felt soft hands patting her down, stroking her like you might comfort a child who's suffered a bad fright. *Cathy*—that wasn't her name—Cathy tried not to panic or to show how much she didn't want any of these women touching her. They looked weird, not the sort of people she'd want as friends. And then she remembered. They weren't her friends.

They were targets. And her name wasn't Cathy. It was Caitlyn.

The women were all dressed in cheap clothing, layered for warmth. Settling back into the pillows, recovering from the un-controlled moment of vertigo into which she had fallen upon regaining consciousness, Caitlyn Monroe composed herself, quickly taking in her surroundings. She was in a hospital bed in a private room, and in spite of the apparent poverty of her "friends" the room was expensively fitted out. Two of the younger women were festooned with colorful protest buttons. A stylized white bird. A rainbow. A collection of slogans: *Halliburton Watch. Globalize Love. Who would Jesus Bomb?* And *Resistance is fertile*.

Caitlyn took a sip of water from a squeeze bottle by the bed.

"I'm sorry," she croaked. "I'm a bit out of it. What happened to me?"

She received a pat on the leg from an older, red-haired woman wearing a white T-shirt over some sort of lumpy handmade jumper. *Celia*. Also known as Aunty Celia, although she wasn't related to anyone in the room. Aunty Celia had very obviously chosen the strange ensemble to show off the writing on her shirt, which seemed to read *If you are not outraged you are not paying attention*. It was hard to tell, because some of the words had bunched up under the woman's breasts.

"Doctor!" cried the woman in the doorway.

Maggie. An American, like Caitlyn. And there the similarities ended. Maggie the American was short and barrel-chested and pushing fifty, whereas Caitlyn was tall, athletic, and young.

She felt around under her blanket and came up with a plastic control stick for the bed.

"Try this," she offered, passing the controller to the young girl she knew as Monique. A pretty, raven-haired Frenchwoman. "See, the red call button. That'll bring 'em." Then, gently touching the bandages that swaddled her head, she asked, "Where am I?"

"You're in a private room, at the Pitie-Salpetriere hospital in Paris," explained Monique. "Paris, France," she added self-consciously.

Caitlyn smiled wanly. "S'okay. I remember Paris is in France." She paused. "And now I am too, I guess. How'd I get here? I don't remember much after coming out of the Chunnel on the bus."

The large American woman standing over by the door to her room—*Maggie, try to remember her fucking name!*—turned away from her post.

"Fascist asswipes, that's how. Attacked us outside of Calais."

"Skinheads," said Monique, seeming to think that Maggie's brusqueness might be too much for "Cathy" to handle. "And you were *magnifique!*"

"I was?"

"Oh yes," the French girl enthused. She couldn't have been more than seventeen years old. The others chorused their agreement. "They stopped the bus and began pulling us out, hitting and kicking us. You stood up to them, Cathy. You fought with some of them. Knocked them down and kicked them before you got hit yourself. You frightened them very badly. Slowed them down long enough for the union men to reach us and drive them away."

"Union men?"

"Workers," Maggie informed her. "Comrades from the docks at Calais. They were traveling in a bus back in the convoy. We were expecting trouble, just not so quickly."

Caitlyn tried to reach for any memories of the incident but it was like grabbing at blocks of smoke. She must have taken a real pounding in the fight. Not for the first time, either.

"I see," she said, but really she didn't. "So I beat on these losers?"

Monique smiled brightly for the first time.

"You are one of our tough guys, no? It was your surfing. You told us you always had to fight for your place on the waves. *Really* fight. You once punched a man called Abberton off his board for . . . what was it . . . dropping in?"

Caitlyn felt as though a great iron flywheel in her mind had suddenly clunked into place. Her cover story. To these women she was Cathy Mercure. Semi-pro wave rider. Ranked forty-sixth in the world. Part time organizer for the Sea Shepherd Conservation Society, a deep green militant environmental group famous for direct and occasionally violent confrontation with any number of easily demonized eco-villains. Ocean dumpers, long line tuna boats, leaky oil tankers. They were all good for a TV-friendly touch-up by the Sea Shepherds. But that was her cover. Her jacket.

She took another sip of cool water and closed her eyes for a moment.

Her real name was Caitlyn Monroe. She was a senior field agent with the Office of Special Clearances and Research, itself a magic box hidden within the budget of the Central Intelligence

Agency's Deputy Director (Plans). She was a killer, and these women were—for a half second, she had no idea. And then the memory came back. Clear and hard. These women were not her targets, but they would lead her to the target.

Al Banna.

Caitlyn cursed softly under her breath. She had no idea what day it was. No idea how long she'd been out, or what had transpired in that time.

"Are you all right?"

It was the French girl, Monique.

"S'cool," said Caitlyn. "It just puts a kink in your day, you know, getting your head kicked in. Have I been here long?"

"It's Thursday," said Monique. "You have been unconscious for three days. We were very worried."

Caitlyn nodded slowly. Any sudden movements sent iron spikes of pain shooting down through her neck.

"Do you mind?" she asked, pointing at the television that hung from the ceiling. "I feel like I'm lost or something. Is there a news channel? I'd like to know what's been happening. How'd the peace march go?"

"Brilliant!" said the red-headed woman. Aunty Celia.

She was a Londoner with a whining accent that really maxed out the fuckoffability scale. "There was 'undreds of thousands of people," she said. "Chiraq sent a message and all."

"Really?" said Caitlyn. "That's great. Was there anything on the news about it?" she continued, pointedly looking at the television.

"Oh, sorry," muttered Monique as she dug another controller out of the blankets on Caitlyn's bed. Or Cathy's bed, as she would have thought of it.

A flick of the remote and the screen lit up.

"CNN?" asked Caitlyn. She knew better than to ask for Fox.

Monique flicked through the channels, but couldn't find the news network. White noise and static hissed out of the television from channel 13, where it should have been. She shrugged. There was nothing on Fox either, but all of the French language channels were available, as was BBC World.

"Can we watch the Beeb then?" asked Celia. "Me French you know, it's not the best."

"Me neither," Maggie chimed in from the door.

"But of course," said Monique.

Caitlyn really just wanted to carve out a couple of minutes to herself, where she could get her head back in the game. She had to figure that her injuries were serious, having put her under for three days, and although her cover was still intact, she didn't want to take any chances. She needed to reestablish contact with Echelon. They'd have maintained overwatch while she was out. They could bring her back up to . . .

"What the fuck?"

It was Maggie, cussing in her broad mid-western accent.

It took Caitlyn a second to realize that the only other American in the room was swearing at the TV. Everyone's eyes were fixed on the screen, where an impeccably groomed Eurasian woman with a perfectly modulated BBC voice was struggling to maintain her composure. The last thought that Caitlyn Monroe ever had in her "normal" life was that the war must have started and this chick was going to lose her job because she couldn't keep it together. Then Caitlyn actually heard what the woman was saying and she lost her cool as well.

". . . vanished. Communications links are apparently intact and fully functional, but remain unresponsive. Inbound commercial flights have either returned to their points of origin or diverted to Halifax and Quebec in Canada, or to airports throughout the West Indies, which remain unaffected so far."

The women all began to chatter at once, and it was Maggie who yelled at them to shut the fuck up, surprising Caitlyn. She'd thought she was going to have to. On screen the BBC's flustered anchorwoman explained that the "event horizon" seemed to extend down past Mexico City, out into the Gulf, swallowing most of Cuba, encompassing all of the continental United States and a big chunk of southeastern Canada. Caitlyn had no idea yet what she meant by the term "event horizon," but it didn't sound friendly. A hammer started pounding on the inside of her head as she watched the reporter stumble through the rest of her read.

". . . from a Canadian airbase have not returned. U.S. Naval flights out of Guantanamo Bay at the southern tip of Cuba have likewise disappeared from radar screens at the same point, seventy kilometers north of the base. Reuters is reporting that attempts by U.S. military commanders at Guantanamo to contact the Castro government in Havana have also failed."

Somebody muttered in French but was quickly "shushed" by three other voices, one of them Caitlyn's. She realized that the background buzz of the hospital had died away. She heard a metallic clatter as a tray fell to the floor somewhere nearby. Caitlyn had a passing acquaintance with the Pitie-Salpetriere. There had to be nearly three thousand people in this hospital and at that moment they were all silent, the only human sounds came from the television sets which hung in every room and ward, a discordant clashing of French and English voices, all of them speaking in the same clipped, urgent tone.

"The prime minister, Mr. Blair, has released a statement calling for calm and promising to devote the full resources of the British government to resolving the crisis. A Ministry of Defence spokesman confirmed that British forces have gone onto full alert, but that NATO headquarters in Brussels has not yet issued any such orders. The Prime Minister rejected calls by the Opposition to immediately recall British forces deployed in the Middle East for expected operations against the regime of Saddam Hussein."

"That'd be fuckin' right," Aunty Celia said quietly to herself.

The reporter was about to speak again when she stopped, placing a hand to one ear, obviously taking instructions from her producer.

"Right, thank you," she said before continuing.

"We have just received these pictures from a French satellite which passed over the eastern seaboard of America less than an hour ago."

The screen filled up with black-and-white still shots of New York. The imagery was not as sharp as some of the mil-grade stuff Caitlyn had seen over the years, but it was good enough to easily pick out individual vehicles and quite small buildings.

"This picture shows the center of New York, as of twenty-three minutes ago," said the reporter. "Our technical department has cleaned up the image, allowing us to pull into a much tighter focus."

Caitlyn recognized Times Square from above. She quickly estimated the virtual height as being about two thousand meters, before the view reformatted down to something much closer, probably about five or six hundred feet. The Beeb's IT guys were good. It was a remarkably clear image, if profoundly disturbing. Her brief curse was lost in the gasps and swearing of the other women. Fires, frozen in one frame of satellite imagery, burned throughout the Square where hundreds of cars had smashed into one another. Smoke and flames also poured from a few buildings. Buses and yellow cabs had run up onto the footpath and in some cases right into shop fronts and building facades. But nothing else moved. The photograph seemed to have captured an unnatural, ghostly moment. Not because they were looking at a still shot of a great metropolis in the grip of some weird, inexplicable disaster. But because nowhere in that eerie black-and-white image of one of the busiest cities in the world, was there a single human being to be seen.

Somebody must have tipped off the ragheads, because they were wailing up a storm. Long ululating cries of *"Allahu Akbar"* rolled around the dusty confines of camp X-ray, drifting over the razor wire and into the hastily convened O-Group meeting in the situation room, the Naval op center at the southern end of the base, a grand title for such a modest facility, a demountable hut with heavy gray air con units rumbling away at the windows. It was a relatively mild Caribbean day outside, late autumn in Cuba was almost but not quite balmy. The Brigadier General knew he could probably run up and down the nearest of the scrubby, low-rise hills that surrounded this part of the base without raising much of a sweat. But the room was stuffy. Dozens of laptops had been plugged into the existing cluster of workstations and they were all running hard, dumping waste heat into a space that was already overcrowded, with at least three times as many occupants as normal.

Having given up on the computers in frustration, however, General Tusk Musso leaned over the old map table, gripping the back of a swivel chair, biting down hard on the urge to pick it up and throw it through the window. His was so angry, and just quietly, so weirded out, that there was a fair chance he could have heaved that sucker all the way down to the water's edge. The bay was deep cerulean blue, almost perfectly still, and the chair would have made a most satisfying splash. Unfortunately, Musso was the ranking officer on the base that day and everybody was looking to him for answers. Guantanamo's naval commandant, Captain Cimines was missing, apparently along with about three hundred million of his countrymen, and a whole heap of Mexicans and Canucks into the bargain. *And Cubans, too*, Musso reminded himself. *Let's not forget our old buds just over the wire.*

"What are the locals up to, Georgie?" he rumbled. His aide, Lieutenant Colonel George Stavros, delivered one brief shake of the head.

"Still hopping around, sir. Looks like someone really kicked over their anthill. Our lookouts have counted at least two hundred of them bugging out north."

"But nothing coming our way, yet?"

"No, sir."

Musso nodded slowly. He was a huge man, with what looked like a solid block of white granite for a head, resting atop a tree trunk of a neck. Even that one simple gesture, spoke of enormous reserves of power. He shifted his gaze from the antique, analogue reality of the map table with its little wooden and plastic markers, across to the banks of the flat screens which even now were refusing to tell him anything about what was going on such a short distance to the north. The faces of the men and women around him were a study in barely constrained anxiety. They were a mixed service group about two dozen strong, representing all the arms of the U.S. military which had a stake in Guantanamo, mostly navy and marines, but with a few army and air force types thrown in. There was even one lone Coast Guard rep, mournfully staring at the map table, wondering where his people could possibly have gone. Their cutter had dropped out of contact. It was easily found on radar, but would not respond to hail.

Musso, ironically, had no permanent connection to Guantanamo. He'd been sent down to review operations at X-ray, the first task of a new job, a *desk* job back in D.C. he really hadn't wanted. A genuine shooting war was about to begin, and here he was, on a fucking day trip to Gitmo, making sure a bunch of jihadi whackjobs were getting their asses wiped for them with silken handkerchiefs, not copies of the Koran. It was enough to test a man's faith. He stood erect, folded his arms as though examining a really shitty used car deal, and grunted.

"Okay. Let's take inventory. What do we know for certain?" he asked, and began ticking the answers off his fingers. "Thirty-three minutes ago, we lost contact with CONUS for two minutes. We had nothing but static on the phones, sat links, the net, broadcast TV, radio. Everything. Then, all of our comm links are functioning again, but we get no response to anything we send home. All our other links are fine. Pearl. NATO. ANZUS. CENTCOM in Qatar, but *not* Tampa. All responding and wanting to know what the hell is going on. But we have no fucking idea. I mean, look at that. What the hell is that about?"

The Marine Corps brigadier general waved his hand at a bank of TV monitors. They were all tuned into U.S. news networks, which should have been pumping out their inane babble 24/7. With the war in Iraq only days away the global audience for reports out of America and the Middle East was huge and nigh on insatiable. But there was the Atlanta studio of CNN, devoid of life. The anchor desk sat in center frame, and dozens of TV and computer screens flickered away in the background, but nobody from CNN was anywhere to be seen. The same over at Fox. Bill O'Reilly's chair was empty. Bloomberg still filled most of one monitor with garishly bright cascades of financial data, but the little picture window in one corner where you'd normally find a couple of dark-suited bizoids droning away about acquisitions and mergers was occupied by a couple of chairs and nothing else. Meanwhile another bank of screens running satellite feeds from Europe and Asia was fully operational, and peopled by increasingly worried talking heads, none of whom could explain what was happening in North America.

"Anybody?" asked Musso, not really expecting an answer.

The silence might have become unbearable had it not been broken by a young naval ensign, who coughed nervously at the edge of the huddle.

"Excuse me, General," she said.

Musso bit down on an irrational urge to snap at her, instead keeping his voice as level and non-threatening as he could.

"Yes, Ms. . . . ?"

"Oschin, sir. I thought you might need to look at these. I've streamed vision from eighteen webcams onto a couple of monitors at my workstation. These cams are all in high volume, public areas, Colonel. Grand Central in New York. Daley Plaza in Chicago, that sort of thing . . ."

Ensign Oschin, who was obviously uncomfortable addressing such a high-powered group, seemed to run down like a wind-up toy at that point. Musso noticed a couple of Army officers glaring at her for having interrupted the big kids at play.

"Go on, Ensign," he reassured her, giving the Army jerkoffs a cold hard glare. "What's your point?"

Oschin stood a full inch taller. "They're live feeds, sir. From all over the country. And there's nobody in them. Anywhere."

That information fell like a lead weight into a dark, bottom-less well, tumbling down out of sight, while everybody waited for the crash. No one spoke as Musso held Oschin's gaze, seeing the fear gnawing away at her carefully arranged professional mask. He could taste a trace of bile at the back of his throat and he was unable to stop his thoughts from straying to his family back home in Galveston. The boys would both be in school, and Marlene would be up to her elbows in blue rinse at the salon. He allowed himself the indulgence of a quick, wordless prayer on their behalf.

"Can you patch it through onto the main displays?" he asked.

"Aye, sir."

"Then do so please, as quickly as you can."

Oschin, a small, birdlike woman, spun around and retreated to the safety of her workstation, whipping her fingers across the key-board in a blur. Other sysops who'd been less successful in their own endeavors to raise anyone stateside snuck peeks over their shoulders at the results of her work as two large Sony flat panels hanging from the ceiling suddenly filled with multiple windows displaying scenes from across the United States. Oschin appeared at the map table again with a laser pointer. She laid the red dot on the first window in the upper left-hand quadrant of the nearest screen.

"With your permission, General?"

"Of course."

"That's the Mall of America. Local time, 1320 hours. You're looking at the main food court."

It was empty. A small fire burned in one concession stand and it looked as though sprinklers may have tripped but the image quality wasn't clear enough to be certain. It reminded Musso of an old zombie flick he'd watched as a kid. *Dawn of the Dead* or something. For some reason his flesh crawled at the memory, even though he'd thought the movie was a dumb-ass piece of crap the first time he'd seen it. Oschin flicked the laser pointer over the next three windows as a group.

"Disneyland, California. Local time 1120 hours. You're look-ing at the concourse just inside the main entrance. Then you have Space Mountain in Tomorrowland. And finally Mickey's Toontown."

Again, the pictures were poor in quality, but no less disturb-ing because of it. Not a soul moved anywhere in them. A breeze pushed litter around the main concourse where some sort of golf buggy had run up on a gutter and tipped over. The young officer, her voice wavering, made her way through the rest of the image windows. The Plaza in Kansas City. Half a dozen cams from UCLA's Berkeley campus. A mortgage brokers convention in Toledo. The main strip in Vegas—which looked like Satan's wreckers yard with cars all piled into one another and burning fiercely. Venice Beach. JFK Airport. The Strand in Galveston.

Musso arranged his features into a blank façade for that one. He'd already recognized the scene before Oschin had explained to the others what they were looking at. Down in his meat, right down in the oldest animal parts of his being, he knew his family was gone.

Oblivious to the personal import of what she'd just shown them, Ensign Oschin carried on, cycling through a list of public gathering places that should have been teeming with people. All of them abandoned, or empty, or . . . what?

"It's the Rapture," whispered an Army major standing directly across the table from Musso. One of the two who'd unsettled Oschin a few minutes ago. "The end of days."

Musso spoke up loudly and aggressively, smacking down the first sign of anyone in his command unraveling.

"Major, if it was the Rapture don't you think *you'd* be gone by now. And where are the sinners? Don't they get to stay and go through everyone's stuff? And anyway, last time I heard, this thing has a defined horizon, not too far north of here."

Chastened and not a little put out, the major whose nametag read "Clarence" clamped his mouth shut again.

Musso wished he had the luxury of shutting up and letting someone else make the running. He didn't know what to make of the video streaming out of his homeland. After 9/11 he didn't think anything could surprise him again. He'd been ready for the day he flicked on the television and saw mushroom clouds blooming over an American city. But this . . . this was bullshit.

"Allahu Akbar. Allahu Akbar."

The distinct popping sound of gunfire in the middle distance reached them through the closed windows and over the drone of the air con. Then came the screams.

"George," growled Musso.

"I'm on it, sir."

His second-in-command hurried out of the room to track down the source of this new disturbance. Musso waited for more shots, but none came.

"Okay," he said. "I'm not sending any more assets into this thing, whatever it is. I think we've established that it's a no-go zone."

Both of the helicopters he'd ordered to fly north over international waters had apparently crashed soon after crossing the line that now defined the edge of the phenomenon. A Marine Corps Harrier jet was still flying, but the pilot had not responded after reaching the same point. The plane was heading north but slowly losing altitude. Musso expected it to crash in a few hours.

"Okay. Let's call up PACCOM . . . ," he started to say.

"General, pardon me, sir? Permission to report?"

A Marine lieutenant in full battle rig had appeared at the doorway. He seemed unperturbed by the freakish run of events.

"Go ahead," said Musso.

"It's the Cubans, sir. They've sent a delegation in through the minefield. They want to talk. Matter of fact, they're dying to. One of their jeeps hit a mine coming in and the others just kept on rolling."

Musso stretched and rolled his neck, which had begun to ache with a deep muscle cramp. He was probably hunching his shoulders again. Marlene said she could tell a mile off when he was really pissed, because he seized up like the Hunchback of Notre Dame.

(Marlene . . .)

"Okay," he said. "Disarm them and bring them in. They're a few miles closer to it, whatever it is. They might have seen something we haven't."

The lieutenant acknowledged the order and hurried away, weaving around Stavros who returned at the same moment.

"I'm afraid a bunch of our guests decided to charge a guard detail," he said, explaining the gunshots of just a few minutes ago. Things were moving so quickly that Musso had stopped caring about the incident as soon as it didn't escalate. "Two dead, five wounded. They've heard something is up. They think Osama's let off a nuke or something. The camps are locked down now."

Musso took in the report and decided it didn't need any more of his attention.

"Folks, right now, I'm gonna say this. I don't think bin Laden or any of those whackjob mutherfuckers had anything to do with this. I think it's much bigger, but what the hell it is, I have no idea."

The live feed from Oschin's webcam trawl stuttered along above his head. Mocking them all.

I wish it was just a nuke, thought Musso, but he kept it to himself.